BORN FOR THE STORM

BORN FOR THE STORM

SAM HOUSTON
BOOK ONE

ROBERT WISEHART

WOLFPACK
PUBLISHING
— EST 2013 —

BORN FOR THE STORM

PROLOGUE

THE TALK of mutiny was like a low rumble of distant thunder that never stopped. Most of the militia were decent men, but they'd been away from home for too long and worried about their families and their farms.

Andrew Jackson was about to teach them all a hard lesson.

What set it off seemed so trivial that no one took it seriously at first. A militia private was on night picket duty with neither food nor enough clothing to keep warm. The officer of the watch gave him permission to stand down early and get something to eat. The private, a sullen runt named Johnny Wood, was wolfing down cold corn meal with greasy fingers when an officer rode up and demanded to know why he wasn't on duty where he belonged.

Wood didn't say anything about having permission. He was tired, hungry, and cold, but most of all he was sick of the damned army, which was exactly what he told the officer.

Being more patient than most, the officer, a captain named Jack Pardee, listened to the tirade for a while. He sighed, shook his head, and leaned down from his horse to look the boy square in the face.

"Private, I didn't ask how you like it here or if you missed your dear old gray-haired Ma," he said softly. "Get your ass moving back to where it belongs."

Blind with the kind of pent-up rage that overwhelms a man before he knows it, Wood jumped to his feet and threw his tin plate at the captain, striking Pardee's horse in the snout instead. The mount reared and screamed while the officer fought to get it under control and suddenly a quiet matter turned into a commotion. The little private did himself no favor when he snatched up his Kentucky rifle, cocked it, and announced with a glare that he'd shoot the first son of a bitch who laid a hand on him.

It didn't work out that way.

The boy's arrest put the militia in an uproar. It got worse when he was sentenced to be shot, the strictest interpretation of the military code. Most of the officers, especially the young ones who didn't know better, assumed that Jackson would reduce the sentence at the last minute and the boy get off with being lashed or branded on one cheek and frog-marched out of camp.

It didn't work out that way either.

On a sun-drenched Alabama morning, little Johnny Wood stood tied to a tree before a firing line of seven army regulars while Jackson looked on from horseback, his mouth a thin slash across his long face. Too proud to ask for mercy, Wood's cheeks were wet with tears. The whole army was ordered to stand at attention and watch the execution, except the men on guard duty or those too sick to stand. At the signal, three fifty caliber balls tore into the paper target pinned to the private's scrawny chest, while three missed altogether and one nicked his ear. The boy jerked once, sagged and met his maker, the ropes that bound him to the tree soaked by his blood.

"That's pretty damn poor shootin'," coldly observed

Colonel John Coffee, who was mounted beside Jackson. He nodded at the officers waiting nearby. "Dismiss the men and have a detail cut that mess down and bury it deep so the critters can't get it."

There was no more trouble with the militia.

1

"SAM, you think we'll hit 'em tomorrow?"

Sam Houston savored the moment as he looked around at the eager faces illuminated by the flickering glow of the small fire. He always enjoyed being the center of attention.

"Well, as I was sayin' to Jackson just this morning, 'Andy,' I said, because he likes his friends to call him Andy, 'don't you think it's about time we stopped fiddlin' around and hit a good lick.' I mean, you boys know how timid the old man is, and how much he depends on advisers like myself. 'Andy,' I said, 'it's about time you got off your skinny butt and *fought* this war.' And that's when he said, 'Sam, I'm glad we had this talk because ....'"

The yarn came to an abrupt end when a half-eaten hoecake bounced off Houston's forehead and the group erupted in a chorus of groans.

With a dismissive snort, Lemuel Main said, "Sam, once again you have revealed your ignorance. As usual, you know even less than I do."

Houston laughed and combed his fingers through his thick chestnut hair. He got to his feet, seized a brand, and stirred the fire, setting off a shower of sparks that scattered into the night like fireflies.

"Lem, it's a widely held notion that I know more than you about a great many things," he said, tossing the brand aside to resume his comfortable sprawl. "But just this once you're right. The fortunate few who know what's in the general's mind sure don't include the likes of us."

The half-dozen junior officers lounged by one of the score of fires lighting up camp on a soft spring night. Earlier, a barrel of flour was broken open, someone found a bit of lard, and they stuffed themselves on hoecakes fashioned on sticks and blackened ramrods and cooked in the fire.

Despite being six inches shorter and sixty pounds lighter than Houston's six feet two inches and two hundred pounds, the twenty-two-year-old Main was Houston's senior in age and seniority and often reminded him of that fact.

Houston's reply never varied. "A temporary condition," he'd say with an airy wave of his hand. "Be sure that when I am *General* Houston I'll remember my friends, especially you, Lieutenant Dotard."

Underneath the youthful hi-jinks, they all knew that it truly might end tomorrow, more than a year after the massacre at Fort Mims by the fierce Red Stick branch of the Creek Indians that left four hundred bodies naked, scalped, and cut to pieces in the smoking ruins.

Led by a mixed-blood named William Weatherford, the Red Sticks had already fought Jackson at Talladega, Enotachopco, Emuckfaw, and Tallushatchee. The grim Tennessean the Indians called Sharp Knife won every time, but never quite decisively enough. Now most of the Red Sticks Jackson hadn't killed were trapped at Horseshoe Bend, a wooded peninsula at a U-shaped bend of the Tallapoosa River, where they built a three-hundred yard log wall for protection while they licked their wounds. The slippery Weatherford wasn't inside, at least that's what the scouts said, but everyone knew that if Jackson won here the war, this part of it anyhow, was all but over.

The fireside talk slowly wound down as the tired men fell asleep one by one. Houston knew that he should be a mass of jangling nerves. Tomorrow might bring his first real battle since he snatched the silver dollar from the recruiting sergeant's drum head and joined the army the day before his twentieth birthday. But instead he was overcome by a feeling of delicious languor that seemed to fill the night and sweeten the air, a longing, stronger than possession, for the indescribable, the unobtainable. The fact that he didn't know what it was only made the yearning that much greater.

"Sam, you still awake?" whispered Main, who was stretched out next to Houston with his feet to the dying fire and his head on a rolled-up blanket. Like all of them, Main slept in his threadbare uniform. They used to have tents, but the things rotted into rags long ago.

"I guess I must be since I've got some crazy man whisperin' in my ear," Houston replied.

"I was just thinkin' about how it was at first, the way the old man scared the hell out of us," Main said. "You remember?"

"'course I remember," Houston answered, cradling his head on one arm. "I'm not addled. And that rough ol' cob *still* scares the hell out of me. I don't think I'll ever forget what he did to Johnny Wood."

"That's true enough," agreed Main. "But even so, I'd say we've come far."

"Sure feels like far," Houston agreed.

2

WAKING WITH A JOLT, Houston propped himself on his elbow and looked around. Blinking fireflies drifted among the tree trunks and a thin crescent moon hung just above the pines. He guessed that it was at least an hour until dawn, but vague movements in the darkness told him that the camp was already stirring.

Main stirred, too. He tossed off the ratty blanket that Houston put over him in the night, rolled over and stiffly rose to his feet, stretching and shaking himself like a big dog.

"Guess I slept straight through." Sleep made Main's voice sound thick and unnatural as he began rummaging through their meager supplies for their usual breakfast of salt pork and coffee. "Anything interestin' happen?"

"Nope," responded Houston, snatching up a bucket to fetch water for the coffee, "but I bet somethin' real interestin' just might happen today."

JACKSON AND TWO COLONELS, John Coffee and Billy Carroll, stood under a pine tree on a small hill three hundred yards from the Red Stick wall and peered through their telescopes. With the land gently sloping down from the wall to the river, about a mile from the wall at the furthest point, they could see that most of the sealed-off area was rough country; tangled brush, a few thick stands of pine, and twisting ravines like corkscrews leading to the shoreline.

"Gentleman, you know your orders," Jackson said, nodding at the colonels as he snapped his telescope shut with a crack of metal on metal.

On duty as a courier to relay Jackson's orders to the wings of the army, Houston couldn't bear the thought of being left out of the fight. With a deep breath, he dropped the reins of his horse, boldly stepped forward, and snapped to attention in front of the general. The horse dropped his head and began cropping the grass as soon as Houston let go of the reins.

"Sir, permission to join the 39th?"

Carroll, a tall man with butter colored hair, bellowed, "Lieutenant, get back ...."

Jackson, his formidable presence enhanced by the gold braid glittering on the shoulders of his dark blue jacket, cut Carroll off with a slashing motion of his hand.

"Afraid you'll miss the fight, son?"

Houston nodded nervously. "Yes sir."

"I don't blame you," Jackson admitted. "If I was your age, I wouldn't want to stand and watch with the old folks either."

Feeling easier, Houston said, "I wouldn't put it that way, sir."

With an impatient glance at Carroll, Jackson said, "Billy, never stand in the way of a man who wants in the thick of it as much as this boy does. You should know that by now."

Embarrassed at being criticized in front of a junior officer, Carroll's face turned crimson. Ignoring his subordinate's discomfort, Jackson looked Houston up and down. Something in the general's eyes made his face seem softer.

"Go join your regiment," he said quietly. "You'll get what you want soon enough."

An aide brought the general's big gray up. Jackson swung into the saddle with a practiced motion, the leather creaking as it took his weight.

"All right, Billy," he barked, "find me another courier."

As Houston ran off to join his regiment, leaving his horse still cropping the grass and waiting for the next rider, the last thing he saw was Carroll's angry glare.

———

LYING ON HIS BELLY, Main peered over the edge of the shallow ravine where the men of the 39th waited for orders, shaking his head at the sight of a wall that seemed taller and more formidable every time he looked at it.

"God almighty, it'll be like chargin' the side of a frigate," he said. "Maybe we should stand outside like Joshua, blow our trumpets, and hope it comes tumblin' down."

"I doubt you've ever even seen a frigate," snorted Houston, who had a vague notion that it might be some kind of ship. "How would you know what the side of one looks like?"

Main slapped a buzzing mosquito away from his face.

"Don't mean I'm wrong, though, does it?"

Houston couldn't think of a retort so they waited in side by side in silence while the army's two pieces of artillery clattered up, pulled by two four-horse teams and followed by pack horses laden with powder and cannonballs. The brass cannon - one six-pounder and one three-pounder - were unlimbered and wheeled to bear on the wall two hundred yards away. The wheels were chocked, powder and ball rammed home, and the smoking matches brought up separately.

Even an inexperienced officer like Houston knew that the little cannon would be no more than a noisy annoyance. The wall's logs were so green the balls would just bounce off. Even so, it never hurt to make a show.

Before opening fire, Jackson asked for a parlay, mostly because he wanted to distract the Red Sticks while Coffee secretly led three hundred men a mile upstream. They had orders to cross the river at a narrow ford the scouts had found and then work their way back toward Horseshoe Bend, where they'd take position to fire across the river at the Red Sticks when the rest of the army drove them back from the wall.

As expected, the parlay with Menewa, Weatherford's main lieutenant, came to nothing. Borrowing Main's telescope, Houston seized the opportunity to take a look. Menewa was short, bow-legged, and deep across the chest, with a Kentucky rifle cradled in his arms. He carried the fighting symbol of the Red Sticks, a distinctive red-painted war club, in a leather sheath across his back.

The cannon opened just after the parlay ended at midmorning. For more than an hour, they hammered the wall to no effect whatsoever.

"Why even bother with those silly pea shooters?" Main complained between blasts, flicking away a formidable-looking creature as fat as a man's finger that was about to crawl underneath his pants leg. "If we stay here much longer the vermin'll eat us to death."

"Why don't you go tell the old man?" Houston suggested with a grin. "Probably change his mind straightaway, what with you being so uncomfortable and all."

While the Red Sticks hooted at the cannons' ineffectual blasts, as Coffee's men quietly took their places on the other side of the river the colonel saw an unexpected opportunity in the hundreds of canoes lining the shore near the village. He had twenty five men swim across to steal almost double their number of canoes and bring them back to Coffee's side of the river. The river was wider and deeper here than where they crossed upstream and most of Coffee's men were poor swimmers, if they could swim at all. But with the canoes they could cross and attack the Red Sticks from the rear while Jackson assaulted their front.

Confident that the general would support him, Coffee sent a messenger to Jackson explaining the change in plan. He ordered the men who couldn't swim to pile into the canoes, along with the arms, powder and ball. The rest clung to the sides while they crossed the river. Careful to land where they were hidden by thick river brush, the men nervously waited while a Cherokee scout named John Rogers led a dozen men into the camp and began setting fire to the lodges.

Jackson saw clouds of black smoke rising from the village at the same time the messenger arrived urging the general to attack before Coffee's men were discovered and overwhelmed. Fortunately, the army was already primed for an assault, with fifteen hundred men divided into three groups. The 39th Infantry was in the middle, flanked by two larger regiments on the right and the militia on the left.

Without lowering his telescope, Jackson barked orders to Carroll.

"Billy, hit 'em now!" The general's skin seemed to stretch tight across his skull and those standing close heard his teeth grind. "The 39th goes first, the militia last. We'll grab 'em by the throat while Coffee kicks 'em in the ass."

Along the line, black powder trickled from power horns into flintlock pans and brass and hickory ramrods slid in and out of muzzles. After scrambling up and down the line to make sure the men were ready, Houston and Main took care of themselves, seeing that their swords were loose in their scabbards and their pistols primed. Main tossed his tall shako to the ground so that he wouldn't be bothered with it in the charge.

"I'm beatin' you over that wall, Sam," he declared. "Get ready for a good look at my backside."

"We'll see about that." Houston replied, nervously eying all the open ground they had to pass to get to the wall. "I've already seen your narrow ass more than I care to. I don't need another look."

"Tell me the truth," Main asked, licking his dry lips. "Are you as scared as I am?"

Houston felt his bowels quiver.

"Me? Scared? Hell no."

3

A LONG ROLLING drum beat announced the charge. The officers moved up, raised their swords, and the 39th Infantry surged out of the ravine with a chorus of whoops and shrieks. After an orderly start, the charge turned into a desperate sprint as the distance among the men widened from the fastest to the slowest and from the eager to the reluctant.

His shako flying off with the first strides, Houston ran as though his heart might burst, his breath coming in hard gasps. As Red Stick arrows flashed past with an evil hiss, he had to fight the instinct to throw himself to the ground. It made no sense, but he feared the arrows more than rifles and muskets. There was something terrifying about how he could see them coming as they rained down from the sky.

Here and there a man fell, but not as many as Houston feared. Their orders were to keep moving and not return fire until they reached the wall. The veterans all said that time seems to slow down in a fight and now he knew what they meant. It wasn't that time moved more slowly as much as he saw everything in extraordinary clarity, as if all of his senses were doubled or tripled in strength.

They hit the wall with a crash. Some men thrust their bayonets into the firing ports, hoping to drive back the Red Stick's on the other side. Others blindly shot into the ports, using the enemy's own defenses against them. Screams of pain, the crack of rifles, the bellows of Jackson's charging army, and the yelping war cries of the Red Sticks filled the air. A thick gray haze surrounded the wall and the acrid smell of gunpowder burned Houston's throat.

Houston and Main started in front of the hard-charging line and stayed there. Houston's legs were longer, but Main was lithe and quick. They hit the wall side-by-side and scrambled up, fingers desperately clawing at the pine. Houston used a firing port as a foothold to boost himself up, passionately hoping that no Red Stick waited on the other side to chop his foot off.

Scaling the wall looked more difficult than it turned out to be. At the top before he realized it, Houston awkwardly straddled the logs, remembering at the last second to make sure his scabbard wasn't tangled with his legs.

Main landed on the other side like a cat, driving his sword into the belly of a Red Stick who tried to club him before he gained his balance. As Main tugged his sword out of the lifeless body, a few feet away screaming brave aimed his musket, pulled the trigger, and a shower of brains and blood exploded from Main's dark hair.

"Lem!"

Houston leaped from the wall, staggered when he hit the ground, but somehow stayed on his feet. Bounding to his stricken friend's side, he fired his pistol and threw it aside without knowing if he hit anything. He drew his sword and fanned the air in great arcs that momentarily drove back the Red Sticks before they gathered themselves and came on again. Standing astride Main's body, Houston sliced open a brave across his body from shoulder to hip. He grabbed a threatening musket by the barrel, yanked the brave off balance, and smashed his face with the hilt of his sword. He seized another brave by the throat and drove his sword through his chest just as the brave's head exploded from a rifle ball fired at close range and a shower of blood sprayed over Houston's face. Half blind, he slashed wildly through the liquid haze, feeling his sword slice through a body with less resistance than if he'd cut open a melon.

Sensing a presence to his right, he whirled to face the new threat, never leaving Main's body unprotected. Someone grabbed him from behind, pinning his arms at his side. As he struggled, a voice screamed in his ear.

"Houston! Houston! Stop it, man! We've driven them back!"

He knew that voice, but it was hard to think clearly. He remembered now; it was Dan Trumball, one of Jackson's staff. He probably came up with the charge to assess the situation and report back to the general.

"Lem's hurt," Houston gasped, his chest heaving. "He's hurt bad."

"He's dead." Trumball seized each side of Houston's head with his hands. "You're the one who's hurt. Look at your leg."

Houston looked down and saw an arrow sticking out from high on the inside of his left thigh. It was strange because he felt no pain, as if he was looking at someone else's leg.

"Lem needs help."

Houston jerked his head free from Trumball's grasp. As he knelt beside his friend's twisted body, a bolt of pain seared through his groin and deep into his belly. He cried out and fell on his side. The fall jarred the arrow and his fingers clawed at the bloody ground in agony.

Through the waves of pain he heard Trumball's voice. "You men, get him out of here! He's too big to lift over the wall. Try to shove him through one of the firing ports. Someone on the other side will have to take care of him. Forget Main. There's nothing we can do."

That was the last thing he remembered.

4

HOUSTON WOKE up on the other side of the wall, sitting with his back against the logs and his legs splayed out before him. He heard the sound of fighting but it seemed more distant now, probably down by the river.

The arrow stuck out of the inside of his thigh, with only a little blood soaking through his trousers. He knew that the arrowhead might be poisoned and had to come out right away, but he wasn't sure if he could stand the pain long enough to pull it out himself. He was terribly thirsty, too. His lips were dry and cracked and his mouth felt like sand.

In the distance, he saw an ensign with three men patrolling the open field, searching the scattered bodies for wounded men. The ensign knelt beside each body and tentatively reached out to touch a shoulder or face, checking to see if he'd found someone whose life might still be saved, or just another gory carcass.

Houston raised his arm and waved. The ensign saw him and trotted over, his men sullenly following. Searching for wounded was unpopular duty usually given to men who couldn't be trusted to fight. The ensign was probably the youngest officer in the army, assigned a gruesome task no one wanted.

As the group drew closer, Houston saw that he was right. The boy had lost his shako and his unruly light-colored hair looked like a badly stacked pile of hay. Someday he might be a great general, but today he was just a frightened youngster assigned to do a dirty job that was almost too much for him.

"Sir ... you're hurt," he stammered, seeing Houston's insignia of rank and the arrow sticking grotesquely out of his leg at the same time.

"That's very good, ensign." Oddly, Houston still felt no pain, only an uncomfortable full feeling in his leg. "Now you're goin' to pull that arrow out."

"Uh, sir, I don't think ... I, uh, don't know if ... ."

"I don't give a damn what you think," Houston said grimly. "Put your hands on it and pull it out. That's an order."

The boy swallowed and glanced helplessly at his men before remembering that weakness was no way to deal with the ranks. He opened a knife and carefully cut open Houston's trousers. With a nervous glance at Houston's face, the boy gingerly put his hands around the arrow. A gentle tug sent such waves of pain coursing through Houston's groin that he had to grind his teeth to keep from screaming.

"Sir, I can't." The boy looked like he might burst into tears. "It won't come out."

Surprised to see his bloody sword in its scabbard, Houston carefully rolled to one side, making sure not to disturb the arrow, and drew the sword, hearing the satisfying rasp of metal on metal.

Without warning, he set the point on the terrified boy's throat, in the hollow just above his collarbone.

"If you don't pull that damn thing out I'll put this sword through your gullet," he snarled. "Now do it!"

The boy's eyes widened with fear. He gulped so that his

Adam's apple bobbed in his throat, took a deep breath, and seized the arrow with both hands, this time close to Houston's leg for better leverage. He put one foot against Houston's knee, bent his other leg under his own body, and tugged, using all his weight and muscle.

Houston screamed in pain as he beat the ground with his fists. Once the pain subsided, it took a long moment before he summoned the courage to look down at the terrible wound. A chunk of meat the size of his fist had come out with the arrow, thanks to the ugly barb on the arrowhead.

The ensign crawled a few feet away where he violently puked up breakfast.

One of the men in the detail produced a dirty cloth. Houston folded it twice and gingerly pressed it to the bloody cavity. Using the same man for support, he carefully rose to his feet while another man found a stout tree branch for a crutch.

With his left hand on the branch and his right hand pressing the cloth into the wound on his thigh, Houston shuffled awkwardly across the bloody field to find someone to treat his leg.

5

HE FOUND the surgeon's tent at a flat grassy area not far from where the charge began. As he hobbled closer he saw two men lift a body from a table inside. They carried it out to the rear of the tent and carelessly dumped it on the ground beside two other bodies. Another aide threw a bucket of water across the table and haphazardly wiped it with a rag.

A bald man with round eyeglasses perched on the end of his nose, the surgeon's black leather apron covered him from chest to knees. Despite his small size, he had the massive forearms of a blacksmith.

Seeing Houston come up, he waved him away. "Don't bother climbin' on the table. You'll only hurt yourself worse than you already did gettin' here." He motioned to his aides. "Help him over there under the trees."

They took Houston by each arm and guided him to where more than a dozen wounded men stretched out in the shade provided by a few scrubby pines. A few moaned softly, but most were quiet or unconscious. Once they laid him on the ground the surgeon knelt over his leg. With quick precise strokes he cut away Houston's trousers where his leg met his torso and probed the wound so gently that Houston barely felt his touch. The little man reached into a leather satchel and pulled out a fistful of rags and bandages that were still clean enough to look almost white. He plugged the wound with the bandages, wrapped the rags around his patient's naked thigh, and tied them with a neat little knot to keep the bandages from slipping.

Without looking up from his work, he said, "When I'm finished, I'll give you some laudanum. Do you know what that is?"

"Yes, sir."

"Drink a little when it starts to hurt so bad that you can't stand it anymore. Wait until you think you can't take it one more minute and then only a few drops at a time."

Houston nodded.

"Here's your situation, son. The arrow wasn't poisoned or you'd be dead or frothin' at the mouth by now. It went in deep and I can tell by the wound it was barbed. I'd have done a better job at gettin' it out, but there's no goin' back now."

The surgeon wiped his sweating forehead with his sleeve. He reached inside his leather apron, pulled out a flask, took a deep swallow, and offered it to Houston.

"Help yourself," he said. "It works almost as well as laudanum and there's a lot more of it."

Houston took a tentative swallow and choked as the raw corn whiskey burned a tunnel of fire down his throat.

"There's not a thing more I can do for you right now," the surgeon explained. "You'll be runnin' a fever by nightfall, but you're young and strong and my opinion is you'll come out all right. By that I mean you'll keep your leg if the rot don't get it."

The doctor took another drink. Relieved by the man's optimism, Houston declined the offer of another swallow. He already felt lightheaded.

"With the crude way the arrow was pulled out, I 'spect you'll have a healing problem," he said. "What I'm sayin' is that it'll take a while to mend. You're lucky it missed everything important or you'd have bled to death. Just stay off your feet. That's the best I can do. Good luck, son. I hope you make it. I've already seen too many that won't this day."

The little man stiffly rose to his feet and returned to his tent, where a long line of wounded waited.

Houston knew that he should sleep, but he couldn't make himself do it, not with the sound of battle still crackling down by the river. After a few minutes, he saw three officers approach the wounded men under the pines. Using his elbows for support, he raised his head for a closer look and realized that it was Jackson and two of his staff. He reasoned that the fight must be going well or the general wouldn't take time to see to the wounded.

Jackson stopped at a man whose face and head were bandaged over, with slits cut into the bandages for his nose and mouth. The general got down flat on his stomach and whispered into the wounded man's ear. Then he rose to one knee, held the man's hand, and bowed his head in prayer.

After a moment, Jackson got to his feet and the trio moved on. When they reached Houston, the general knelt by his side.

"I know you," he said. "You were the one who was in such a hurry to leave me this mornin'. Your name's Houston, isn't it?"

"Yes, sir." Houston made a sudden decision. "Sir, please tell the doc to let me get back in. I walked all the way here so I figure I can still make a fight."

Jackson's long face seemed to split in two with a crooked smile revealing a row of even white teeth. Good teeth were unusual on the frontier, especially for someone the general's age. Houston guessed that the man must be at least forty. The smile was shocking, like seeing a marble statue grin.

"My boy, I saw you go over that wall. I heard about what

happened on the other side, too," he said. "I'm sorry about your friend. He was a promisin' young officer. I don't want to lose you both on the same day. The army can't afford it and neither can I. You just stay right here."

A rider galloped up. The horse was lathered and blowing hard. Without dismounting, the rider saluted.

"What is it?" Jackson asked.

"Sir, Colonel Carroll says to tell you we have some hold-outs. We tried to get 'em out but their position is awful strong. The colonel would like you to see for yourself, sir."

At Jackson's signal an ensign came up leading three horses. With a final nod to Houston, the general mounted and galloped away with the two staff officers trailing behind.

Jolted by the mention of Main's death, Houston cursed himself for a disloyal and unworthy friend. How could he forget that he saw Lem's brains blown out less than an hour ago? It already felt unreal, almost as if it never happened. Good God! What kind of man was he?

Throwing his arm over his face, Sam Houston wept, humiliated by how he failed to live up to the standard he set for himself, but too young to know how impossibly high that standard was.

When the storm passed, he wiped his face with his sleeve and struggled to his feet. Fortunately, the surgeon was busy in his tent. He found his old tree limb where it was tossed aside and limped back toward the sound of the fighting, downing all the laudanum in one long gulp.

When he got to the wall, he found wide open a gate he didn't know existed. It was easier to pass the second time.

6

DRIVEN FROM THE WALL, the Red Sticks fell back in confusion only to have Coffee's men hit them with a deadly volley followed by a bayonet charge that cut them to pieces. Struck from two sides and with half their fighting men dead or wounded, the Red Sticks broke into groups. In a series of small but brutal stands, they fell in heaps until there was only one remaining pocket of resistance; with about fifty holding out under the river bluffs behind a natural redoubt of fallen logs and brush. The only approach was through a ravine that gave the defenders a clear field of fire. When one assault was beaten back with heavy casualties, Carroll refused to try another, at least not on his authority.

Jackson sent in the faithful Coffee with the offer that those who surrendered would be spared. But the Red Sticks refused mercy from the hated Sharp Knife. For the time being, it looked like a stalemate. The army's riflemen kept the defenders pinned down so they couldn't escape, but the position was too strong to storm without heavy losses.

Determined to take the last of the Red Sticks by nightfall so that not one escaped in the darkness, Jackson decided on another assault, this time with overwhelming numbers. With only a half-hour of daylight left, there wasn't much time.

Houston limped up just as the order to get ready rippled down the line. Drinking all the laudanum at once made his head feel slow and muddy. It was hard to keep his mind straight, but at least his leg didn't hurt. All he knew for sure was that he'd better get started if he wanted to be part of the assault.

Covered with blood and with one trouser leg cut away, Houston stumbled to the front on the side of the line furthest away from Jackson and his staff. Snatching up a discarded rifle without checking to see if it was loaded, he began a slow grotesque shuffle toward the waiting Red Sticks. It took all of his concentration just to put one foot in front of the other. A weak cheer from a few men in the twilight was his only support from the rest of the army. Without the order to advance, no one was eager to follow the strange apparition.

From a distance, Jackson saw a lone man with one bare leg lurch forward while the men on that side of the line cheered him on.

"Good God almighty! What in hell's that?"

An aide who'd accompanied Jackson when he visited the wounded rose in his stirrups, balanced expertly against his mount's nervous sideways jitter, and peered through his telescope.

"By God, I believe that's Lieutenant Houston, sir."

"What the devil is *he* doin' out there?" the astonished general asked.

As he closed on the Red Sticks, Houston knew that he would die, but for some reason it didn't matter. A rifle cracked and a hard blow on his right arm spun him around. With his bad leg, he lost his balance and fell heavily to the ground. The fall jarred his earlier wound and blood coursed down his naked leg.

Jamming the butt of the rifle into the ground for balance, using his good arm he struggled to his feet. It seemed to take forever. His leg still didn't hurt. He couldn't feel his new wound either, but his limbs felt awkward, as if he couldn't make all of his parts work together. He heard the men behind him as their cheers turned into pleas to stay down, but it seemed like their shouts came from far away.

He staggered forward again, using the rifle as a crutch with his left arm while his right flopped uselessly at his side. After a few tottering steps, the Red Sticks fired again. This time he felt his shoulder blow apart as the heavy blow from a seventy five caliber ball put him flat on his back.

He feebly reached out to find the musket so he could use it to get back to his feet, but all his clutching fingers found was black Alabama dirt.

After a moment, he stopped trying. What did it matter? All he wanted to do was lie there and look up at the sky. It looked like it might rain. That was good. He was very thirsty.

7

It was a beautiful warm day, with a crackling blue sky and a gentle breeze that rustled through the trees like music. The forest floor was soft and springy, free of almost all undergrowth except a few shade-growing ferns.

With a worn copy of *The Iliad* on his lap, Houston sat under a big sycamore that was inside the tree line but still within sight of the whitewashed two-story house. He didn't know how many times he'd read *The Iliad* but he never grew tired of it. The story touched some chord that ran so deep he couldn't explain it. The few times he tried he could only stammer in self-conscious embarrassment, as if the experience was too personal to share, something that was uniquely his and impossible to talk about.

He'd gained twenty pounds since a detachment of east Tennessee militia on their way home dumped him on his mother's doorstep, lice-ridden, filthy, covered with sores, and helpless as a baby. He needed twenty more to get back to the two hundred pounds he weighed before the Red Sticks almost killed him. His chestnut hair had grown so long he tied it in a queue. The hollows in his cheeks had mostly filled out and his gray eyes gleamed with their old luster. His arm felt better, too, although he still couldn't raise it above his shoulder.

According to Doc Willows, who rode from Knoxville down to the Houston homestead every two weeks, a man's muscles often compensated for what other muscles couldn't do. When Willows recommended that his young patient exercise the arm and force it to move beyond the boundaries set by the pain, Houston tied a heavy rock to one end of a rope, threw the other end over a tree limb, seized it with his bad arm and hauled the weight of the rock up and down. He made himself do it every day, even when it brought tears to his eyes. At first the popping and crackling from deep inside the shoulder scared him more than the pain, but he got used to it just like he got used to the thin slivers of bone that painfully worked their way to the surface of his arm and shoulder. Willows said there were so many bone chips in there that it might be years before they all worked their way out, assuming they ever did.

The thigh wound was a worry, too. It was smaller now, but slow to heal. The ugly hole still oozed blood and puss and the dressing needed to be changed twice a day. Willows said it was suppurating; a word Houston asked him to explain.

Despite his progress, Houston claimed that he still wasn't well enough to help with the farming, not even light chores. His mother knew better, but curbed her usual acid sarcasm. The truth was that he hated farming. He always did. From the moment the family arrived in Tennessee after his father's sudden death, clattering along the trail from Virginia with two wagons stuffed to overflowing, a cavalcade of nine Houston children, two female slaves, *their* three children, four saddle horses, and a handful of barnyard animals, he detested the miserable work of farming and the dull company of farmers.

But he was just a boy then and there was no way out of it.

Elizabeth Houston supervised her children with a sharp tongue as they knocked together a temporary three-sided cabin and began the grinding labor of carving a home out of the wilderness of sycamore, poplar and willow trees. Pens and huts for livestock were built of poles, split rails, and brush. They cleared a small kitchen garden and built a fence to keep out the deer, raccoons, and wild hogs. Clearing room for corn, wheat, barley and rye demanded weeks of chopping and sawing, girdling trees, digging out stumps, and grubbing up roots. Brambles and vines grew everywhere, grimly battled by scythe and ax. The ground meal from their first small harvest of corn was used to make cornbread, hoecakes, mush and spoon bread. Until the farm was up and running well, most nights family supper was nothing more than hot cornbread and some sweet cow's milk. They slept under quilts and bearskins on bedding and mattresses stuffed with dried corn shucks and goose feathers.

From spring to autumn the endless cycle of digging up stumps, splitting rails, plowing, planting, weeding, and harvesting kept the family busy every daylight moment. Houston resented every drop of sweat that dripped down his forehead to sting his eyes and curdle his spirit. There was no rest even when the crops were in, not with more of the forest to be cleared and prepared for the plow. The awful humdrum life of farming - or occasionally clerking in the tiny Maryville mercantile where his mother owned a small interest - seemed to steal his soul a little piece at a time. The thought of a future where every day was the same as the day before horrified him.

So he would not farm. Not now and not ever again. His mother's displeasure be damned.

The only domestic task he enjoyed was tapping the maple trees for syrup. Maple syrup didn't have to be cultivated. It grew in the forest like game and was tapped as the sap rose from the deep roots. Once the sap was wept into buckets, the buckets were carried to a boiling furnace kept a safe distance from the house. Forty gallons of sap boiled down to one gallon of syrup and ten gallons of syrup made one gallon of sugar. Syrup and sugar were valuable commodities in east Tennessee. Elizabeth Houston cooked with it, bartered with it, gave it away as presents, and sometimes sold it for cash money. Houston told himself that working to supply the family with such a valuable commodity was contribution enough.

Mostly he liked to sit out in the woods, read, sleep, and think about the future. It occurred to him that he had more options than the average lieutenant, one of the benefits of being a hero, even if his heroism was more of an accident than a decision. He didn't even remember most of it, though he was careful never to mention that part. Once he got his strength back, he thought that Washington might be the best of those options, assuming he could finagle the orders. All the real fighting was back east anyhow, despite talk that the British might make a move somewhere along the Gulf. He'd like to see Washington, too. Things happened there, important things done by important people.

His drifting reverie was cut off by the astonishing sight of John Coffee riding up to the house on a big chestnut mare.

Houston watched open-mouthed as Coffee swung down from his mount and tied it to one of the wide-spreading limbs of the big oak tree in front of the house. With Elizabeth Houston away in Maryville, Houston's sickly younger brother, John, who was chopping kindling beside the barn and making a mess of it, as usual, pointed the visitor in Sam's direction. Coffee grabbed a wooden stool from the verandah, carried it out to the tree, and sat down without waiting for an invitation. Houston scrambled to his feet, but the older man waved him back down.

Coffee was on leave to see his family and Jackson told him

to look in on Houston even though it was two days' ride out of his way. It did not occur to Coffee to mention the inconvenience just as it did not occur to Jackson to consider it.

Houston admired John Coffee. Everyone did. As much as anything, it was his initiative that whipped the Red Sticks at Horseshoe Bend. He not only was one of Jackson's oldest friends, he was family, too, by way of marrying Rachel Jackson's niece, Mary. He was almost as big as Houston, with a round face framed by a helmet of dark hair, and they said he was so strong that he could bend a horseshoe straight with his bare hands.

For all his brawn, John Coffee was a subtle and charming man when he wanted to be and Houston got the full treatment. Coffee poured it like syrup over the young invalid. Houston knew there was a point to all this. Otherwise Coffee wouldn't ride so far out of his way to tell stories and hand out compliments to someone he barely knew. He suspected that if he waited long enough, eventually he'd find Coffee's track and figure it out. But until then it was pleasant to sit in the shade and talk to someone from the outside world.

"You can't imagine how angry Andy was when he learned how they let you wander off and get all shot up," Coffee's said. "You should be flattered."

Houston *was* flattered, but didn't want Coffee to see it. He'd noticed that men who made things happen in the world rarely acted flattered or pleased at a compliment. They simply took it as their due, which somehow raised them even higher in the esteem of those who offered flattery and compliments. He didn't fully understand it, but until he did he resolved to act as he thought a man of the world would act.

In the meantime, he was grateful for news of the war. He'd heard bits and pieces, of course, but they didn't get many visitors and details were scarce. Coffee was the first visitor who knew the whole story.

"It was an ugly end to an ugly war, even if it had to be done," Coffee declared, a scowl darkening his broad face.

After Houston was shot down, Jackson came up with a less costly way to take the last of the Red Sticks. Once the lieutenant was dragged to safety, Jackson's friendly Cherokee rained fire arrows on the log-and-brush redoubt. Most of the Red Sticks who were left died screaming in the flames. The few who tried to run were cut down by Jackson's riflemen. The sickening sweet stench of burned human flesh lingered over the village for days.

All told, the bodies of more than nine hundred Red Sticks lay in the smoking ruins of Horseshoe Bend, piled behind the wall, on the slope leading down to the shore, and floating in the Tallapoosa, where the river's quiet pools turned pink with blood. The count was unusually precise because Jackson ordered the tip of every dead Red Stick's nose cut off for a tally. There were nine hundred and seventeen dead, plus three hundred prisoners, all but four of them women and children. As always, Jackson treated the prisoners with precise courtesy.

"The river swept some of the bodies away, but more than nine hundred dead will do," Coffee said, leaning forward and putting his elbows on his knees as he warmed to the story.

Although he was wounded at least twice, Menewa escaped in plain sight.

"He pretended to be dead and floatin' in the river while the current carried him away," Coffee explained. "When one of the militia waded out to cut him for the tally, he rose up, put a knife in the poor bastard's gizzle, and got away."

Jackson's losses were heavy, with forty seven dead, along with twenty three Creek and Cherokee allies. One hundred and fifty nine whites and forty seven Creeks and Cherokees were wounded. Altogether, more than ten percent of Jackson's army was either killed or wounded.

Houston wasn't surprised to hear that the 39th suffered the heaviest casualties. It proved what he already knew; his regiment was engaged in the worst of the fighting.

The war was marked by incredible cruelty, Coffee admitted, even by the brutal standard of the frontier wars. Teeth pried out with knives became necklaces and ears became trophies. Both sides took scalps and more than one officer steamed the flesh and hair off a Red Stick skull, cleaned out the brains, and took it home to use as an inkwell.

Houston swallowed hard to keep his bile down. He'd already heard some of the stories but refused to believe them. Now he knew better.

To break the power of Red Sticks for all time, after Horseshoe Bend Jackson marched his army across the width and breadth of Alabama, laying waste to every village, orchard, and field in his path, and slaughtering what livestock his army couldn't eat. It didn't matter whether it belonged to the Red Sticks or to friendly Creek and Cherokee. The general swore that by the time he finished if a crow flew over the land it would have to carry its own rations.

Seeing Houston's grimace at the destruction to friend and foe alike, Coffee asked, "We heard you lived with the Cherokee as a sprat. Is that true?"

Surprised at the man's information, Houston nodded. "Three years down on the Hiwassee River. They even adopted me."

"I'll tell you a story," Coffee said. "Maybe it'll help you understand how some of the men felt if you haven't already figured it out for yourself. Back when the fightin' started, before your bunch joined us, my men raided a Red Stick village on the lower Tallapoosa. They knew we were comin' and the place was deserted. I went inside the council house with three men. There must have been fifty arrows stickin' out on the central pole and on those arrows hung the scalps of the men, women, and children of Fort Mims, hundreds of 'em. When those devils attacked, they swung children by the feet and bashed their brains out against the stockade walls. Pregnant women were cut open and their babes pulled out of the womb to die on the ground. The men who went to the fort to bury the dead found vultures and wild dogs fightin' over the putrifyin' bodies. Two of the boys with me in the council house that day had family there. So don't try'n tell them that anything we did was wrong. They hit us hard. We hit them a damn sight harder."

Coffee reached into an inside coat pocket, withdrew two thin cigars, and offered Houston one. He shook his head. Smoking made him dizzy. Coffee returned one cigar to his pocket, bit the tip off the other, and spit it out. He flicked a match with his fingernail, brought the flame close to the cigar's end, and puffed until it drew to his satisfaction. Houston was fascinated. He'd heard about the new sulfur matches, but this was the first he'd seen up close. It seemed like some kind of miracle.

For Houston, the best part of the story was the remarkable surrender of William Weatherford.

"He rode right into camp, swear to God." Coffee took another puff, expelled the gray smoke, and gazed reflectively at the cigar's glowing end. "We had so many Creek and Cherokee with us that nobody marked him at first."

Weatherford slowly eased his horse through the crowded camp like he belonged there. No one thought to challenge him. He stopped in front of Jackson's big blue and white tent, waiting patiently until one of the guards called out, "General, there's someone here to see you."

"Well, who is it?"

"Don't know, sir," the guard said. "Maybe you should come out?"

Jackson impatiently lifted the tent flap with one arm and

glared at Weatherford, who was dressed in an eccentric mix of Indian and Scottish regalia that would have looked ridiculous on another man.

"Who the hell are you?"

"I'm William Weatherford."

The air filled with the sound of a dozen rifles, muskets and pistols cocked and aimed at the notorious Red Stick leader.

After a tense moment, Jackson asked, "Give me one good reason why I shouldn't drag you off that horse and hang you right now."

"I can't, not one that matters to you," Weatherford replied, returning Jackson's stare. "I've done you all the harm I could. If it was up to me I'd be at your throat now. But my braves are dead and the women and children are starving. Do as you please to me, but I beg you to save what's left of my people."

Jackson frowned as he thought it over, never taking his eyes off Weatherford.

"Get down off that horse and come inside."

"It was the bravest thing I ever did see," Coffee marveled. "He was surrounded by a whole army that wanted to murder him on the spot and didn't seem to give a tinker's damn. Andy finally let him go after a warnin' that if he ever attacked a white settlement again he'd be hanged for sure. Weatherford only laughed and said if he made war again he'd probably be hanged by his own people.

The Red Sticks had other leaders, but Weatherford was the one who mattered. The rest either surrendered or, like Menewa, headed south to join the Seminoles in Florida.

With the Red Sticks finished, Jackson saw an opportunity. Without bothering to get approval from a government that would only dither away the moment, he negotiated a treaty granting twenty three million acres of Creek and Cherokee land to the United States. As a reward for acquiring the land as much as for his military success, Jackson was promoted to major general in command of the Seventh Military District, a vast area that included Tennessee, Louisiana, Alabama, and the entire Mississippi Territory.

Coffee tapped the long gray ash off his cigar and watched it fall to the pine needles between his polished boots.

"Now tell me about yourself," he said. "I hear the shoulder's comin' along."

Once again, Houston marveled at Coffee's information. What was all this about?

Reluctantly, almost shyly, he explained his thoughts about Washington.

Coffee looked skeptical. The idea seemed to amuse him.

"That might do for the short haul, but it's a fool who pegs his future on the army," he said. "Everything'll change once the war's over. The peacetime army is a dull place for dull men to do dull things. You might not make captain for twenty years. Do you *really* want to be a lieutenant at forty?"

Nettled by Coffee's abrupt dismissal of what seemed like such a good idea just a few minutes ago, Houston hated to admit that he didn't know what he wanted. He always envied men who knew what they wanted and how to get it. To him, the future was like a puzzle he couldn't solve. The best he could do was take advantage of opportunity when it came. But that wasn't enough and he knew it. A man should make his own opportunity.

But he didn't want to admit that, certainly not to John Coffee. He didn't want to say anything at all, but the more experienced man waited him out.

"All right, what do *you* think?" he asked, not bothering to hide his pique.

Coffee seemed to gather his thoughts, although Houston suspected that the pause was a sham. The colonel was about to reveal why he went to so much trouble for someone who was hardly worth his time and attention.

"Son, Andy holds you in fair regard," he said. "You impressed him and that's not easy. You might consider a future with him. He can help you at first, just as you can help him once you've established yourself. The men who join him now will be part of his inner circle and rise as he rises."

Houston still didn't understand. As he rises? Andrew Jackson was already one of the most famous men in the country.

"How can someone like *me* help a man like him?"

Coffee allowed himself a smile that he hoped wasn't too patronizing. He liked this naïve youngster who showed so much promise.

"You won't always be what you are now," Coffee explained. "Neither will Andy."

Houston still didn't understand, so Coffee brought it out in the open.

"I'm talkin' about the Presidency, son." He smiled again at the shocked look on Houston's face. "This country is movin' west and power is movin' with it. We've been dominated by Massachusetts and Virginia for too long. Andy wants you to join him. You're young and you need seasonin'. Do what you'd like for a while, at least until we win this war with the British. Go to Washington, if that's your pleasure. But then join us. A great man holds out his hand. You'd be wise to take it."

Coffee's smooth manner was almost hypnotic, leaving Houston dazzled by the new world suddenly laid out before him.

Pulling himself together, he asked, "Does the general really want it, to be President, I mean?"

Coffee shrugged. "Andy goes where duty calls him. If he's persuaded that it's his duty to accept the Presidency, then he'll accept it."

"In other words, he doesn't want it yet, but he will," Houston said.

Coffee nodded. "Not in other words," he said with a smile. "Those *are* the very words."

8

PICKING out the best of the family's five horses, Houston rode east in easy stages to Staunton, Virginia, where he sold the horse for a good price and used the money for passage in a coach to Fredericksburg. There he boarded a small steam boat that slowly chugged up the Potomac to Washington, its passengers packed on deck like cattle.

The boat tied up to a rickety wharf high above the mud along the river's edge. Carrying a leather satchel stuffed with everything he owned over his shoulder, after making his way through more than a mile of crowded hovels and shanties packed with more slaves, free niggers, and poor whites than he'd ever seen in one place, he passed through a thick grove of trees, trudged up a hill, and came out in an open space to find Washington spread out before him.

What he took to be Pennsylvania Avenue ran straight as a rifle shot, with full-grown trees lining both sides. Even from a distance, he saw more cattle, hogs, and goats than people moving along the broad avenue. The few substantial homes were scattered far apart and mostly away from the main streets, with privies, pig sties, cowsheds, and poultry pens cluttered in the rear like ducklings following their mother. Later, he came upon a phrase that exactly captured his first impression of Washington; a place of houses without streets and streets without houses.

It was not exactly the golden city he dreamed about, but then it was not at its best after the British burned it.

It happened with shocking ease. Led by a pugnacious general named Ross, a British force of four thousand men sailed up Chesapeake Bay, landed unopposed on the Maryland shore, and marched toward the capital. The way Houston heard it, the blockheads running the war in the East had convinced themselves that the city wasn't in danger. Why attack Washington when it offered nothing of strategic value, asked Secretary of War John Armstrong, who thought himself a master of war. The ports of Baltimore or Annapolis were the logical targets, he declared. It is there that the enemy will strike, not Washington.

With professional efficiency, the British proved him wrong. Ross so easily brushed aside a small American force at Bladensburg, Maryland, that the embarrassing pell-mell retreat was known as "the Bladensburg races." With her husband, the President, safely out of town and British infantry marching down Maryland Avenue, Dolley Madison escaped just ahead of the British cavalry after bravely lingering behind to stuff her carriage with as many irreplaceable state treasures as it could carry.

After pillaging the Madison's personal possessions, eating their food and drinking their wine, the British mercilessly set fire to the President's House. As the flames roared out of the windows, they put the Capitol, Treasury, State, and War Department buildings to the torch, too. Secretary Treasury Albert Gallatin's estate was one of several private homes burned. Even now, months later, Washington's empty lots still were scarred by the remains of charred wooden beams and naked chimneys. When the British marched away after two days, an even larger fire blazed to the south, where the retreating Americans set fire to the Washington Navy Yard to keep the warehouse and munitions from falling into enemy hands.

Even now, much bitterness remained. Down at his Virginia estate, old Tom Jefferson raged at the British "infamy" in a pamphlet that made for exciting reading in the pubs and taverns that survived the fires. It didn't take Houston long to notice that the number of red coats slain in defense of the capital rose in direct proportion to the amount of rum, whiskey, corn liquor, brandy, and beer consumed.

The more Houston listened to the blather the more he realized that most of these fools didn't know what real war was. Until recently, war happened somewhere else, even when it was as close as Baltimore, where the British were beaten back after a night-long bombardment. There was already a popular poem circulating about the battle, written by a lawyer named Key. Hearing the poem bawled repeatedly by its drunken admirers until he thought he'd go mad, Houston hoped that Key was a better lawyer than poet, otherwise the man might starve.

In Houston's view, the burning of Washington was the inevitable consequence of a stupidly fought war, at least in the East. Didn't Jackson do the same thing to the Red Sticks? The only difference was that if Jackson led the British Madison would be his prisoner and there would be nothing left of Washington at all.

Of course, he kept these thoughts to himself, as a wise junior officer should.

Once Houston got to know the city better, it struck him as not much more than a glorified country town with its nose in the air. Too many of the men he met were of the plump and pink-cheeked sort who were eager to take on the airs of someone more important than they were. Built on a swamp, Washington's fine wide boulevards turned back into a swamp after even a short rain so that a man crossing the street could easily sink up to his knees in the bog. The summer heat was the worst he'd ever known. He couldn't walk fifty feet before he felt his shirt sticking to his back underneath his uniform jacket.

Despite the damage of war and the crude nature of the capital, wealth and finery were all around him. The silver snuff boxes, velvet and silk dresses, crystal and chocolates, intricate clocks and satin-lined trinket boxes amazed him in a world populated by diplomats, congressmen, cabinet members, and high-ranking army and navy officers, all of them engaged in a constant whirl of official business and society functions.

But there was ugliness lurking beneath the veneer, too. During a party at a prominent congressman's home, Houston heard a muffled cry from inside a pantry. He opened the pantry door to find the host with his pants around his ankles pressing himself on a struggling servant girl with her dress ripped off to the waist.

His duties in the Quartermaster's Department began to bore him after just a few weeks. He shuffled papers and made copies in his find round hand as the government slaved to recreate the files that the British destroyed, as if more paper would win the war. His boredom led to an enthusiastic consumption of alcohol as he drank anything he could get his hands on. Over time, he became particularly fond of Jamaican rum, telling himself that he drank to ease the pain of his wounds.

Worst of all, it looked as if the war might end soon. Word spread that a peace conference had convened in Belgium, where the American delegation included Gallatin, John Quincy Adams, the brilliant but prickly son of the second

President, and Henry Clay, a fast-rising rising political star from Kentucky.

Remembering Coffee's warning about the peacetime army, the thought that the war might end before he gained promotion made Houston so restless that he was close to panic. He knew now that coming to Washington was a terrible mistake and spent most of his off-duty time lobbying to be posted where there might be more fighting, or at least more active duty. Most of his failed efforts consisted of sitting hour after hour in the waiting rooms of various cabinet members, generals, senators, and congressmen, surrounded by other officers with similar hopes. He rarely saw anyone of importance and nothing came of it when he did. Even with the war, there were too many officers and too few places for them. Why advance a cripple like Sam Houston when there were so many able-bodied young men to choose from?

His lone success was a meeting with Tennessee Congressman John Rhea in Gilhooley's, a popular tavern on F Street near Newspaper Row, a shabby block on Fourteenth Street that held the offices of every newspaper circulating in Washington, all fifteen of them.

The six-term Congressman resembled a badly packed sandbag, with an out-sized head on one end and skinny legs on the other. While Rhea stuffed himself with pickled eggs and beer, Houston made his case in a short speech that he'd prepared in the tiny room he shared with two other impover-ished army officers, Stephen Burke and Hector Grafton, at Mrs. Trout's boarding house. Two of them slept in the bed, the other slept on the floor, and they rotated every day.

Although he didn't need it anymore, he made sure to wear his sling to impress Rhea with his sacrifice.

"Congressman, I *must* be allowed to take a more active part in the war," he begged. "I'm fully recovered and ready for active duty. Consider my record. It seems to me that any truly virtuous government is obligated to reward such a man."

Rhea burst out laughing, which was not the effect that the lieutenant intended. The unfortunate result was that the Congressman sprayed a mouthful of beer across the crowded tavern, including a disastrous-looking woman with mostly exposed breasts who appeared to be painted for war. Her eyebrows and lashes were astonishingly blacked and her mouth a fearsome daub of vermillion. She was about to close a transaction for an afternoon's entertainment with a well-dressed young man who was shifting his weight from one leg to the other with excitement. Her business affairs interrupted, the woman glared at Rhea and marched out of the tavern muttering about her *toilette*.

Bowing his apologies to the remaining patrons, the amused Congressman turned back to Houston.

"Lad, did you write that ghastly speech yourself? 'Virtuous government' indeed. Who put *that* idea in your thick head? Virtuous is the one thing government most decidedly is not!"

Being hard of hearing, Rhea had the habit of bellowing almost everything he said. Now everyone within earshot knew that the young officer had made an ass of himself. Fortunately no one seemed to care. Asses weren't rare in the nation's capital.

Seeing the effect of his scorn play across Houston's expressive face, Rhea took pity on the crestfallen young man, who was, after all, paying for lunch out of his obviously meager resources. To make amends, the Congressman lowered his voice as if engaged in a conspiracy.

"My boy, you don't have the hang of this at all," he explained. "You come to me with your arm in a sling and tell me you're ready for active duty. What I see and what you tell me are two different things."

Taking another gulp of beer, Rhea gazed thoughtfully at

Houston. He placed his mug on the counter and wiped his mouth with thumb and forefinger.

"Tell me, how *are* your wounds?" There was a mischievous glimmer in the Congressman's not-quite sober eye. "It seems to me I saw you on the street a day or two ago, but without the sling. Or was that your twin who also happens to be assigned to the Quartermaster's Department? Tricky things, these infirmities. Believe me, I know. I suffer from a touch of gout myself."

Catching the bartender's eye and waving for another round, Rhea's multiple chins jiggled with amusement.

"Houston, I like you, which is neither here nor there. But it seems to me that anyone who wants what you want so badly probably deserves it. So I'll do what I can, which consists of writing a letter on your behalf to the War Department that will make you sound like a second Alexander. Will that do?"

Seeing the young man's relief, Rhea smiled happily. "Now, buy me another beer before I change my mind."

Houston wobbled out of Gilhooley's two hours later, leaving the Congressman peacefully snoring in a corner chair tilted back so that it was precariously balanced against the wall. As he staggered down the street to Mrs. Trout's, he knew that he'd learned a lesson by trying to be too clever with a more experienced man. He was lucky. Not everyone was as good-natured as Rhea. He needed bigger guns firing on his behalf, too.

After spending most of a day sweating over the composition, he sent off two letters. One went to Secretary of War James Monroe, the man who everyone said was most likely to follow Madison and put another Virginian in as President. Except for John Adams' single term, the state had a stranglehold on the office. The other letter went to Tennessee Senator Joseph Anderson.

To Monroe: *"I have given repeated proof of my honor and*

fidelity in the cause of liberty. In return I carry scars for the many wounds I received at the battle of Horseshoe Bend. You will no doubt want to acquaint yourself with my character. I refer you to the Congressional delegation from East Tennessee. I have the pleasure of acquaintance with the members. In all candor, without influential relatives to support me if merit alone is not enough for advancement, then I must sink."

Bit of an exaggeration there. Well, more than a bit. Rhea was the only Congressman he knew. With luck, Monroe wouldn't check.

His letter to Anderson concluded: *"I proved to the world that I am willing to risk my life for my country. If you feel yourself justified in using your influence on my behalf you may rest assured that I will be ever grateful."*

There was no way to tell if the letters would help, but Houston had learned that it was better to do something, even if it turned out to be wrong or pointless, than to do nothing and regret it.

9

As THE DAYS and weeks passed, Houston made the dismal discovery that Washington's winters were every bit as dreadful as its summers. The air was so thick with smoke from hundreds of burning fireplaces that a smelly haze blanketed the city twenty four hours a day. The wet and miserable cold made him long for the wet and miserable summer while the stultifying boredom of routine drove him out of his mind.

Two events turned his already dark mood utterly black. The first was Jackson's smashing victory at New Orleans, which left the proud British army shattered and its commander, Lord Pakenham, dead on the field. Houston bitterly regretted that he wasn't there instead of playing the paper-shuffling cripple stuck in a half-burned mud hole of a city that baked a man in the summer and suffocated him in the winter.

The second event was peace and it hit him hard. Although the news about the Treaty of Ghent reached Washington well after the news of New Orleans, it turned out the battle took place two weeks after the peace treaty was signed, but no one knew it at the time.

Several weeks after news of the war's end blazed through

the capital, Houston found himself back at Gilhooley's, at a raucous *soiree* to see off Erasmus Spendlove, Houston's superior officer in the quartermaster's office. Only a few years older than Houston, Spendlove was more friend than superior. With the war's end, he resigned his captaincy to return to the family dairy in upstate New York, but only until his sickly father died and he inherited everything. At that point, he intended to sell it all and never work again.

Envying his friend's prospects and overwhelmed by self-pity in the midst of revelry, Houston stood alone at the end of the long bar and stared morosely into his rum. A group gathered around the tavern's stone fireplace at the other end of the tavern was bellowing Key's poem, "The Defense of Fort McHenry," to a tune to which it was recently put, a drinking song called "To Anacreon in Heaven."

Seeing the unhappy Houston by himself, Spendlove made his way through the boisterous mob, a pretty dark-haired tavern maid at his side. After working with the younger man for many months, Spendlove knew his friend's moods well and recognized a bad one.

"I must say, Sam, you bring a certain depressing posture to the festivities." Spendlove's long arm was draped around the shoulder of his buxom companion so that he could conveniently fondle her breast. "A true friend would be happy for me."

"You know I am, Razzy. It's just ... oh, never mind. It doesn't matter what I think."

Spendlove's long face brightened with an idea.

"I know just the thing to cheer you up," he announced.

Houston took a small sip of his rum. This one had to last because he couldn't afford another. Why didn't Spendlove just go away and leave him alone?

Giving in to Spendlove's eager look, he finally asked the question that was so clearly expected if him.

"And what might that be, Razzy?"

Spendlove removed his arm from the girl's shoulders, placed his hand at the small of her back, and gently pushed her toward Houston.

"Take her," he announced grandly. "She's yours."

Incredible as it seemed, Spendlove was serious. Houston looked into the girl's bovine eyes and saw nothing resembling a protest, or much of anything else, for that matter.

"Don't worry about Sally here," Spendlove explained with a fond slap on the young woman's round rump. "She thinks one's as good as another. Isn't that right, old girl?"

The tavern maid answered by boldly snuggling under Houston's arm so that he felt her large breasts pressed against his side and her delicious thighs against his leg.

His despondency replaced by a rising sense of urgency, Houston resolved not to dawdle.

"What about you?" he asked over his shoulder, guiding the young lady toward the door with one hand on the small of her back and the other on her arm.

"Oh, don't worry, I'll find another one," Spendlove shouted, happily diving back into the crowd. "Now that I'm rich it seems that I've become quite handsome."

Houston didn't hear a word. He was already out the door with whatever her name was. Sarah? Sally? Susan? Something like that. Where could he take her? The situation called for privacy. He'd think of something.

10

HE FINALLY WAS DELIVERED from purgatory with orders to report to Southern District headquarters in Nashville. From there, he'd travel south to New Orleans for duty with the 1st Infantry.

Houston was one of the fortunate few and he knew it. With the end of the war, scores of other officers, most of them his senior, either left the service voluntarily like Spendlove or were dismissed with cursory thanks from an indifferent government. He sensed Jackson's powerful hand at work on his behalf. There could be no other explanation.

He rode out of Washington shielded from the worst of the foul weather by a new coat made of India rubber that shed most of the rain. As he plodded along mile after soggy mile, the young officer's thoughts naturally turned to his benefactor. Andrew Jackson's spectacular rise was remarkable considering that only a few years earlier he'd been linked to Aaron Burr's infamous plot to set up an empire for himself somewhere beyond the Mississippi, most likely in the Mexican province of Texas.

The scheme seemed more alarming than it turned out to

be once the scanty evidence was displayed at the former Vice President's trial. Despite Burr's political success, until then the suave New Yorker was best known for killing Alexander Hamilton in a duel. In Washington, Houston met several people who'd known the insufferable Hamilton and privately applauded Burr's marksmanship. Jackson's involvement in Burr's plot seemed to consist of the expected hospitality when Burr passed through Nashville, along with a few bland letters. Once Jackson realized what Burr might be up to, he promptly backed away and sent word to Washington about Burr's scheme. But none of that mattered now. Real or imagined, Jackson's past sins were forgotten in the euphoria of New Orleans.

As Houston drew closer to the Hermitage, Jackson's plantation east of Nashville, he began to worry. What if his assumption was wrong and Jackson had nothing to do with his assignment? What if it was just dumb luck or coincidence? What if Jackson didn't remember him at all? What if he humbly offered his gratitude and the great man laughed in his face?

The rain that followed him all the way from Washington had turned into a cold needling drizzle by the time he rode up to the big house in the darkness. When he dismounted his boots squished deep into the mud. A slave carried Houston's saddle bags with his meager possessions to an outlying cabin while a groom led away his horse, a handsome stallion named Achilles that was worth more than everything else he owned put together.

Chilled to the bone, Houston was escorted into the parlor by a massively dignified house slave, who took his rubber coat and and made it clear without saying a word that he was appalled by how the visitor's muddy boots tracked into the house and that only an unmannerly oaf would commit such an unpardonable sin.

Entering the parlor, he was greeted by an image he'd never forget; Andrew Jackson sprawled on the floor in front of a great stone fireplace with a small lamb and an even smaller boy between his long skinny legs. The general explained that the boy had cried because his favorite lamb was out in the cold and wet and begged Jackson to bring it inside. Now boy and lamb were happily sleeping in front of the toasty fire.

"Forgive me if I don't rise and greet you," Jackson said, waving toward a hickory rocker. "Help yourself to a glass of Madeira, take a seat and warm yourself. Don't bother pourin' any for me. A glass at this hour would only trouble my sleep."

Spying a decanter on a silver tray surrounded by six beautifully cut crystal glasses, Houston poured a glass and gingerly eased into the rocker. Turned and polished with remarkable craftsmanship, the rocker seemed so delicate that he was afraid it might shatter from his weight, but he managed to settle in with only a few small creaks of protest.

Searching for something to say, Houston nodded at a brace of pistols displayed above the mantel.

"Beautiful weapons, sir," he said. "I've never seen the like."

"Lafayette gave those pistols to George Washington," Jackson explained with obvious pride. "After New Orleans, the Washington family was good enough to present them to me."

Houston's nervousness quickly disappeared in the warm and comfortable room. Looking back on it, he marveled at how easily Jackson drew him out without seeming to try. The talk turned to Houston's family, starting with his father. Also named Samuel, he was a colonel in the Virginia militia and fought with Morgan's Rifles during the revolution. Constantly on the move around the state inspecting local military units, he rarely stayed more than a few nights at a time in their comfortable frame house with the imposing white columns on Timber Ridge, a rise overlooking the beautiful Shenandoah Valley.

At the end of a routine inspection trip, Colonel Houston stopped overnight at a tavern on the Old Kentucky Road only a days' ride from home. He had dinner at six, said goodnight to his host at eight, and was dead by ten.

Sam was only thirteen. His father was gone so much that he barely knew him, and now he never would. He couldn't even remember what his father looked like, or even *how* he was, the sense people have about other people that makes them whole. All he had was a few wisps of memory.

It was only after his death that Colonel Houston's private failings became known; a gambler and spendthrift with a long history of unwise investments that he'd managed to conceal from his family, which suddenly found itself in a state of barely genteel poverty.

At over fifty years of age, with creditors yapping like jackals, Elizabeth Houston started over. She sold the farm, most of the livestock, their furniture, all but two female slaves, and struck out for Tennessee, where the family had distant relatives and a parcel of land. It was hard to leave the home where her children were born, but sentiment did not get in her way. It was necessary to leave the place she loved and so she left it. If there was pain, and there had to be, she kept it to herself.

Young Sam hated their new life. As troubled as he was troublesome, he shirked his work and escaped into the woods whenever possible, often for days at a time, until he finally found the courage to run away. Heading south, he skirted the flank of the Appalachians, with no idea where he was going or what he would do. Nearly weeping from hunger, he burst out of the woods on a bluff above the Hiwassee River two weeks later. The loud rustle of his movements started a grazing doe, which ran in sure-footed leaps down the fern-covered bluff.

"I thought there might be a buffalo in the woods, but I see only a clumsy boy."

Houston's heart jumped to his throat as he whirled around, his hand grasping the bone-handled knife in his belt. He didn't see anything until a figure moved out from behind a tree. Tall for a Cherokee, he had a long face and melancholy brown eyes. His hair was dark, with silky gray whiskers down his jaw. He wore a blue jacket embroidered with red designs, a homespun shirt, and baggy white trousers with a red sash.

"I didn't know you were there," Houston said.

"I didn't want you to."

"Why are you followin' me?" Houston demanded, his hand still clutching the knife. "What do you want?"

The Cherokee smiled at the boy's bluster.

"Why don't you come down to the village?" he asked. "You look hungry."

"What village?"

The question brought another smile.

"The one you didn't know was there."

Without bothering to see if the boy followed, the Cherokee started down a narrow path mostly hidden by ferns. His hunger stronger than his pride, after a moment's hesitation Houston followed. After a few steps the village came into view. He couldn't imagine how he'd missed it, especially with smoke from the cooking fires rising high in the air until it disappeared like vapor.

It was the most beautiful place he'd ever seen. The river was cold and clear as it poured out of a notch in the Great Smoky Mountains. There were fields of corn, beans, pumpkins, tobacco and potatoes. The grass sheltered thousands of strawberry plants and the ground was stroked with crimson. There were plums, peaches, and wild apples, too. A thick forest of oak, pine, maple, hickory and sour wood trees grew down to the river shore. As they drew closer, his senses were overcome by the mouth-watering scent of barbecuing meat.

His benefactor's name was Oolooteka and he was leader of the small Hiwassee branch of the Cherokee Nation. His name meant "he puts the drum away" and everyone, including the Cherokee, most of whom spoke English, called him Drum.

Taking pity on the unhappy boy, Drum persuaded him to stay in the village called Drum's Town, at least for a while. It didn't take much persuasion because the lonely youngster loved the place from the moment he saw it.

Two months later, Drum adopted the strapping youngster as his son, giving him a Cherokee name; Colonneh, or Raven. Houston's pride that Drum thought so highly of him was deflated when he learned that the good-hearted Cherokee had adopted at least a dozen other needy youngsters over the years, his way of keeping them under his protection. Well known to white settlers all over eastern Tennessee and north Georgia, Drum got a message to Houston's mother explaining her son's whereabouts, along with a promise to keep him safe for as long as necessary.

When Houston asked why he was named Raven, Drum explained that the bird was a symbol of good luck.

"You were lucky I found you, otherwise you might still be stumblin' around or starved to death," he said, his large expressive eyes shining with humor. "And if I didn't give you a name, someone else would, maybe 'Fool Who Couldn't See the Village Under His Nose.' It's better to be called Raven than Fool, I think."

Sam Houston became a man in that village. He adopted Cherokee dress and Cherokee ways and became fluent in their language. Being Drum's adopted son brought him no favors as he suffered through the same rigorous training given to the other young men. Although he lagged behind at first, in time he caught, and then surpassed, his peers. He learned to run five miles with a mouthful of water and spit it out at the end of the run to prove that he hadn't swallowed it, training that forced him to properly breathe through his nose, which increased his endurance. To toughen his feet, he ran with moccasins packed with river sand. While he never really got the hang of how to use a bow and arrow, he was the best wrestler in Drum's Town and never beaten in competition with other villages.

Although the youngster thought that he had reasonable woodcraft before coming to the village, he quickly realized just how much he didn't know. Over time he learned that the bear was by far the most valuable animal in the forest and the most difficult to hunt. He learned to look for claw marks on tree bark and how to assess the freshness of scat to see how long ago a bear had passed through the area. Scat also revealed what the bear had recently eaten. While a bear's diet might include everything from berries, nuts and acorns to carrion, wild honey and insects, if the droppings were dark and runny it meant that the bear had recently eaten meat and might linger in the area for several days as it fed off the carcass.

A good sized black bear not only provided delicious meat, it was a rich source of fat and fur. The thick pelts were turned into a variety of goods, including rugs, bed robes, coats, and fur caps. Great quantities of bear fat and oil stowed in barrels or sewn in watertight deer skins were shipped by barges down the Mississippi River to New Orleans and then to markets in the east, where they was used for lamp and cooking oil.

Early in Houston's second year at Drum's Town, he learned that folk medicine was just as good and maybe better than any other. A Cherokee boy out picking berries was accidentally shot by another Cherokee who was deer hunting. The boy was brought into the village and Houston watched while Drum carefully examined the belly wound. Although the rifle ball had miraculously passed all the way through without hitting any vital organs, Drum knew that deadly infection still was a possibility. The wounded boy was laid on a table before the large hearth in Drum's house while Drum wrapped a silk handkerchief around the ramrod from his rifle. While Houston and several other braves held the writhing boy still, Drum inserted the ramrod into the wound and pushed it out the exit hole in his back. He then took both ends of the handkerchief that remained in the bloody wound and pulled it back and forth from one side to the other, which cleaned out the debris and helped keep the wound from festering.

His years in the village were easily the happiest time of Houston's life. But as much as he loved it, he knew that someday he had to go home. When he finally did after almost three years, he regretted it immediately. He knew his mother too well to expect a warm welcome, but her unrelenting scorn cut him deeply, although he refused to let it show. He didn't know it, but her dreamy son reminded her too much of her dreamy husband.

When the war came, at only nineteen Houston needed his mother's permission to enlist. She gave it, but Elizabeth Houston was not pleased. He couldn't remember a time when she *was* pleased, at least not by him.

He remembered the day he left. As they faced each other in the parlor of their white-washed two-story home south of Maryville, his mother looked into his crisp gray eyes and presented him with a gold ring of his father's with the word "honor" inscribed on the inside.

"Do your best," she said, slipping the ring on the little finger of his right hand. "That's all we can ask."

As goodbyes go, it lacked, well, everything; as if she expected him to come crawling back like a whipped dog.

But Sam Houston thrived in the army. He made sergeant in a month, mostly because he was one of the few enlisted men who could read, write, and do sums. Not much later he was commissioned lieutenant and transferred to the 39th Infantry, where he met a friendly Georgian named Lemuel Main.

A clock gently chimed somewhere out of sight. Counting the chimes, Houston was abashed to realize that he'd babbled for well over an hour. The fire was down to a pile of glowing ashes.

"Sir, I do apologize," he said, placing his big hands on the slender rocker arms and rising to his feet. "I had no idea ...."

"Don't apologize, lad, I wanted to hear it," Jackson said, stroking the dark hair of the boy whose head was cradled on his skinny thigh. "It seems to me that you and I are much alike. I never knew my own Pa. He died before I was born. A thing like that leaves a mark on a man. You and I were born for the storm, I think. Calm does not suit us. It does not suit us at all."

"But we've talked enough for now. It's time to put this little fella in a proper bed. Why don't you go on to your cabin for the night and I'll give you a tour of this little place of mine in the mornin'."

Houston dutifully allowed himself to be led to his cabin by a house slave. Following Jackson's instructions felt like the most natural thing in the world.

11

HOUSTON SLEPT WELL and woke early to find that the rain had stopped. After a light breakfast of one egg and coffee, true to his word Jackson led him on a tour of the Hermitage.

Seeing it in the daylight, Houston was surprised by its simplicity. Where he expected a grand mansion, he found a collection of primitive log cabins built around a two-story log house with a limestone chimney. About thirty slaves ran the thousand-acre plantation, with the indefatigable Jackson overseeing every detail. In addition to a stable of race horses regarded as the best in Tennessee, Jackson raised cattle, sheep, and hogs. Cotton was the cash crop, about a hundred acres of it, while corn fed the livestock and the slaves.

"It's still a modest place, but it won't be that way long," Jackson explained, guiding his strapping young visitor along a dirt path that ran parallel to a meandering creek. "We have plans, by God. Big plans!"

The rain had cleared the cool morning air and Houston felt as if he could see for miles. As they walked the Hermitage grounds, Jackson waved his long arms to indicate the location and size of all the new structures he intended to put up.

Before long Houston was so confused that he had no idea what Jackson planned to build or where he planned to build it.

"The main house was already here when I bought the property," Jackson continued. "I hired a Nashville man to dress it up with French wallpaper and painted trim. We've made a few improvements since then (a wave to the right). I put in a distillery, a dairy, a carriage shelter, a cotton gin, a smokehouse, and more cabins for the slaves. But I haven't been home enough to do near everything I want."

"For one thing, I want to build a proper house for Rachel, with a decent verandah for our Tennessee summers. That'll go up over there (another wave). The new stables will be over there (another wave) and the guesthouse over there (yet another wave). We'll need at least fifty slaves because we're gettin' into cotton even more than we already are, as much of it as we can grow. Demand will triple now that we're tradin' with England again. I don't like the British, but I'll take their money. This year I'll sell more than seventy bales of cotton. At five hundred pounds a bale, that'll bring in a pretty penny."

By the time the tour ended, Houston was overwhelmed by phantom buildings and invisible architecture. He wasn't surprised to learn that Jackson was a self-taught student of architecture. While never a scholar, the man learned what he needed to learn and never forgot it.

Was *this* the implacable martinet who ordered boy privates executed, Houston wondered? How could such different personalities exist in the same man? The childless Jacksons had even adopted two children. One was a Creek boy named Lyncoya, an orphan the general found in the smoking ruins of war and sent back to the Hermitage. The other was the son of Elizabeth Donelson, the wife of Rachel Jackson's brother, Severn. The couple had twin boys, but didn't have the means to raise two babies, so Rachel and Andrew Jackson took one as their own. That was the boy Houston saw sleeping with the lamb.

As they walked back to the big house, Houston unconsciously massaged his shoulder.

"How's the wound, son?" Jackson asked.

Houston admitted that he still didn't have full use of his arm. Worse, it looked as if a full recovery wasn't likely, an unhappy thought for a young man in the prime of life.

"You're posted to New Orleans, aren't you?" Jackson knew the answer perfectly well because he arranged it himself. "I know a surgeon there, the best I've ever seen. I want you to contact him when you get there. I'll send word ahead so he'll be expectin' you. If anyone can mend your shoulder, he can."

Flushing with embarrassment, Houston stammered that he had no money for special care and made do with what treatment the army provided, which was none at all most of the time. On the rare occasions that he received treatment, being worked over by army doctors made him feel like a side of beef.

Jackson put his long arm around Houston's broad shoulders. Although famously skinny, his wiry strength was surprising.

"You're not to worry about it," he said gently.

When Houston feebly protested, Jackson made a cutting motion with his other hand.

"Say no more about it. I'm not offerin' charity. You'll repay me tenfold before we're through."

As the days passed and he got to know Jackson better, Houston began to suspect that the general's legendary rages were more calculated than real. He could explode with a fury that took a man's breath away, but he wasn't above using his volatile reputation to get what he wanted. A glare usually was sufficient to get most men hopping.

However, in the long series of surprises that jolted

Houston all through his weeks at the Hermitage, perhaps the biggest surprise of all was Rachel Jackson, the great love of Andrew Jackson's life.

Houston knew the story. Everyone on the frontier did.

Young Rachel Donelson was pretty, flirtatious, and remarkably unlucky in love. The popular dark-eyed daughter of one of Nashville's pioneer families, she made a poor choice when she married at eighteen. Jealous to the point of madness, Lewis Robards threatened to shoot one man just for being alone in the same room with his wife and took a whip to another for nodding hello. The unhappy couple lived at her mother's boarding house in Nashville, in those days a small settlement on the edge of the frontier where the Indian threat still was very real. Not many years earlier, Rachel's father was killed and scalped while out surveying.

And then an ambitious young lawyer named Andrew Jackson rode into town.

Tennessee was part of North Carolina then and Jackson was the new prosecuting attorney for the western district. He took a room at the Donelson boarding house and promptly fell in love.

"Ah, Sam, my boy, you should have seen them," recalled John Overton.

It was twilight at the Hermitage. The warm day slowly cooled as cicadas chirped their symphony in the woods. Overton and Houston smoked cigars as they strolled through the stables. Houston had acquired the smoking habit in Washington, where almost everyone did it. The air was thick with the smell of horses, manure, feed grain, and straw, enriched by the rich scent of polished leather from the saddles and tack hanging from the walls.

A frequent visitor, Overton was one of Jackson's oldest and dearest friends. Everyone called him "judge," thanks his time on the Tennessee Supreme Court. Overton certainly looked like a judge, or what a judge *should* look like, in Houston's view, with his dark hair, widow's peak, and folksy dignity, although most of the younger folks thought him too fond of long pointless stories and gruesomely bad jokes.

"Rachel was the prettiest girl in Tennessee, but with Robards the way he was none of us had the gumption to do anything about it, except young Andy," Overton recalled, a description that left Houston struggling to conjure up a vision of a *young* Jackson.

As they left the stables and turned toward the little creek that meandered through the property, Overton's face softened with the bittersweet memory.

"It all started innocent enough. With Robards was away more than he was home, Andy and Rachel naturally fell in together. They danced and rode and talked and walked and then talked some more. We all knew they were in love long before they knew it."

When Robards confronted Jackson about being too familiar with his wife, the fiery young lawyer dared him to do anything about it and threatened to cut off his ears. Robards countered by having Jackson arrested. When his accuser didn't appear in court, the judge set Jackson free. A rumor spread that when Robards returned to Nashville from wherever he was he intended to challenge his rival to a duel. Rachel was terrified of what might happen. If Robards killed Jackson, she'd lose her lover. If Jackson killed Robards, he might be charged with murder given that dueling was illegal in Tennessee. Rather than wait, she fled south to relatives in Natchez, hoping that her absence might help cool off both men.

Months later, word filtered back to Nashville that Robards had divorced Rachel in Virginia. Hearing the news, Jackson gleefully galloped to Natchez. Married within a week, the couple eventually returned to Nashville and Jackson began his rise.

Two years later, to their horror they learned Rachel was *not* divorced when they thought after all. In fact, Robards' petition for divorce was not granted until more than a year after they married. The couple prayed their innocent mistake would be forgiven, but it was a naïve hope. As he grew more prominent in the public eye, Jackson's enemies made sure that the story of Rachel's bigamy was never forgotten. The slander tormented her until she grew to hate crowds and strangers. In recent years, she turned ever more religious and was rarely seen without a Bible.

"Andy needs her more than I've ever seen anyone need another human bein', even though they're opposites in most ways," Overton said. "She's drawn to the plantation and the fireside; he's drawn to the world. She hates politics; he dearly loves the cut and thrust of it. She's content with what they have; Andy'll never have enough. But no matter how much she hates it, she'll never deny him his future and she's the only one who *could* deny it to him."

Overton took a last draw on his cigar and flicked the stub into the rocky little creek trickling beside the worn path.

"So that's the story," he said. "What do you think of it?"

Houston dropped his own cigar and crushed it under his boot. While everyone knew the broad strokes of the tale, he was fascinated to hear it from someone who was there. Romantic to the core, it tugged at his heart, even if he knew that most of it was nonsense. The truth was that Jackson did what he always did. He wanted something, in this case another man's wife, and took it with the same surety that he grasped everything. The couple lived together well before Robards petitioned for divorce and didn't think twice about it. No one did until the general became a public figure.

Jackson was outraged by the charges of impropriety not because they were false, but because they were true.

"Well, Judge, I don't think that what they have comes along very often," Houston said, choosing his words carefully. "The general is a lucky man."

"... and you shouldn't be spendin' your time listenin' to a gabby old feeble-wit like Johnny Overton."

The husky voice came from around the bend just up the path. Rich with personality, it was low but quick, with short and slightly wheezing breaths.

Houston glanced at the smiling Overton. A few more steps found him face to face with the fabled Rachel Donelson Robards Jackson, who was sitting on a rough wooden bench between the path and the creek, a pile of knitting in her lap.

Obeying an impulse, he stepped up and seized her plump hand. With a deep bow, he said, "Madam, I salute you."

"Well, what do we have here?" A chuckle rose from the depths of her vast bosom. "You'd best watch yourself, Judge. This handsome youngster just might replace you in my heart."

"Rachel, darlin', to be anywhere near your heart is more than I deserve," replied Overton, adopting the bantering tone they apparently used all the time.

She threw back her head and laughed. "At least you've got that right," she said, giving Overton's arm a fond squeeze.

Like the Hermitage itself, Rachel Jackson wasn't at all what he expected. Her dark face was open, friendly, and still showed hints of her once-considerable beauty. At barely five feet tall, she seemed almost perfectly round, with an enormous bosom that resembled the bow of some stately ship. Her mouse-brown hair was tucked under a mob cap, with a few odd strands flying wild from beneath it.

Plain as she was, happily puffing away on a small cherry-wood pipe, Houston loved her immediately. He thought later it was because she was so unlike his own stern mother. Having been judged so much herself, she did not judge others.

"So *you're* the young man Andy's been talkin' about," she said mischievously. "He thinks the world of you, you know."

Embarrassed and at a loss for words, Houston offered another deep bow, feeling ridiculous even as he did it.

"I am greatly honored," he mumbled, knowing even as he said the words that he sounded like a fool.

Sensing how smitten he was, she moved to put him at ease.

"Please stop that nonsense, Samuel. Watching you bob up and down is like being out in a pirogue on a choppy day. There's no need. We're all family here."

12

No MATTER how much he enjoyed life at the Hermitage, Houston was still an officer in the United States Army. Duty didn't call. It insisted.

And he did not object. He was eager to see New Orleans. The city's cosmopolitan promise excited him. If the stories were true, it was a place where excess was ordinary and behavior considered scandalous elsewhere was accepted with a sophisticated smile and a desire to hear the details.

To reduce expenses, he arranged to travel with a young man who was returning home to study law. They pooled their limited resources and bought a battered skiff. To Houston's dubious eye, it was no more than a large rowboat with a much-patched sail.

Although he looked younger than his twenty one years, Ed White claimed to have made the river trip once before and assured Houston that the skiff was river-worthy and plenty big enough for both of them. As a soldier, the young officer knew nothing at all about aft and port and starboard and jib your something.

What finally convinced him was White's promise that the

little craft were so popular on Louisiana's endless lakes, rivers and bayous that they could easily sell the skiff down river at a profit. To hear White describe it, half the man's home state must be under water.

Leaving Nashville, their route would take them northwest on the Cumberland River to the Ohio, down the Ohio to the Mississippi, then hundreds of miles south to New Orleans. While Houston looked forward to the adventure, he realized that he'd picked an unlikely traveling companion. With a narrow face topped by a shock of wiry black hair, White was skinny, pale, and painfully shy, an astonishing trait considering that he intended to get into politics one day. With one exception, Houston had yet to meet a politician who didn't jabber at marathon length. Jackson was that exception and he wasn't really a politician. Years ago, the general's brief time in the Senate had so infernally bored him that he resigned after only a few months. While it was possible that White might be among the first of his kind, in Houston's opinion if he didn't learn how to assert himself he'd more than likely be the last of his kind.

Not that he minded White's reticence. If he had the money he would have traveled alone. He hungered for solitude, an opportunity to gather himself and try to make sense of everything that happened in the last two years. If he couldn't be alone at least he found someone who wouldn't fill every moment with empty blather and chat.

He was pleased to see that White packed a box of books for their journey. Houston brought a few books himself; a few were all he could afford. He still had his tattered copy of Pope's translation of "The Iliad." After hard dickering, he also acquired a worn edition of Shakespeare's works, along with battered copies of "Robinson Crusoe" and "The Vicar of Wakefield."

They set off from Nashville on a gray and blustery morning. The river was rougher than it looked from the safety of the shore shore and they were soaked after only a few minutes. Despite the ominous start, White's prediction about the journey's ease proved to be true. Pushed along by the current, they never even broke out the small sail. Houston didn't know how to use it anyway, although White did, or said he did. It was easy enough to use the oars to maneuver the little skiff. At first they took turns, but after the first day Houston did all the rowing. Even with a bad shoulder, his strength was a match for anything the river threw at them.

A routine was quickly established that they always put ashore an hour or so before sundown, where their first task was to start a fire before dark. They didn't need it for warmth, but the smoke helped keep away the thick clouds of mosquitoes flourishing along the river shore. They usually read themselves to sleep by the fire's flickering light, although many nights Houston was content to lie on his back, fill his lungs with the heavy river air, and look at the stars in all their glorious smears and clusters.

It was impossible not to gape when they came to the fabled Mississippi. The great river seemed to mysteriously change with the color of the sky. One day it might resemble a lightly done biscuit, especially if the sun was bright in a cloudless sky. Sometimes it was slate gray, and seemed as flat and motionless as a billiard table.

Only the speed of their passage gave a clue to the river's enormous power. Even when there was no other craft in sight, they had to stay vigilant because so many dangerous snags lurked just below the surface. Twice they saw boats jolt to a stop when they hit a "sawyer," a collision with a sunken tree that could easily rip a hull wide open. They had to watch for eddies, too. Once a boat was drawn into the swirl it could go on indefinitely, or until it collided with the ever-accumulating drift and sink out of sight. Houston was astonished at what floated downriver with them, everything from trees, huge logs, and wooden boxes to barrels and dead livestock. Once they saw an entire house spinning crazily downstream. True, it was a small house, but still, a house!

As they drifted south, Tennessee's fresh green scents were replaced by a dank humid odor that smelled like freshly plowed ground after a hard rain. The not unpleasant smell filled Houston's senses and never entirely disappeared. Most of the time, thick walls of dark and inscrutable forest came down to the shore. The river itself was always beautiful, at least Houston thought it so, but the nature that beauty changed from moment to moment. Unless it was raining, the birds always sang at sunrise, with the initial blush of the rising sun and the shifting light and shade and dappled reflections. At the end of most days, when the sun went down it briefly turned the great river into gleaming bars of gold and crimson that quickly faded from sight.

River traffic increased as they traveled south. At first there were only a few small boats, along with the occasional flatboat carrying passengers, cargo, or, most often, both. Lumber, everything from barrel staves to large planks, was a popular item stacked high on the decks. Other boats were loaded with livestock, nails, kegs of gunpowder, tobacco, hemp, and whiskey. Solitary canoeists, usually trappers or Indians, glided past, too, along with a progression of rafters and flatboat men.

The two young men always kept their distance, even after a friendly hail and a hearty invitation to tie the skiff to a passing flatboat for a visit. River men were a notoriously rough crowd. Houston knew how to defend himself, but he didn't want to put White in danger. As far as he knew, his companion had never fired a pistol or pulled a knife in anger. With just the two of them, it was best to be cautious.

As they grew comfortable with each other, they talked more than Houston anticipated they would, one way to keep from feeling overwhelmed by their insignificance on the vast river.

"Sam, what do you want?" White abruptly asked one hot afternoon.

"What do I want?" Houston answered dumbly, as if repeating the question was a kind of answer. "How do you mean?"

"What do you want to *do?*" insisted White. "What do you intend to make of yourself? You're talkative enough, most of the time, but you don't really say much."

As usual, Houston was at the oars. In the bow, White lounged with his head on a stack of books, one ankle propped on the other knee. Houston rowed energetically to cut across the river and gain position closer to the shore, not because he needed to, but to avoid giving a reply.

It seemed as if he was asked that question all his life, and it irritated him that he still didn't have an answer. First his mother, who seemed so unhappy with him because he was his father's son. Then John Coffee. And now Ed White. He asked it of himself a thousand times, but he was no closer to an answer now than ever. He hated the thought of drifting through life the way they drifted down river.

Cutting across the current, he rowed hard until his breath came in bursts and sweat dripped from his brow. Muscles tingling pleasantly, he rested a forearm on each oar as a counterweight to keep the oars out of the water. All the rowing had thickened his arms and shoulders with muscle, although he still couldn't lift his bad arm high enough to scratch his head. With the added bulk, his three shirts were too tight across the shoulders. He'd even ripped one down the middle of his back, a devastating loss of wardrobe.

White refused to let him off without answering and stared at Houston the way a hook pierces a fish's mouth.

"Hell, I don't know." Houston looked down at his big feet in the bottom of the skiff. Going barefoot gave them a better foothold when the river grew choppy. "I wish I did. I don't feel ... I don't know how to explain it exactly ... I don't feel complete without knowin'. Maybe that's why I'm still in the army. Most of the important decisions are made for you."

He raised his head and stared at White, who rolled to one side and propped his head up on one hand.

"What about you?" Houston asked irritably. "I 'spose you're one of those people who know exactly what they want and how to get it."

White's head bobbed emphatically, as if nothing could be more natural than to know at twenty one what you intend to do with the rest of your life.

"I'll practice law for a few years, establish myself, marry well, have a hundred children, and run for Congress. The way this country's growing what better time could there possibly be for someone our age?"

When Houston rolled his eyes White responded with an impatient sniff. How could his large friend miss what seemed so obvious?

"It'll take a few years, of course. I know that. But think of the possibilities for young men like you and me! We can do anything in this country. Anything! In all of history, there's never been anything like it."

Houston remembered something Jackson said not long before he left for New Orleans. They'd wandered into the woods before dark, walking off dinner. A storm was blowing in from the west, although it still was too far away to hear the thunder. They watched from a distance as a breeze kicked up and the air rapidly cooled.

Picking up the dinner conversation, Jackson said, "You know, Sam, trust is a rare thing."

He idly poked a hole in the rich black dirt with his walking stick. The general seemed incapable of being completely still. Even when seated, a foot jiggled or his fingers drummed on a table.

"As you get older, you'll find that there aren't many men worthy of your trust and it takes a while to figure out who they are."

"How do you know?" Houston asked. "How can you tell one from the other?"

"It's time and patience, mostly," Jackson replied. "The trick is to have apparent confidence in everyone, but real confidence in no one until experience shows they're worthy of it. Trust no one except those who prove themselves, but at the same time never let those who fail *know* they failed."

At that moment, Houston realized that he trusted Ed White. They hadn't known each other long, but he knew that this man would pass Jackson's test, no matter what. Being sure of such a profound and personal thing was rare, and Houston felt his heart lift.

"Oh, you'll be fine, I 'spect." White said, interrupting Houston's thoughts. "One of these days you might even grow up. In a world where carpenters are resurrected, anything is possible."

With that, White stretched, got to his feet, dropped his pants to his ankles, widened his stance for balance, and began to piss over the side of the skiff.

Houston quietly slid forward, caught White on his pale skinny butt with the flat of his big foot and sent him over the side with a surprised yelp that was cut off when he hit the cold water.

Houston quickly worked the oars into the water and held the boat against the current while White floundered to the skiff, gasping with laughter and holding his pants with one foot so the current wouldn't carry them away. He hooked one arm over the side and held it there while he threw a bare leg over and weakly hauled himself back into the skiff.

Houston laughed so hard his belly hurt.

"I figured it was time for the Congressman's bath. It *is* Friday, you know."

13

It was hard to say goodbye. They'd see each other again, but the great adventure was over, already tucked away in the vault of memory, and the only way they could do it over is to remember.

Since no one knew that he'd arrived in New Orleans, Houston decided to wait for a day or two and explore the city before reporting for duty. It was easily the most exotic and alluring place he'd ever seen. There were so many languages and colors on the streets that New Orleans was truly a city of the world. Especially at night, it was as if some rare and intoxicating perfume filled the air.

The heart of New Orleans consisted of several dozen neatly laid out blocks on the northwest side of a crescent bend in the Mississippi River. The public square, the *Place d'Armes*, opened to the river on one side. The double-towered St. Louis Cathedral faced the square, plastered and painted to give the appearance of marble, along with the *Cabildo*, or the City Hall. Other public buildings nearby included the Ursuline Convent, two hospitals, the army barracks, a theater, and a ballroom.

Most of the buildings on the main streets were built of brick, with roofs of tile or slate. Others were made of wood with shingle roofs. The better houses were decorated with delicate iron latticework. Arched entrances led to courtyard gardens luxuriously planted with lush tropical shrubs and flowers.

The streets were mostly unpaved and haphazardly drained by open ditches. Garbage and slop thrown into the gutters created a formidable stink, and it was only after a hard rain that the drains were flushed of their smelly contents. Fortunately, hard rain came often in New Orleans. The *banquettes*, or sidewalks, were either paved with brick or made of cypress planks.

Money was New Orleans' blood and commerce its heartbeat. The city boasted four foundries, a rope factory, a flour mill, two potteries, a paper mill, two shipyards, one pianoforte manufacturer, and a brickyard. The air was alive with the sound of clanging blacksmith forges, the grind of saws on wood, the percussion of hammer on nail, and the boisterous voices of men in the riverfront bars. The great port held all manner of craft, including many-masted vessels from a dozen countries. Open boats and skiffs scattered around the great ships like ducklings. The docks bristled with activity twenty-four hours a day, as busy in the middle of the night as in the middle of the afternoon, and the great warehouses bulged with goods waiting to be exported or imported.

The city's social life was as active as it was notorious. While most of the population was Spanish or French, the Spanish, French, and English languages were equally popular. Single officers were in great demand as escorts and Houston quickly found himself in more demand than most, a handsome young officer who cut a dashing, broad-shouldered figure in his blue-and-white uniform. Even his wounds enhanced his stature as a war hero and a friend of the great

Andrew Jackson, New Orleans' savior. Houston wasn't above exaggerating that friendship to get what he wanted, and what he usually wanted was women.

Most of his duties were light, mainly confined to the morning and early afternoon. The Crescent City's balls, coffeehouses, taverns, and nearby plantations became familiar ground as he moved among them during his off-duty hours. He'd start with cognac or absinthe in the late afternoon and end his revels early the next morning at an outdoor café with a cup of rich chicory coffee and a delightful flour and sugar concoction called a *beignet*.

Between the first drink of the night and duty the next day, he gorged himself on pleasure. The Creoles dominated the social life. Vain about their breeding and fastidious in their manners, they possessed a limitless courtesy that somehow was vaguely insulting and hospitable at the same time. The plantations surrounding the city throbbed with life. Guests amused themselves by dancing, drinking, dining, fox hunting, and playing cards. A three-tiered racial structure – white, free black and mulatto, and slave – prevailed. If a man wanted feminine company on a more or less stable basis, a mulatto mistress was an acceptable alternative to participating in the heavy and sometimes cutthroat competition for the city's few eligible white women.

Intent on avoiding commitment, but rarely fond of whoring, Houston favored the elegant quadroon balls, especially one held weekly at a cavernous dance hall on St. Phillip between Bourbon and Royal Streets. It was operated by a colorful character named Cloquet, who claimed to be a veteran of Napoleon's Waterloo campaign, as did what seemed like most of the Frenchmen in New Orleans. The balls promoted a custom called *placage*, where free mixed-blood women hoping to make a match of convenience brazenly paraded themselves before any eligible men who showed up.

It was common for mothers to try to place their young daughters with white men, including married men looking for mistresses, a business arrangement that allowed a free black woman – some of them with so little African blood they were nearly white – to rise in the world. Houston's resources were meager, and he was not interested in anything for the long term, but he found that vague promises cost nothing and accomplished much.

Sam Houston had come a long way from Tennessee. Whatever plans Jackson had for him seemed as distant as the moon. During frequent trips into New Orleans from his family's plantation south of the city in Plaquemines Parish, White was surprised at how quickly his friend came to regard his army duty as inconvenient to his social life. Alarmed by the change, he gathered himself to confront Houston and tell him just that when they met for a lunch of white wine and oysters at Tessier's, a bustling café just off the river on the broad boulevard called Canal Street.

"Sam, it sure looks to me like you've discovered a genuine talent for dissipation." White took care to make his words sound like a tease rather than an accusation. "Just be careful you're not consumed by it." He waved his arm to take in the bustling city. "This place is seductive. It devours people. I've seen it happen."

Houston tilted back his head and let a raw oyster slide out of its shell and down his throat.

"Ed, if I knew being devoured felt this good I'd have tried it a long time ago," he laughed, wiping his mouth with the back of his hand.

In time, he sensed something almost feverish to his life in New Orleans. It was as if he no longer possessed a will of his own. The city's seductive atmosphere burned away ambition and judgment, leaving only an unquenchable thirst for pleasure. He *did* have a talent for dissipation. He realized that now. He enjoyed it without remorse, too. Why not? Hadn't he earned a little pleasure? There was plenty of time.

If he hadn't injured his shoulder perhaps he never would have bothered to find Jackson's surgeon.

Her name was Marie Villars. After a determined siege of several weeks, he finally spent the night with her in her family's large, multi-pillared home on Esplanade Avenue. After going at it until they glistened with perspiration in her candlelit bedroom, they stepped out on the balcony to cool themselves in the night air. Wearing a flimsy silk dressing gown that barely concealed her magnificent breasts, she settled on a cushioned settee with Houston's head in her lap.

"I cannot tell you how wonderful this night has been, *Mon Cher*," Marie said, speaking in the lilting French-accented English he found so charming.

"My love, we'll have many nights like this one," he purred. "The nights will become weeks, and the weeks become months."

He was not about to let *that* happen, but he'd learned that such nonsense was part of the ritual.

"But tomorrow ...." she said.

"Tomorrow my mind will not be on my duty because my heart will be with you," he said dreamily, smiling to himself at the well-turned phrase.

"Tomorrow I am to be engaged."

The next thing he knew, he was sitting bolt upright.

Marie sighed as she reached out to touch his flushed cheek with her cool hand.

"I know you must think it capricious of me, but I wanted a night like this before pledging myself to the old fool Papa picked out for me," She shrugged and her dressing gown slid down to reveal a delectable shoulder. "Still, at least he is wealthy. And perhaps we can still find a way, you and I."

"Capri ...." He heard his voice crack and tried again. *"Capricious,* you say?"

His mind raced as he searched for a way to escape while leaving no hurt feelings behind.

"Well, perhaps a little," he said with a smile, holding his thumb and index finger an inch apart. "Just the tiniest bit."

His rose to his feet. Marie started to rise, too, but he held out his hand to stop her. It was time to retreat. Hell, it was time to run. This was trouble he didn't need.

"No, Marie, I want to remember you just as you are, perfect in every detail. I ...."

"Marie! Is that your light? What are you doing up at this hour?"

Heavy booted feet clumped up the stairs inside. Houston suspected more than one pair, too.

"Oh, Papa! You're home early! It's nothing. I couldn't sleep," Marie replied, her eyes wide with alarm.

"It's my father and brother," she whispered, her voice shaking with fear. "You must hide! The scandal ...!"

Whatever Houston's faults, indecision was not one of them. He seized his uniform jacket, boots, and sword, took a deep breath, placed one hand on the balcony's wrought-iron railing and vaulted over the rail. He couldn't see the ground in the darkness, landed awkwardly, and cracked his bad shoulder on the flagstones, barely managing to stifle a cry of pain before crawling under the balcony.

"What was that?" asked a younger male voice directly above his head.

"What?" Marie asked innocently. "I didn't hear anything."

After a few minutes, she coaxed her brother and father inside and Houston scrabbled away, clutching at the pain in his shoulder.

14

HE FOUND Jackson's surgeon two days later. The man gruffly introduced himself as Cambronne. No first name, no title, just Cambronne, a Frenchman whose hooked nose, long neck, and spindly legs gave him the appearance of an ungainly water-fowl. He lived and worked in an airy suite of second-floor rooms on Royal Street.

The examination was brief but excruciating. As Houston writhed on the table, the surgeon probed his shoulder while muttering about "army butchers" and "ignorant rustics."

Washing his hands after the examination while Houston fumbled to button his shirt with a numb arm and painful shoulder, Cambronne wasted no time.

"Lieutenant, that ball must come out and the bone frag-ments with it," he declared, his precise English all but devoid of accent. "If I don't operate you risk being crippled for life. As it is there may be some restricted movement, but nothing such as plagues you now. If you'd come to me sooner I could have done more, but that is in the past."

Houston explained that he had no money to pay for such an operation.

"Do not insult me," Cambronne replied curtly. "This city owes everything to Jackson. He asked that I help you, and I will. As you see, I live simply. Money is not important."

Cambronne operated three days later. A stick covered in leather was jammed in Houston's mouth. Despite a few drops of laudanum, it took four men to hold him down while Cambronne sliced open the old wound and dug in his shoulder for the musket ball. An explosion of lightning shot from Houston's shoulder through his neck and burst in his head with a white flash while he struggled against the eight strong hands holding him on the table.

A scalpel carefully re-opened the wound, knotted thick with scar tissue and muscle, and the probe slid deep into the mangled flesh, searching for the ball. Finding it, Cambronne forced the long-necked forceps into the incision to get a purchase on the ball. Houston's mind told him that the instruments moved only the barest fraction at a time, but the sensation was of vast distances as he felt the horrible scrape of metal on bone.

Through the fog of pain, he heard a distant cry of triumph, followed by a grunt and a muttered *"Merde!"* as the doctor strained to drag the ball out of the flesh already closed around the forceps. There was a sharp clank as something dropped into a metal pan beside the operating table.

———

WHEN HOUSTON CAME to he was lying in a feather bed. A down comforter covered him in the sticky New Orleans' heat. He started to toss it aside, but stopped when he remembered why he was here. Better to remain still and swelter beneath the comforter than risk the pain that might come from sudden movement.

It's a blessing that the body has no memory of pain. He

remembered pleasurable in all its many forms, but he couldn't recall pain with the same detail. He remembered that the operation hurt, but not *how* it hurt. He didn't *feel* it in his memory the way he felt how it was to make love to Marie. As he gratefully sank back into unconsciousness, he thought that it must be the body's way of protecting itself. If so, he was glad of it. Some things he did not want to remember.

Cambronne sitting on the side of the bed awakened him again. He didn't feel the surgeon's presence as much as sense it. As usual, the Frenchman wasted no time on pleasantries.

"We were successful, Lieutenant," he said. "It was difficult. Working through all that muscle and scar tissue wasn't easy. I hurt you more than I intended, but there was no other way."

The doctor held up a badly misshapen musket ball between thumb and index finger.

"This is the rascal that caused the trouble. I removed many bone chips, too. Once you're healed, months from now, you'll have much better movement of your arm and shoulder. I doubt that you'll notice what little you can't do."

For the first time since they met, Cambronne smiled. For a moment, he seemed almost human.

"You will stay here for a few days, perhaps a week. I have a woman to care for you. You will be a long time healing and it is my recommendation to your commanding officer that you go home. Your army likes its cannon fodder to be healthy, I believe."

With that, the surgeon stood and walked out of the room. Houston never saw him again.

As Cambronne predicted, Lieutenant Sam Houston was granted permission to go home to Tennessee, although he was in no condition to travel right away. Unfortunately, his weakness kept him from diving back into New Orleans' revels and there was nothing to do but wait. After three weeks of mind-numbing boredom, relieved only by frequent visits from Ed White, he finally was deemed well enough to travel with a detachment headed to Detroit.

And then? He wasn't sure. Once again, he was drifting.

15

HE WAS uncomfortable from the moment he walked through the door of the family homestead on Baker's Creek.

What once was so familiar - the cast iron stove, the faded Persian rug, the horse hair sofa and chairs, and the leather hinges on the doors and windows - now seemed dreary beyond belief. Maryville itself was depressing and provincial, a place where nothing ever happened and nothing ever would. He was embarrassed to be there, ashamed that someone might think that this was where he belonged.

Certain that the world had forgotten him, after just a few weeks Houston wanted to lash out in frustration. Even what little amusement he found wasn't satisfying for long. Maryville's young ladies were smitten with his handsome figure and the worldliness that went with it; a war hero who'd traveled to faraway places to do exciting things. He enjoyed their attention for a while, but the lemonade intimacies paled after the delights of New Orleans. Home was an even smaller world than he remembered, and it was not his world. It never was.

Houston's shoulder healed quickly. Cambronne did his

work well. The problem wasn't physical. He roiled with the old feeling that events were passing him by. All he could do was wait for orders, but waiting was the hardest thing of all.

He hated to wear his uniform when he went into town. It made him feel self-conscious, as if he was showing off in a place that wasn't worth the effort. Unfortunately he had no other decent clothes. The trip down river added so much muscle to his big frame that none of his old clothes fit. His mother and sisters made a few things for him, but he was embarrassed to be seen in the rough country clothes and wore them only when there was no other choice.

As time passed, Houston began to notice barely concealed hostility from a few of Maryville's young men, mostly belligerent glares and dark muttering just out of earshot. He didn't have to hear it to recognize it for what it was. He'd heard the story many times from others like himself. The stay-at-homes his own age resented his presence because it made them feel like lesser men. The young women always noticed when he passed and the older men made sure that he never paid for a drink. Comparisons were inevitable and the locals were not happy when they came up short.

The worst of it came from a gang led by Obadiah Brock, a local tough whose shaved head resembled a cannonball and whose short arms were thick with muscle. Brock's followers consisted of the stupid, the dishonest, the lazy, and one soft-brain who tagged along like a pet dog because no one else would have him.

On a warm and cloudless morning, Houston rode the buckboard into Maryville to pick up supplies for the farm. The mundane errand gave him time to reflect on how far he'd fallen and the glum thoughts stoked the simmering frustration that never seemed to go away.

After dickering for everything the farm needed - another task he found demeaning - by mid-afternoon he was ready to go home. As he mounted the heavily loaded wagon in the little town square, just in time he saw the lumpy mess of horse shit dumped on the wagon seat, still steaming in the hot sun. Stepping back to the ground, he spotted the leather bucket they'd used turned upside down on a barrel of flour in the back of the wagon.

From behind, near the entrance to Dexter's Mercantile, Houston heard a half-stifled giggle. He turned to see Brock leaning against the logs of the mercantile front, his huge arms folded across his chest and one leg bent at the knee with the bottom of his foot resting against the wall. Two of his gang lounged on the ground to his right, passing a jug between them. At least one of the men was drunk. Houston guessed that was probably the one who giggled. They'd all been drinking. That was clear enough. Who was drunk and who wasn't was just a matter of who held it better.

"S'matter, is the hero 'fraid to get his pants dirty?" Brock's smirk twisted his face into something even uglier than it already was. "Sure seems like yer too good for jus' 'bout everything goes on 'round here, sol'jer boy."

The anger was a clean feeling because Houston didn't have to hold it back anymore. Feeling relaxed and confident - relieved even - he casually moved toward Brock with his arms at his side, taking his time and savoring the moment. When he was close enough, he planted his left foot, swung his right leg with all his strength and kicked Brock between the legs, feeling the satisfying jolt all the way to his hip. Brock gasped, clutched himself, and crumpled to his knees with a sound between a whimper and a moan.

The two on the ground were stunned, astonishment written all over their faces. No one had ever made the first move on their leader, much less put him down. Responding to Brock's half-growled, half-groaned "Get him!" they scrambled to their feet, the sober one moving just a little faster.

It was almost too easy. The first one charged like one ship trying to ram another. Houston stepped aside, put one hand on his collar, the other on the small of his back, and used the fool's own momentum to send him out into the middle of the square, where he hit the hard-packed dirt and skidded painfully on his chest.

While Brock struggled to his feet, hands between his legs and his face purple with pain, the other one snatched up a hoe leaning against the mercantile wall and barreled at Houston, carrying the hoe as if he was making a bayonet charge.

But Houston was faster. He seized the end of the hoe with one hand, slipped to the side and yanked it toward his own body, jerking the charging man off balance. Houston twisted the hoe away, held it horizontally with both hands and snapped forward with his right hand, cracking the man on the jaw with hoe's end. The blow sent him reeling backwards.

Houston heard himself keening a mad noise. He enjoyed the fight, if he knew anything of what he felt. He sensed only ecstasy blotting out fear and driving him forward. Like at Horseshoe Bend, he saw everything with astonishing clarity, as if the enemy was slowed to half speed.

Rising to his feet, Brock charged, too, bellowing like a bull. At the same time, someone grabbed Houston from the back, trying to pin his arms to his side, while another pair of hands clawed at his legs. The hoe was still in his hands, spread about eighteen inches apart. He jerked his powerful forearms and wrists up and cracked Brock under the chin with the handle. Brock staggered, bleeding from a deep gash on his chin. Houston rammed Brock in the belly with the hoe's wooden end and the blow put him on his hands and knees again.

Houston whirled around, throwing off whoever was trying to pin his arms. He seized the end of the hoe with one hand, twirled it around his head and hit the side of an ugly pock-marked face. Dull and dirty as it was, the hoe's metal ridge sliced the man's face open from forehead to chin. With Houston's heightened senses, it was as if he could see the long gash sluice open.

Desperate hands still clawed at his legs. Houston stomped on a skinny chest, and then dropped his whole weight on one knee, pulverizing flesh and shattering ribs. To make sure his foe stayed down, Houston kicked him twice on the side of the head.

Brock was on his feet again and breathing hard, his fleshy lips parted and chin dripping blood. Houston dropped the hoe and grabbed Brock by the shirtfront with his left hand. He pulled him close and hit him on the side of his face with his right fist. He backhanded Brock with the same fist and kept the rhythm going, three, four, five times. Brock sagged and Houston realized the only thing keeping him upright was his hold on the shirt. He let go and Brock crumpled to the ground.

Suddenly there was no one left to fight. It didn't seen right that it was over so quickly.

He felt something wet run into his eye and down the side of his nose. He wiped it with his sleeve and it came back red with blood. His eyebrow was slashed open. He didn't even feel it happen.

Three bodies were scattered on the ground, all of them still breathing. Not that he cared.

Heads hesitantly appeared at windows and doorways around the square. Feeling lightheaded, Houston walked to the horse trough beside the mercantile, knelt, and stuck his head in the foul water.

He came up gasping. A shake of his head sent the water flying. He combed his fingers through his hair, went over to Brock, reached down, ripped off his shirt, and walked back to the trough. He soaked the shirt in water and walked to the wagon, where he wiped the horse shit off the wagon seat.

After flinging the leather bucket away, he tossed the shirt on Brock's face.

He saw Dexter, the white-haired old man who owned the mercantile, standing in the doorway, as if he was afraid to come outside.

"I'm sorry about your hoe," he said, motioning toward the shattered hoe on the ground beside one of the bodies.

"My hoe?" Dexter gaped. He did not believe what he'd just seen, shocked by the naked ferocity of the young man he'd known since he was a boy.

When Dexter didn't say anything else, Houston climbed onto the wagon. He felt empty and tired. But home was ten miles away and he'd have to unload the wagon when he got there.

———

NO ONE SAID a word about the brawl, then or later. His mother didn't even say anything about the cut along his eyebrow. Except for the cut, it was as if it never happened. His wounded shoulder wasn't even sore.

He never saw Brock again. No one did, at least not around Maryville. When Houston returned to town the following week, although no one mentioned the fight he saw how people looked at him. He didn't care.

His orders came two weeks later, delivered by courier, a sandy-haired ensign who stood rigidly at attention at the door, his shako cradled under his arm. Too impatient to be mindful of his dignity and open the orders in private, Houston used the edge of his hand to knife through the heavy wax seal, tearing the paper in his haste.

And what splendid orders they were! He was "requested and required" to proceed with all possible haste to Nashville, where he was assigned to Jackson's staff.

There was a personal note, too.

"Sam,"

"We heard about your little tussle. It's about time we got you out of there. Hope you hit a lick for me."

"Gnl. Jackson"

16

THE DAYS PASSED in a blur as Houston got to know Jackson's staff, advisers, friends, and the hangers-on who followed the general like flies on a bull. In time he'd separate those who mattered from those who didn't, but for now he had only fleeting impressions. The inner circle was divided into long-time friends and a handful of men a generation younger:

* A slender, sharp-eyed patrician from South Carolina, the ambitious James Gadsden was not much older than Houston. A graduate of Yale College, he served the general with thin-lipped efficiency.

* After fighting at Jackson's side from the Creek War to New Orleans, handsome Johnny Eaton followed the general like a puppy. While it was impossible not to like the affable young man, to Houston he seemed more surface than depth.

* Two young newcomers had recently joined the group. James Knox Polk was an intense North Carolinian with dark hollows around his eyes and brown hair swept straight back from a broad forehead. James Buchanan was a soft-looking Pennsylvanian. Polk rarely laughed, or even smiled, while

Buchanan seemed constantly amused by something only he knew.

* Finally there were Jackson's oldest and most trusted friends, John Coffee, Billy Carroll, and John Overton.

Rachel Jackson was away visiting relations when Houston arrived and it was almost a month before she returned to the Hermitage. She was knitting in a rocker under an elm tree in front of the main house when Houston strode up the gray flagstone walk after riding in from Nashville, a saddlebag stuffed with Jackson's official and personal correspondence slung over one shoulder. With some effort, she heaved her bulk out of the rocker and enveloped him in a hug.

"Samuel!" Her shout was muffled, the noise going directly into his chest. "I made Andy promise he'd get you back here. He'd of done it anyhow, but he likes to pretend he did it just for me. Of all his young men, he knows you're my favorite."

She looked the same as he remembered, even down to the small cherry-wood pipe that was clenched in her teeth and painfully jabbing him in the breastbone. If anything, she seemed even more perfectly round than before. Touched at how pleased she was to see him, he was surprised by how easily he returned the feeling.

Extricating himself from her fleshy grasp, he put his hands on her shoulders and held her at arm's length.

"Aunt Rachel, do you think *anything* could keep me away?" he asked.

Houston glanced over her head toward the porch of the big house. Apparently he'd interrupted an informal gathering of some kind. He was curious to see the reaction to Rachel's declaration that he was her favorite among the younger men. Gadsden's cool eyes narrowed as he reassessed the challenger. The good-natured Eaton offered a grin and a wave. Buchanan smirked at his usual inner delight while Polk simply stared, his face expressionless as stone.

Aware that he was staring, too, Houston took a step back and recovered from his lapse with a flamboyant bow. With his left arm tucked at his stomach, his right swept through the air. As he bowed, he repeated the words he'd spoken when they first met.

"Madam," he said grandly, "I salute you."

Rachel erupted with one of her wheezing laughs and hugged him again. He would have been disappointed if she hadn't remembered.

———

HOUSTON'S DUTIES kept him constantly on the move. Although he usually spent one or two nights a week at the Hermitage, he was in Nashville so much that he eventually took a small room at the Nashville Inn. The upper floor of the rambling whitewashed inn on the busy town square was a rabbit's warren of suites and single rooms, with a popular well-stocked tavern dominating the ground floor.

With its ideal location on the main road west, Nashville, and, thus, the Hermitage, was a seething hothouse of news, rumor and gossip. There were so many visitors to the Hermitage that as far as Houston could tell the general and his wife never dined alone. Guests knew to go to the parlor an hour after dinner, after Jackson's customary brief after-dinner nap, where the local, national, and international issues of the day were debated, analyzed, and discussed. Fast friendships and bitter rivalries developed, split, and then reformed, with the composition constantly changing and reforming along new lines.

The atmosphere was intoxicating. Houston felt himself being molded and shaped by everything he saw and heard. At first he hesitated to take part for fear of embarrassing himself. Until now some of the issues hadn't even crystallized as issues in his mind. It wasn't a case of not knowing *what* to think about them as much as not knowing *how*. At the urging of Jackson and Overton, he gradually became a participant, at first reluctantly, then enthusiastically. With his keen memory, intelligence, and natural rhetorical gifts, Houston discovered that he possessed a talent for debate.

"You're not here to be mute, son," Jackson explained one rainy afternoon during one of their frequent chess matches in the parlor. "A man learns by doing. You risk being bested sometimes, but there's no avoidin' it. There's been plenty of times in my life I felt like a fool, but feeling foolish never yet killed a man."

Learning to play chess was a genuine trial for the young man, especially with a teacher as ruthless as Jackson.

"Sir, I just don't have the patience for this," Houston protested in frustration after Jackson scolded him for a particularly blundering move.

"Then you'll just have to learn," Jackson replied mercilessly. "Patience can be acquired like anything else. Chess is all about tactics, strategy and foresight. Believe me, you'll need 'em all. Mostly it's a matter of discipline. Just take your medicine like a man until you figure it out."

———

HOUSTON'S PROMOTION to first lieutenant was a surprise, an unexpected advance in rank with a generous allowance for traveling expenses. Thrilled to be earning such a magnificent sum, for the first time in his life he had money to spare, a condition that didn't last long. He wasn't the first young man to discover that the more he had, the more he spent.

As Jackson's eyes and ears in military matters, which often were political matters, too, he was constantly in the saddle and got to know Tennessee as well as anyone, just as

Tennessee became familiar with the young giant who had the ear of the most powerful man in the state.

Despite the hard work, he'd never been happier. Not that his life was all work. He eagerly looked forward to the monthly balls and soirees that rotated among the plantations scattered across the Cumberland. After refining his skill in New Orleans, despite his size Houston was an excellent much-in-demand dancer and enjoyed the spectacle of the well-dressed men and women capering across the dance floor in an infinity of swirling petticoats.

If he lived to be a hundred he'd never see a stranger sight than the long skinny general and his short dumpling of a wife capering to the wild melody of "Possum Up de Gum Tree" at Houston's first Christmas ball. Waving a glass of eggnog in the direction of the frolicking couple, Buchanan chuckled, "By God, the old gent looks like a man trying to stomp out a campfire, doesn't he?"

Houston looked forward to the frequent horse races, too. Jackson's stable was one of many in Tennessee, a state where horses rivaled religion. The races in no way resembled the decorous affairs of those Houston sometimes attended around Washington. Cheating was not only common, it was expected. Jockeys were as likely to apply the whip to each other as to their mounts. Bets ran as high as twenty thousand dollars a race and passions ran even higher. As a young man, Jackson himself fought a duel as a result of hot words exchanged after a race. He killed his opponent, but still carried the man's pistol ball in his chest.

———

HOUSTON'S first important assignment was to work with Polk and Gadsden to come up with a candidate for sheriff in a newly-created west Tennessee county. With its control of information and manpower, the sheriff's office was a vital position and Jackson wanted to be sure the job went to the right man; the right Jackson man, in other words.

Unfortunately, Polk and Gadsden supported different candidates, with Houston on the fence, not knowing either man well enough to venture an opinion, although the real reason for his silence was that he didn't want to get between Polk and Gadsden when they had their claws out. After two hours in one of the Nashville Inn's meeting rooms, with sleeves rolled up and collars undone, the trio was tired, frustrated, and angry. Polk and Gadsden were too much alike to get along at the best of times. Each one adamantly refused to give in to the other and somehow managed to blame Houston for the stalemate.

Overton quietly opened the door, entered the smoky overheated room, and took a seat at the table. After listening to the argument for a few minutes, he tilted his chair back on its rear legs and entwined his fingers over his paunch.

"You know, that reminds me of a story."

Houston, Polk and Gadsden looked at each other in disbelief. What on earth did anyone say that could possibly remind Overton of one of his awful stories? This was hardly the time another meandering yarn.

"When I was a young man you might be surprised to hear that I was somewhat wild in my ways. Like most young men, I was always on the lookout for a little easy money. And then I had a bright idea. I captured a badger and put him in a barrel right out there," he said, waving toward the town square. "I put up a sign declarin' to anybody who had a dog that I bet their dog couldn't get my badger out of the barrel. Silly as it seems, just about every day somebody'd give it a try. We'd drop the dog in the barrel and they'd go at it, snarling' and snappin' until the barrel tipped over and my badger took off with the dog on his heels, though he always came back when the dog got tired of chasin' him. Never known a badger to wander home like that before, but it happened every time."

"Now it's been quite a few years so I can't say how much money I lost, but I could see there wasn't much future in this line. Eventually I solved the problem."

Someone had to ask, so Houston did.

"How?"

Overton grinned and slapped his knee.

"I shot the damn badger."

The story wasn't particularly funny. In fact, it wasn't funny at all. But Polk started giggling. Usually as humorless as a pine board, on those rare occasions when something hit him right Polk might titter about it for the better part of a week. His unexpected laughter drove the tension out of the room like smoke flowing through a window. When they returned to business, Houston thought of a compromise candidate who managed to satisfy both Polk and Gadsden. More important, it allowed them to save face so that neither man gave in to the other. To the relief of them all, the session finally broke up a few minutes after midnight.

Seeing Houston's questioning look, Overton waited outside on the deserted square after the others left. Although he wore a wool jacket, Overton still folded his arms across his chest in an attempt to keep warm.

"You know, as I get older, it's hard to stay as warm as I like," Overton muttered as he looked out on the street, huffing into the air so he could see his own breath. "Come winter I'll probably be so bundled up you can just roll me down the street."

He turned to Houston. "What's on your mind, Sam? Spit it out before I freeze to death."

"How did you do that?" Houston asked. "I mean, how did you know *when* to do it? It's as if you appeared by magic exactly at the right moment, like you were listenin' outside.

I've seen you do it, or somethin' like it, before, too. How do you know?"

Overton shrugged. "It's not so mysterious. For one thing, I know my young gentlemen. I figured Polk and Gadsden'd more'n likely get into one of their wet hen fights."

"But that story was ...." Houston struggled to find the right word, one that wouldn't be insulting.

"Pointless?" Overton chuckled. "It surely was. I'm not sure it was entirely true, either. But once the bullshit stopped flyin' and the three of you relaxed a little someone came up with the right name, didn't they? I believe that someone was you, by the way."

Doubting that he'd ever learn what Overton seemed to know intuitively, Houston said good night and started to walk back into the inn and up to his room.

"One more thing, Sam."

"What's that?" Houston asked, turning on his heel.

"You don't much like Polk, do you? Or Gadsden either, for that matter. "

"They're a little hard to warm up to."

"No argument from me on that," Overton nodded. "But you might consider a little Christian charity, especially when it comes to Polk. There's a lot of grit in that young man. If you ever broke through the crust he'd probably make a good friend. Anybody ever tell you what he went through when he a youngster?"

"No, what happened?"

"Seems he had a sickness in his gut for years. Almost died of it, in fact. When he was sixteen his family took him to a Kentucky doctor who said he had some kind of stones in his pisser. The doc gave him a little brandy, put him jay bird naked on a table and strapped his legs up in the air. Then the doc took a monstrous thing called a gorget and bored right through Polk's balls to his innards to get the stones out. I don't know if what they say it did to him is true, and you sure didn't hear any of this from me, but it'd be a hell of a thing for a man to carry around for the rest of his life."

Houston shivered and knew it wasn't from the night air.

"All I'm sayin' is you might consider givin' Polk the benefit of the doubt sometimes," Overton concluded. "He'll be a good'n. Along with you, he's the best here."

With a cheery wave goodnight, Overton sauntered down the street, leaving the weary Houston to trudge up the stairs to his room. It wasn't until just before he went to sleep that he realized exactly what Overton said. He slept well that night.

17

IT WAS NO LONGER enough to talk about what everyone called the Indian problem. Something had to be done.

Everyone knew that Jackson and Houston had opposing views. Houston respected and sympathized with most Indians, especially the Cherokee. Jackson might respect individuals like Weatherford, but he offered not an ounce of sympathy. It was their only significant disagreement. For that reason, they never talked about it. Houston owed Jackson too much to disagree publicly and it wouldn't do any good to try to hash it out privately because each man knew that he couldn't change the other.

As usual, it fell to John Overton to bridge the gap idling near the Hermitage stables on a hot summer afternoon when Houston rode in from Nashville.

"Walk with me a while, Sam," Overton said, catching up to Houston after the young officer turned his horse over to a groom to be watered, fed, and rubbed down. "It'll do you good to stretch out the kinks. Unless we're at war again, whatever you're supposed to deliver can wait a few minutes."

Houston was instantly alert. John Overton was anything

but a horseman. At best, he regarded horses as a necessary evil and he certainly didn't waste his time lounging around the stables for no good reason. The canny old gent had something on his mind.

Leaving the stables and all their pungent scents behind, they walked out to the trees beyond. The ground was dappled with shade and sunlight and insects buzzed softly in the background. Houston was in his shirtsleeves after throwing his military jacket over the split-rail fence. Overton removed his dark coat, hooked it on his finger, and carried it over his shoulder. He offered a drink of whiskey from his flask and Houston gratefully accepted with a long thirsty swallow.

After making small talk while they walked far enough for Overton to be sure that they wouldn't be overheard or interrupted, he came to the point.

"Sam, I wanted to talk to you about our little Indian issue," he said. "We all know you and Andy disagree somewhat. But if you look beneath the surface I'm thinkin' you'd find more to agree on than argue about."

Uncomfortable with how quickly he was put on the defensive, Houston protested, "Judge, I've never disagreed publicly with the general and I doubt I ever will."

"No one thought you would," Overton said, smoothing the young man's ruffled feathers. "No one questions your loyalty. Not one soul."

They walked a bit more, the silence punctuated by the crunch of twigs under their feet, before coming to a small clearing. Overton, who was at least thirty pounds overweight, with a hard round belly he concealed with excellent tailoring, gratefully sank down on a stump. Sweat had soaked through his shirt and made large circles under his armpits.

Houston remained standing and pressed the heels of his hands against the small of his back, stretching out after the ride from Nashville.

"As I see it, Sam, the problem with our so-called Indian policy is that we don't really have one," Overton began.

He reached into his waistcoat pocket for a couple of cigars. Houston declined the offer. It was too hot to smoke, though that didn't stop the judge.

"Not only do we treat every tribe different from every other tribe, we treat factions within 'em different, too," Overton continued. "Half the time we're at cross-purposes with ourselves. Despite what they say about how Andy hates 'em all, the fact is that if they don't get in the way he's content to leave 'em alone. But if they *are* in the way either they move voluntarily, or they'll get moved, and that means war. Believe me, he'd much rather they go voluntarily. Any sane man would. He'll support any reasonable plan to compensate for the loss of their lands and move 'em west beyond civilization's reach."

Houston was puzzled. What was Overton up to? This was familiar ground and they both knew it. As he did many times before, Houston pointed out that no amount of money could compensate the Indians for the loss of their lands, just as no amount of money could compensate Jackson if he lost the Hermitage. There was no such thing as "beyond civilization's reach" either. Eventually civilization reached everywhere, at least everywhere that mattered.

Overton drew deeply on his cigar, releasing the smoke in a long relaxed hiss.

"I know, and I agree, too, mostly," he admitted. "But we're both realists. Sooner or later they've got to go and you know it. Settlers are pourin' in from the East. There's no way to stop 'em even if we wanted to. Your family did it just like everyone else. Maryville and everything around it used to be Indian land. Hell, the whole country used to be Indian land, but here we are. Do you want us to give it back?"

Overton was fond of Houston. But more to the point, the

young man was in a position to do something important for Jackson and Overton intended to make sure he did it. It was time to plant the thought in the lad's head and let it simmer for a while.

"Wouldn't it be best for the tribes to strike the best bargain they can instead of fightin' to delay the inevitable?" he asked. "Better for them and better for us. They can't win and you know it. The only choice they have is how they lose. It may be a poor selection but if they wait too long they'll have none at all."

Overton was right, but Houston still didn't like it. He felt trapped between what was right and what was real, between what could be done and what should be done. Seeing the world from two points of view wasn't easy. Young as he was, hard experience had taught him that the truth is not often simple. It is almost never all of this or all of that. The truth is full of elusive shapes and strange mixtures, a mingling of subtle shadings that can be difficult to grasp and impossible to hold.

They walked back to the stables, stopping to retrieve Houston's jacket and his saddlebags. Once again he admired the older man's skill. Overton obviously was recruiting him for something, however gently, but he still didn't know what.

Overton ambled toward his cabin and Houston continued to the big house.

"Sam, I'm glad we had this little talk," Overton said. "Now I believe I'll take a nap. I can use a rest."

18

THREE DAYS LATER, when Houston came downstairs from his room in the Nashville Inn on the way to a light breakfast in the tavern, the innkeeper handed him a note that asked him to meet with Overton, Gadsden, and Jackson that afternoon at the Hermitage.

Houston wryly noted that he was "asked" to attend. As close as they were, Jackson still was his superior officer, so far above him that the general might as well be God. He could order Lieutenant Houston to do anything and go anywhere. Yet, he was cordially *asked*, as if he had a choice.

If the sugar coating was meant to put him at ease it failed. It was clear that something unusual was in the wind and it had to do with his strange meeting with Overton. But what was it? Filled with suspicious but no conclusions, riding out to the Hermitage the next day was like approaching a bear's den. With all of his senses vibrating, it was if Houston could feel the blood coursing through his veins.

It was another warm afternoon. Rachel Jackson sat in a rocker on the veranda, wearing a blue-and-white checked apron and languidly cooling herself with an ornate Spanish fan. As he bent over to kiss her cheek, she whispered, "You'd best watch yourself in there, Samuel. I don't know what it's all about, but they're layin' for you, sure as can be." Houston winked and received a fond smile in reply.

He straightened himself, took a deep breath, and entered the big house to find Overton, Gadsden, and Jackson gathered around the dining table in their shirtsleeves. He noticed that they were careful to not all sit on the same side, which would force him to sit by himself on the opposite side. This way they didn't seem aligned against him. It was a small touch, but he'd learned that small touches were important.

Taking his seat, Houston looked around to assess the mood of the opposition, although he hated to think of them in that way. Gadsden was his usual self; single-minded and cold as frost. At times he seemed like more of a mechanism than a man, as if made up of cogs and wheels. Irritation that turned into anger when he didn't get his way and impatience with anyone he considered less than his intellectual equal were the only emotions Houston recalled seeing from the South Carolinian.

As for Jackson, the general radiated a blend of power and warmth; a man who treasured his friends and his enemies. His white hair looked more than ever like a lion's mane, topping a long face that was weathered and brown from life spent outdoors.

And while Overton seemed genuinely pleased to see him, practically bubbling with good cheer, Houston sensed something at work under the surface, too.

And what did they see when they looked at him, he wondered, trying to see himself objectively? A tall young man forged by experience. With gray eyes set wide apart and unruly chestnut hair, his vitality attracted men and women alike. He had growing confidence in himself, knew that he was given to excess, and possessed considerable vanity, sometimes too much.

"Sit down, Sam, sit down." Overton beamed like he was welcoming a guest to a Christmas party. "Can we get you anything? Whiskey? Beer? Rum? A little corn liquor?"

Taking a seat next to Overton and across the table from Jackson and Gadsden, Houston desperately wanted something to calm his galloping nerves, but another quick glance told him that no one else was drinking.

"Water will do fine," he said.

Overton rose, poured a glass of water from a crystal pitcher and placed it on the wide dining table in front of Houston. He returned to his chair, tilted it back so that it balanced on its rear legs, made a steeple with his fingertips in front of his chin, and got down to business.

"Sam, we have a problem and we think you're just the man to take care of it," he explained.

Not long ago, Houston would have puffed up at the compliment. But he'd learned a great deal. Without commenting, he sipped his water and waited for Overton to continue.

Seeing Houston's response, or lack of it, Overton dropped his hands, along with his avuncular pose, and eased his chair to the floor.

"As you know, the war with the Creeks eliminated any Indian threat in the South except for down in Florida, which I'll get to later. As you also know, earlier this year Andy and Governor McMinn negotiated another treaty with the Cherokee for more than a million acres of land in exchange for certain long-term annuities, enough land west of the Mississippi for them to comfortably settle, and an agreement that they'd begin to move as soon as possible."

"And now the lying treacherous savages refuse to go," interrupted Gadsden with his usual impatience.

He was about to further vent his spleen when Jackson

made a cutting motion with his hand, the signal for Gadsden to keep his mouth shut. It amused Houston to see Gadsden choke down his unspoken words and sink back in his chair.

Overton began to build his case.

The Cherokee, Creek, Choctaw, Chickasaw, and a few other minor tribes occupied land that sprawled over parts of Tennessee, North Carolina, South Carolina, Georgia, and Alabama, an extraordinary amount of territory for such a sparse population. About six thousand Creek survived the war, all but a few hundred of them women and children, while the Cherokee numbered about twelve thousand. Add the other tribes and altogether between twenty five and thirty thousand Indians lived scattered across a vast area of land that was much coveted by white settlers who were moving in fast.

It was an old story. The two generations since old Dan Boone led the first settlers through the Cumberland Gap saw almost constant war with one tribe or another. The Cherokee signed the first treaty of any kind with the United States in 1785, eight years before Houston was born. They supported the French during the French and Indian War and the British during the War for Independence. When their allies lost both times, a treaty with the victors seemed the wisest course.

Unfortunately the settlers flooding across the mountains ignored the treaty. Most of them probably didn't even know about it and wouldn't have cared if they did. As the white pressure increased, the Cherokee naturally pushed back, but without much success. The state governments vigorously supported the settlers while the federal government made a feeble effort to honor the treaty. But Washington was far away, with too many other problems and too few resources to deal with them.

The cycle was predictable: A new round of treaties made

the Indians secure, but only until the next wave of settlers, which led to a new round of treaties.

The idea of moving the tribes somewhere beyond the Mississippi was not a new one. Many years ago, President Jefferson sent a delegation west to find and inspect land for just such a thing, ignoring the inconvenient fact that the tribes there considered the land their own. Several years later, two thousand Creek and Cherokee left for the new country, although, as far as Houston knew, precious little had been heard from them since. It was as if they disappeared into the mist.

Now it was time to try again. The Cherokee were the most respected of the Five Civilized Tribes - Cherokee, Creek, Choctaw, Chickasaw, and Seminole. If they, or at least a sizable number of them, began serious preparations to move west, others would follow. But, as Gadsden said, so far they refused to go. In other circumstances, war was the next inevitable step, but, fortunately for the Cherokee, the timing was against it. According to reports out of Georgia and Florida, the Seminole were showing surprising aggressiveness, although most of the experienced hands Houston knew thought they were being manipulated by the Spanish. It wouldn't be the first time the Dons used the Seminole as a buffer to protect their Florida settlements.

Houston had read the reports, having delivered most of them to Jackson himself, and doubted that the Seminole were as hostile as they were made out to be. Another Indian war was just a convenient excuse for the United States to snatch Florida from Spain's weak grasp. If Jackson moved south, he'd no doubt seize the opportunity to claim that while pursuing the Seminole they took refuge in Florida and he no choice but to follow. Once there, it would be easy to either provoke a war with Spain, or bully Spain into giving up Florida for a few minimum concessions.

Considering everything that Houston heard about the place, he didn't understand why anyone coveted Florida at all. Why not leave it to the snakes and alligators?

Whatever the reason, real or artificial, Jackson intended to move south sooner rather than later, so for now a separate campaign against the Cherokee was out of the question.

Jackson spoke for the first time. "It's simple enough, Sam. I don't want a war on two fronts. For now I intend to offer the Cherokee an olive branch. But they must be made to understand this is the only chance they'll have. If they don't take it …."

The general didn't finish. It wasn't necessary. Everyone at the table knew exactly what he meant.

Now Houston understood the reason for the earlier talk with Overton. It was so obvious that he berated himself for not seeing it earlier. As he made his case then and then repeated it today, Overton didn't say anything that Houston didn't already know. If anything, he understated the problem. It was much more complicated and they all knew it.

One unspoken detail that would no doubt remain unspoken was that Jackson and McMinn were partners in land speculation and held options on thousands of acres bordering Cherokee land. They stood to profit immensely if the Cherokee were forced out. Despite the Hermitage, Andrew Jackson was not a wealthy man. In fact, if the rumors were true, like most planters Jackson was heavily in debt. But if his speculation schemes worked out he would certainly become wealthy. Houston didn't know how much it influenced Jackson's thinking, or if it influenced him at all, but it was wise to keep in mind that there is no interest stronger than self-interest.

Houston also knew that the latest treaty with the Cherokee was a fraud. There was no other word for it. It was true that a handful of malleable minor headsmen made their mark, but that was all. What the whites never understood, or refused to acknowledge, was no one spoke for all the Cherokee, or for any other tribe. To pretend otherwise was a farce, which never kept the whites from pretending otherwise. It was always easy to find *someone* to sign a treaty.

Another problem ran even deeper. Houston knew that Jackson, Overton, and Gadsden wouldn't be sympathetic when he explained, but they had to understand the magnitude of what they were asking. If all of this was headed where he thought it was, if they wanted him to do a hard thing, then they must be made to know just how hard it was. This was no time to play the brainless swashbuckling hero.

"I think I understand, sir," he said. "But please allow me to share a few thoughts."

When Jackson nodded, Houston shoved back his chair, rose to his feet, and began pacing back and forth along the length of the dining room. He always thought better on his feet. The movement seemed to free his mind. It made everyone look up at him, too, and there was advantage in that. He'd learned to enjoy these games within games.

He stopped pacing and put his big hands on the back of his ladder-back chair.

"In Cherokee mythology, the spirits of the dead travel to the West, where the rivers and creeks are paths to the underworld," he explained. "Because the sun rises in the East and sets in the West, they think of the East as the sun and the West as darkness."

"Mythology?" Gadsden muttered. "Oh, for Christ's sake!"

Houston ignored Gadsden and continued speaking directly to Jackson. It nettled Gadsden to be ignored and Houston knew it.

"The Cherokee have their mythology just as we have ours. What is most religion if not mythology in one way or another?"

he explained. "In all the legends of the Cherokee, the West symbolizes darkness, death and defeat. Travelin' far to the West, especially by water, is thought to be very dangerous, even fatal."

Jackson looked skeptical but at least he was listening.

"Sir, imagine if hell was a specific place on earth," Houston said, trying another way to make his point. "And we knew exactly where it was and how to get there. What would happen if we were asked - if we were *ordered* - to go to this place we knew to be hell? What kind of inducement would it be to be offered tens of thousands of acres of it, or to be told that no one would bother us? Of course, no one would bother us. How much of hell does a man want?"

Gadsden responded with another skeptical snort. Houston knew that only Jackson's presence kept him from walking out of the room.

"Aren't you exaggeratin' a bit?" Jackson asked softly.

"Not as much as *some* think, sir," Houston replied, still refusing to even glance at Gadsden. "We're askin' the Cherokee to defy their own beliefs for our benefit while our past behavior gives them no reason to believe our promises. How many treaties have there been already? We say, 'Trust us.' Then we say, 'Sorry, It didn't work out.' Then we say, 'Trust us' again. Can you imagine how we'd act if it was turned around. What if ...."

"But it's not turned around, is it?" Jackson interrupted, his hand on the table turning into a fist. "Young nations, like young men, sometimes make promises they can't keep in their maturity. It may be unfortunate, and it may be regrettable, but it also happens to be true. Nations, like people change along with circumstances. Notions of 'what if' and 'imagine' mean nothin'. We are what we are. Life is what it is, not what we'd like it to be. There's no point pretendin' otherwise. Believe me, Sam, I hope the Cherokee accept the inevitable. Those who do will be our friends. Those who don't will be our enemies."

Jackson was right, of course. Houston *was* exaggerating. Like many Cherokee, Drum had as much white as Cherokee blood. While he offered his respect to the Cherokee myths and ceremonies, he did not take most of them literally any more than Jackson believed the devil had cloven feet, horns, and a tail. White or Indian, it was possible to offer fealty to some higher power without believing all the filigree that went with it.

The heart of the problem was that the Cherokee were being told to leave their homes for an uncertain future in a faraway place where enemies who resented their coming surrounded them. Pushed and pushed and pushed for years, they were being pushed again. When would it stop? Would it *ever* stop?

Houston tried again, putting his argument in different terms.

"Sir, you know as well as I do that if we could build a wall all the way from Canada to the gulf, so high that no Indian could scale it, white people would go crazy trying' to find a way over it, under it, or through it. Eventually they'd do it, too."

"Sam, maybe you're right and maybe you're wrong, but it's nut cuttin' time," Overton said. "We're not askin' you to build a wall. We're askin' you to help make this thing work. Your background puts you in a unique position. We need a man the Cherokee trust, but a man we can count on, too. Like it or not, you're that man."

It came mostly as he expected. They wanted him to persuade the people of Drum's Town to give up their land and move across the Mississippi, taking everything they owned with them, until they were somewhere so deep in Arkansas territory that it probably wasn't Arkansas territory anymore.

Among his people, Drum was an influential man. Where he went, others would follow. How Houston did it was up to him. To give him the proper legal status, he'd take temporary leave from the army and accept an appointment as federal agent to the Cherokee Nation.

They did not wave a bone in front of his face without a little meat on it. To sweeten the offer, his agent's salary, plus a generous allowance for expenses, would more than doubled his army pay. Promised the closest thing to a free hand anyone in his position was likely to get, he'd report directly to Jackson and be responsible only to Jackson and Secretary of War John Calhoun. By any measure, Houston had to admit that it was a heady offer.

Jackson leaned forward, chin in hand and with eyes somehow fierce and warm at the same time.

"Sam, one way or the other this *has* to happen." Houston felt the power of the great man's personality surround and overwhelm him. "We need you. *I* need you. Will you do it?"

It was the first time that Jackson asked him for anything. He was being used and he knew it. But that didn't bother him. He knew that one way or another, all men are used, if not by their work then by other men. If not by other men, then by their beliefs. He wasn't even surprised to hear that the paperwork was already in place. All he had to do was sign his name.

As usual, Overton moved in to smooth any ruffled feelings.

"Please don't be offended, Sam," he said. "We didn't take you for granted. But we've got to get this movin'. If it didn't work out there was no harm done in havin' it ready."

Overton squeezed his shoulder. "By the way, you're good at this, very good. I'm proud of you."

"Glad you noticed," Houston replied. He was pleased with himself, too, but didn't want to show it.

At Jackson's command, a house slave brought an ink pot

and quill into the room. As Houston dipped the quill in the ink and prepared to sign, his self-satisfaction was punctured by a disturbing thought. He considered Jackson his surrogate father, but Drum cared for him when he desperately needed help and probably saved his life. How does a man serve two fathers, especially when they're on opposite sides?

Impatiently, he pushed the thought aside. There wasn't anything he could do about it now. He'd think of something. He always did.

19

DESPITE THE BEST OF INTENTIONS, Houston didn't get underway for more than two months. Not even Jackson could make the government move any faster.

As he rode out of Nashville, traveling alone through the fertile rolling hills of Tennessee, early fall overwhelmed the countryside as the leaves died a brilliantly colorful death and left the trees extravagantly splashed with gold, brown, red, and orange. The water in the rivers and creeks that veined the land was as cold and clear as the air.

For the first time in years he was on duty but not in uniform. Instead of army blue and white he wore a homespun shirt with buckskin pants and a fringed buckskin jacket. He'd ordered the skins stitched in Nashville, so new that they glowed like warm butter in the cool sunlight. If he kept them long enough they'd turn stiff and brown with sweat and dirt. He'd often seen trappers wearing buckskins so old and grimy they were nearly black. The thought of wearing years of accumulated filth appalled him.

Fond of flamboyance in their own dress, the Cherokee respected it in others. Already self-conscious in his new clothes, Houston figured he might as well give his eccentricities free reign. He wore boots instead of moccasins because he won a pair of fancy new spurs at the last race of the season and needed proper boots to show them off. He liked the way the big three-inch rowels fashioned as stars jingled when he walked. As a final touch, he wore a long red feather in his old-fashioned tri-corner hat, a style at least twenty years out of date.

Instead of taking the direct route to Drum's Town, he added a half day to his journey so that his first sight of the village was from above the river, the way he first saw it as a lost and starving boy. It had grown since he left it; probably to more than five hundred men, women, and children. A man of means among the Cherokee, Drum lived in a clapboard house with a wide porch offering a fine view of the river. He owned more than a hundred cattle, with oxen to plow fields of corn, potatoes, pumpkins, and tobacco. The harvest season was over and the countryside was checker-boarded with empty squares where the crops once grew. Thick forests of oak, maple, pine, sour wood and hickory bordered the fields. Along the river shore, deep green forest closed down against the river, and here and there a thick tangle of vines dropped into the water.

Whites and Indians had rubbed up against each other for so long that from a distance their villages looked more or less the same. From whites, Indians learned to use firearms and metal tools and build log cabins and make woven cloth. With metal axes, saws, adzes and augers, they erected structures like the peaked and windowless council house that dominated the center of the village. For some reason Houston never understood, Indians preferred to notch their logs on the underside, while whites notched their on the top. In turn, whites learned the ways of the woods, how to hunt deer and bear, and how to trap beaver, otter, mink, raccoon, muskrat, and pine marten. In Europe the warmth and luxury of fur was exclusively reserved for the wealthy. In the forest, fur was available for anyone with the skill to take it.

The Cherokee social structure was more sophisticated than most whites suspected, or cared. On one side, Drum was a descendant of the highland Scots who came into Charleston, moved west, and eventually married Cherokee women. Most of the chiefs and headsmen who fought with Jackson during the Creek war had similar lineage. Even so, according to tradition, all Cherokee were descended from seven clans and clan loyalties were strong. Families were mother-led. When a Cherokee man married, he joined his wife's family. Women had an equal voice in the council and if a wife wanted to get rid of her husband all she had to do was pack his things and put them outside the door.

After watching the village for a while and finding himself awash in memories, Houston rode down from the ridge, letting his horse pick the way along the winding path. As he entered Drum's Town, a knot of chattering children gathered in his wake. He was amused at the thought that some of the children likely were the offspring of friends he made years ago. It occurred to him that if he'd stayed, he'd probably be a father, too. The thought made him shiver. Maybe someday, he thought. But that day was far away.

As Houston worked his way toward the village center, he saw Drum emerge from his doorway. Houston dismounted in front of the council house just as Drum came up. They hugged and then held each other at arm's length. He was surprised at how much he towered over the older man. The years had diminished one while filling out the younger.

"It's been a long time," Houston said. "We have a lot to talk about. I've come here to help, if I can."

"We'll see about that," Drum said.

20

HE SETTLED into village life with an ease that surprised him.

Knowing that success depended on the Cherokee trusting him to deliver on his promises, in his role as Indian agent Houston wanted to appear to represent the Cherokee to the government, not the other way around. Eventually he'd make them see that it was in their best interest to move west, especially once they learned to trust him and, through him, the government he represented.

He moved in with Drum, who lived in the big house by himself. His wife had died long before Houston first came to the village as a boy. Unlike most Cherokee men, he did not take another, claiming that he was too old and set in his ways.

When Drum admitted that he worried about the disastrous effect of whiskey on his people, Houston's first official act banned the sale of whiskey on Cherokee land. Did he have the authority to take such a drastic step? He wasn't sure, but decided to do it and argue about it later, if necessary. For the sake of Drum's people, the whiskey sellers had to go. They howled and made threats, but Houston ignored them.

As he investigated the long list of complaints submitted by

the elders, Houston was shocked at the extent of the profiteering, price gouging, and outright thievery by the traders who were licensed to deal with the Cherokee. He threw one trader out of the village when he discovered sand mixed with flour in the barrels. In his anger, he clouted the man on the jaw. Four men carried the unconscious man deep into the woods and dumped him on the ground, leaving him to find his own way back to where he came from.

When he heard about slave smugglers slipping niggers across Cherokee land on their way to the Carolinas, he led ten braves to intercept a gang of eight smugglers with fifty slaves. After holding the terrified smugglers for two weeks in an abandoned lean-to while they pissed themselves in fear, Houston ordered them lashed out of the village with the message that he'd hang the next slave smuggler caught on Cherokee land.

As usual, the government was the root of the problem. While slavery was legal, importing slaves into the country was not, which made slave smuggling irresistibly profitable. In Houston's view, the idiotic conflicting policies would cause trouble as long as they existed.

In the meantime, he gave out hundreds of blankets and household utensils for the women, especially the coveted cast-iron kettles, plus tools, traps, rifles, and high-quality gunpowder for the men. Most of the suppliers screamed when he refused to accept the poor quality goods they usually offered, but he ignored them, too.

As he heaped the booty on Drum's people, he knew that on some vague moral level what he was doing amounted to bribery, but if it helped his cause, then so be it. He boldly signed requisitions for thousands of dollars of superior supplies with no notion of how to pay for them. That was someone else's problem. He was an Indian agent, not a clerk. Didn't Jackson promise him a free hand?

The double-dealing wasn't all played against the Cherokee. Renowned horse traders, they regarded cleverness and dishonesty as more or less the same thing. A generous application of bootblack on an aging nag made it seem years younger, at least for long enough to sell it at a good price, while a spike of ginger up the ass made even the laziest horse awful sprightly for a while, too.

With the reluctant consent of the elders, who'd engaged in the same sort of trickery when they were younger, as did their fathers before them, Houston posted notice that any Cherokee horse trader caught using bootblack and ginger would have the same done to him.

Once he had Drum's Town and the surrounding area more or less under control, Houston rode throughout southeastern Tennessee, north Georgia and the western Carolinas meeting headsmen, elders, and leaders from other villages. Most were hostile at first, but gradually he made them - some of them - understand. Cherokee names were on a treaty ceding their lands to the United States. Yes, they might resist, but what chance did they have against the dreaded Sharp Knife? Didn't they remember what happened to the Creeks? He promised that if they agreed to go west they would be generously provided for. The Cherokee could trust the Raven. Didn't his actions prove that his word was good?

As he rode from settlement to settlement, to his dismay he found that the Cherokee were in even worse shape than he thought. Their world was breaking apart, with nothing to replace it. While some responded to the new order better than others, a few simply ignored it. They clung to the old ways, refused to speak English, even if they knew it, danced the old dances, worked the old spells, and acted as if nothing changed and nothing ever would. They didn't care if the whites thought there were twenty fours hours to a day, seven days to a week, and 52 weeks to a year. What did such nonsense have to do with them? And it was simply unthinkable that marks on a piece of paper could dictate where and how a man lived.

At the other extreme were the Cherokee who all but stopped being Cherokee. They owned slaves - some owned sizable plantations - ate off expensive china, and used fancy cutlery imported from England. They dressed like well-off whites, sent their children to white schools, either couldn't or wouldn't speak their own language, and scornfully looked down their noses at other Cherokee.

But most were caught in the middle, like the people of Drum's Town. With so many settlers biting off great chunks of land for cultivation, the hunting was worse every year. While many Cherokee learned to be good hard-working farmers, others disdained it and refused to even try, a feeling Houston understood all too well. Too many of the young men drank too much and worked too little, while the older men spent too much time lamenting how life used to be. The strength of the clans weakened as Cherokee numbers shrank, attitudes changed, and the population scattered in bits and pieces to avoid the relentless white pressure.

It was sad to see. Lethargic and confused, they weren't Cherokee anymore, at least not as Cherokee used to be, but they weren't white either. They weren't anything at all, parts of this or that but not a single whole thing.

Drum did better than most at keeping the new world at bay, or at least cooperating with it without surrendering the essence of his people. But he couldn't keep it up forever and he knew it.

After going off by himself for a day and night to get his arguments in order and come up with reasonable answers to the likeliest questions, Houston finally made his case at a formal meeting with the elders in the council lodge, where the only illumination came from the fire pit in the center and the small smoke hole in the peaked roof. It was the first of what he assumed would be many such meetings while he argued to overcome Cherokee resistance and haggled over countless details.

But he was nervous and it showed. Negotiating with Jackson and the others was one thing, but negotiating with Drum and his people struck close to his heart. He wanted to help more than he wanted to win. His nervousness made him talk too much and his sympathy made him a poor negotiator. He babbled away his position, revealed all the concessions he was authorized to make, added others he was sure that he could wheedle out of the government, and threw in even more that occurred to him on the spur of the moment.

Overton, who'd warned Houston against exactly what he was doing, had a name for it; "givin' away the pig before the barbecue."

After speaking for more than thirty minutes, Houston left the council house so the elders could talk. To his surprise, he was summoned to return only a few minutes later. He'd barely taken his seat on the rough wooden bench when Drum assumed his place at the center of the lodge. Speaking for the elders, he admitted that the time had come to give up Drum's Town, but he was so matter-of-fact about it that Houston wasn't quite sure what had just happened.

"Say something," Drum urged, breaking the silence. "You look like a stunned duck."

Feeling the pressure of every eye in the council house, Houston realized that he'd been outwitted. Ever the realist, Drum always intended to take the government's offer. Short of a war the Cherokee couldn't win, there was no other option. But he was determined to delay as long as possible and strike the best bargain he could, especially when he learned that his adopted son was the government's representative. With his fondness for the Cherokee, Houston gave up much more than Drum ever thought possible.

Burning with humiliation, Houston blustered, "You used me!"

Drum, who expected Houston to react exactly as he did, smiled benignly.

"Of course, I used you. Jackson knew that sendin' you here was an advantage and it was ... for all of us. We get what we want, you get what you want, and Jackson gets what he wants."

Faced with such an undeniable truth, Houston slumped, utterly defeated.

"You tricky old devil!"

Drum shrugged in rely. "We use what weapons we have. Jackson has his army. I have my few tricks. There was a time when we had a whole wilderness to range in. But whites have a passion for land they can keep and till and hold close and then they always want more. Soon the world was not big enough for both. Because we want to be friends, we learned your ways because you would never learn ours and the two cannot exist at once because the whites won't let it. All the whites give us in return are laws and more laws to tell us that we can't do this or we can't do that. In my lifetime, there have been five different treaties. You say this is the last time, but it isn't. Then you say *this* is the last time, but it isn't. There's never a last time."

Seeing Houston's questioning look, Drum put it another way.

"You people are a lot of damn trouble."

21

WHEN TWO OTHER bands of Cherokee agreed to join the migration west, Houston forgot his pique and congratulated himself on a job well done. As usual, Drum was right. It looked like everybody got what they wanted.

A hard-riding messenger from Nashville brought the bad news: Led by a venerable old warrior named Talon, after a long silence the Cherokee who west west years earlier were making trouble that could bring down the whole scheme. First, they discovered that the land promised to them was already home to several western tribes, especially the Osage, who hit the newcomers from the East hard and often. The Cherokee retaliated until the whole territory was on the verge of a full-scale Indian war.

It didn't help that the government was far behind in the payment of annuities promised to Talon's people for giving up their homeland and that the annual shipment of supplies guaranteed by treaty hadn't been seen for two years. So far the western Cherokee were holding their own, but they weren't properly equipped to either farm *or* fight.

What happened was obvious. Once the Cherokee were out

of the way, the government that promised so much forgot all about them. Such neglect did not bode well for the people from Drum's Town.

The angry Talon wanted nothing more to do with treaties others made for him. He came up with the idea that if his people resigned from the central government of the Cherokee Nation and were recognized as an independent entity by the United States, they could negotiate on their own and decide their own fate. The plan for Indian removal would fall apart if the remaining Cherokee thought the government couldn't be trusted, especially if the unpredictable Talon was permitted to go off on his own. Houston could not imagine what might happen then.

To Houston's astonishment, Drum revealed that Talon was his older brother. Despite all their time together, Houston didn't even know that Drum *had* a brother. A grim warrior with nothing of his brother's peaceful nature, Talon believed that occasional war helped Cherokee bloodlines remain strong. He agreed to go west only to get away from the hated whites.

The messenger reported that Talon was leading a small delegation of Cherokee to Washington to make his case for independence. Fortunately, he'd stopped on the way to meet with Governor McMinn, who contacted Jackson, who sent the messenger galloping to Drum's Town with orders for Houston to accompany Talon to Washington and do everything he could to soften him up along the way. Once in Washington, Houston was to work with Secretary of War Calhoun to keep Talon from making more trouble. He'd never get what he wanted, but there had to be a way to make him like what he got until time solved the problem and the old man finally dropped dead.

At the same time, McMinn sent a courier to Washington warning Calhoun about what was headed his way. He sent a copy to Houston and the young man had the heady experience of reading a private dispatch about himself. According to the Governor, *"Sam Houston is a man of extraordinary vigilance and judgment who can be trusted by the highest areas of government. His close tie to the Cherokee places this young but enterprising officer in a position of extreme importance critical to the success of our plan."*

After a hasty goodbye to Drum, Houston left the village at a high lope. He picked the dun-colored gelding out of the corral for its endurance. He'd need it. There was a lot of ground to cover.

IT TOOK the better part of a week to track down Talon, who seemed to move around a lot without going anywhere in particular. Houston finally found him at a Tennessee mountain settlement near the North Carolina border where the hot sulfur springs attracted the sick and infirm of all ages in hopes that the springs' curative powers might ease what ailed them.

Settled comfortably in one of the hot springs, Talon dozed with the water to his chest and his back against a rock, gently snoring with head back and mouth open. Awakened by Houston's approach, he rose out of the hot water stark naked. Despite the winter cold, he stood nude on a bed of pine needles while he dried himself, water dripping from his wizened haunches. According to Drum, Talon took a Choctaw arrow in the left eye as a young man and Houston saw that the eye was milky white. With stringy shoulder-length gray hair and skin like aged parchment, he seemed beyond cares of the flesh.

It was two days before they started for Washington and Talon set a slow pace. They traveled north and east toward Virginia, working their way through the barren mountains before turning into the Shenandoah Valley. The countryside was a drab gray. The air was brittle with cold and the leafless trees looked like giant scarecrows against the sky, except there was nothing for them to frighten. Even the birds took cover for the duration of this hard winter.

Talon's moccasins were old and tattered and his hunting shirt was threadbare, but his only concession to the cold was to throw a ratty old blanket over his shoulders as the party of seven plodded along day after day on their durable Cherokee ponies. Although Talon had never been this far east, he took in everything with the same implacable gaze. When Houston tried to strike up a conversation, he gave no sign that he heard, much less deign to reply.

As the days passed, Houston dreamed of wrapping his hands around the old man's scrawny neck and squeezing until his eyes popped out of his head. He suspected the aged chief traveled so slowly because he knew that it infuriated his young escort, who he all but ignored for the same reason. Gritting his teeth, Houston told himself that if Andrew Jackson could learn patience, then, by God, he could, too, if it didn't kill him first.

The events of one afternoon made him see Talon in a different light.

As usual, they stopped early and made camp. It was another cold miserable day and the heavy gray clouds seemed so low it was as if Houston could reach up and touch them. He decided to reload his pistol in case the priming was wet. As he finished, he realized that Talon was standing beside him. He'd moved so quietly that Houston didn't hear him approach. As always, Talon seemed ready for war, with his bow in one fist, a quiver of arrows across his back, and a tomahawk in his belt. He never carried a rifle or a pistol and seemed to disdain modern weapons.

"Good?" Talon asked.

"Good?" repeated Houston, surprised that Talon finally considered him worthy of attention, although he was talkative enough with the other Cherokee. "What do you mean?"

"With that," Talon said, motioning toward the pistol. As usual, he spoke Cherokee. After all their time together, Houston still wasn't sure if the old man had any English

"Not many are better."

Although only adequate with a rifle, Houston was an excellent pistol shot. Normally there would have been more modesty in his answer, but Talon's tone was challenging and he instinctively responded in kind.

"Show me," Talon said.

The chance to put the old bastard in his place for once was irresistible.

"Why not?"

He looked around for a suitable target and pointed to a tree.

"See that knot, just below the lowest limb?'

When Talon grunted a reply, Houston raised his pistol, took aim, and fired. He didn't have to wait for the smoke to clear to know he'd hit the target.

Almost faster than the eye could follow, Talon fired three arrows before Houston lowered his pistol, much less start the long process of reloading. With the last arrow still in the air, Talon dropped the bow, pulled his tomahawk, and threw it with a powerful windmill motion.

Houston was stunned. He'd seen Cherokee marksmanship many times, but never with anything like Talon's speed. It did not seem impossible that the arrows or the tomahawk could have hit anywhere close to the target, yet the tomahawk was buried in the middle of the knot, buried halfway up the blade.

Houston walked to the tree and tugged out the tomahawk with a grunt. It landed in the middle of the arrows, shattering two of the shafts. The three arrows were so close together that Houston could cover the arrowheads with his palm. One of them landed on the ball from his pistol and drove it deep into the tree. He'd never seen such a breathtaking combination of speed and accuracy.

Talon pulled a knife, intending to work the valuable arrowheads out of the tree.

Houston stopped him with a hand on his arm above his elbow. It was like grabbing a knotted rope.

"Leave them," he said. "Anyone who passes will know a master was here."

As he hoped it would, the suggestion appealed to Talon's pride.

His hand still locked on Talon's arm, Houston added, "No one is better with bow and tomahawk. But the day is coming when the whites will have guns that fire many times without reloading and giant guns that fire such a distance they will be too far away for you to even see them. Cling to the old ways and you and your people will die."

Talon removed Houston's hand from his arm and looked him in the eye.

"Everyone dies," he said in perfect English. "But a man should live so that fear of death never enters his heart."

22

As INSTRUCTED, they stayed at Brown's Indian Queen Hotel on Pennsylvania Avenue at government expense. For all of its drab inconvenience, the hotel possessed two outstanding virtues; it was cheap and it accepted Indians.

Indian delegations were such a common sight in Washington that no one paid them any mind. So many emissaries from far off tribes wandered through the capital that they were regarded as more of a nuisance than a novelty. The routine rarely varied, as both sides took part in a ritual that neither one truly believed in. A mincing functionary from Calhoun's staff led the six Cherokee on a tour of the city, expecting them to be impressed by sights they mostly cared nothing about, found absurd, or didn't understand. To Houston's eye, Washington was as ugly as ever. There were still only two large government buildings, the rebuilt President's house, which seemed forlorn sitting out in the middle of empty farmland, and the large capitol building looming some distance away. Cheap presents, gaudy trinkets for the most part, were heaped on the visitors, Talon in particular. At the same time, Calhoun's ridiculous lackey chattered endlessly about the generosity of "the great white father" and his great regard for his "children."

Houston stopped translating the worst of the drivel and made it up as they went along. He knew that Talon didn't need a translation, but the rest of the Cherokee delegation did and it amused Talon to pretend that he had no English. The only event Talon seemed to enjoy was the half day they spent in the Turkish baths. Although Houston couldn't be sure, the old man might even have smiled once or twice as the steam worked its way into his bones.

After three days, the time came for the delegation's interview with the Secretary of War, which was to be followed by a formal reception with President Monroe. Houston was eager to see what Talon and the rest of the Cherokee might make of that.

A tall cadaverous aristocrat whose dark hair was slashed with gray, John C. Calhoun's critics joked that the South Carolinian was a self-made man who worshiped his creator. A plantation owner turned famously adept politician, he was so utterly convinced of his own righteousness that he did not believe he was on the side of the angels as much as the angels were on the side of John C. Calhoun and they damn well better stay there if they knew what was good for them. So far Jackson and Calhoun were allies more often than opponents, but it was well known that neither man trusted the other. It seemed only a matter of time before they'd bump heads and the crash would be heard from New England to Florida.

But just now Calhoun's hands were full. The war against the Seminoles had blown wide open with a series of bloody skirmishes in Georgia and north Florida. If the secretary took Jackson's advice, the fact that the country was already fighting one Indian war should make him more inclined to cooperate with the Cherokee.

After much brooding over what to wear, Houston decided

on a coat of soft doeskin that reached his knees. A gift from Drum, it was edged in fringe and emblazoned on the back with elaborate designs in red and blue beads. He tucked a pistol and a tomahawk into a belt with a big brass buckle. Two leather straps crisscrossed his chest, one supporting a powder horn, the other a pouch for personal effects. His legs were covered with fringed deerskin leggings, with moccasins decorated with more bead work. His long hair was pulled back and bound into a queue.

Houston assumed that the significance of his dressing as a Cherokee and not as an army lieutenant or an Indian Agent wouldn't be lost on someone as attuned to diplomatic nuance as Calhoun. It might reassure Talon, too, who probably felt surrounded by enemies, although he gave no sign of it.

When the delegation was escorted into the secretary's office, Calhoun rose, stiffly walked around from behind his desk, and bowed formally to the old chief, a conciliatory gesture that Talon ignored. After the usual bland preliminary comments from both sides, Talon abruptly demanded that Calhoun put in writing his understanding of what was due the Cherokee under the terms of the much-violated treaty that sent them west in the first place. Speaking through Houston, he declared that putting promises on paper was something the whites seemed to hold in great regard, even if they never kept any of their promises. Doing it again would insure that there was no misunderstanding between them this time.

It certainly was not Houston's plan to start negotiations with the blunt declaration that the representatives of the United States government were a pack of liars, even if it was mostly true. In his translation, he did what he could to soften Talon's challenging words, but judging by the flush that crept up the Secretary's face he was not successful. Nevertheless, speaking in a soft Southern drawl, Calhoun agreed to have such a document ready the next day, written in his own hand.

Houston doubted that Talon cared if the document was written by Calhoun or by some soft brain he found lying in the gutter. It was obvious that Talon's goal was to embarrass the white government and everyone associated with it. Strange diplomacy, he thought, but not surprising, given Talon's combative nature.

Regarding the chief's demand that his band be recognized as an independent nation apart from the other Cherokee, Calhoun's response was much less specific. Using many words to say as little as possible, he explained he needed time to confer with others in the government, President Monroe in particular, before making such an important decision, although he was sure that something satisfactory to both sides could be worked out eventually.

"Great chief," he explained, "think of the complexities if Wales, for example, demanded to be recognized as an independent nation apart from Great Britain."

A grimace crossed Calhoun's face, which Houston suspected might be as close as he could come to a smile.

"You will recognize, I'm sure, the difficulty in what you ask. We are not averse to your request, although obviously it will take some time to craft a suitable response, which I'm sure you fully appreciate as a leader of men yourself."

Considering that Calhoun and Monroe already had plenty of time to talk it over, and that Talon didn't know Wales from a walnut, Houston knew a stall when he heard one. As expected, Talon would never get any such concession, or anything close to it. Of course, he'd never get a direct rejection either. There would be bland assurances without end until he did the decent thing and dropped dead, hopefully somewhere far from Washington, and couldn't make any more trouble.

Pleased that he hadn't met with Calhoun privately, Houston could honestly tell the Cherokee that he had no part in the secretary's diplomatic misdirection. At the same time, he'd do everything possible to take credit for whatever superficial concessions Calhoun was sure to make.

Unfortunately, even before Houston finished translating the Secretary's double talk, Talon recognized knew it for what it was.

"I thought it was your way for one to speak for many," he growled. "You demand it from us.' Speaking to Houston, he added, "We have come a long way to see and hear nothing that matters, especially from this fool."

Thinking frantically, Houston hesitated - not too long to be obvious, he hoped - while he put together a "translation" that might satisfy Calhoun, assuming that Talon kept his mouth shut.

"He said that would be acceptable, sir. Although he'd naturally prefer to see events move as swiftly as possible, considering the importance of his request, he understands your need to be cautious."

"Judging from his tone and expression, he said nothing of the kind," Calhoun coldly replied. "In the future, lieutenant, tell me exactly what he says, not what you think I want to hear or to keep insults from my tender ears. I suspect that he understands more English that I was led to believe, too."

After that fiasco, there wasn't much left to say. Calhoun promised that every line of the original treaty would be adhered to, and that wagon loads of seed corn and other vitally needed supplies would shortly leave for the Cherokee settlements, carefully leaving out any mention of money or arms, although Houston assumed there would be a little of both, just enough to keep the Cherokee mollified. With that small comfort, Talon and the other Cherokee were escorted to the reception with President Monroe. As they filed out of the room, Houston could have sworn that he saw Talon smirk;

probably, he thought bitterly, at all the torment the old bastard had caused Sam Houston.

He did not envy the President, who had a reputation as an old fashioned, if rather dull, gentleman. Fortunately, Talon was unarmed. Beneath the smirk, the chief was an angry man.

As Calhoun rose to graciously bow the delegation out the door, out of the corner of his mouth he muttered, "Houston, remain here with me."

When the door shut, the color in the Secretary's face changed from its usual gray to bright pink as a small vein throbbed on his forehead.

"Just what do you think you're doing?" His once-soft voice had a harsh grating sound, like small rocks being crushed. "How dare you come before me dressed like a savage! You will explain yourself and, by Christ, you will do it this instant!"

Stunned by Calhoun's anger, Houston involuntarily stepped back like a man trying to put some distance between himself and a mad dog. Of all the things the Secretary might have said, nothing could have surprised him more. If anything, he expected praise. Instead, he received … this.

"Goddamn your eyes!" Calhoun shouted, spittle flying from his mouth. "Stand at attention while you explain yourself! I assume you remember how to do that at least!"

Although Calhoun's slim body practically vibrated with anger, it was not as impressive as one of Jackson's wild, earth-shaking rages, a thought that Houston found strangely calming as he snapped to attention and answered in the sing-song cadence popular among junior officers when they weren't sure of their ground.

"Sir, to keep the trust of the Cherokee I felt it necessary to appear to align myself with them, to be one of them, if you will. Particularly here in Washington, where they are in a place foreign to them and which they regard as hostile at best, I felt it best to give the appearance that I am their ally."

He paused to give Calhoun an opening if he wanted to say anything. When he didn't, Houston plunged ahead.

"As you know I've been traveling with Talon for some time, and lived in a Cherokee village discharging my duties as agent before that, all the while dressed more or less as I am today. I believe that it would have made Talon suspicious if I suddenly appeared in uniform. If I offended you, sir, I apologize. I only did what I thought best under the circumstances."

With long angry strides, Calhoun returned to his desk and sat down. Houston heard the squeak of wood on wood as the Secretary rocked back and forth, the muscles rippling across his jaw.

After an uncomfortable moment, Calhoun returned to his paperwork. Without looking up, he said, "You are dismissed, lieutenant. You will await further orders."

Seething, Houston snapped off a salute, smartly turned on his heel and marched out of the office. Everything was a blur as he fumbled to find his way out of the building.

Finally outside on the busy street, as Houston leaned back against the building's cold marble wall he felt as if his head might explode. In five years of service, he'd fought in one war and was so badly shot up that he almost died. He received poor medical treatment when there was any treatment at all. He risked his career on an assignment he didn't want and made a success out it. Drum had as much to do with it as he did, but Calhoun didn't know that. By God, he wasn't even on active duty! He had a right to wear anything he damn well pleased! And after all the uncertainty, hardship and pain, *this* was his reward, a royal reaming out over haberdashery by a bilious blowhard who spent his life in drawing rooms and over-heated offices!

Humiliated and furious, in long angry strides Houston marched down the wide boulevard of frozen mud and horse dung, intending to enter the first tavern he saw and drink the place dry. To hell with John C. Calhoun! To hell with Talon! To hell with them all!

23

THERE HAD BEEN HANGOVERS BEFORE, too many to count, but this one was brutal. It felt like shards of glass were caught behind his eyelids and slowly working their way into his brain.

As Houston lay groaning in bed without the slightest idea how he got there, he vaguely remembered a fight. He wasn't sure if there were several fights or one fight with several men. He couldn't remember any details at all, although the painful acorn-sized lump on his head proved that he did more than watch.

It took him full two days to recover and by then Houston received orders to report back to Calhoun. He hadn't brought his army uniform to Washington. It was stored in Nashville and there wasn't time to detour and get it before leaving with Talon for the capital. He appeared in Calhoun's office wearing a new uniform cadged from an old friend in the quartermaster's office. His brass buttons gleamed and the white trousers were so new and stiff that they made a harsh rustling sound when he walked.

After so long out of uniform he felt like he was strangling.

It took all of his self-control to keep from tugging at the high stock. Still angry about Calhoun's tongue-lashing, he reminded himself to be patient and hear what the Secretary had to say, not that he had much choice.

After waiting for almost an hour with his shako in his lap in the outer office, Houston finally was admitted into the great man's presence. From behind his desk, the gaunt, hollow-cheeked Calhoun looked him up and down. With an approving nod, he told the lieutenant to take a seat.

"Lieutenant, serious charges have been brought to me regarding certain actions during your recent duty with the Cherokee," he announced. "Given your record of service, it seemed only fair that I conduct the investigation myself."

Shocked into silence, Houston tried to read Calhoun's face for clues but saw only an expressionless mask. What on earth was the man talking about?

"Sir, I'm sorry but I don't understand," he said. "What charges do you refer to?"

"It's a lengthy list that boils down to two substantial items." Calhoun reached inside his coat pocket for his reading glasses before picking up a sheet of paper from the desktop. "The first is that while acting as agent to the Hiwassee branch of the Cherokee Nation you were secretly engaged in smuggling slaves from Florida. The second is that you made private transactions to sell alcohol to the Cherokee for your own profit after illegally banning all other competition."

Calhoun removed his spectacles and placed them carefully on his desk.

"Lieutenant, you must understand that charges such as these are not to be taken lightly. My man in the outer office will give you documents with the particulars in order that you may answer two weeks from this date. If either or both of these charges are found to be true, I can assure you that you will be punished to the fullest extent of the law."

Feeling numb and lightheaded, Houston accepted the packet from Calhoun's assistant and once again found himself out on the frigid Washington street, this time without remembering how he got there. As he frantically ripped open the papers, he felt trapped in some horrible nightmare.

A quick reading of the material showed the charges could be refuted, assuming that Calhoun gave him a proper chance to defend himself and then believed him when he did. After all, instead of smuggling slaves he'd broken up a smuggling ring and punished the smugglers. The charge of selling whiskey must have come out of his banning alcohol. Either someone thought that he intended to corner the market for himself, or this was their way of getting back at him. Maybe he *was* too high-handed, but what was he supposed to do? Ironically, the thing he worried most about at the time, the thousands of dollars of requisitions on no authority but his own, wasn't even mentioned.

Once his heart stopped pounding and he calmed down, Houston realized that delivering the charges informally might have been Calhoun's way of softening the blow. Maybe the starchy blowhard wasn't so bad after all?

Houston spent the next two weeks gathering information to refute the charges. Fortunately, following on Overton's sage advice, he'd kept impeccable records. Signed and dated requisitions, letters and reports helped prove his whereabouts and actions. He also intended to offer Drum and other Cherokee as witnesses on his behalf, although it would take a long time to get them to Washington. To summarize his defense, Houston labored over a nine-page letter that he intended to present with the documents.

When the day came, Houston again found himself in the large office with Calhoun and the same assistant. This time the anonymous little man sat against one wall with a sheaf of paper on his knees taking notes for the record. Houston tried not to squirm while Calhoun carefully read his long letter and all of the accompanying material, then went back to reread certain sections two or three times. He wanted to appear as an innocent man should, but wasn't sure exactly how an innocent man looked. The more he struggled and squirmed, the harder it was to adopt the right pose.

When the Secretary finished reading, in a soft drawl he asked a few direct questions about the events that Houston believed triggered the charges.

Finally the secretary sat back in his chair and rubbed his eyes.

"Lieutenant Houston, I believe these charges to be false, as I suspected from the beginning. In my opinion, this is crude attempt by enemies of General Jackson to injure him through you. You are the friend of a powerful and controversial man. I'm afraid there is a price to be paid for that friendship. Unfortunately, in the halls of power here and elsewhere it is not unusual for ambitious men to do whatever they can to destroy other ambitious men. It also appears that certain of your actions – intemperate actions, shall we say? - were taken upon men who have friends in Washington and they used those friendships to seek revenge."

With more heat than he intended, Houston asked, "Sir, if you thought these charges false from the start, why did you continue to pursue them and persecute me?"

The old flash returned to Calhoun's eyes. He did not like to be challenged, especially by lowly lieutenants from out in the canebrake.

"Serious charges such as these must be investigated, whatever the source. There is no other choice. You will note that I conducted the investigation outside the boundaries of formal procedure, which is why there will be no written statement of exoneration. Lieutenant Houston, if you truly believe that you have been persecuted, then I suggest that you don't know what real persecution is."

Calhoun might be unpleasant, but at least he was honest. Houston didn't like this self-righteous, stiff-necked bag of bones, but it was time to back down.

"Sir, I apologize," he said with a bow of his head. "This whole affair has been a strain, as you might imagine, an assault on both my character and my career."

Calhoun nodded but said nothing more. And that, apparently, was that. Houston thanked the Secretary, got no reply other than a perfunctory wave of his hand, rose to his feet, saluted, turned on his heel and left the office. The Secretary of War was on to other business before he was out the door.

Finding himself out on the bustling street once again, Houston took a deep breath and steadied himself against a lamp post, his mind whirling with anger and relief. Yes, he'd cleared himself, but only that. It was galling to be confronted by the charges, then left to fret about them for weeks, if Calhoun didn't believe them in the first place. Not only was there there was no statement of exoneration, there would be no action against the men who tried to ruin him, no thanks for a job well done, and no apology for the false accusations. He told himself that he wasn't so naïve that he expected the world to be fair – although, in truth, that is exactly what he expected - but this was too much.

Fuming, he marched to his tiny room at Browns, where he found his pen, ink, and a sheet of writing paper:

"Washington City

"March 1st, 1818

"Sir,

You will please accept this as my resignation, which is to take effect from this date."

"I have the honor to be your most obedient servant,"

"Lieutenant Sam Houston, 1st Infantry"

Even in Houston's white-hot anger, the timing was not lost on him. It was one day before his twenty fifth birthday, five years to the day since he picked up the silver dollar from the sergeant's drum head in Maryville and joined the army. Once again, the feeling of fate at work in his life was overpowering. But if fate truly had a hand in all this, he decided, then fate had a macabre sense of humor.

And fate, it seems, was not his friend. He had no money, no prospects, and hard wounds to show for five years.

He did have a few influential friends. Perhaps something might come of that?

24

EVERYTHING THAT CAN BE DONE HAS BEEN *done.*

His will was witnessed a week ago, his affairs are in order, and nothing has been left to chance. He spent two days at the Hermitage practicing his marksmanship. To make sure that the rifled pistols are accurate, he molded his own pistol balls. There will be no flaw that might cause him to miss and helplessly wait to be shot down.

Too restless to sleep any longer, he rises in the darkness and dresses by candlelight, moving quietly so not to disturb the others. He is sure that his friend, Sanford Duncan, who lives here with his family, will be up in plenty of time.

As is his habit, he carefully laid out last night what he'll wear this morning. Fond of expensive and flamboyant clothes, when he finishes dressing he looks at his image in the mirror. In the flickering candlelight, he sees a tall, broad-shouldered man with a cleft chin, high forehead, and thick chestnut hair never quite tamed by the comb. He's wearing a broad-brimmed black beaver hat set at a jaunty angle, white ruffled shirt, black vest, and a buff-colored coat. Around his waist is a brilliant red sash with elaborate bead work, a gift from Drum when he was elected to Congress. A large silver

*buckle holds the sash in place. His trousers are tucked into soft calf-
skin boots that come almost to his knees.*

*He steps outside and finds his horse already saddled and waiting.
That tells him that Duncan rose early, too. The high-tempered gray
he'll ride this morning snorts and impatiently paws the ground.*

*Joined by his second, Colonel John McGregor, who carries the
weapons, along with Duncan, they ride north to a pasture just across
the border in Kentucky. With dueling illegal in Tennessee, it is a
necessary inconvenience.*

*It's still more dark than light when they arrive. The three men
dismount and Duncan leads the horses away. He doesn't want to
pace and show his nervousness, but waiting is hard. It takes all of
his self-control to stand still. Following Jackson's advice, he slips a
pistol ball out of his pocket and pops it in his mouth. When the time
comes, he'll slip it between his teeth and bite down to steady his aim.*

*Just after dawn, William White and his second, Colonel John
Erwin, ride out of the trees into the pasture. The hoof beats on the
soft ground are startlingly clear in the quiet morning.*

*The duelists offer each other a curt nod while their seconds draw
lots and decide who'll get choice of position and which side will give
the word to fire. Erwin wins both choices, not that it matters. The
sun is barely over the horizon. Whatever happens, it will not be a
factor.*

*The stocky White removes his coat and hands it to Erwin. With
the exception of his black boots, which are so highly polished that the
moisture from the grass beads on the boots, White wears all gray -
trousers, waistcoat and a shirt with an open collar.*

*McGregor opens the cherry-wood box with the twin dueling
pistols. White selects one of the weapons and hands it to Erwin.
When Erwin finishes loading, White expertly balances the pistol in
his hand to test its weight before lowering to his side with the barrel
pointing at the ground.*

*He sees White's hand tremble slightly and wills his own hand to
remain steady. He takes the other pistol from the box and hands it to*

McGregor to be loaded. When McGregor returns the pistol the weight feels comfortable in his hand. White takes his position in the pasture. They are fifteen paces apart, close enough to see that White's eyes are bloodshot. Probably didn't sleep well either, he guesses. Under the circumstances, who could?

He feels as if he's standing outside of himself, watching the duel instead of taking part. But at the same time he never felt more concentrated. He feels his heart thumping in his chest and the blood rushing through his veins. He goes over the procedure in his mind. When Erwin says, "Present!" they raise their pistols. Then Erwin will count out loud and they must fire before he reaches five.

From his position off to the right, Erwin asks, "General Houston, are you ready?"

Not used to being called "general," he is momentarily startled before he realizes that Erwin addressed him according to his appointment as commanding general of the state militia.

"I am ready."

"Mister White, are you ready?"

"Ready, sir."

"Present!"

They raise their pistols.

"One, two ..."

Houston hears the pop from White's pistol an instant before he pulls the trigger and feels the recoil jerk his hand. Partially shrouded in smoke, White drops his pistol and slowly sinks to a sitting position, clutching his stomach.

McGregor rushes forward. Houston hands him the pistol, and they walk toward the horses.

He hears White call his name. He returns to kneel beside the fallen man.

"Damn you, Houston, you've killed me."

"I'm sorry. You know I never wanted this to happen."

White gasps from a sudden spasm of pain and clutches at his

belly, pressing down with his hands as if to force the pain back into his body. When the storm passes, he looks up, his face twisted.

"It's over, Houston. You win. You and Jackson, god damn you both."

He reaches out to touch White's shoulder, but thinks better of it and withdraws his hand. He rises to his feet and walks to McGregor, Duncan and the horses. Before mounting, he turns his head to one side and spits out the pistol ball. He'd forgotten all about it.

HE THOUGHT about the duel every day since it took place over a year ago. His life might have ended that morning. It easily could have been him and not White lying gut shot in a Kentucky pasture.

The anti-Jackson forces in Tennessee knew couldn't get to the general, so they found a way to maneuver his protégé into a duel over some damned trifle. Forced into it by the iron idiocy of the *Code Duello*, if he refused the challenge there would have been talk of cowardice and a ruined political career. If he lost, he might be dead or crippled for life.

Instead here he was, governor of Tennessee only nine years after he left the army, pride hurt, pockets empty, and prospects unknown.

He succeeded Billy Carroll, who was kept from serving another consecutive term by the state constitution, although there was no doubt he'd return one day to the office he loved so dearly. The opposition, the pompous Newton Cannon, was easily brushed aside. When it came to campaigning - the chaotic hurly-burly of politics on the hoof - Sam Houston was the best in the state.

He caused a stir wherever he went. Not the least of the reasons was his flamboyant dress. It was something he learned from the Cherokee, who believed it was a man's duty to be noticed. Who else campaigned for high office wearing a bell-crowned beaver hat, a patent-leather military stock, black velvet vest and trousers, and his old beaded red sash with the polished silver buckle, topped off by the most colorful Cherokee hunting jacket in his increasingly large wardrobe?

At their first debate in Nashville, Cannon, whose dismal oratory could kill flies at ten paces, tried to make an issue out of his foe's eccentric dress.

"My opponent's ridiculous apparel is not suitable for a clown or a buffoon, much less for a governor," he sneered.

Houston's reply was repeated all over the state: "You see before you a man made by God, not by his tailor."

"And now it's time to start usin' the power I won," he announced. "The man I'm about to see is in need of a lesson and I intend to teach it to him."

Houston leaned back in his leather chair, picked up the tumbler of whiskey on the desk and rolled his wrist, watching thoughtfully as the yellow-brown liquid swirled in the glass.

"But I suppose we shouldn't include that observation in this little project of ours, should we?"

On the other side of the desk, a scholarly young man with the dirty brown hair and watery eyes bobbed his head in a series of quick jerking motions that resembled a bird trying to tug a stubborn worm out of the ground.

What was his name? Johnson? Hanson? Something Scandinavian.

"No, sir." His prominent Adam's apple moved up and down as he gulped. "It wouldn't be wise at this time. Such candid notions might come a bit later, I think, when you - or perhaps, we, although I would never want to presume - write your memoirs, softened a bit with the proper wording, of course."

Good God! Houston was only thirty four and this young-ster jabbered about writing his memoirs, as if he was some gnarled old relic who spent his time looking back because there was nothing left to look forward to. He laughed to himself that this "youngster" was more or less his own age. He'd risen so far in such a short time that it was sometimes hard to keep all it in perspective.

He had the name now; Swenson. His memory for names never let him down.

"Well, Mister Swenson, I think that's enough for one day, don't you?"

"Yes, Governor. This new material should keep me busy for some time." He gathered up his scattered notes and rose to leave. "When should I schedule our next meeting?"

Houston waved a hand toward the office door. "See one of my people outside. They'll fit you in. On your way out tell them to wait a few minutes before sendin' in my next appointment."

Swenson was writing Houston's official biography. The things took hold a few years back and now everybody worth noting had at least one in circulation. He'd already read Swenson's passages on the Creek War, when bold Lieutenant Houston, arrows sticking out of his body like a pin cushion, apparently won the battle of Horseshoe Bend single-handedly. He made a mental note to tell Swenson to ease off a little. A little exaggeration was expected, but not that much.

Houston himself helped write a biography of General Jackson a few years back. Just about everyone agreed that "A Civil and Military History of Andrew Jackson" was an improvement over Johnny Eaton's flabby "The Life of Andrew Jackson." Eaton, now a United States Senator, was testy about it to this day.

He knew that he'd better watch that sort of thing. Jealousy among rivals was inevitable. Just the other day, Carroll complained to John Overton about "Emperor Houston's vanity," a sneer that Overton, who liked Carroll less and less these days, happily passed on. Houston reminded himself to be careful to show the correct amount of modesty. The world loves a humble hero. But not, he thought, too humble. A man should know his worth.

The truth was that he enjoyed the time spent with Swenson. There were few moments of quiet in his busy life. The interviews gave him an opportunity to savor the remarkable events of the last nine years.

After deciding on law because it offered the fastest route into politics, Houston took Overton's advice and studied under old Judge Trimble in Nashville. He read law books, ran errands, researched cases, attended court as much as possible, and listened to anything the canny Trimble had to say. He finished his studies in six months and passed the oral examination with ease. At their next meeting, Houston would have to explain to Swenson that eighteen months was typical. It was clear from what he'd written that the scribbler didn't properly appreciate the achievement.

Law was his practice, but politics was his calling. Under Jackson's guidance, after a few months in private practice Houston became the Davidson County district attorney. One of the position's virtues was that it allowed him to remain in Nashville, the Davidson County seat. He was elected to congress at thirty and governor at thirty four.

Along the way, Houston discovered that one of the pleasures of a successful life was watching old friends rise with him. Eaton was in the Senate. Ed White, his old Mississippi River traveling companion, was a judge down in New Orleans and a rising political power in Louisiana. Jimmy Polk had Houston's old seat in Congress. At times he felt as if he belonged to a great brotherhood that was destined to run the country one day. No more of that Massachusetts-Virginia cabal. Of the six Presidents so far, four were Virginians, two were Massachusetts men, and all of them were from the gentry.

But there was a new movement rising in the land as Andrew Jackson formed a new constituency, a constituency of the people, not the upper classes. Power was shifting to the West at last, just as John Coffee predicted so many years ago. The East was the past. The West was the future. His future.

Sometimes Houston's enthusiasm got the better of him as he set sail on great gusts of oratory. At a time when a typical speech was measured in hours, Sam Houston was considered exceptionally windy. In Congress, they joked that it took him thirty minutes to clear his throat. He could speak for any length of time on seemingly any subject. Official Washington still remembered the time he started a speech in the early afternoon, spoke until recess, and then picked up the next day where he left off and spoke until lunch.

He was particularly proud of his first major speech as governor, one that his friends praised as exceptional and his foes dismissed as exceptionally long. He invoked Jefferson, Madison, and Monroe. He mentioned Greece, Rome, Troy, and Nazareth. He referred to Cato, Cicero, Jackson, and Lafayette. Then he closed with a long quotation from "The Iliad." By God, it was beautiful.

Ironically, it was Jackson himself who suffered the only setback these last years. As expected, Monroe easily won re-election in 1820, more of a coronation than an election. With Monroe finishing two terms, it was time for the old guard to step aside so that a westerner – Andrew Jackson, for example – could step in. But the old guard refused to give ground. From Jefferson on, each president chose as secretary of state the man he preferred to follow him in office. For Monroe, that man was John Quincy Adams. But Adams and Jackson weren't the only men who coveted the Presidency. The election of 1824 offered no less than five serious candidates. The crowded field also included John Calhoun, Treasury Secretary William Crawford, and Speaker of the House Henry Clay.

It resembled a fight among rabid dogs. The common people revered Jackson for his victories in the Creek War, at New Orleans, and in Florida, where he added another huge section of someone else's land to the country. The general easily won the popular vote, but the decision lay with the Electoral College, which fell into chaos when the credentials of several of the electors came in dispute.

For weeks the country bubbled with speculation. Jackson was the clear leader, with Adams a strong second. But who would finish third? If the leading candidate failed to receive a majority in the Electoral College, the House of Representatives would choose from among the top three. If Clay finished third, his long tenure and close alliances in the House could make him the next President. But if Crawford edged Clay, Jackson would be the favorite.

Once the dispute about the electors' credentials was worked out, as expected, no candidate won an Electoral College majority. The tally was Jackson ninety nine, Adams eighty four, Crawford forty one, and Clay thirty seven, with Calhoun, who had withdrawn from the race, lurking in the background to offer himself as a compromise if the House couldn't reach a decision, an uncharacteristically passive strategy devised by his aide, John Gadsden, who, as far as the public knew, voluntarily left the Jackson camp in favor of his fellow South Carolinian.

Houston was one of the few who knew the truth. Gadsden was run out of Tennessee after writing a letter to a friend in Charleston that was astonishing for its careless arrogance. After rattling on about how Rachel Jackson's "crude ways" and "sordid history" made her such a political liability that she might cost Jackson the election, Gadsden concluded, "If the fat old boot would do the decent thing and die, the sympathy vote alone would be enough to make the old man President. As it is, her sluttish reputation could very well deny him – and his supporters – the success they have worked so hard to achieve."

When Jackson learned about the letter he had to be restrained from taking a cane to Gadsden, who galloped out of the Nashville as fast as he could find a horse. Back in South Carolina, he was welcomed into the Calhoun camp.

Before the House could vote, the election took a shocking turn when a stroke disabled Crawford. With Crawford out of the way, the only thing that Clay and Adams had in common was their loathing of Jackson, but it was enough to unite them. After a late-night meeting, Clay threw his votes and influence to Adams, who promptly named Clay as his Secretary of State.

But public outrage crippled the new administration from the first day. Although Adams was scorned as "the Clay President," the deal itself was not the problem. All politics involved deals. People didn't like having their noses rubbed in it. Thanks to Adams' blunder, Jackson's path to the Presidency four years later was that much easier. True, the General wasn't elected yet, but there was little doubt that Adams would be a one-term President just like his father.

In the meantime, Houston had big dreams for Tennessee. He wanted solid accomplishments for his first term as governor. What better way to guarantee a second? He intended to push through an internal improvements program of roads, canals, harbors, and bridges. He knew firsthand the marginal livelihood of the farmer unable to bring his produce to market without a dependable way to get it there. And he meant to browbeat the legislature into providing relief for the poor homesteaders and squatters who couldn't afford to pay for the land they worked so hard to improve. Then there was his plan to establish a statewide public school system. It was a marvel. Everyone said so.

At that moment, Houston's next appointment, state Senator Augustus Wiley, entered his office. Houston felt himself tingling as a feeling of anticipation traveled pleasantly down his loins.

He didn't bother to offer the pudgy west Tennessean a chair. Let him stand there and take it.

"Wiley, you have been a great deal of trouble and it's time for your obstructionist nonsense to end," Houston announced. "I can't remove you from office, but I *can* make sure you're buried, and as long as I'm Governor, buried you shall be. No bill of yours will ever get out of committee and you will never again be recognized to speak on the Senate floor. Politically, from this moment you cease to exist. Every door that I and my friends influence will be closed to you and I think you will find that *your* friends are no longer quite so friendly. By the time we're finished, there won't be enough of you to scrape off my boot. You have thwarted the will of the people long enough."

"The will of the people, or the will of Sam Houston?" he asked, lifting his flabby chin as if to absorb the blow and at least give the illusion of defiance. "Despite what you and your cronies seem to think, they are not one and the same."

"For purposes of this conversation and this state, they are identical," Houston snapped. "I wanted the pleasure of telling you face to face. Now get out of here."

After a last glare, a sour mix of frustration and defeat, Wiley shuffled out the door as if he'd received a whipping.

Some said that revenge was an unworthy desire, but Houston didn't believe it for a second. There were times when nothing but revenge would do.

Not ten seconds after Houston dismissed Wiley, John Overton stuck his head through the open door.

"Governor, I couldn't help but overhear," he said. "I hope you're not angry with *me* today. I'm not quite ready for a burial."

Houston laughed. "Never, John. When you finally go, I may prop you up in a corner just to inspire me." He waved to a chair. "Take a seat."

As Overton settled in, Houston asked, "What can I do for you?"

"As it happens, not a thing, at least not today." Overton fumbled through his pockets for a cigar. "I was makin' a few rounds and thought I'd stop by."

Houston reached across his desk and flipped open a beautifully carved humidor to reveal a row of rich cigars.

"Help yourself. They're better than those vile things you smoke."

Overton selected a cigar and sniffed appreciatively along its length.

"I appreciate it, I surely do," he said. "But it's strange how those 'vile things' used to good enough for the Sam Houston I used to know."

Houston didn't bother to answer. What on earth was that supposed to mean?

"You were pretty hard on Wiley," Overton observed.

"He deserved it and you know it. Sets an example, too. People'll see what happens when they oppose us."

"Maybe so." Overton nodded, still gazing at the unlit cigar. "But it's best to leave a man with a little dignity. You might need him somewhere down the road."

"Not a creature like that."

"Probably not," Overton amiably agreed. "After today, he won't be there for you anyhow."

25

AUNT RACHEL IS DEAD. Even as Houston heard the words in his head, they had no meaning.

Andrew Jackson was about to become the seventh President of the United States, but he would do it without the love of his life.

She was sick and they all knew it, forever short of breath and complaining about pain in her chest. But she was in poor health for so long that no one thought much about it. It was a fact of life, the way some people are tall and others short.

They said the campaign killed her, although as far as Houston knew, she never heard the worst of it. It easily was the most vicious in the young nation's history, with vitriol flowing both ways like a mighty river. Some over-zealous Jackson supporters claimed that when John Quincy Adams was minister to Russia he routinely procured women for Czar Alexander to gain favor with the Russian potentate. It was a lie, but that didn't stop too many of Jackson's people from asking if the nation really wanted a pimp for President. In return, Jackson's wife was called a whore and bigamist and his mother a camp follower during the revolution. The general was attacked for his temper, his history of dueling, for atrocities during the wars against the British, the Spanish, and the Indians, and for stealing another man's wife.

When her husband won the election, Rachel Jackson dutifully prepared to leave for Washington. She even consented to wear the beautiful ball gown her husband had specially made for her.

How she must have hated the prospect! It was impossible to see the woman that Houston knew - informal, pipe-smoking, and badly overweight – in such a gown. But Jackson saw her through eyes of love. After almost forty years, to him she was as beautiful as the day they met.

One night at the Hermitage, while Jackson was away, she revealed her dread of leaving the shelter of the Hermitage for Washington.

"Samuel, I would rather die than go to that terrible place," she confessed, breaking into tears as they sat alone in the parlor. "Andy's enemies will dip their arrows in wormwood and gall and skewer me with them."

Alarmed by her terror, Houston took her in his arms while she quietly wept on his shoulder. Once she calmed down, he urged her to tell the general. Perhaps she could arrange to remain at the Hermitage when Jackson went to Washington? Such a thing had never happened, but that didn't mean it was impossible.

Regaining her composure, Rachel shushed him by placing her fingers over his lips. "Not one word to Andy about this. If I didn't go, he wouldn't either. He'd give it all up, everything he's worked for, and I can't have that. It would kill him."

When Houston started to argue, Rachel silenced him again.

"If you have the slightest regard for me, if you truly love me as you know I love you, you will not speak of this to anyone," she said, her expressive brown eyes pleading with him. "Promise me, Samuel, and forget my weakness."

Bowing his head in submission, Houston made his promise.

She was stricken in the parlor, where Jackson was writing letters before stepping outside for some night air. Suddenly she felt terrible pain in her left shoulder, arm, and side. He heard her cry out, dashed inside, and somehow managed to carry her to bed. Jackson sent to Nashville for the doctor, but after the usual treatment of bleeding her once a day and dosing her with mercury and castor oil there was nothing to be done. She lingered for three days and did on the fourth. Her grieving husband holding her so tightly that she had to be pried from his arms to be prepared for burial.

They said that her heart gave out, but Houston was as sure as he could be that Rachel Jackson willed herself to die. True to his promise, he told no one about their conversation. How could he?

Winning an election - even the Presidency - seemed so empty now.

They would bury Rachel Jackson today.

———

As the funeral cortege left the house and moved slowly down the walk to the burial site in a private corner of the Hermitage garden, Houston's dulled mind refused to accept the incredible number of people. Only a few were invited, and yet hundreds came, all of them touched by Rachel Jackson's warmth and kindness. Of every class and description, they seethed with emotion but did not make a sound. The silence was like a living force as Houston marched through the gentle rain with the other pallbearers toward the grave site with the edge of the coffin carefully balanced on his shoulder.

He'd never seen Jackson like this. His thin body racked with violent sobs, he fought to regain his composure only to be devastated again. For the first time, Houston saw that the general was truly old, as if he aged twenty years in a few days. He was supposed to say a few words at the grave site, but Houston did not see how he could. It did not seem possible that the old man would survive this blow, or wanted to.

Calling on a lifetime of discipline, Jackson steeled himself and stood erect when the pallbearers gently set the coffin at the grave. He turned to face the throng of mourners, people Rachel Jackson touched with her own life over so many years.

He cleared his throat and gathered himself with terrible effort.

"My Rachel never liked crowds," his said, his voice thin but holding firm. "But I am sure that looking down from above she is as pleased as I am to know how many people loved her."

He weaved slightly and his face quivered as he fought to hang on just a little longer.

"My beloved wife was so virtuous that while slander might wound her it could never dishonor her." He stopped as the tears flowed down his gaunt cheeks. He tilted his head and looked up into the gray sky. "Dear God, please accept into your heart the purest soul of all."

With a nod, he turned away and slowly walked back toward the big house, erect and ready for what might come. Life would be much harder now.

Choking with the greatest sorrow he had ever known, Sam Houston bowed his head and wept.

26

HE DIDN'T KNOW exactly when he fell in love with Eliza Allen. It wasn't as if one day he wasn't and the next day he was. It was just ... there.

"When I try to explain it never comes out right. Hell, Johnny, you know me. Most of the time, I can talk the ears off a jackass. But when it comes to Eliza I can't get near to what I want to say. I even struggle when I talk *to* Eliza. I'm the governor of a great state, but around her I stammer like a schoolboy."

They occupied a table in the otherwise empty tavern of the Nashville Inn. Snow was falling outside and the big stone fireplace put out so much heat that Houston and John Eaton, who'd left the frozen swamp of Washington to come home for a few weeks, were forced to retreat to a more temperate zone on the other side of the tavern.

This time of year was always slow and Governor Houston and Senator Eaton agreed that it might be the highest and best use of their time to drink the heart out of the afternoon. Houston slouched in a chair with one knee hooked up on the battered plank table, his Jamaican rum within easy reach.

Holding a mug of beer in his lap, Eaton had both feet up on the table and crossed at the ankles while his chair tilted on its back legs.

If Eaton seemed distracted, he had good reason. It was fast closing in on necessary for the senator to change his position, except that the situation was awkward. Being half drunk, if he moved without careful planning there was a chance that he might lose his balance and topple over backwards, which was not suitable for a man's dignity. But he had better make a move soon because pissing in his pants wouldn't exactly enhance his dignity either.

Houston peered blearily at Eaton, who was concentrating on his dilemma and did not seem to be paying attention.

"Johnny, does anything I'm sayin' make sense?"

"Not one bit." Eaton erupted with a belch impressive for its tone and length. "A man in love isn't s'posed to make sense. You should know that by now. As I recall, you've been in love ten or twelve times. Nobody I know falls in love as often as you do. That's enough to muddle any man."

"But ...." Eaton interrupted Houston's boozy protest by swinging his feet off the table while simultaneously shifting his weight so the chair's front legs hit the floor with a crash. With a broad grin, Eaton raised his beer triumphantly, having executed the difficult maneuver without spilling a drop.

He slammed his free hand on the table and glared at his friend. "Sam, I will say this ..." Eaton blinked and tried to remember what he intended to say. Like a dead fish floating belly up to the surface of a stagnant pond, the thought returned and he seized it before it got away again. "If you're serious this time you'll never find a better catch than Eliza Allen. She's a rare beauty and her family's one of the richest in Tennessee. Good God, man, you positively roll in luck."

Eaton took a deep swallow of his beer. He'd need it to fight off the elements when he went out back to turn the snow yellow, it being much too cold to walk all the way to the privy. As the senator rose from his chair and weaved toward the back door, another thought floated to the surface.

"Does the general know?" he asked, stopping in mid-stride. "If he doesn't, you'd best tell him right away. The poor man's has been tryin' to marry you off for so long he'd be mad as hell if he heard it from someone else before he heard it from you. God knows he could stand some good news, too."

The question flooded Houston with memories. Yes, he made sure to tell the Jacksons about his engagement before announcing it to anyone else. He had the added satisfaction of interrupting one of the general's frequent lectures on the virtues of married life, and how Houston ought to settle down if he was going to make something of himself, as if being governor was a puny achievement open to any dullard.

The old man meant well, but when he cranked up one of his lectures Houston felt like a little boy with skinned knees and a runny nose. Jackson's long and happy marriage convinced him that everyone could enjoy the same happiness that he did, if only they put their mind to it. Over the years, Rachel and Andrew Jackson introduced him to enough eligible young women to populate a harem, which was not, Houston reflected, an unpleasant thought, however impractical.

Pacing back and forth in the Hermitage parlor with his usual restless energy, Jackson rattled off the same old arguments. He apparently believed that sheer repetition might somehow penetrate his protégé's thick skull.

"Sam, what are you now, almost thirty six? I'm afraid for your future, I truly am. I hate to be the one to tell you, but you have a lamentable reputation for drinkin', carousin', and, well, you know the rest. That kind of life weakens a man. Just think what might happen if the details of your debauchery were made public? Son, believe me, people want a steady hand at the helm, and that means a married man."

Houston knew all about his reputation. He never bothered to deny it either, no matter how exaggerated some of it was. If anything, he suspected that his critics were envious. But there was no point telling Jackson that. The General's deep moral streak showed up more often as he grew older, to the dismay of the many friends who suffered through his interminable lectures.

"Sir, if I may." He threw up both hands like a dam to divert the ceaseless torrent of words. "I have some news. I believe you will find it pleasin'."

Houston waited for a few heartbeats, savoring the expectant look on Jackson's face. After suffering through so many lectures, he couldn't resist the temptation to keep the older man in suspense.

"I am to be married."

With a mighty whoop Jackson trapped Houston in a bear hug while be bellowed for Rachel so they could tell her the good news. It was the last time he saw her alive and it tugged at his heart to think about it.

"Well I'll be damned, Sam Houston is gettin' married," marveled the beaming Jackson, tugging the cork out of a bottle of champagne to toast the occasion. "You're sure about this? You're not pullin' my leg just to get the old man to shut up, are you?

He assured Jackson that no leg pulling was involved.

"Eliza Allen, eh? That's a fine match! Splendid girl! She could use a little more meat on her bones but that'll come when you two start havin' babies. And she comes from a fine family, too. Good work, Sam. That's a brilliant alliance."

Houston winced at the word alliance, although it seemed like everyone insisted on describing his engagement exactly that way. People assumed that he was more calculating than he was and most of the time he let them think it. But not this time, not with Eliza. As he explained more than a few times, although no one seemed to listen, he was a man in love, not a man negotiating a treaty.

True, the Allens *did* have power, influence and wealth. There was no denying it. Allenwood, the family plantation outside of Gallatin, featured a spectacular mansion set high on a wooded bluff overlooking the Cumberland River. Houston met Robert Allen, Eliza's uncle, during the long convalescence from his wounds after the Creek War. Like most of Tennessee's plantation aristocracy, the Allens were enthusiastic horse breeders. Over the years, they ran into each other from time to time at races around the state. The Allens were gentry, and old gentry at that, at least by Tennessee standards, well connected to all the right people from Nashville to Washington.

And Sam Houston was always a welcome guest at Allenwood. At first, he was drawn by his casual friendship with Robert. Later, there were practical considerations, too. It was wise for any ambitious politician to stay in contact with Tennessee's influential families and no family was more influential than the Allens.

In time, he developed a friendship with both Robert and John, Robert's brother and Eliza's father, even though the brothers had little in common. Robert was easy to like while John was a prickly patrician who devoted his life to expanding the family holdings and influence. As time passed, his stronger personality dominated Robert, who grew sickly and old before his time.

Houston knew that the flinty-eyed John Allen was his friend because of *what* he was, not *who* he was, but that hardly made Allen unique. Yes, Eliza was a catch, but Sam Houston was the best catch in Tennessee. There was already vague talk about the possibilities after Jackson's presumed two terms as

President. One of the Philadelphia newspapers even called him "King Andrew's crown prince."

To Eliza's father, the marriage *was* an alliance. The fact that Houston happened to love his daughter was a happy coincidence, but entirely unnecessary for matrimony. Houston tried not to let it bother him, although he couldn't keep the thought from niggling a little. At least Eliza's feelings for him were genuine. He was sure of it.

At barely half his age, it was only natural that he didn't notice her at first. She caught his attention about five years ago with a pair of startling blue eyes looking out at the world with more self-assurance than any thirteen-year-old girl should possess, along with some of the best riding he'd ever seen. As she grew older, she learned to ride in a more ladylike fashion, but that first impression stayed with him because he loved the way that it captured her spirit - long blonde hair flying in the wind as her lithe figure melded to the horse. Her favorite mount was named Wildfire and when she rode it was as if they were made of a liquid shaping horse and rider as one.

Although she rarely left Allenwood, Eliza grew into a poised young woman who took her throngs of beaux for granted. Despite his greater experience, Houston felt clumsy and oafish when he was with her. Teasing him unmercifully, she wasn't intimidated by his position or his reputation and casually assumed that he worshiped her because everyone did. One day he realized there was an undertone to their banter that hadn't existed before. It was no longer man to girl. It was man to woman.

One afternoon after a picnic as they strolled beneath the plantation's massive oaks, driven to distraction by her teasing, he blurted out, "Do you treat all your admirers this badly?"

"Why yes, I believe that I do," she said, laughing at his fit of temper. "In fact, I'm sure of it. Ask anyone."

To Houston's ears, her laughter resembled the tinkling of bells. He adored it. He adored everything about her.

"But I save the real torment for the special ones," she added, gaily thumping him on the chest with her Spanish fan. "Only you, Sam Houston. Only you."

It was starting. He hoped that it would and now it had. He loved the feeling in his stomach when it started, the first sign it was more than flirtation. He'd known for weeks that he wanted to marry her and this was her first hint that such a thing was possible. As time passed, the possibility grew into a certainty. True, they didn't talk about it much; hardly at all, in fact. In Houston's mind, it wasn't necessary. All was understood.

Romantic to the core, it was his nature to be ardent, to want to move things along as quickly as possible. This time there was a practical reason. A long engagement was impossible. Houston's re-election campaign would start soon and he was running against the canny Billy Carroll, who wanted his old job back and would do anything to get it.

The Carroll faction even started a rumor about a so-called agreement that Houston would walk away after one term and leave the field open for their man. Of course, there was no such agreement. Carroll aimed to brand Houston a liar for going back on a pact that never existed.

A bitter campaign could lead to serious trouble in Tennessee politics. Fortunately Houston had the President-elect's tacit support, although he couldn't offer it publicly. As Jackson explained, "I'm the President, or soon will be, not a nursemaid for feuding youngsters. You two will have to work it out on your own. Billy knows how I feel."

But if Carroll was willing to defy Jackson's wishes, it promised to be a long hard fight.

The inauguration was another reason for the couple to marry as soon as possible. Many of Houston's friends were going to Washington for Jackson's swearing in and he wanted the wedding to take place before they left. They set January 22 as the date, only a little more than a month after announcing their engagement. He knew that the unusually short engagement set tongues wagging, but the truth was that nothing had happened between them. They rarely even kissed, which only made him want her all the more.

If Eliza was willing, Houston would happily elope, but the Allens demanded the pageantry of an extravagant ceremony, although the bride seemed oddly disengaged from the preparations. He put it down to the fact that all her life she had a large family and many servants to care for her. A spoiled young woman who never did anything for herself, she behaved as if there was no other way. For Eliza, the bothersome details of everyday life simply did not exist.

Not long after Aunt Rachel's death, over a quiet dinner at the Hermitage, Houston offered to postpone the wedding, but Jackson wouldn't hear of it.

"My son, we appreciate your offer more than I can say, but no one will be more pleased than my Rachel to see you married," he said. "She'd hate it if she caused any delay in your happiness."

Since his beloved wife's death, Jackson had taken on the habit of talking as if she still lived. Some thought him unhinged by grief, but it pleased Houston that they were inseparable even in death.

"I know what they say," acknowledged Jackson, as if reading Houston's mind. "Let them talk."

Just the same, it was good to see the general so consumed by the details of his coming presidency that there was little time for him to mourn. To Houston's disappointment, Jackson couldn't stay for the wedding. He'd already delayed too long. There was too much to do in Washington.

The night before Jackson left Nashville by steamboat, they

met at the Nashville Inn. The general was in a pensive mood. With his wife's death, his long face had lost much of its restless vitality, although the old fire still burned deep within. If he wasn't quite the man he used to be, even a lesser Andrew Jackson was still the most formidable man Houston that had ever known.

After dinner they relaxed over port and cigars in Houston's suite of two rooms. At the general's command, a servant raced down to Jackson's carriage and brought up two heavy wooden boxes covered with rich velvet cloth. Jackson produced a silver key and opened one of the boxes, careful to keep the contents hidden from Houston's view.

"Here, Sam, I wanted to present you with our wedding gift before I left."

With a flourish, he stepped aside and Houston saw the Jacksons' own sterling silver flatware, imported from England. He'd seen it many times at occasional formal dinners at the Hermitage.

"Sir, I don't know ... I can't ...."

Jackson glowed with pleasure. He loved to surprise friends with gifts large and small.

"We had no money when we married," he said, laying a long bony hand across the other box. "It was a while before we could afford gee-gaws like this. Rachel always said it didn't matter but I was young and full of pride. I swore that I'd have fine things for her one day. We didn't use it often. But I know my Rachel loved it because it was a part of us, a promise kept."

"Sam, we would be honored if you accepted it," he said. "It means a great deal to us both."

Jackson offered the key and Houston took it from his hand, struggling to control his emotions.

The general perked up, intent on lightening the mood before they parted.

"Now why don't I get out of here before we both start

blubberin' like two old ladies? I don't know how often I'll get back to Nashville these next few years, or if I'll get back at all, but I expect to see you in Washington before long. The folks back east had better get used to westerners in charge, though I know some of 'em expect me to show up in Washington with a tomahawk in one hand and a scalping knife in the other. Anyhow, there's a Senate seat comin' up in two years that'll go a long way to set you up as a national man. After that, well, we'll see how things work out. Just you make sure and beat Billy Carroll. He can wait a little longer to be governor again. We have great things to do, you and I, great things!"

It was peculiar to think back on it, but the only person who didn't seem overjoyed at his engagement was Rachel Jackson, who Houston assumed would be happiest of all. The night that he told the Jacksons, the general had to leave the parlor for a few minutes to greet a late-night visitor and escort him to his cabin. With her husband gone, Rachel Jackson took Houston's hand in both of hers, a question in her eyes.

"Samuel, are you sure about this?" she asked.

"Of course, I'm sure, Aunt Rachel," he replied. "I love her. Truly, I do."

"No, I don't mean sure about how *you* feel," she explained with a shake of her head. "I mean Eliza. I don't know how to say it exactly, and please don't be offended, but Eliza and her family are …" Unable or unwilling to finish, she gave a worried little shake of her head.

What a strange thing to say, he thought. But before he could ask what she meant, Jackson returned from tending to his guest and Houston never got the chance. Now it was too late. Aunt Rachel was gone and he would soon be married.

27

AS HE WATCHED Eliza slowly descend the great staircase of Allenwood, Houston felt as if his heart might pound right out of his chest. With her blonde curls and shimmering white dress, she was the most beautiful thing he'd ever seen. He could swear that he saw a golden glow swirl all around her.

As she floated down the staircase on her father's arm, the soft light enhanced her coolly elegant beauty. There was a look of triumph in the way her eyes darted around the room, like a hunter coming home after a successful kill. A few days ago, the Nashville Banner and Whig gushed that Eliza was the "Belle of the Cumberland" and the wedding the "event of the year," with a guest list "worthy of a monarch." To be seen and adored by others is what Eliza Allen was made for, and this was her moment.

Eliza did not meet the eye of her husband to be until her father stepped back and she stood at Houston's side before the Reverend William Hume, pastor of the Nashville Presbyterian Church. She looked every inch the queen and Houston did his best to live up to her high standard, with a suit of rich black velvet and a Spanish cloak lined in scarlet. No one could accuse him of under-dressing for his own wedding.

The ceremony passed in a blur, with a strange roaring in Houston's ears the whole time. Hume, who was barely five feet tall, with multiple chins and a mellifluous voice, for some reason spoke so quietly Houston had to lean forward to hear him. Even then he only caught an occasional word. He responded at what he guessed was the right time and hoped that he wasn't making a fool of himself.

Suddenly it was over. He didn't actually hear Hume say that he could kiss the bride, but he knew it was time by the way Eliza turned her regal face to his. He put his big hand at the small of her back and gave Mrs. Houston her wedding kiss.

As such things go, it was a disappointment. Her lips barely brushed his before she turned to face the huge gathering and let loose a radiant smile, leaving his head awkwardly hanging over her shoulder. Beneath her glowing self-assurance, Eliza must be nervous, Houston thought. That must be it. His own heart was beating like a hammer pounding iron on a smithy's anvil.

The weather had turned freezing that afternoon. Another big snow was coming; if not tonight, then overnight or early in the morning. The guests crowded in front of the mansion's many roaring fireplaces, sipping refreshments offered on silver trays by the house slaves resplendent in their scarlet and gold livery. They talked about the handsome bride and the beautiful groom. They talked about the weather. They talked about Andrew Jackson and what his presidency might mean for the country. They talked about the upcoming campaign that pit Houston against Carroll, and what it meant that Carroll refused to withdraw even though everyone knew that Houston was Jackson's chosen man.

"So tell me, Sam, I mean, Governor, where are you two spendin' the night?"

Houston turned to see the bright red face of Willoughby Williams, an old friend who stood at his side the day he snatched the silver dollar from the sergeant's drum head and joined the army. The portly round-faced Williams was the Davidson County sheriff, one of the most important political positions in the state, and one of the most lucrative. With the sheriff allowed to keep a percentage of every fine he collected, after only two years in office Williams was well on the way to becoming a wealthy man.

When Houston didn't answer, Williams plowed ahead. "You know, Sam, where will it, uh, happen?"

Williams' eyebrows bounced up and down and his round red face contorted comically. Houston realized that he was seeing a drunken attempt at a leer. Given the ocean of alcohol being consumed everywhere he looked it was no surprise that Williams was drunk. No doubt he wasn't the only one.

"Easy, Willie, easy," laughed Houston, who'd grown used to this kind of rough but good-natured ribbing. "We'll spend the night here and ride to Nashville tomorrow. If you don't stop hittin' the champagne so hard you'll have a bad time of it come mornin'."

Williams was offended as only someone who is drunk but doesn't know it can be offended.

"Well aren't you just a fine one to talk of moderation?" He raised one hand and snapped his fingers. "I give *that* for moderation."

Williams stopped as a notion barreled through the alcoholic fog, squinting as he tried to focus.

"Here?" he asked. "You're stayin' here?"

Houston nodded while he looked around for a way to escape without offering insult, a valuable skill that any successful politician learned in self-defense.

"That's a bad sign, a *very* bad sign, if you ask me." Williams pointed his index finger under Houston's nose, as if lecturing a dense student. "A man's weddin' night should not . . . ah, ah, *transpire* under his father-in-law's roof. It's awkward, that's what it is, awkward. I'd beware, Sam, I'd beware."

He drew even closer and whispered, "What if she hollers? Sometimes they do, you know."

While Houston was amused rather than offended by Williams' boozy advice, the truth is that he wasn't pleased with the arrangement either, preferring that the two of them strike out on their own as soon as possible. Somehow spending their first night at Allenwood didn't feel right. But it seemed churlish to refuse, especially when Eliza weighed in so prettily on the side of acceptance.

"Oh, Sam, it will be so lovely here with Mama and Papa." She seized his hand in both of hers, held it to her magnificent bosom, and gazed up at him with those irresistible blue eyes. "After all, you're part of the family now! Say yes, Sam, please?"

He gave in, of course. How could he do anything else?

———

THEY SET out for Nashville after a night that was even more confusing than it was disappointing, and it was very disappointing.

He knew that Eliza was inexperienced. In fact, he was confident that she had no experience at all beyond flirtation. But where he expected timidity, he found indifference verging on hostility.

He would have understood if she was afraid. But she wasn't, or didn't seem to be. She accepted him as she might accept foul-tasting medicine - with a grimace, or something close to it, but without a word or a sound, a woman grimly determined to do her duty and get it over with.

She retired well before he did. In a fever of anticipation, he waited in his room until he heard her two servant girls shut her door and giggle as they scuttled down the hall. Once they were out of earshot, he practically leaped across the hallway, knocked gently, opened the door, and eased through.

Eliza faced the door, her face a pale cameo against the darkness of the bedroom illuminated by a small fire in the fireplace. She wore a night gown of sheer white silk that poured over her breasts like a milky cloud. She braced her hips against the scrolled foot of the bed and the pose was at the same time provocative and defiant. Her hands clenched at her sides, she leaned back a little as he stared, but said nothing.

In two strides he crossed the room and she was in his arms, but no more yielding than a block of stone. In a fever of wanting her he kissed her hard on the lips, but she did not answer him. He picked her up and carried her to the bed, but he might as well have carried a statue. The night was not pleasant for either one of them.

They left Allenwood accompanied by Mattie and Louisa Martin. The twin daughters of Robert and Martha Martin, they were the flower girls at the wedding. The Martins lived at Locust Grove, a middling plantation on the road between Gallatin and Nashville. Robert Martin was an invalid whose spine was shattered when he was thrown from a horse. When Martha rushed home immediately after the ceremony to be with her husband, Houston promised they'd escort the twins to Locust Grove, where they'd have a light meal before riding their carriage on to Nashville.

As expected, it snowed overnight. As they passed through the white rolling landscape, the snow muffled the horses' hoof beats so that they rode in ghostly silence, with only an occasional squeak from the carriage. He wanted to talk to Eliza about last night, but with the girls present a conversation that promised to be difficult at best was impossible.

The snow began to fall again, lightly at first, then heavier. The wind blew harder and the snow seemed to fall almost horizontally. If Houston were alone he'd push on to Nashville. The turnpike was impossible to lose even in heavy snow. But with the girls they had to stop at Locust Grove. If the weather didn't improve, they'd probably spend the night there, too.

That night was even worse than the one before. He hoped that getting away from Allenwood might relax Eliza, but if anything she was even more unresponsive. Her soft skin was warm to his touch, but it was the only warmth she displayed. Instead of going through the charade of lovemaking again, he stopped trying.

He wanted to help her, but didn't know how.

"What's wrong, Eliza?" he asked. "Please, what is it?"

Her only response was to screw her eyes shut. A tear escaped from the outer edge of one eye and rolled silently down her cheek.

He propped himself up on one elbow and lightly caressed her cheek with his hand.

"I understand, at least I think so," he said quietly. "It must be hard to be thrown into a new life that's so different from everything you've known. You need time to adjust, that's all. I'll wait as long as you want. We have all the time in the world."

He tried to hold her, if only to comfort her. But she was so rigid with tension it was like holding a pine board. Finally, he gave up, rolled over, and tried to sleep.

It was a long and tormented night. Neither of the newly-weds slept, although both pretended to.

The next morning was clear, cold and exhilarating, with a sky of such brilliant blue that it almost hurt to look at it. The freshly fallen snow didn't have a track on it, as if a new world was created overnight, full of purity and possibilities.

Houston rose early, dressed quickly, and went downstairs. The Martin girls coaxed him to help them build a snowman, with a carrot for a nose and rocks for eyes. It wasn't until Eliza heard Houston's laughter outside that she came downstairs, too. Hugging herself, she stood at a bay window watching her husband and the girls have a snowball fight. Houston roared with feigned anger while the girls chased him around the snowman and pelted him with snowballs. When he let them catch up, they jumped on him, and all three fell down in a laughing heap.

Eliza didn't hear Martha Martin come up beside her with a cup of steaming tea.

"My goodness, Eliza," she said with a smile, watching the battle outdoors. "I think poor Sam's getting the worst of it from my girls. Maybe you should go out and even things up?"

Eliza Allen Houston turned toward her hostess and the sorrow in her eyes seemed to fill the day.

"Have you ever made a mistake, such a big mistake that you knew it right away?" Eliza asked. "Something so awful it ruined your life?"

Surprised at the question, Martha could only shake her head.

"I've made mistakes, Eliza. Everyone has. But ruin my life? Never."

"Well I did," Eliza said.

28

HOUSTON WAS CAUGHT in the maelstrom of the campaign almost from the moment they got to Nashville. The unintended result left Eliza mostly alone to make a new home in a strange place surrounded by people she didn't know. His wife desperately needed more support and he knew it. But there was no time. With Jackson in Washington, most of the General's political responsibilities in Tennessee fell to him, on top of the crowded days and nights that came with being the governor of a growing state who is facing a challenge from a popular three-time governor. The whirlwind of activity meant long days followed by late-night meetings, sessions that invariably ended with a drink or two. Eliza was usually asleep by the time he got home, although most nights he suspected that she was only pretending.

Sensitive to the contrast between her sheltered life at Allenwood and the rough-and-tumble nature of her new life, Houston berated himself for not seeing it earlier. It simply never occurred to him. He loved her and, being massively self-centered, he assumed that was enough.

He didn't own property. He never wanted any. Property tied a man down. Someday he'd have his own place, but that was in the future. Until his marriage, his modest suite in the Nashville Inn was more than enough for his needs, although Eliza contemptuously regarded it as little more than inadequate closet space. When her clothes were delivered from Allenwood they almost filled all of one room. When he insisted that most of the clothes be stored because there wasn't enough space for them all, she collapsed on the floor and began to cry. Between sobs, she wailed pitifully, "But what am I supposed to wear?"

Houston had no good answer, at least none he dared say aloud. It seemed to him that with what she dismissed as the "pitiful few things" she kept on hand Eliza could go for weeks at a time and not wear the same thing twice. It was not his nature to keep silent, but he learned there are times when nothing is the best thing a husband can say.

Their second argument came when she complained that the campaign consumed too much of his time.

"It's still months until the election." There was a shrill whine in her voice he hadn't noticed before. "Why do you have to start so *early?* I never *see* you! Why do you leave me *alone* all the time when you know how much I *hate* it! I must be the *loneliest* woman in all of Tennessee!"

There was no answer to that either, other than to explain that he'd have to start early and run hard to beat Carroll. In a weak effort to lighten her mood, he joked, "If I don't start now come election day I'll be the ex-Governor and then you'll see way too much of me." Eliza was not amused.

The Nashville Inn, once so comfortable, accommodating and convenient, now seemed shabby, crude and cheap. Nashville itself wasn't much better. He couldn't imagine how it must look to Eliza.

Until recently, Houston was proud of Nashville's rough edges. To him, it represented the future. Full of restless energy, the town practically created itself as he watched it. Now, seeing it through Eliza's eyes, he was embarrassed by it, although he was ashamed of himself for thinking that way. His marriage had forced him to give up something important, some vital part of himself, but he couldn't identify what it was. As the days passed, he felt restless, discontented, and irritable without remedy.

Years ago in Washington, he was told that with its wide boulevards and huge, if still mostly non-existent, government buildings, the capitol was designed to intimidate foreign dignitaries, which he conceded that it just might do one day if they ever finished the place. He doubted that Nashville intimidated anyone, or ever would. Originally laid out by surveyors as a long rectangular grid of streets at right angles to each other, it overlooked a thriving riverboat landing on the Cumberland River. Nashville was crowded, noisy and boisterous, a ragged frontier town thrown together without thought or plan, with ten hotels, eight taverns, three billiard halls, two military armories, and five newspapers.

The public square was the city's throbbing heart. The courthouse stood on one side, fenced off by a long hitching rail. With its unusual three-story colonnade, the Nashville Inn stood at a right angle to the courthouse, faced by the smaller City Hotel on the other side of the square. The opposing locations were rich with symbolism. The Nashville Inn was the informal headquarters of the Jackson Democrats while the Whigs adopted the City Hotel as their own. A large vacant lot in back of the inn was used for the almost daily cockfights, which added to the general sense of bustle and noise around the square. The stocks and a whipping post stood next to the courthouse, and rarely a week passed that they weren't used.

The inn's popular tavern was directly below their rooms. When Eliza complained about having to listen to "drunken brutes" all night, Houston agreed to arrange for other rooms the moment they became available, although he knew that it wouldn't make any difference.

This wasn't the life Eliza was bred for and it wasn't the life she expected, but for now it was the only life Houston had to offer. Many times he tried to coax her into talking about it, but after a few minutes she'd begin to weep. In the face of her tears, a vague promise of something better at some distant time seemed so weak he finally stopped making it. It was a bitter thing that the silver-tongued Sam Houston couldn't talk to his own wife.

She was still cold to him, too. That it came from her unhappiness was the only explanation he could think of. He'd known all kinds of women in his life, blue bloods and women from hardscrabble farms, prostitutes and wives unhappy with their husbands, Creoles and Indians, mulattoes and quadroons. Women were always attracted to him, all kinds of women, every kind of woman. Except his wife.

One afternoon he decided to surprise her. Leaving a formidable pile of work on his desk, in his eagerness he practically ran across the bustling square from his courthouse office, burst through the double-doors of the inn, and bounded up the stairs, waving off several acquaintances loitering in the tavern as he passed by. He thought that they might take advantage of the pleasant day and go riding. Eliza loved to ride and went out alone many afternoons.

He found her curled up in a rocker in their small parlor, crying and dabbing at her face with a perfumed handkerchief. A slave he recognized from Allenwood stood awkwardly at her side.

He got down on one knee and gently put his hand on her shoulder.

"Eliza, what is it? What's wrong?"

Wordlessly, she showed him a note written by her father and obviously delivered by the slave:

"Dear Eliza,"

"Your poor brother, Charles, passed away last night. Your mother and I are devastated. Can you find it in yourself to come home for a few days?"

"Papa"

A sickly boy whose racking coughs were painful to hear, Charles was an accidental child born eleven years after the next youngest of the Allen children. His death was sad, Houston thought, but not surprising.

"Eliza, I'm so sorry," he said tenderly. "Do you know what happened?"

"This is all I know." She crumbled the note and threw it on the floor. Her eyes were red and the traces of tears ran down her splotchy face. He felt his heart jump. To him, she never looked more beautiful.

"I'm going home," she said.

"Of course, you have to go," he agreed. "I understand."

He had to arrange it. Eliza couldn't do anything for herself. He rose to his feet and turned to the waiting slave.

"Did you bring a coach?"

"No, sah," he said. "Ah rode myself."

"That's all right," Houston said, thinking rapidly. "We'll pack a trunk for Mrs. Houston, then I'll hire a coach and you can drive her to Allenwood. If your horse isn't coach-trained, we'll hire a horse and hitch yours to the back."

"You're not coming with me?" Eliza asked, her blue eyes narrowing as she rose from the rocker.

"Eliza, I can't," he said. "Not now."

He hated what he had to say because he knew how she'd take it.

"The legislature convenes tomorrow," he explained. "I've

183

got to be here, especially with the campaign. There's no other way. I'd go with you if I could. You know that."

"Yes," she said, her voice cold as frost, "of course you would."

29

ALMOST MIDNIGHT, time to turn in after another long day. Might as well take his whiskey with him. Why waste it? Eliza wouldn't be awake. Ever since she buried her brother she slept at least a dozen hours a day. He still felt guilty about not getting away for the funeral. She never said anything about it, but she didn't have to. Her silence was enough.

With a round of bleary good nights to Overton, Williams and three state legislators, Houston headed toward the stairs. Wherever they took place, sometimes these late-night get-togethers were work, sometimes they weren't, and most of the time it was impossible to tell the difference. Good things came out of them, at least sometimes; new legislation, obstacles avoided, compromises made. He knew that he attended too often and stayed too long, but that didn't make him stop. It was a good way of staying on top of things.

He felt tired and heavy-footed. Each step seemed unnaturally loud as he climbed the stairs and opened the door. To his surprise, Eliza was awake, sitting on the floor in front of the pot-bellied stove with her skirts spread around her. The nights still were cool, Eliza liked a fire, and she had a hot one

going. The stove's door was open and sheets of paper surrounded her, scattered across the floor.

Although she didn't turn around, he could tell by the set of her shoulders that she heard him come in. He watched as she picked up a few of the sheets with one hand, glanced over the contents, and tossed them into the fire.

"You're up late," he said. "Is anything wrong?"

She looked at him standing at the door with the whiskey in his hand, disapproval gleaming in her eyes.

"No, nothing's wrong," she replied. "I'm just burning my old letters and things. We have so little room I thought it best to be rid of it all. I've always saved everything. I don't know why. It's just a lot of girlish nonsense."

Irked by her gibe, it made him feel guilty and that irked him even more. The problem wasn't that there was "so little room." It was that Eliza had so many ways to fill it up. If they lived in a palace Eliza still wouldn't have enough room.

He sat down in a rocker near the burning stove, already sweating from the heat. Eliza seemed as cool as a fall day.

A small bundle of letters neatly tied with a scarlet ribbon caught his eye. Settling the whiskey on a table beside the chair, he picked up the bundle from the floor. Intent on her work, Eliza paid no attention. He untied the ribbon, let it fall across his knee, unfolded the top letter, and began to read. As hot as it was, he suddenly felt clammy as his heart flopped in his chest.

"My beloved Eliza,"

"I ache to be with you. I can't sleep at night because I think of you and nothing else. My practice suffers because you are always in my thoughts. When I should see my clients, all I see is you. I miss you so much. How much longer must I wait?"

"My love, give me just the smallest sign and we can run away and live as destiny intends - together forever."

"I yearn to be with you and feel the warmth of your touch. Listen to your heart, my love, listen to your heart."

"Until tomorrow, your devoted slave,"

"William"

Dread seeped through his soul like a dark fog creeping in off the river. Houston unfolded another letter and another one after that, his fingers tearing at the paper. In an elegant script flowing across the pages, the writer rhapsodized about her "sweet kisses" and the "stolen moments" that were a prelude to their "future happiness."

He had no idea who William was until he found a letter signed, "Your love, Tyree."

Willie Tyree! Houston had him marked now. Pale and handsome, he was the kind of man most women either loved or mothered. His Gallatin law practice often brought him down to Nashville. They said he was a lunger, but Houston didn't know if it was true. Good God! How could any of this be true!

As the thoughts ricocheted through his mind, he felt dizzy and disoriented, lost in some strange and terrible place.

Tyree! He wrote about their love and their kisses and God knows what else! How could it be? When did it happen? His mind lurched. Wait! That explained why Eliza was cold to him. Now he understood her long afternoon rides, too. They met somewhere. Of course! That had to be it! It was so obvious now! Eliza thought she could be the governor's wife - his wife! - and carry on with another man! And not even a man! A ridiculous boy like Willie Tyree!

Did anyone know? Had she told anyone? Of course, she did! Everyone in Nashville must know! How could they not? He must look like a fool! There goes poor Sam Houston! Did you hear about it? Only married a few weeks and his wife already needs another man. He runs the state while she runs him.

Did Eliza mean for him to see the letters? Was that possible? Was she flaunting her affair and daring him to do anything about it? Yes, that must be it! Why else would she leave them out like this? Was the woman *that* brazen?

The emotional turmoil swept through him like an explosion. He jumped to his feet and the violent motion scattered the rest of the letters across the floor.

When Eliza looked up, he crushed a letter in his fist and held it out.

"What ... what is this?" His voice was a croaking whisper.

"If you let me see it perhaps I could tell," she said sarcastically.

Damn the woman! How could she be so smug?

He threw the letter on her lap. Smoothing it over her skirts, as she read Eliza's wistful smile stoked Houston's rage until he choked on it.

"Childish isn't it?" she said softly. "How naïve!"

Houston seized the whiskey glass on the table and threw it against the wall. The glass shattered with a pop and whiskey dripped down the white-washed wall.

"You are a lying treacherous bitch!" he roared. "Once I throw you out on the street, I'll find that little bastard Tyree and beat him to death, you goddamned slut!"

Desperate to vent the rage searing his soul, he raised the rocker over his head and smashed it against the wall again and again until it splintered into kindling, leaving long dark slashes in the wall. He pulled the drawer out of his writing desk, flung it across the room, and then smashed the desk into pieces with his bare hands.

Breathing hard, he glared at Eliza, who matched him glare for glare, contempt seething in her cold blue eyes.

"You fool! You pathetic clown! You ridiculous alcohol soaked blowhard!" Hissing at him like a snake, from her place on the floor she scooped up a handful of letters. "Look at the dates, you monumental idiot."

He snatched the letters from her hand. The one on top was dated more than two years ago. Heart pounding, he frantically shuffled through the rest. They all ranged from between two and three years ago, long before there was anything but banter between them.

Houston's hands fell to his sides and the letters fluttered to the floor like falling leaves. He stumbled backward until he bumped against the wall by the door. Without knowing it, he slid down the wall until he found himself sitting on the floor.

Eliza rose to her feet and stood with her back to him, facing the hot stove as if she was talking to it and not her husband.

"I was just a girl when it started," she said, her voice low and wistful. "You know how young people are, how intensely they feel everything. We even talked about running away. It was just a fantasy, but I didn't know. It felt so ... so pure. Papa found out – I don't know how – and threatened to horsewhip Willie if he ever caught us together. He would have, too. You know Papa."

Eliza seemed to gather herself as she lifted her head and stared off into space.

"Willie's from a poor family and he's utterly without means, though they say he's a very good lawyer. But I thought he was wonderful. A more gentle and romantic soul never lived."

She finally turned to face him. "Do you know the real reason Papa refused to let me see him?"

Houston didn't answer. After his frightening violence there was nothing to say.

"Willie has the lung disease. I told papa that I loved him and didn't care. But he wouldn't let me marry a dying man, especially one so poor. I haven't seen Willie in almost two years. If what they say is true, I imagine he'll be dead soon, but I really don't know."

Eliza went to the liquor cabinet next to the wall. She opened a bottle, found a glass, and carefully poured whiskey into the glass until it was half full. Houston expected her to give it to him, but to his surprise she raised the glass with both hands, hesitated, and took a sip. As far as he knew, except for the champagne at their wedding it was the first time that alcohol touched her lips.

She choked reflexively, and then took a longer sip, this time without choking.

"I always wondered what you saw in this, why you enjoyed it so much," she said, her eyes tearing from the whiskey's sting. "I was confused when you began to be so serious about me. Just the *idea* of you was overwhelming. It was out of control before I knew it. The great Sam Houston was everything my father ever wanted for me. Especially after Willie, he was afraid I'd run away with someone who wasn't suitable. I went along with it. Why not? It was obvious that what I thought, what I wanted, didn't matter. You were charming and attentive and you cared so much. If I couldn't have Willie then I might as well have you, especially if it made my family happy."

Eliza found an overturned chair, put it up right and sat down. Holding the glass with both hands again, she took another drink. The whiskey seemed to renew her and give her the nerve to tell him what she'd kept hidden, never raising her eyes from the glass.

"Our courtship, if that's what you'd call it, was never real to me until the day we married. It was as if we were playing some harmless little game that had no consequences. By the time I realized that I'd rather die than marry you it was too late. Do you remember our first night?"

When he didn't answer, she looked up with a grim smile.

"Yes, I'm sure you do. I was terrified. I didn't want to be with you. I wanted to be *anywhere* but with you. But I didn't know what to do about it. There wasn't anything *to* do about it. I'd waited too long and there was no one to turn to. For the first time in my life, I didn't have someone to take care of everything for me. I never felt so alone and afraid."

Eliza laughed, a bitter laugh filled with disappointment, and her eyes examined him as if seeing him for the first time.

"Do you have any idea how repulsive you are? How much you disgust me? I don't know what you're like without the stink of cigars and whiskey I shiver to think about those horrible scars all over your body and the thought of being touched by your great crude hands makes me ill."

He wanted to speak, to say something that would make it all stop so they could somehow go back in time, but he couldn't. There was nothing to say.

"You're not even a companion to me. You were so attentive during our courtship, but it all stopped the instant we came to this awful place. I don't even think you want a wife. You want a prize, something to display and show how wonderful and successful you are. You love the *idea* of love, but the thing you love most is yourself. At first, I thought I could at least *seem* to love you, to pretend that it was all right even if I hated every minute, but you never gave me the chance. And *now* you're jealous after ignoring me all this time? What did you say when you were bellowing like an ox and making a fool of yourself, something about throwing me out of your life? Tell me, when was I ever *in* your life?"

Without realizing it, Eliza was on her feet and screaming.

"Damn you, Sam Houston! Damn you to hell! I hate you! Do you understand me? I hate you! I hope you die!"

At dawn the next morning, Eliza hired a coach and driver and left for Allenwood. Astounded at her new-found initiative, when Houston wasn't pleading with her to forgive him, he spent the hours trying to talk her out of leaving.

"We're beyond talk. Even a fool like you should know that." She didn't bother to look up from her packing. "Things were said last night that can't be ignored or forgotten. Why should they be? It's over between us. It never really started, did it? You'll ever love anyone as much as you love yourself."

Eliza seemed almost giddy as she stepped into the coach in front of the inn. She was a girl again, the Eliza of old, the girl he'd fallen in love with.

30

HOUSTON WAS surprised and shaken at how quickly word spread that Eliza left Nashville. He should have known better. People were curious. It was only natural.

He recovered his poise, came up with a plausible-sounding tale, and refined it with every telling until he put together a reasonable yarn about how Eliza's mother still suffered from her son's death and needed her daughter at her side. As far as he could tell, it seemed so reasonable that no one thought anything of it.

He felt foggy and disoriented all day. Everything happened so fast that there was no time to collect his thoughts. His first instinct was gallop north to Allenwood and try to set things right. But the day after tomorrow he was supposed to debate Carroll in Corkrell's Spring. As the first debate of the campaign, it was impossible to postpone because it would look like he was afraid of taking Carroll on face to face. Even if he called it off, the only possible excuse was Eliza's mother, and he didn't want to call more attention to his rickety deception than was absolutely necessary.

He had to be in Corkrell's Spring in two days. There was no way around it.

Their argument made a hell of a racket, too, hardly the behavior of a happily married couple. Everyone in the inn must have heard it. He was surprised that someone didn't connect it with Eliza's sudden departure. They probably did, but were too tactful to say anything, at least not yet. Knowing how quickly gossip spread in Nashville, Houston knew that he didn't have much time. It would ruin him. It was just that simple.

The more he thought about it through the strange and muddled day, the more it seemed that going ahead with the debate might work in his favor. For one thing, it would give Eliza time to think. A scandal would ruin her reputation, too. She had as much to lose as he did. John Allen might be a cold man, but he loved his daughter. Houston couldn't imagine that Allen would do anything other than to try to keep the illustrious marriage from falling apart.

That was it! Eliza's father was the key! Why didn't he think of it earlier? He'd send a letter to John Allen explaining what happened and then go on with the debate. Once that was out of the way, he'd ride up to Allenwood and persuade Eliza to come back to him. Sam Houston knew himself to be a persuasive man. Looking at it as a lawyer, he thought that this was a case he could win.

With their rooms a wreck and the writing table smashed to pieces, he shut himself in his courthouse office to compose the most important letter of his life.

By the time he finished hours later, wadded up paper littered the floor around his desk and his fingers were stained black by ink. It was hard to find the right words, harder than he ever imagined. They more he tried, the more elusive they were. He finally decided to explain what happened as an enormous and regrettable misunderstanding, but at the same time dismiss it as the kind of thing that sometimes happens in marriage. He suggested that while Eliza's running away was an overreaction, it was not without reason. Yes, he was mad with jealously, but only for a moment, and knew now that his jealously was without foundation. After all, it was his great love for Eliza that caused the jealously in the first place. He'd leave it to John Allen to do the right thing. With his help, they'd straighten everything out and go back to being a happily married couple with a glowing future.

April 9, 1829

John,

As you know by now, a most unpleasant & unhappy event took place, one that was entirely unnecessary and entirely my fault. Whatever my feelings and expressions at that time, I know Eliza to be a virtuous wife.

She was cold to me and as a result I thought she did not love me. You yourself can judge how unhappy I was to think I was united to a woman that did not love me ...." After rattling on in that self-pitying vein for some time, Houston closed the letter by pleading with Allen to "*let me know what is to be done and I will eagerly do it.*"

By now he had gone thirty six hours without sleep. His nerves were raw and his usually sure-footed instincts dulled by fatigue and worry. Convinced that he'd written a master-piece of persuasion instead of the contradictory and self-serving gibberish that it was, Houston signed it, sealed it with the governor's seal, and sent it off by courier.

The seal was a good touch, he thought. It was a reminder of just how much the Allens had to lose.

For now, he'd done everything possible. The rest would come later. He'd think of something. He always did.

31

THE DEBATE WENT WELL. Everyone said so.

With Willoughby Williams at his side, Houston rode into Cockrell's Spring an hour before noon to find more than four hundred people already gathered in front of the church on the little town square. Driving a horse and buggy, Carroll arrived thirty minutes later. It was a warm day and the crowd kept busy by sampling the barbecue and dipping into the liquid refreshments, mostly alcohol.

The contrast between the candidates was stark. Houston wore a hunting shirt decorated with beads and fringe, buckskin pants soft as butter, Drum's flamboyant belt, and beaded moccasins. Instead of the statesmanlike appearance he intended, Carroll looked out of place and uncomfortable in a claw hammer coat, tall beaver hat, cravat, and waistcoat. His attire, combined with his pinched mouth and florid face, gave him the look of a disapproving preacher who imbibed too much before Sunday services.

By previous agreement, each candidate spoke for two hours, followed by a thirty-minute rebuttal. To pack the crowd with supporters, Houston instructed Sheriff Williams to muster a few militia and have them attend out of uniform. As a militia general, Houston knew that the men were loyal to him. He also asked Williams to meander through the crowd and get the drift of what voters were saying. He was relieved that no one mentioned Eliza, at least not to his face. It looked like his story held. Just a little longer and he wouldn't need it anymore.

When the debate ended, Houston lingered for another hour to do a little more politicking. In normal circumstances, he'd spend the night with one of his supporters, but instead excused himself with vague talk of duties of governance in Nashville.

Houston and Williams rode out of town early in the evening just as a brief but torrential rain came thundering down like heaven's wrath. Their horses seemed to hang close together as if for comfort, and now and then Houston's left foot in its stirrup brushed against Williams' right as the horse's hooves squished in the sodden ground.

Shouting to make himself heard through the rain, Williams reported that most of what he heard during the debate was good. After an uncharacteristically wobbly start, most of the crowd thought that Houston had bested Carroll. As far as Williams could tell, there weren't many present who saw any reason to turn him out of office after only one term.

"I'd say most think Billy'll be governor again, but not yet," Williams explained. "They figure it's still your time, Sam."

All things considered, Houston was pleased. It *did* take him a while to find his stride. He knew that. But once he did it felt as comfortable as ever. While one debate did not make a campaign, today was a good start. If he could find a way to mend this business with Eliza everything would be back to normal. She had to come around. She *had* to. The alternative was simply not possible. He'd make her see. He could do it. He was sure of it.

In a jovial mood, they rode up to the Nashville Inn. Soaked from the rain, Houston hankered for a beer or two, just the thing after a speech and long ride. He dismounted, tossed the reins to the boy waiting by the door, flipped youngster a coin, and got a gap-toothed grin in return.

"Water, feed, and a good rub," Houston instructed. "Do it right and I'll double that."

As they entered the tavern, he heard a voice call out, "Sam! Wait! Over here!"

John Overton emerged from the courthouse and hurried across the square. The passing years had put more gray in his hair and dark bags under his eyes, but Overton was still one of the most astute men in the state. Houston often sought his advice on matters large and small and never regretted taking it.

But more than that, John Overton was his friend. Houston knew himself to be a man with hundreds of acquaintances, but not many close friends.

Without saying a word, Overton grabbed Houston's elbow and guided him inside the inn to a private corner. Alerted by Overton's agitation, Houston asked, "What's got you so fired up, John? Did you hear? I put a whippin' on Billy today."

"Governor, right now you've got more problems than Billy Carroll," Overton whispered urgently. "Half of Gallatin showed up last night to burn you in effigy. It's got somethin' to do with Eliza. Sam, what the hell's going on?"

Staggered by the news, Houston's big frame sagged in the chair. He ran his fingers through his chestnut hair while Overton waited for an answer.

"What else did you hear?" Houston asked. "Any details?"

"They seem to think Eliza's been wronged without knowin' how exactly," Overton replied. "Rumors are flyin' and you don't want to hear the worst of it. There's no doubt John Allen's behind it. The family owns Gallatin and everyone in it.

The Allens could fart and those people would swear they smelled roses. Until you married Eliza, that part of Tennessee was never really your country anyhow."

Overton put a comforting hand on his friend's forearm.

"Look, Sam, your marriage is your business, but now it's a public problem. I heard somethin' about your situation the other night. Nashville has too many wigglin' ears to keep it a secret. It can't be coincidence that Eliza went back to Allenwood the next mornin'. We've known each other a long time and you know I'll do everything I can to help. If there's no truth to all this, we'll punish those who spread the rumors. If there's truth there, we'll do what we can to make it well. Either way, this isn't just about you and Eliza anymore. It's out there and it'll get worse if we don't do somethin' fast."

Houston took a deep breath, lifted his head, put his big hands on the arms of the chair and pushed himself to his feet so that he towered over Overton.

"John, I appreciate the offer, but I think I can fix it myself. Just give me a little time, that's all. A day or two is all I need."

"You *think* you can fix it," Overton responded dubiously, looking up at Houston's great height.

Realizing that he wouldn't get any more information, Overton gave in.

"All right, Sam, you do what you have to do, but this better get taken care of one way or another. Good God, I can't begin to imagine what Carroll might do when he gets hold of this, whatever it is."

32

AFTER A RESTLESS NIGHT, he rode out of Nashville the next morning.

As his horse's hooves thudded along the Nashville Turnpike and the countryside rolled past in all of spring's resurgent glory, Sam Houston saw none of it. It was only now that he realized how badly he'd blundered.

Overton was right, of course. John Allen was behind the uprising in Gallatin. He had to be. Houston didn't count on Eliza's father seizing the initiative so quickly. He naively assumed that his father-in-law would wait to hear his side of things. He didn't know what Eliza told her father either. Her version would do everything to shape his thoughts. He couldn't imagine that she'd lie, but he couldn't imagine a lot of things that happened lately.

He did know one thing: If it turned out badly, with his reputation the court of public opinion would find him guilty and not think twice. There was no way around it.

As he rode north, his confidence evaporated like the morning mist.

OLD JOSEPH, the Allen's ancient house slave, opened the door with a flourish as Houston crossed the spacious veranda of Allenwood.

"The young lady is in there, suh."

With his usual massive dignity, Joseph managed to bow and at the same time nod toward a drawing room off the main hall dominated by the massive staircase that Eliza so beautifully descended on their wedding day only three months ago.

Houston handed Joseph his hat and entered the room to find Eliza perched on a small settee against the opposite wall. As the sun poured in through the window at her back, the deep blue of her dress made a dramatic contrast to her shimmering blonde hair. She looked like she wasn't getting enough sleep, but somehow it only added to her beauty. There was something different in her face, too. It took a moment for Houston to find it, a new firmness around her eyes and mouth.

Eliza's Aunt Margaret, a twittering pigeon of a woman who'd lived at Allenwood for longer than Houston had known the family, was seated in the far corner of the room with her hands primly in her lap while she pretended to stare at nothing. She was far enough away to offer the illusion of privacy, but still close enough to hear everything that passed between them.

Her presence made Houston self-conscious. Did John Allen really think that he needed a witness to what passed between his daughter and son-in-law?

Obviously, the answer was yes.

Eliza patted a spot on the settee beside her.

"Sit down, Sam. You look terrible."

"And you never looked more beautiful, Eliza," he replied gallantly. "A man would be a fool not to love you."

The settee was too small for his big frame and it was hard to find a comfortable position. After some squirming, he decided to keep his back straight and teeter on the edge. His legs were too long for the distance between the settee and the floor, so he awkwardly straightened one leg and bent the other at the knee.

It didn't help that he was too aware of Aunt Margaret's over-perfumed presence. The old maid tried so hard not to stare that she drew even more attention to herself.

Houston jerked his head toward Margaret and whispered in the vain hope that only Eliza heard.

"Does *she* have to be here?"

"I'm afraid so." Eliza didn't bother to keep her voice down. "This is as private a meeting as father will allow."

"Eliza, we should be able to talk in privacy," he protested. "We're husband and wife."

Inside, Houston cursed. This was not how he wanted to start.

A patronizing smile played across Eliza's thin lips.

"We are husband and wife in name only. I thought I made that clear."

"No! That's not true!"

In the small room with its high ceiling and polished oak floor, Houston's desperate protest boomed out louder than he intended and startled Eliza's aunt, who dropped her pretense and openly stared at the couple, mouth gaping wide. All of the eloquent things he planned to say flew out of his head as he struggled to gather his scattered thoughts.

"Yes, we quarreled, but married couples sometimes quarrel," he stammered. "Ask your parents. Ask anyone. For God's sake, Eliza, one quarrel is no reason for us to destroy our marriage."

Impulsively, he reached out and seized her slender white hand with his big hands.

"God knows I'm sorry. I behaved like a madman. For a while I think I *was* mad. If I could take it all back, I would. You know that. But if I didn't care so much about you I wouldn't have acted the way I did. I can't do anything about it now, except to promise you that nothing like it will ever happen again. We can't go back. We can't undo what's been done. We can only move on. Please, Eliza, come back to me. I need you."

He was ashamed of himself even as he said the words. Sam Houston was a proud man who knew that his words sounded weak and foolish. He was begging and he hated it.

Worse, it did no good at all. With a look of contempt, Eliza lifted her hand from his as if he'd soiled it.

"You great ridiculous fool! How can you call what happened *just* a quarrel? Did you hear a word I said that night? Do you *ever* listen? What do you and I have that's worth saving? 'Destroy our marriage?' How absurd you are! What you really mean is destroy your precious career. I was miserable and so were you. I don't love you. I never did. Not for one minute. And you didn't even know it. How can you be so blind?"

"I said it all that night. I will not be second to your ambition. I will not stay at home while you go out carousing night after night. I will not live one more minute in that awful place. I will not pretend to be happy when I am miserable. I will not pretend to love you when I don't. I can't bear to be touched by you and the very thought of touching you makes me ill. I married you to please my family and found out to late that the price was too high. If that makes me the disgusting names you called me, then so be it. Before it's finished, the world will think otherwise, my family will see to that."

Eliza's eerie calm eroded with every word until she was practically snarling. Her cheeks flushed and her blue eyes seemed as wide as silver dollars as she rose to her feet, her skirts rustling.

"I despise everything about you! Go crawl into bed with some Indian woman, or wallow in some bordello, but leave me alone! I never want to see you again, you great drunken pig!"

She drew back her arm and slapped Houston across the face with all her strength. He felt an explosion in his head, a red and black rush of heat obliterating everything around him. Before she had time to withdraw her hand, he seized her wrist and jumped to his feet, unintentionally twisting her arm as he rose. Aunt Margaret screamed. Growling like an animal, Eliza fought to escape but his grip was too strong.

The red haze passed as quickly as it came. He released her wrist, stepped back, and made an ironic half bow.

"I believe you've made your feelings clear enough so that even I can understand them," he said, speaking through clenched teeth. "Good-bye, *Mrs.* Houston."

As he turned on his heel to leave, John Allen burst into the room with a pistol in his hand.

"Houston, touch my daughter and I'll kill you!"

Eliza's father was not a fighting man. Houston knocked the pistol away with a sweep of his arm, seized the smaller man by the shirtfront, lifted him off his feet, and smashed his back against the wall. The blow caused a large portrait of Allen's grandfather to fall from its place on the wall, its frame shattering on the floor.

"Sam! Stop it! You'll kill him!"

Eliza's terrified voice cut through the murderous feeling in his heart. He released his hold and Allen fell to his hands and knees, one hand groping for the pistol on the floor.

Houston contemptuously kicked the weapon out of reach and faced the room, the image frozen in his mind for all time: Allen helpless on his hands and knees, groping for a pistol that wasn't there; Eliza stunned and absolutely still; and Aunt

Margaret staring wide-eyed with her hands covering her prim mouth.

"No matter what happens now, I'm damn well rid of you," he said, glaring at Eliza. "All of you!"

Forgetting his hat, he marched outside to his horse. Ignoring the stirrup, he mounted by throwing one leg over the saddle, angrily jerking the reins as the startled animal wheeled.

Galloping down the long oak-lined road leading from the great house to the turnpike, he heard Allen screaming in the background.

"Houston, you're finished! Do you hear me! You're finished!"

33

IT WAS as if he dreamed the ride back to Nashville. He couldn't force himself to think clearly and after a while stopped trying.

Exhausted and desperately wanting sleep, after two miles he left the turnpike and eased the horse down to a glade where he knew that a small stream ran. He felt the way he did as a boy when he was sick with fever. The world around him seemed distant and distorted. He had no energy and even simple tasks were beyond his strength. He took off his coat, rolled it up to make a pillow, collapsed under a tree, and fell asleep.

His horse finally woke him up, pushing at his body with his snout. He was stiff and cold. He knew that he'd slept for hours but still didn't feel refreshed. If anything, he was more tired than before. Even his bones hurt. He felt so weak it that was hard to mount his horse. Once he did, it climbed up to the turnpike on its own. It knew the way home well enough and Houston let it carry him there.

He was a mile down the turnpike before he realized that

he'd left his coat rolled up under the tree. It wasn't important. Going back was too much effort.

Houston plodded into Nashville, slumped in the saddle and indescribably weary. Fortunately, it was so late that the square was empty and there were no questioning eyes. He weakly slid down the horse's side and let the reins fall to the ground. It would wander away in the night looking for water and food, but he didn't care.

He entered the back door of the tavern and climbed the stairs. Each step seemed to take more effort than the one before. He leaned his head against the door while he fumbled with the key and didn't bother to shut the door behind him. He staggered to his bed and collapsed.

All he wanted was to sleep. No one could bother him then.

34

THERE'S a big storm coming as the skiff violently rocks back and forth on the river. He's got to get to shore before the storm breaks, but they won't leave him alone. They keep pushing and clawing . Now they're yelling at him. Why won't they stop? Why can't they let him be? Please, just a little longer....

"Governor Houston! Wake up! Sam! You've got to wake up!"

Why is Johnny Overton out here on the river? What the hell?

With a groan, Houston rolled over, opened his gummy eyes, and saw Overton's worried face hovering above him. There were other faces in the background, too. It took a moment before his eyes focused and he identified Willoughby Williams, Doctor John Shelby, and Colonel John McGregor, all of them anxiously peering over Overton's shoulder.

"Let me sleep." He rolled over on his face so the pillow muffled his voice. "Leave me alone!"

"No, Sam," Overton said, shaking Houston's shoulder again. "I'm sorry, but we can't. I don't know how long you've been here, but there's trouble and you can't sleep your way through it."

When Houston didn't respond, Overton snarled, "Get up! I said. Get up, goddamn you!"

The lash of the older man's words shamed Houston into wakefulness. He slowly sat upright and put his feet on the floor, surprised to see that he still had his boots on.

What's going on? Why was John in such an uproar?

It all came back in a giant wave of pain that washed through his soul and destroyed everything in its path ... Eliza . . . their quarrel ... Allenwood ... Aunt Margaret ... Eliza's slap ... he felt the sting on his cheek and the madness coursing over him ... Allen and his pistol ... holding Allen up against the wall and wanting to kill him with his bare hands... "Houston, you're finished!"

He remembered it all with terrible clarity. Sitting on the side of the bed, he groaned and buried his face in his hands. Oh, God! What would he do now?

―――

TRAPPED IN A SELF-MADE FEVERISH MADNESS, it wasn't that he lacked the strength to break out of it as much as he felt it was what he deserved. His only escape was sleep, and he slept long and often. The best time was when he came out of a deep sleep, but before he was really awake. Then it was as if he'd only dreamed the horrors of the last few days, that none of it was real. If he held on to the moment - desperately clung to it somehow - none of it *would* be real and he wouldn't have to face the awful void of his life. It was such a warm and comfortable place that he never wanted to leave. No one could hurt him there. He fought to hang on, but sooner or later it always slipped away and then he knew it wasn't a dream. He had to get up and face life but he didn't know how.

Sometimes he could behave almost normally, but it never lasted long. There always came a time when everything seemed to catch in his chest and throat and a crushing feeling churned through his insides until he felt like he was choking on it. Whenever he felt it coming, he found a way to get away by himself before it overwhelmed him the way it always did.

A few times he met with his friends in the conference room next to his office, usually the same men who came to his bedroom the first day - Overton, Williams, Shelby and McGregor. Others joined them at first, but they dropped away one by one. Not that it mattered. Houston told himself that he didn't deserve friends. It would be better for everyone if they stayed away from him.

Every day he listened as they talked and argued, pretending that what happened was politics as usual. They all knew better, but no one dared say it.

This morning promised more of the same, except he knew something they didn't. It was time to end it. He couldn't bear the awful weight any more. He rubbed his eyes with his thumb and index finger. Strange, he thought, despite all the sleep it was never enough. He was always tired, and the burden grew heavier day by day.

"Any more demonstrations?" he asked, although he didn't particularly care anymore. "Any new places join the list?"

"There's Gallatin, as usual," reported Williams. His position as Davidson County sheriff gave him the quickest access to information about what he mildly called the "upsets" across the state. "Knoxville, too. Bigger'n last time. There was a report about somethin' happenin' in the bottom lands out near Memphis, but we're not sure exactly what yet. And then, uh, well ... I'm not ...."

Williams' eyes danced around the table, the dark eyes of an honest and simple soul pleading for help. Houston had known Willoughby most of his life. He was a good and loyal friend and the news must be especially bad if the sheriff couldn't look him in the eye. It was painful to see. He hated the idea that his friends suffered for him. This was the kind of thing a man should bear alone.

"Well, what is it?" he demanded.

"Governor, I ..."

To Williams' relief, Overton spoke up. "They burned you in effigy last night here in Nashville, just outside of town. Some of 'em even threatened to move on the inn. Thanks to Will here, we knew it was comin' and took the precaution of calling out a few militia. A small demonstration of force shut it down, but that won't be the end of it by a long shot. We've got the militia standin' by until things settle down."

"John, do you really think it'll settle down?" Houston asked.

He saw them glance at each other, waiting for someone to speak up. No one would say it, but they all knew the answer. It would only get worse. There was no way out. He was trapped.

"What are they sayin'?" he asked, breaking the awkward silence. "What is it that I'm supposed to have done? What makes me such a monster?"

Overton bought time by opening his cigar case. He used a pearl-handled clasp knife to cut off the end off one of the thin cigars he favored lately, and took his time striking a match underneath the table. He worked longer than necessary to get his cigar going. It gave him an excuse to avoid eye contact with the Governor. He didn't like having to say it, but he was the only one who would.

"Some say you abused her, Sam, that's why she ran home to Daddy. Others claim you made her do certain ... things you'd learned from the Cherokee, things no self-respectin' white woman would ever do, whatever that's supposed to mean. There's another story that you were so wild with jealousy you kept Eliza locked her in your room and beat her. There's all manner of contemptible rumors. What they're sayin' today is worse than what they said yesterday and what they'll say tomorrow will be worse than today."

With his index finger curled over the cigar, Overton eased back in his chair and waved his hand to take in the outside world, making a thin curlicue of smoke in the air.

"The whole thing's feedin' on itself as it spreads. Nobody knows what the hell they're talkin' about, of course, but that doesn't make it any less dangerous."

Something occurred to Houston. He should have thought of it before. He must be losing his wits.

"What's Billy Carroll doin' with all this?" he asked. "He probably wet himself considering the rich possibilities."

The men around the table chuckled, their first laughter in days.

"Billy's not involved personally, of course, at least not directly," explained Shelby. "He's been careful to avoid it for appearances sake."

A deliberate man whose word carried weight, the gray-bearded doctor had no political ambitions and never asked for favors, which made him someone to regard.

"Pious Billy announced that he does not want to ride to re-election on the back of your personal problems, meaning he wants it both ways. He managed to call more attention to your trouble and at the same time drape the golden mantle of virtue around his shoulders. In short, he's a lyin' hypocritical horse's ass."

"We've spotted a few of his people at the burnin's, mingled along with Allen's crowd," added Williams. "Carroll and Allen are workin' together, one way or another. Maybe it wasn't that way at first, but it's sure true now. You can take big odds on that."

Houston exhaled loudly, like the air leaving a bellows. He

leaned back in his chair and tilted his head so that he looked at the ceiling.

"Don't blame him too much," he said. "If it was turned around we'd do the same thing."

"No we wouldn't." Overton was quiet but firm. "Don't you think that for one damn minute."

Houston shrugged. "I 'spose it's nice to think so, but I wonder."

Overton reached into a pocket inside his coat and brought out a letter.

"By the way, this just came in from Washington."

"What is it?" Houston jerked to attention, his dread about how Jackson would react to the mess he made boiling to the surface.

Overton patted himself down searching for his rimless reading spectacles. He found them and slipped them on, the spectacles perched on the end of his nose.

"Andy says he'll give Carroll an ambassadorship to the South American country of his choice in exchange for his withdrawal from the governor's race," he said, paraphrasing the letter. "He also guarantees his full support if Carroll decides to withdraw now and run for governor at any later date."

"John, are you sayin' the General doesn't know about any of ... this?" asked Houston.

"I 'spect he does by now," replied Overton. "This letter probably crossed on the road with the news. It's all over the country, or soon will be. By the way, Carroll already put together his reply, though he hasn't sent it off yet. He said circumstances might soon require someone to step into the breech in Tennessee, so he respectfully declines the offer. He described what's goin' on as 'a chaotic situation verging on anarchy through lack of leadership, one that requires a strong and experienced hand,' or some such bullshit."

Williams pounded his fist on the table. "Andy ought to name that holier-than-thou hypocrite ambassador to some island of cannibals. I'd happily supply the cooking pot."

"Sam, Billy Carroll isn't our problem, not really," Overton said. "You *must* say somethin'. You've *got* to defend yourself. So far you haven't given the people anything to hang on to. When you give them nothin' else to believe, it's only natural they believe the worst. You *must* fight back. If you wait any longer I swear to God it'll bring you down."

"What would you have me do?" Houston asked gently. "What do you want me to say?"

"Tell the world John Allen is a treacherous pile of shit and his daughter is a lyin' bitch," said Williams, his chubby body squirming with pent-up emotion. "Then show how Allen and Carroll have their lackeys stirrin' it up. We can prove it easy enough. Just give us the word. Sam, we can turn this thing around sure as we're sittin' here. But you have to start right now 'cause this state's ready to explode."

Houston rose out of the chair, put his hands flat on the table, and leaned forward so he dominated them all.

"If I hear anyone insult Mrs. Houston again, that man will answer to me," he said. "I am the cause of whatever trouble I face, me and no one else. Do all of you take my meaning?"

His eyes moved from one face to the next. Poor Williams looked as if he wanted to disappear into a hole in the floor. Shelby, usually steady a rock, turned pale. McGregor looked like he might burst into tears at his friend's unfathomable folly. Overton seemed heartbroken, as if watching a loved one slowly die.

Point made, Houston sat down. The feeling was coming on him again. He had to end the meeting before he lost control.

"There is one more thing."

They leaned forward, desperately hoping to hear what

they wanted him to say. Mouths gaping in anticipation, they looked so comical he wanted to laugh.

He smiled at Williams to soften the blow he'd delivered to a loyal friend.

"Will, your prediction that I won't be governor much longer is truer than you thought. I intend to offer my resignation tomorrow."

He reached into a valise at his feet, removed two sheets of paper, and pushed them to the center of the table.

"Here's my letter. I wanted you all to see it first. I owe you at least that much."

They all started talking at once and he raised his hand for silence.

"Don't try to talk me out of it. You can't. Everything that's happened makes it impossible for me to continue. I am a ruined man and everyone here knows it, whether or not you want to say it to my face or admit it to yourselves."

"*Executive Office, Nashville, Tennessee, 16 April 1829*"

"*It has become my duty to resign the office of Chief Magistrate of the State.*"

"*In dissolving the political connection which has so long existed between the people of Tennessee and myself, no private afflictions, however deep or incurable, can forbid an expression of the grateful thanks due to the kindness of an indulgent public.*"

"*From my earliest youth, whatever talent was committed to my care has been expended for the common good, and at no period of life have any views of private interest or private ambition been permitted to mingle in the higher duties of public trust.*"

"*I can only regret that my capacity for being useful was so unequal to the devotion of my heart. It is one of the few remaining consolations of my life that even had I been blessed with ability equal to my zeal, my country's generous support in every vicissitude of life has been more than equal to them both.*"

"*That veneration for public opinion has taught me to hold no*" *delegated power which would not daily be renewed by my constituents. I am, by my own misfortunes more than by the fault or contrivance of anyone, overwhelmed by sudden calamities. It seems the respectful thing that I should retire from a position which, in the public judgment, I might seem to occupy by questionable authority."*

"Sam Houston."

As they passed it around the table, he gave them a chance to read it, one by one. When the last man finished, they all began to speak at once. Houston silenced them with a short chopping motion of his hand, a gesture of authority he'd picked up from Jackson. He had to get out before he broke down. It happened so easily now.

"This is the most painful thing I've ever done." His rumbling voice was so low that they strained to hear it. "I appreciate your friendship more than I can say. But what happened between myself and Mrs. Houston is private and will remain private. Others can say what they want and I'm sure they will, but I will say nothin' more on the subject."

"Sam, what will you do?" asked McGregor

"I have no idea," he admitted. "Let's do one thing at a time. These days, I can barely do that."

Without another word, Houston rose from his chair and hurried out the door. Keeping his head down to avoid eye contact, but knowing that every eye was on him, he walked across the bustling square to the inn where he could be alone with this awful weight that was breaking his heart. What would he do? Where would he go?

What did it matter?

35

HE SPENT the days and nights in his room, drinking, brooding, burning personal papers, giving away possessions that didn't mean anything to him anymore, and seeing the few people who bothered to come around.

At first it hurt that there were so few, but he decided that he was such a wretched creature they were right to leave him to his misery.

One of his visitors was Congressman David Crockett, who'd stopped in Nashville to pay his respects to the Governor before traveling on to Washington. After Houston waved Overton out the door so they could be alone, Crockett apologized for intruding.

"I'm sorry for comin' at such a bad time," said Crockett, whose ruddy face was topped by a thick mass of gray-flecked hair. "I knew there was trouble, but livin' clear out on the Obion River I never got a handle on exactly what it was 'till I got here. Even then, I figured you of all men would ride it out. I've been on the road and didn't know 'bout your resignation till I got to Nashville."

"It's not your fault." Houston rubbed the stubble on his

cheek. When did he last shave or take a bath? It was embarrassing to be seen like this. "At least I can be hospitable. He took a jug of corn liquor out of the cabinet. "Care for a drink, Congressman?"

Crockett accepted the jug from Houston, tilted it up in the crook of one arm and took a long swallow.

"I wanted to make your acquaintance before headin' off to Washington," Crockett explained, wiping his mouth with the back of his hand. "I hoped you might have some advice for a well-meanin' man who still can't figure out how the hell he got elected in the first place."

He passed the jug back to Houston, who took a long pull of his own.

"As you can see, I'm in no position to offer advice, much less expect anyone to listen to it," Houston said, lowering the jug. "But I have a feelin' you'll do well enough as long as you keep your humor. There's so much in Washington to laugh at."

They chatted awkwardly for a few minutes before Crockett excused himself, obviously eager to get away from an embarrassing meeting. Houston continued to drink alone, sneering at Crockett's false modesty. "Can't figure out how the hell he got elected?" What humbug! Crockett served two terms in the state legislature before winning election to Congress. None of that happened by accident. Crockett was a politician who didn't want to be caught acting like one. Houston's advice was just something to say. His last thought before sleep was that Washington would more than likely eat the poor man alive. He seemed decent enough, but he was badly out of his depth.

Despite Houston's resignation, now that he was on the run the demonstrations grew larger and more threatening. One even took place after dark on the square beneath his window. A liquored-up mob illuminated by a half-dozen torches demanded that he reveal what he did to "wrong poor Eliza." If he did not respond, they threatened to storm the inn and drag him out, where tar and feathers waited.

One of Williams' people managed to sneak in through the back door with a message urging Houston to get out of Nashville for his own safety. The sheriff was waiting with an armed escort. Houston replied that while he appreciated the offer, he'd leave when he was ready. He would not be run out of town.

The messenger, a one-armed veteran of the Creek War, made the mistake of trying to leave by the front door, where the mob pinned him against the wall and demanded to know Houston's intentions.

Hearing the commotion, Houston stepped to the window so that he could clearly be seen from outside. The mob grew quiet when it saw him lift the curtain. With all eyes on the disgraced ex-Governor, the messenger slipped away into the darkness.

"I have no intention of sayin' anymore than you'll find in my letter of resignation," Houston announced, using the same voice rattled the rafters when he gave a speech. "If that isn't satisfactory, I have two pistols and a knife waitin' for the first men through the door. If you're feeling brave enough, then start the ball. There's enough of you to get the job done if you're willin' to pay the price."

When no one moved, he let the curtain fall. He knew they wouldn't come. And what did it matter if they did? They'd be doing him a favor if they killed him.

Despite his defiance, he desperately wanted a way out of his misery. He had dark thoughts of suicide, but that would leave an even worse scandal for Jackson to clean up. He couldn't go to Washington for the same reason. There, he'd be a living embarrassment. But where could he go? What would he do?

The answer came to him one sleepless night: Drum!

The thought was so clear it jolted him upright. Drum! He found a home with the Cherokee once, why not again? He'd at least stay until next spring. After that he might go on to the Rockies, or maybe all the way out to the Spanish lands in California. He'd have to borrow money, but that wouldn't be a problem. The wealthy McGregor would loan any amount he needed.

The last he heard, Drum's band was somewhere west of Little Rock. He wasn't sure of the geography that far west. He'd figure it out on the way. At least he had somewhere to go.

36

SAM HOUSTON LEFT Nashville early on a dank and overcast morning.

With McGregor, Shelby and Williams, he followed the winding cobblestone street down the hill to the river landing. The quartet walked in awkward silence. What was left to say?

The night before, Overton sent his regrets that he couldn't see him off. Houston was disappointed, but didn't blame his old friend for not wanting to be part of this sad day.

At the same time the four men made their way down to Houston's riverboat, the Red Rover, Overton was in a room at the Nashville Inn giving last-minute instructions to young Hugh Haralson. He'd arranged for Haralson to take passage on the Red Rover, too, plus a generous sum for the young man's trouble, time and expenses.

The lanky redheaded son of an old friend of Overton's from Georgia, Haralson was touring the country before settling down to take over the family plantation near Savannah. He was in Nashville less than forty eight hours when Overton made his remarkable offer, based partly on the fact that Haralson and Houston had never met. Overton reasoned that if the young man was anything like his father he could be trusted. Not that there was any other choice. It was either Haralson or no one at all. As Overton reminded himself, there's no sense complaining about the air if there's nothing else to breathe.

"I want you to go with him at least as far as Little Rock," he explained for the third time, urgency making him even more voluble than usual. "You're to be his guardian angel. In his state, he's likely to throw himself off the boat or do somethin' foolish that'll get him shot. Sam's playin' the martyr now. The big fool always had a streak o' that nonsense in him. If he didn't feel so miserable he'd probably be enjoyin' himself. I want you to watch over him and be friends with him. Right now there's nobody on God's earth who needs a friend as much as Sam Houston. But I don't want him to know what you're doin', or that we know each other. Sam has more pride than is good for him and he wouldn't like this little scheme of ours one bit. And I don't want you getting drunk, either, though it's for sure and for certain he will. Report to me as often as you can, every stop, if that's possible. If he changes his plans, I want to know it. Are you with me, son? Do you understand?"

Eager to get down to the landing, Haralson pulled his watch from his waistcoat pocket, checked the time, and snapped it shut.

"I'd best get going," he said. "There is one last thing; what should I do when we get to Little Rock?"

"Once you're sure Sam's on his way to the Cherokee like he says, you get yourself back here," Overton replied. "If he asks, tell him you're lookin' over property for your family. He'll believe that. Half the people headed out that way are up to their noses in land speculation."

Before Haralson could leave, Overton seized him by the shoulder.

"Son, I know I'm askin' a great deal of you, but you'll not only have my gratitude, you'll have the gratitude of the President of the United States," he said. "Andy Jackson remembers his friends. For that matter, so do I."

With that, Haralson, who regarded the whole affair as a grand and unexpected adventure before settling into the routine of plantation life, left to board the waiting riverboat, a slave carrying his trunks in a cart and his pockets bulging with Overton's money, plus a bank draft for more if he needed it.

———

As the Red Rover slowly steamed away on the muddy river, Houston leaned against the railing and watched Nashville disappear from his sight just like it was disappearing from his life. Fourteen years ago he made a voyage of self-discovery downriver to New Orleans with Ed White, a journey that changed his life. He was an army lieutenant then, a young man who thought too much and too little of himself at the same time. In the years since, he exceeded his wildest dreams only to fall from a greater height than he ever thought possible.

Just yesterday, he heard about Billy Carroll's gloating letter to Jackson: *"Poor Houston! He rose like a rocket and fell like a stone. But then he was always of weak and unsettled mind, incapable of manfully meeting a reverse of fortune. Charity requires us to place it to the account of insanity."*

Maybe Carroll was right, Houston thought bitterly. Maybe he was insane? How could he tell? Does a man know it if he's mad?

He could not imagine what he would do in the years ahead. All he knew is that he lost the essence of what he was somewhere on the road between Allenwood and Nashville.

Now there was a gaping chasm between the man he was then and the man who stood at the rail watching his life, hopes, and dreams disappear in thin wisps of river fog. He could remember the man he was, but he couldn't ever be him again. It was as if that person died or disappeared somehow.

There was no going back, no matter how much he wanted to. The sheer pain of it burned in his chest. It was finished. All of it. And he had nothing to replace it. Nothing at all.

37

Traveling down river was pleasant enough, at least when he was mostly sober and aware of his surroundings, before he drank until he was either physically helpless or passed out.

As long as the liquor supply held, it turned out that limbo wasn't such a bad place after all. It might even be a fine thing to stay on the river for the rest of his life. The plan's only flaw was money, though he could always turn a few dollars as a living exhibit, the empty wreck of what used to be Governor Sam Houston of Tennessee, a living testimonial to what to avoid in life if only you saw it coming.

Standing with his elbows on the rail as the deep green forest of the shoreline slowly passed by, he expounded on that very thought to a congenial redheaded young man who seemed vaguely familiar. But the more he talked the more the idea lost its shine. Faced with the demise of what seemed like such a grand notion only a moment ago, when his boozy rambling petered out he took a good look at the youngster whose accent he placed from Georgia or Alabama.

"By the way, who the hell are you?"

"Sir, don't tell me you've forgotten," Haralson replied, a

225

well-practiced imitation of hurt feelings passing across his face. "Governor, you wound me. I'm Hugh Haralson of Georgia. We met a few nights ago in the gambling salon. You weren't feeling well and your head kept falling on the table."

By now Haralson was familiar with Houston's alcohol-induced memory lapses. Just last night he carried the big man back to his cabin after he passed out on deck with his head resting against the bulkhead and a bottle of brandy precariously balanced on his chest. With Houston outweighing him by at least sixty pounds, it was more work than the Georgian had done in years.

Ah, yes, Houston remembered now. This was the youngster who looked at him in such an odd way. He noticed other people doing that, too. Strange folks on this boat, the way they openly stared at a man. Not what he'd call the manners of polite society.

"But haven't we changed boats at least once?" he asked, groping for a shred of dignity in what had become an embarrassing conversation. "I seem to recall just that thing. If that's so, why are you still here?"

"I see you've forgotten our talk, too," Haralson said, sticking to the story concocted by Overton. "I'm headed to Little Rock, just as you are, I believe. My family is interested in land speculation. When we talked about it earlier, you offered some very sound advice."

Now that the boy mentioned it, Houston did remember doing a lot of talking. That must have been the sound advice. A faint chord of memory thrummed through his consciousness, something to do with being helped back to his cabin. This was a good boy, he thought. It was a fine thing to have a friend handy. A fine thing, indeed.

So far, Haralson found the journey fascinating, much more entertaining than his brief trips on the squalid little riverboats and miniscule rivers of the east. Once the governor was safely in his cabin for the night, or tucked away in some out-of-the-way place where he could do no harm, Haralson enjoyed prowling the fantastic three-tiered craft. The Orion was a nothing less than a floating palace, with twin thirty-foot smokestacks belching vast plumes of black smoke and soot into the air. A gigantic stern paddle wheel roiled the water, powered by the deep coughing of the engine and occasionally punctuated by a series of shrill whistle blasts. From the lowest deck to the high pilothouse, the riverboat was gaily decorated with banners and pennants, with its name written in gold script across the paddle-wheel casing. The world inside seemed to come out of some fairyland; ornate chandeliers, brass fittings, gold-framed mirrors, thick red carpets, skylights of colored glass, and rich oil paintings. The passengers were as colorful as the riverboat itself; Southern planters in wide-brimmed hats, accompanied by wives with faces hidden under deep bonnets, dandified merchants and gamblers in fancy velvet jackets, uniformed military men, whores searching for prey, a few politicians, and, most exotic of all, the wild and hairy trappers with knives in their belts and Hawken rifles cradled in their arms.

It was a captivating journey, and its many distractions made Hugh Haralson careless.

38

AIMLESSLY STROLLING the riverboat with a bottle of Jamaican rum in hand, Houston spotted Haralson at a table in the lounge, drinking coffee and writing, deep in concentration.

Feeling lonely and depressed, he decided to go over and visit for a spell. The boy always seemed so interested in what he had to say. But before Houston got close enough to call out, Haralson rose and walked away, leaving his pen, ink pot, and portable secretary on the table.

Houston took a chair at the table and waited for Haralson to return. As the long minutes passed, he became curious about what was obviously an unfinished letter. The lad probably had a girl back home. Good for him, he thought. Every young man should have a girl back home. The thought produced a heavy and vaguely painful feeling in his chest, which he attempted to remedy with a long pull from his bottle.

Feeling better, and thinking he'd tease Haralson about his girl, Houston reached across the table and pulled the paper toward him. A reading of the first few words scrawled across the page jerked him back to sobriety:

"My Dear Judge Overton,

"I'm afraid to report that Governor Houston has been nothing but trouble on our journey, much exceeding the worst fears of one and all. I feel certain that if the voyage were much longer he would be put off the boat, to the great relief of most of the passengers."

"Just last night I found him singing and capering wildly on the deck outside the entrance to the gambling salon. That alone would have been embarrassing enough, but the Governor had removed all of his clothes and tied a long red ribbon around his manhood. It took some time, effort, and a considerable amount of money to persuade the boat's owner, a Pennsylvanian named Rawlings, who is making the voyage with us, not to put him off. The money aside, only my repeated mention of the Governor's well-known association with President Jackson kept him out of this most dire difficulty."

"I am not sure what the Governor's intentions are when we reach Little Rock. Perhaps they have not changed. It is impossible to tell. He talks a great deal, but his thoughts are muddled and his plans seem to shift and evolve from day to day, and sometimes even from hour to hour. While it was not in my instructions, I may accompany him beyond Little Rock under the pretense of scouting the area looking for property to buy. The story seems to have satisfied him, probably because every time I tell it he forgets it and I am forced to repeat it when next we meet. Such, I fear, are the ravages of excessive spirits, of which the Governor's consumption is, dare I say, Herculean."

"Wherever he goes and whatever he does, the longer I am with him, the more accurately I can gauge his true intentions, per your instructions. I will send this note to you from Little Rock, which I am told is our next stop. After that, I do not know when you will hear from me again. Hopefully it will ..."

In a rage, Houston pounded his fist on the table. Fortunately the lounge was mostly empty. The few passengers present either didn't notice or didn't care. The boy was a goddamned spy! It wasn't enough that his life was blasted into rubble, now his friends spied on him, too! Why couldn't they just leave him alone? Wasn't he already miserable enough?

"Why good day, sir, I see ..."

Haralson's ruddy face paled when he saw his unfinished letter under Houston's big hand. He was certain the man would sleep at least until mid-afternoon, as usual. Good God! How could he have been so careless?

Houston gathered Haralson's pen, ink pot, and portable secretary, walked to the railing outside, and flung them into the river below. Still in a rage, he marched back to the lounge and shoved Haralson backward until his big hands were flat on the bulkhead on either side of the cowering young man's head.

"I understand that our next stop is Little Rock," Houston said, cold menace vibrating in every syllable. "If you're not off this boat by the time we leave there I will throw you off myself, you contemptible pissant. Do you understand me?"

Panic bulging in his eyes, Haralson managed to duck under Houston's arm, squirm away, and edge along the bulkhead toward the doorway.

"Yes, sir. I understand, sir. Believe me, I'm sor... "

Houston slammed the bulkhead with such force that he put his fist through the wood. By now, the other passengers in the lounge were following their every word with wide eyes and whispers, not that he gave a damn.

"Get out of my sight you goddam viper!" he bellowed. "And the next time you write John Overton, tell him if I ever see his ugly face again it'll be over a pistol!"

By now, Haralson's panic had crossed the line to blind terror. He scuttled up the stairs, ran down the hall to his cabin, slammed the door, locked it, and barricaded it with a chair.

Houston spent the rest of the day drinking his way into another stupor, his thoughts bitter and morose. He foolishly thought that he might have a few friends left in this world, but now he knew better. He was alone, utterly alone. Why couldn't they just leave him be? Was that so much to ask? Convinced that no one was ever as miserable, once again dark thoughts of suicide came to him. He dismissed the idea with a sneer; he'd only make a botch of that, too.

He was awakened the next day by the bright afternoon sun streaming into his cabin. As usual, he hadn't taken off his clothes the night before. His mouth felt like a vulture's crotch. He weakly raised one hand to his eyes and whimpered. Oh, God! Eliza was right. He was a fool.

He saw the truth now. Overton was only trying to protect him. He did it in secret because he knew how much Houston would resent if it he found out. In his usual stupid headstrong way, he made a mess of it, the way he made a mess of everything he ever did. He already owed Overton more than he could ever repay and now here he was acting like God's own idiot. How could he be so blind? There must be something wrong with him. That was the only explanation. Billy Carroll was right. He must be addled. He'd end his days dressed in rags and squatting on a filthy street corner begging for pennies.

With no way to hold his head that didn't hurt, he rolled over, put his feet on the floor, tried to stand, and reeled helplessly to the bulkhead. Head throbbing, he clung there with his eyes closed and his face on the cool lacquered wood until the room stopped whirling.

A few minutes later, stooped and holding fast to the back of a chair because it hurt too much to stand upright, he'd recovered enough to pour a pitcher of water into a bowl on the table at the foot of his bed and plunge his face into the cold water. He held his face under until red spots danced in the darkness of his closed eyes. With a gasp, he brought his head out of the bowl, sending a shower of water across the room. He blindly groped for the towel beside the bowl and furiously rubbed his face and head, the knuckles of his hand swollen and aching from punching it through the bulkhead the day before.

Unless he started drinking again, Houston knew that he'd have a brutal hangover for the rest of the day. But this time he wouldn't get drunk. He owed John Overton an apology, even if Overton didn't know it yet. He told himself that he wasn't capable of much anymore, but at least he could do that.

He rang his service bell and ordered coffee. He threw up the first cup, drank another, threw it up, forced another one down, and that one stuck. The first time he put pen to paper he made a mess of it. He couldn't control his trembling hand and the ink made great black splotches across the paper. The second attempt was only a little better, but he managed to write a readable word on his third try:

"To my valued friend,"

"By the time you read this you may have already heard the sordid story from your man Haralson. If not, I'm sure you will hear it soon enough."

"Whatever he tells you, I'm sure it will be the truth. But please understand that it was the pathetic babbling of a drunken fool who did not mean a word of what he said."

"I would be sadly lacking in fairness were I to suppress the expression of my most grateful and friendly regard for you. In prosperity you always regarded me well and generously, but when the darkest hour of human misery was passing by you sustained me by your friendship."

"My soul feels all that conscious gratitude can bestow upon you, gratitude to a man who tried to diminish the awful weight of misery that I have been doomed to feel as an exile from my home and my country."

"I am your friend, as I hope you are mine, and I beg your forgiveness."

"Sam Houston"

It was shorter than he liked, but it had to do. His hand was shaking too much to write another word.

He didn't bother to see Haralson get off at Little Rock. The boy was too scared to do anything else.

39

HARALSON WASN'T the only one who got off the boat at Little Rock. All the passengers headed further upriver had to transfer to the Felicity, a small stern wheeler owned and operated by Captain Phillip Pennywit. When Houston discovered that the tee totaling Pennywit did not allow alcohol on board his little boat, he frantically scoured Little Rock to find other arrangements, only to discover that the Felicity was one of the few riverboats that could travel further up the Arkansas River. The reason was Watson's Falls, a series of dangerous boulder-strewn rapids that took their name from a trading post run by a half-breed named Watt Watson. The big boats drew too much water to negotiate the rapids, leaving river traffic to smaller and more nimble craft like the Felicity.

Depending on the season and how high the river ran, a daring captain could jump the rapids by surging at full speed through the falls one by one, a bruising adventure that had to be repeated a half-dozen times. At best, it bounced the passengers and cargo around more than most thought proper. At worst, the rapids could crack a boat's spine.

If the boat wasn't powerful enough to jump the rapids, or

the captain wasn't bold enough, or didn't trust his pilot enough, the other option was to run six-inch thick ropes to teams of oxen on shore and tow the boat through the falls. It was less exciting and much slower, but less risky, too. Most passengers, captains, and owners preferred duller, slower, and safer.

Considering the Felicity's appalling lack of alcohol, jumping the rapids seemed like a fine idea to Houston. He'd agree to just about anything to move this miserable little floating chamber pot along.

It was after sundown by the time the Felicity approached Watson's trading post. Pennywit announced only a fool would try to negotiate the falls in the dark, so they'd put in for the night. Once the Felicity was tied to the wharf, Houston elbowed his way to the front of the line to get off, ignoring the dark looks from the other passengers. He was desperate to see if Watson's little settlement had anything fit to drink, which, in his view, was anything with alcohol in it.

His first impression wasn't encouraging; no more than a few log cabins and an unfinished two-story clapboard house set in a notch in the river surrounded by water on three sides.

To his delight, Houston discovered a small tavern hidden on the other side of the clapboard house, with several wagons drawn in a cluster around the tavern and a row of horses, mules, and ponies tethered to the hitching post at one side of the entrance. Lifting the worn bearskin flap that served as a door, he paused for a moment to get his bearings in the wavering light from the big river-rock fireplace. Warm tobacco smoke and the heartening smell of food being prepared washed over him as he stepped into the tavern. Customers sat at rough benches along the length of a long plank table. A few smoked pungent pipes filled with cheap-smelling tobacco or ground-up corn stalks. Others drank liquor or beer out of horns. Two weary souls rested their heads on the table. Whether they were sleeping, drunk, satiated from their meal, or just waiting patiently for it Houston couldn't tell.

He must need a drink even more than he thought because he could swear that he saw Drum step out of the shadows in a far corner. Houston blinked, rubbed his eyes, and looked again. In the weak light of the crowded and noisy tavern, he felt as if he was dreaming. It took another moment before he was able to convince himself that the vision was real. By God, it was Drum, along with a half-dozen other Cherokee!

Without a word, the old man hugged Houston as hard as his aging muscles allowed. He stepped back as they clasped each others' arms in their familiar greeting and the seams of the chief's weathered face split with a smile.

"My boy, it's good to see you. How long has it been? Too many years, I know that much."

Houston was dying to ask how Drum knew he was on the Felicity, but the old man disappeared to make arrangements for Houston's trunk to be unloaded, held overnight, and delivered to Drum's settlement.

When Drum returned, the band of eight went outside and mounted the ponies Houston saw earlier. He hadn't ridden one of the tough little Cherokee mounts in years. With his long legs dangling nearly to the ground, he knew that he looked every bit as ridiculous as he felt. When Drum joked that he wasn't sure if Houston should ride the pony, or the pony should ride him, he couldn't help but laugh. For the first time in months, he thought that maybe he wouldn't drink himself to sleep.

Drum never did explain how he knew Houston was on the boat, except to grin and say, "You haven't changed much. You still make a lot of noise."

"I still don't know where the hell I'm going either,"

Houston admitted, shifting his weight on the worn saddle in a vain effort to get comfortable.

"Then maybe you haven't changed at all," Drum laughed.

Bypassing Fort Gibson and its small garrison, for two days the group followed a narrow winding trail that led to the crest of a knoll at the fork where two rivers joined. From there, they split off to another trail leading to the thick grove of cottonwoods and sycamores that Drum and his people called home.

40

ALTHOUGH HE'D GROWN PORTLY and hard of hearing, now that Talon was dead Drum was the sole leader of the western Cherokee.

Houston was surprised at the feeling of loss that shivered through him when Drum told him about his brother's death.

"It was time," he explained. "He was old and tired. One day he walked out and never came back. It was a week before we found his body. He wrapped himself in a blanket, laid down under a tree and waited for death to take him."

Like his people, Drum lived simply; a small farm with a few fat cows and enough crops to get by. It didn't take long for Houston to realize that the Cherokee had no choice but to live simply. Their resources were few and shrank with each passing year.

Three days after his arrival, a dance was held in Houston's honor. Sensing that it was more than a simple welcoming, for the first time in a while he took pains with his appearance, shaving the beard he'd grown mostly through neglect and keeping only a neatly trimmed mustache and goatee. Drum presented him with a beautiful doeskin shirt for the occasion.

Softer than velvet, it came down to mid-thigh, worked with intricate patterns of beads on the chest and back. He wore it with a leather belt, buckskin leggings, and moccasins.

He chided himself for forgetting what a warm-hearted people the Cherokee were. The afternoon was full of laughter, music, dancing, bright colors, and couples walking along the bluffs by the river while beef and pork slowly turned on the spits in front of the council lodge. Watching the men and women who represented the clans, leaders who'd attend the council meeting that night, Houston saw people who knew their worth even in hard times. Their faces, some dark and some lighter, depending on the mix of Cherokee and white blood, were thoughtful and deliberate, with a troubling undercurrent that was obvious to see.

He had only a vague idea of Cherokee history since he galloped out of Drum's Town so many years ago. At first, he told himself that Drum's people were far away and he couldn't concern himself with every detail, but knew it to be the shabby excuse of a self-absorbed man. Eliza was right, he admitted. So consumed by ambition there wasn't room in his life for anything else, the moment the Cherokee were of no more use he forgot all about them.

After the dance, listening to the clan representatives speak at the council meeting in the smoky triangle-shaped lodge, Houston pieced their story together.

The people of Drum's Town, along with four hundred other Cherokee, left Tennessee at about the same time Houston and Talon rode into Washington that cold hard winter. Their migration stopped at the large tract of fertile land in north central Arkansas Territory that had been guaranteed to them by treaty Houston helped negotiate. Unfortunately, it was the same old story. Within three years, pressure from white settlers led to another treaty and more land, this time further west in what had become known as the Indian

Nations, or sometimes just the Nations, where the government someday intended to dump all the southern tribes.

Drum's people found themselves badly outnumbered in the midst of enemies. Even in their reduced state the Cherokee were well off by Indian standards. Their livestock made them fat targets for the raiding Osage, Pawnee, and even the dreaded Comanche from the plains to the west. Although badly armed and outnumbered, the Cherokee fought back, and the result was a small but deadly war that saw their numbers whittled down year by year.

Fort Gibson was supposed to keep the peace, but its commander, Major Matthew Pilchard, was helpless. According to Drum, Pilchard was sympathetic, but he only had infantry under his command and not many infantry at that. Foot soldiers were worthless against the well-mounted Pawnee, Osage and Comanche. It didn't help that Fort Gibson was the worst posting in the country. Only the dregs were assigned there. Even if he had proper troops and equipment, initiative was no longer part of Pilchard's nature, if ever it was. According to Drum, he preferred a hot toddy and a warm fire to action in the field.

As usual, the worst enemy of all was the white government. The various treaties over the years called for substantial annuities to be paid to the Cherokee in compensation for twice giving up their home, including a fifty thousand dollar lump sum indemnity, plus annual payments ranging from two thousand to five thousand dollars. But when the lump-sum payment came due, the Indian agent in charge, the self-styled "Major" E.W. Du Val, announced that it would not be paid in gold, as expected, because that much gold was too difficult to transport over long distances. Instead the Cherokee were paid in government certificates of indebtedness.

It was an old trick. Houston knew it well. The certificates were always discounted from their official worth, sometimes by as much as thirty percent, because hard money was scarce on the frontier. But cashing the certificates was much easier for an Indian agent, so Du Val's cronies bought them from the Cherokee at an even more steeply discounted rate, often only half their worth, then cashed them at a higher rate and pocketed the difference.

Liquor was a serious problem, too. Drum wanted to ban it, just as Houston did in Tennessee. But Du Val's brother had made himself king of the whiskey sellers, with more than a hundred barrels a week passing through his hands. Given such a lucrative business, Drum's request to ban alcohol was turned down without a hearing and Du Val refused to pass his appeal on to Washington.

And, once again, the profiteering was extraordinary. The Cherokee were forced to pay ten dollars for a barrel of flour, more than five times its normal price. Gunpowder cost even more than that. Instead of the promised rifles, they got old revolutionary war-era muskets that were rusted and falling apart. Supplies often had a way of not showing up at all, mysteriously "lost" along the way, another way of saying they were stolen and sold elsewhere. Most of the meat they received was rotten, or well on its way.

There *were* a few honest traders, but only a few. Watson was one. Until he resigned last year, fed up with government bungling and dishonesty, a Frenchman named Chouteau was another. But most honest traders didn't last long. They either gave up in frustration or were run out of business by their crooked peers.

Bad as it was, Houston wasn't surprised. The Bureau of Indian Affairs was corrupt from top to bottom and everyone knew it. Bureau chief Thomas McKenney was either a thief or a fool, and possibly both. But the ultimate fault fell on President Jackson and John Eaton, who, as Jackson's Secretary of War, was McKenney's superior. It was no mystery why the

President sustained a dead branch like McKenney, one of the few holdovers from the Adams administration. McKenney had influential friends in Washington and Jackson needed their support to get a bill through Congress that would finally make the Indian-removal policy official, instead of the informal and inefficient tool it was for so many years. Once the bill passed, Jackson wouldn't have to rely on bribery, persuasion, and promises to get what he wanted.

Drum's voice interrupted Houston's thoughts. "... so we ask you to use your influence to help us. You know Washington. You know those people. You know what to say. You have friends there. They'll listen to you."

Houston was afraid that it might come to this. He rubbed his eyes, red and irritated from the smoky lodge, and felt the need for a drink from his head to his toes. He'd always found alcohol to be a fine lubricator of thoughts.

Reluctantly rising to his feet to address the council, Houston tried to explain. "You don't understand. I'm in disgrace. It's true that once they might have listened to me, but now I'd likely do more harm than good. I'd like to help, but I can't, not anymore. I'm ...."

"Is *this* the man you spoke of?"

The growled words were like a slap across the face. They came from a hulking brute with a purple scar running in a jagged line across his nose and down his cheek.

"Is *this* your son, the one you praised so often you put us all to sleep? This can't be him! We expected a man! All I hear a dog that whimpers and cries. He says no one listens. Well I have listened and I think he is afraid. Someone stepped on this dog's tail too often."

The ugly clansman turned his hard eyes on Drum.

"We've been patient with you long enough. You're like your brother, an old man who outlived his time, too worn out and feeble to lead us. We need new ..."

Clenching his fists without knowing it, Houston glared at the ugly clansman.

"Be careful what you say next, unless you want more scars than you already have. We'll see who whimpers like a dog."

Instantly the atmosphere changed. Feeling it but not knowing why, Houston looked around the lodge and saw every man and woman grinning, especially Drum and the ugly clansman. Then they laughed outright, nodding at each other as if they approved of something he didn't understand.

"You were right," said the ugly one to Drum, only he was not as ugly now that he was bubbling with laughter.

Seeing Houston's confusion, Drum explained, "I'm sorry, but we had to test you. It wasn't enough to provoke you. Prod him enough and any man will fight. We wanted to see *what* would provoke you. You did nothin' when *you* were insulted, but defended me when *I* was insulted. The spark is still there."

Drum motioned at the other Cherokee, obviously pleased with themselves at how well their deception worked.

"The ugly one over there is Sam Sixkiller, my first daughter's husband." The chief gave an exaggerated shrug. "Who knows? He probably thinks I *am* old and feeble."

Sixkiller rolled his eyes. "You *did* put us to sleep talking about your mighty son."

Drum's smile left his face. "So I ask again; will you help us?"

Houston felt his resistance crumble and his spirit lift. Drum's faith was better than a tonic.

"Of course, I will," he blurted out. "I'll do everything I can."

And exactly what would that be? Houston didn't know. But it felt good to have something to do again.

41

HE DECIDED to attack the closest problems first, starting with Major Matthew Pilchard, the commander at Fort Gibson.

Assuming that Pilchard didn't offer to help, Houston hoped to persuade the major to at least stay out of the way. A meddlesome incompetent could be more trouble than an intelligent enemy. Pilchard also filed reports and those reports were read in Washington. Any report with the name "Sam Houston" in it would draw attention he didn't want, at least not now. If possible, he wanted to make an ally of the man, even if he still didn't know exactly what he was going to do.

He also wanted to make an impression and for that he needed a real horse to ride to Fort Gibson, not one of the little Cherokee ponies. After dickering with a New Orleans trader who was passing through with a dozen horses and three wagons loaded with goods, he traded an old beaver hat, a bright red waistcoat, and a twenty dollar gold eagle for a spirited white stallion named Renard.

On one of those Cherokee ponies Houston felt like a jack leg circuit-riding preacher on the way to harangue a reluctant congregation. Mounted on Renard, he looked and felt like a man on a mission.

Fort Gibson was widely known as the worst posting in the army; a career-killer for officers, too. It wasn't unusual for an officer to resign rather than accept assignment there. A combination way station, trading post and army barracks, there wasn't much remotely military about it, a "fort" that looked like it needed protection more than it could give it. Riding into the outpost, the half-dozen mounts Houston saw in the ramshackle corral were either spavined or swaybacked, so scrawny that even the Comanche wouldn't eat them. The men weren't in much better shape. He'd seen a better class of men in jail. For man and beast, Fort Gibson was the end of the line.

As he neared the center of the sloppy collection of log and thatch cabins that passed for the garrison quarters, Houston's eye was drawn to a demented old beggar picking through a trash heap while he sucked on old melon rinds.

"At least there's one person here knows what doin'," muttered Houston.

But, appearances to the contrary, Matthew Pilchard was a surprise; a profane, rotund, intelligent, hard-drinking bachelor who deserved better treatment from the government he served and the army that employed him.

Houston was escorted to Pilchard's one-room cabin and office by a private whose patched uniform was at least two sizes too short in the legs, exposing his pasty-white shins. Before calling out to announce the major's visitor, the private stopped outside the door, reached down his backside, groped around in his pants with a look of dim concentration, and removed his hand with a triumphant cry that signaled the death of some tiny vermin.

Motioned to a chair in front of his desk, a wide plank resting on two sawhorses, Pilchard offered Houston a glass of home-brewed alcohol. After a few sips and minute or two of preliminary chat, Houston decided to risk offending his host and come straight to the point. One more drink of this rot might kill him. His feet were already numb.

Without bothering to soften the question, he blurted out, "Major, for God's sake, what are you *doin'* out here?"

"I wondered when you'd get to that," replied Pilchard as a smile creased his round face. "Most men don't have the decency to wait even a few minutes. I appreciate the courtesy."

The major shifted on his fat haunches and unleashed a fart that seemed to shake the cabin walls. He acknowledged the thunderous release by sighing, "Ah, sweet relief."

Returning to the conversation as if nothing unusual happened, Pilchard continued, "Politics, Houston. That's the reason I'm here; politics, pure and simple."

Grunting with the effort, the big-bellied major hiked his feet up on his desk.

"There was a time when I had a genuine career, at least until I ran afoul of Winfield Scott, old Fuss and Feathers, as they call him now. In one of my reports, I made the foolish mistake of suggesting that Scott was something less than the military genius he believes himself to be, an observation I expanded on in person at a later date. It's well known that Scott's most vulnerable spot is his vanity and he rather vehemently disagreed with my assessment of his meager skills. Although I am the older man, he is my superior in rank and greatly my superior when it comes to influence. As a result of my gross impertinence, they sent me here, and here I shall remain until retirement two years hence, when I can tell Scott to go bugger himself."

Houston's opinion of Scott was higher than Pilchard's, but the general did have a reputation as a man mightily impressed with himself, someone who saw slights where none were intended, although in this case it sounded like the slights were very much intended. He'd seen Pilchard's kind before, a good man who was broken for no good reason until he was no good to anyone, including himself. Pilchard's tragedy was that he was smart enough to know it and let himself go until he'd become a bloated, booze-soaked wreck.

Now it was Pilchard's turn.

"And if *I* may inquire, sir, what in blazes is a former congressman, governor, and rising star in the national firmament doing *here?*"

Pilchard erupted with another of his explosive farts, followed by the inevitable, "Ah, sweet relief."

"Forgive me for saying so, but I know something of your recent difficulties," he continued. "Surely you came to this godforsaken place for some reason other than a failed marriage. If that was the case, half the country would be here with us."

Ignoring Pilchard's curiosity about his marriage, Houston explained his long relationship with the Cherokee. Laying on the flattery with a trowel, he revealed his promise to help, adding that he'd appreciate hearing Pilchard's thoughts on the matter given his experience and obvious intelligence.

Pilchard flashed a knowing smile to indicate that while Houston piled it on awfully thick, he enjoyed the application.

"If the government was honest and we did our job properly the Cherokee wouldn't need help," Pilchard explained. "Drum's a good shepherd for his people. Unfortunately, my crack troops in this wilderness citadel could not protect the Cherokee from a litter of kittens."

Pouring another tumbler of his gruesome home brew, Pilchard offered a cogent assessment.

"There are two key points, as I see it." He held up one fat finger. "First, the Indian agents. They're mostly either crooked or incompetent. There's a saying that when an agent comes out here it takes one bag to carry everything he owns. But when he leaves, it takes a whole steamboat. Document the dishonesty and incompetence, then convince the government to replace 'em with decent people, and you'd go a long way toward solving the problem, all of which is easier said than done, as most things are. No doubt having Jackson's ear will help."

Houston saw no reason to tell Pilchard that he wasn't sure if he still had the President's ear. He'd learned long ago that the perception of power can be as effective as the real thing.

Pilchard raised another sausage-like finger.

"Second, make friends with Chouteau up in Osage country, although if you ask the Osage, it's all their country. If you want to keep 'em off Drum's back you've got to deal with Chouteau. There's no way around it. The man commands their respect. If he can be roused into action he'd likely calm them right enough. I'm sure they could be bought off if anyone had the sense to make the offer in the right way. As always, it's not what you do, it's how you do it."

In Pilchard's opinion, the Comanche and Pawnee were minor problems. Yes, they raided and always would. But if the Osage were persuaded to end their hostility to the Cherokee, the major raids would cease. If the Osage, Comanche, and Pawnee wanted to kill each other that was their problem.

Leaving Pilchard's office, they walked outside to where Houston hitched Renard. Eyes sparkling with delight, the major slowly walked around the stallion, touching flank and chest as he assessed it with an expert eye.

"That's a fine animal, a fine animal indeed," he declared. "If you ever want to sell him, I'd be interested in buying. I'm sure you've noticed the quality of the officers' mounts we have here. In most cases, a large dog would be an improvement."

As Houston began to swing into the saddle, he was checked by Pilchard's meaty hand on his shoulder.

"By the way, don't think I failed to notice how you evaded answering my question about why you're here," he said. "I am not quite the fool I appear to be. I assume you have plans beyond what you expressed and prefer not to reveal them to a talkative old sot like myself. But unless your activity is a clear violation of law, I shall not hinder you in the slightest, not by letter and not by deed, not that I could do much by deed. It will be amusing to see it all transpire. Watching you promises to be the most entertainment I've had since my banishment to this Eden of the West."

Although he didn't let it show, Houston felt sorry for Matthew Pilchard. The man deserved better. He doubted that fat major would live until retirement. He had the feeling Pilchard knew it, too.

42

To Houston's surprise, a handful of letters waited for him at Fort Gibson.

Recovering the letters from the sutler's store, where the shelves featured a pathetically thin inventory of whiskey, tobacco, needle, thread, soap, combs and other items the soldiers bought on credit and paid for on payday, he was pleased to read that several old friends offered their support, including old John Coffee, who was stone deaf and living in Alabama. The most satisfying letter came from John Overton. The great-hearted man dismissed Houston's apology by declaring "there need be no apologies among friends." A more generous soul never lived.

"Just to give you the lay of things here," Overton summarized a letter from Carroll to Jackson repeating Carroll's claim that he always suspected Houston to be of "unsettled mind." Overton added that Carroll would be elected governor by default. With Houston out of the picture, there was no real opposition.

But others were less forgiving, Polk one of them: *"Houston, what a mighty fall was yours, one of your own choice, too. I must say that it was a deep and abiding wound to your close friends who thought you had more grit."*

Houston wasn't surprised at Polk's reaction, although he *was* surprised that Polk considered him a close friend.

The worst of it came from Jackson, as Houston feared that it would. Apparently the President relied on Overton to send his letter along. Houston couldn't bring himself to read it until after he fortified himself with several glasses of whiskey late one night at Drum's settlement. The words seemed to flame across the pages:

"My God, man, have you gone mad? When last we saw each other, you were about to be united in marriage to a beautiful young lady and seemed on the brink of happiness. No one in my acquaintance showed more promise than you, and now you have thrown it all away."

"I do not know what led to the break with your wife, but I do know that no challenge ever yielded to flight. The brave and honest man stands his ground against whatever life throws at him. He does not take refuge in distance and the bottle. That way is cowardice. Your behavior has been disgraceful, tragic, and deeply disappointing to all those who cared for you."

Jackson's sharp words cut deep because they were true. He *did* run away and he *did* behave badly. There was nothing more to say.

But none of that mattered now, he thought, watching The President's letter curl and burn to ash in Drum's fireplace. The past was the past and there was no going back. It was as if Jackson and the others wrote about someone else. Whoever he was now, he was no longer that man. At least he had a chance to make himself anew.

That's what he told himself, except the ache in his heart told him something else.

43

GUIDED by a sullen Osage guide with a gnarled stump where his left hand should have been, Houston went looking for the infamous Auguste Pierre Chouteau.

As they rode, the deep green hills of the river country left off and the land gently rolled away to the west as far as sight could go. From everything Houston heard it wasn't too long before the countryside flattened out like a frying pan all the way to the Rockies. The distances were incredible out here, he thought. A mile was still a mile, but there were so many more of them.

Houston did not know what to expect from Chouteau. He'd heard the tales, of course, but, as the subject of more than a few wild yarns himself, he didn't know what to believe and resolved to reserve judgment.

A West Point graduate, trapper, explorer, trader, and one of the founders of the Santa Fe Trail, Chouteau came from a legendary family. His father founded St. Louis, the greatest city in the West, and ran the family's fur and trading empire with an iron hand. Years earlier, on a trading expedition along the upper Arkansas River, the Spanish captured Chouteau and held him prisoner in far off Santa Fe for six months until he escaped and made his way back to St. Louis with nothing but the rags on his back. They said that he kept a white wife in St. Louis and two Indian wives at the isolated home and trading post he ruled like an eccentric squire. Incredibly, all of his wives knew about the others and somehow he kept them all happy. He spoke French, Spanish, English and Osage with equal ease, plus enough Cherokee and Pawnee to be understood.

After several days, as Houston and his silent guide rode up to the whitewashed log house on the picturesque Six Bull River, a formally dressed servant in silken livery and bare feet opened the gate to let them pass. What made the gate so bizarre was that there was no fence, just an ornate iron gate on open land. Yet everyone behaved as if the gate was the only way in. A gilded carriage with one wheel missing sat tilted to one side between the gate and the house. According to Pilchard, Chouteau went to the trouble and expense of transporting the carriage all the way from New Orleans and then never even hitched a team of horses to it. A half-dozen Osage braves lounged under a big shade tree at one side of the house, roasting venison on a spit. Children of various blood mixes were everywhere, laughing, running, squealing, and crying. There were even more animals than children running loose. Dogs, cats, horses, cattle, goats, and pigs roamed free while hens fluttered and geese marched with great dignity to nowhere in particular.

The house was built in the dogtrot style common on the frontier, but bigger in every way. The downstairs rooms were separated by an open breezeway running front to back through the house, with several smaller rooms upstairs, plus a hodge-podge of outlying buildings of various shapes, sizes, and purposes.

As they drew closer, a man Houston took to be Chouteau

came bounding out of the house. Dressed in a loose-fitting white linen shirt and worn buckskin pants tucked into high black boots, he was short and dark, with black hair swept back from his forehead and falling to his shoulders. When Houston dismounted, Chouteau offered a broad smile as they shook hands.

"You must be Sam Houston," he said. "I heard you were headed my way. Welcome to my home."

Houston liked Chouteau immediately. The man's natural warmth was irresistible.

After exchanging a few words in Osage with Chouteau, Houston's guide led his horse over to the braves roasting venison under the tree.

"Broken Hand didn't talk your head off, did he?" Chouteau asked, eyes gleaming with amusement.

"Not hardly," Houston replied. "I don't think he said twenty words the whole time and I didn't understand a one."

"He must like you then." Chouteau guided Houston toward the doorway, stopping to gently lift a sleeping white cat out of the way. "That's his idea of a major speech. He's probably ashamed of himself for jabberin' so much. He might not say another word for a week."

"What happened to his hand?"

"I cut it off."

Although the revelation pulled Houston up short, Chouteau was so matter of fact he might have been talking about fishing in the river in front of his house or the prospect for his crops this season.

"We fought when I first came out here," he explained. "I could have killed him but I only took his hand. By his choice, he's been my man ever since."

Seeing the wary expression on his visitor's face, Chouteau laughed. "Don't worry. I wouldn't try anything like that with you."

"Probably best for us both if you didn't," Houston said evenly.

Chouteau looked Houston up and down, measuring size and muscle.

"Yes, I can see that."

The exchange gave Houston something to think about an hour later as he smoked a good cigar, savored a glass of fine whiskey, and luxuriated in the hot water of Chouteau's massive iron bathtub, enclosed in its own cabin next to the main house. For all his cheerful eccentricities, Chouteau was not a man to be fooled or cowed. Persuasion was Houston's best - and only - weapon.

They settled into the dining room for a dinner of venison steaks, bread, beans, a bottle of red wine, and chicory coffee, with French chocolate for desert, served by the half-breed sister of one of Chouteau's Osage wives. Port and cigars came after dinner.

The inside of the big house turned out to be just as chaotic and messy as the outside, only its daffy contrasts seemed even more outlandish in the confined space. Three handsome Irish Wolfhounds grandly wandered from room to room. Some-one, a white man from the looks of him, was curled up and snoring on the floor in a corner of the parlor. The house had glass panes and lace curtains and the meal was served on fine English china.

Chouteau kept a well-stocked wine cellar and generously offered Houston the run of his large library. He employed a Jesuit priest to tutor his children, white and Osage, and built a nearby racetrack as fine as any track in the west, except no one ever raced on it. There was an array of scientific para-phernalia scattered about, too, for Chouteau's studies in botany, astronomy, and geology.

Unable to stifle his curiosity any longer, over a glass of port Houston asked why Chouteau built a race track but didn't use it, much less import a fancy carriage and never ride in it.

The Frenchman replied with an eloquent shrug.

"Ah, Sam, I have these ideas and then time passes and ... pffft, I lose interest. It seems that I have energy, but my attention wanders."

They stayed up all night talking, slept most of the next day, and talked through the next night, seriously reducing the contents of Chouteau's wine cellar. By the time they finished, they knew most of the details of each other's lives, although Houston steadfastly refused to divulge what passed between himself and Eliza. The well-mannered Chouteau backed away from the subject once he sensed his visitor's reluctance.

More important, Houston exacted a promise that Chouteau would do what he could to keep the Osage quiet, at least for a while. In exchange, Houston would do everything possible to help the Osage, who were caught between the Cherokee on one side and the Comanche and Pawnee on the other. Like the Cherokee, they were plagued with dishonest Indian agents, too. The worst of them was John Hamtramck, who ran the agency in Three Forks, a day's ride west of Chouteau's homestead.

"He's a pig who keeps the Osage around Three Forks liquored up while he steals them blind," Chouteau sneered, refilling Houston's wine glass as they took their ease in front porch rocking chairs at sunset on the second day.

"He's generous to the few who are friendly to him and gets rich by stealing from the rest. That's one reason why they raid the Cherokee, though mostly it's their natural inclination. Most of the other agents out here aren't any better. The whole lot of 'em should be ... well, it'd be easy enough. They'd just be made to disappear and no one would ever know what happened. I've thought about it myself more than once ... but then good judgment gets the better of me."

Houston pointed out that less drastic options were available, but Chouteau impatiently waved the thought away.

"I played at being an Indian agent for a time only because not many others who're honest want the job. It didn't take long to see why. It's as if your government encourages stupidity and dishonesty. The strong are bribed and the weak coerced. I agreed to do what I can to help you because I like Drum, I like you, and war is bad for business. For myself, I want nothing more than to be left alone to live my life the way I want."

"My government?" Houston asked. "Isn't it your government, too?"

"Not if I can help it," Chouteau replied with a wide grin.

Laughing, Houston conceded that Chouteau might be right. Maybe he *was* on a fool's mission.

"But right now, I don't have a hell of a lot else in my life. A man needs to do something."

Chouteau only shook his head.

"I used to think that, but I learned better. Most of what men do is bullshit. They only think it matters because it feeds their pride."

Again, Chouteau might be right, Houston admitted. But he hoped not.

44

HOUSTON SPENT most of the next three months in the saddle, all but wearing out Renard as he rode from Osage, to Cherokee, to Creek, to Choctaw, to Fort Gibson, to Pawnee, to Chouteau, and back again. He argued and cajoled until his voice was near giving out, trying to persuade the feuding tribes to give him time to see about getting fair treatment from the government that either abused or ignored them.

Sometimes he rode with Chouteau, especially when he met with the Osage. Given Houston's long friendship with the Cherokee, they had no reason to trust him, but Chouteau trusted him and that was enough for them. At least for now.

But most of the time he rode alone. He wasn't surprised to find the Choctaw and Creeks in the same fix as the Cherokee. They'd come west filled with glowing promises, too. Their agent, old Will McClellan, who had a withered right arm from a mauling by a grizzly back when he trapped beaver in the Rockies, seemed honest enough. But the simple mountain man was so easily manipulated by the likes of Du Val and Hamtramck that it seemed worse than outright thievery.

Traveling alone as much as he did gave Houston plenty

of time to form a plan, one that would place himself in a position between the government and the tribes. Day dreaming as he covered the miles on the faithful Renard, he envisioned an official post with genuine clout, something like federal overseer in charge of Indian policy in the Nations, and, by necessity, in charge of the Indian agents themselves.

The territory badly needed an honest man with vision and experience. Why couldn't that man be Sam Houston? Look what he'd already accomplished: gain the confidence of the commander of the territory's army garrison; ally with one of the most influential white men on the frontier; and establish temporary control over more than twelve thousand Indians over a vast area stretching from Missouri to Texas and from the Mississippi to the plains.

By God, he'd even managed to stop most of the fighting. Working with Chouteau, he hammered out a treaty between the Creek and Osage stipulating that anyone breaking the peace would be tried by a joint council made up of ten Creeks and ten Osage. Theft from one tribe by a member of the other was punishable by ten to thirty lashes, with the exact number set by the chief of the offender's nation. The fragile truce was only temporary, but with a little luck he'd make it stick and go on to make others like it.

Drum was right. Who else knew the Indian mind *and* the ways of Washington?

During a stop at Fort Gibson to pick up supplies - he always made it a point to keep Pilchard informed, but without revealing too much detail too soon - Houston found a letter waiting from someone he'd known back when he was in Congress. He remembered Thomas Hart Benton well. A big man with a hooked nose, a booming voice, and more self-esteem than ten men, Benton was impossible to forget. Along with the letter, the Missouri Senator included two newspaper articles he'd written on the subject of westward expansion, a popular theme in Washington these days.

"Sam,"

"I want to take this opportunity to renew our old friendship and ask that you call upon me if I can be of any service."

"You have too much energy to be idle, despite your unfortunate setback in Tennessee. I can only assume that you have some great and secret goal in mind to which you are quietly devoting your tongue, your pen, and your considerable ability."

"I have no wish to pry. I am sure that you will reveal your plans when you feel the time to be appropriate. All I ask is that you remain in contact. Whatever you plan, and I'm sure it will be some extraordinary endeavor, please remember that I am ready to render any service an old friend can provide."

"Your friend and ally,"

"Tom Benton"

While Houston appreciated the flattering words, Benton's assumption that he was engaged in some kind of mysterious plot was infuriating. Dangerous, too. If he wasn't careful, people might think he walked the same dangerous path as old Aaron Burr.

RUMORS WERE FLYING ALMOST before he got here! Some fool even put out the preposterous notion that he married Eliza with the plan of forcing a premature end to the marriage in order to have a public excuse to leave Tennessee and get beyond Washington's direct influence. According to another mad fantasy, he was secretly negotiating with Mexico about some idiotic plan to purchase the province of Texas for untold millions, this at a time when he didn't have a dollar to his name. There was another rumor that he somehow intended to conquer a fat section of Mexican territory with the help of the

Cherokee, people who couldn't properly defend themselves. There was no end to the nonsense.

Practically every white man he met and many more that he did not assumed he was involved in some outlandish scheme when all he wanted was build a new life. He desperately needed to stay active. He knew himself well enough to know that faced by a long period of inactivity he'd rack himself to pieces if he didn't drink himself to oblivion.

What was there about him that attracted such widespread cynicism? Did he possess some terrible flaw than made men – at least white men - distrust him, that made them all assume he spent his days lying, scheming, and plotting?

Apparently the answer was yes.

Late one night by the flickering light of a candle in the small room he sometimes used in Chouteau's house, Houston scratched out a letter to Overton explaining what he'd accomplished so far, and hinting at his hopes for the future. His conclusion reflected his frame of mind: *"I find it strange that while I have yet to be wronged or deceived by an Indian, every wrong that I've suffered in my life was the work of those of my own blood. Tell me, who are the savages and who are the civilized men?"*

To be any real help to the tribes and to achieve his personal goal, Houston knew that eventually he had to go to Washington, something he dreaded and looked forward to at the same time. He had to persuade Jackson that what he proposed was best for both sides, not just to satisfy Houston's ambition, or as a favor for a down-and-out friend, assuming the President was still his friend. After Jackson's blistering letter and the silence that followed, who could say? As naïve as it seemed, he had to show that what he proposed was the right thing to do. So much the better if there was a place for Sam Houston in it.

With Drum's backing, the Cherokee council was convinced to approve Houston's petition for citizenship in the

Cherokee Nation. As a Cherokee citizen, he wouldn't be bound by the complex regulations the government mandated for all United States' citizens who were granted a license to trade with the Indians. The lawyer in him saw that having Cherokee citizenship might be a way to wiggle through a convenient loophole. If his mission to Washington failed, at least he could start an honest trading post, one run by a Cherokee for the Cherokee.

But everything changed when he met Tiana Rogers.

45

THE MESSAGE CAME from a Cherokee rider who'd spent the better part of a week searching for him: Drum was seriously ill. The old man might not live.

Houston was attending an Osage council north of Chouteau's place when the rider found him. Within thirty minutes, he was galloping south on Renard, naked fear tearing at his heart. For all he knew, Drum was already dead.

By the time he rode into the village Houston felt like a creaky old man. With groaning joints, stiff legs, a sore back, and enough dirt on his face and in his hair to grow crops, he dismounted, stepped up to the cabin porch and rapped on the door. From inside, a female voice he didn't recognize said something he couldn't make out, which he interpreted as an invitation to enter.

The window was open and the small bedroom drenched in sunlight. Drum's eyes were closed and a quilt covered him up to his chest in the big feather bed. The round face acquired as he grew older had fallen away until it looked as hard and bony as a death mask. Beads of sweat glistened on his forehead and around his eyes. His breathing was harsh but regular.

A woman with long dark hair cascading down her back sat on a stool at the side of the bed with her back to the door, her sleeves rolled up past her elbows. She gently wiped the old man's throat and face with a cloth soaked in a sweet-smelling mix of herbs and water from a bowl on a small bedside table.

When she turned to face the intruder Houston's heart flopped in his chest. He'd never seen anyone so beautiful. Her dark hair fell down her back almost to her waist, pulled together at the nape of her neck with a silver ring. Her eyes were dark pools beneath a wide forehead on a lively oval face.

They stared at each other for a moment.

"You're Sam Houston," she said.

The way she put it wasn't a question; it was a statement of fact.

"How did you know?"

"You're not a man to be mistaken for someone else."

He was embarrassed to be so unkempt and stinking in front of someone so beautiful.

"There's no one as filthy as I am either," he admitted. "I came as soon as I got word, but it was a long way."

He nodded toward the sleeping Drum.

"How is he?"

"We almost lost him, but the worst is over." She rose from the stool and wiped her forehead with the back of her wrist. "He had the sweating sickness but the fever broke two days ago. He'll be weak for a long time, but he'll live."

Her eyes moved from Drum to Houston. He felt her look down to his toes and it made his skin tingle.

"You know, we've already met," she said.

Taken by surprise at the sudden change of subject, he fumbled for something to say.

"How? I mean, when? I don't think I'd forget you."

The smile that acknowledged his compliment showed even white teeth against her lightly bronzed skin.

"I was ... different then," she said.

Seeing him frown a question, she explained, "It was at our village on the Hiwassee. I was very young, just a girl. You were just a boy, too, only a little older."

He fidgeted in the awkward silence, shifting his weight from one foot to the other.

"Who *are* you?"

Another quiet smile. It made him nervous and excited at the same time.

"I'm Tiana Rogers," she said. "Drum is my uncle. You used to watch us play. You thought you were too grown up and serious to play in the river with the children, but I could tell you wanted to."

The scene came back to Houston in vivid detail, although he couldn't link the lithe sprite that seemed as nimble as an otter as she played half-naked in the river to the tall beautiful woman standing uncomfortably close in this small bedroom. The memory of seeing her without most of her clothes made him flush, even though the memory was at least twenty years old.

To hide his embarrassment, he asked about her older brothers, John, James, and William. They'd served under Jackson in the Creek War, although he never met them.

A mischievous grin played around her eyes and mouth, as if she read his thoughts.

"They're fine, all of them," she said. "Alive and well."

One of Drum's daughters, the chubby one who was married to Sam Sixkiller, came in to relieve Tiana, who edged past Houston and went outside, her head tilted back to savor the air after the close warmth of the cabin.

Houston walked with her, a half step behind.

"Why haven't I seen you before?"

"I don't live here," she said. "I came when I heard he was sick. It was hard to see him the way he was, but he asked for me." She stopped so he could catch up. "He asked for you, too. No one knew where you were, so we sent riders out."

"Will you stay here 'til he's well?" he asked.

At this moment he wanted nothing more in the world than for Tiana Rogers to say yes.

She stared at him for a moment with the same disquieting effect as before.

"Yes, I will," she said. "At least until Uncle is better."

46

WITHOUT BEING OBVIOUS ABOUT IT, he found out everything he could about Tiana Rogers. Using Drum's illness as an excuse to remain in the village, his heart and mind were so full of her that he couldn't think about anything else. He thought that he was being clever, but everyone saw what was happening and laughed behind his back.

She was the daughter of "Hell Fire Jack" Rogers, a Scot trader who married Drum's sister and made his reputation as a hard-fighting Tory captain in the Carolinas during the revolution. Decades later, by then well into his sixties, he fought alongside his sons with Jackson during the Creek War. It was Tiana's bother, John, who led the party across the river at Horseshoe Bend to steal the Red Stick canoes for John Coffee.

Like many Cherokee, she had several names: Tiana was her Cherokee name, but she was Diana to the whites and Talahina to the Creeks. In one way or another, she was related to most of the principal families of the Cherokee Nation. Well educated by frontier standards, after missionary school Drum hired private tutors to work with her until she was eighteen. At twenty, she married a white blacksmith named David

Gentry, who was killed in one of the fights between the Cherokee and Osage.

Houston knew that he shouldn't be pleased at another man's death, but he couldn't help it. He found himself making excuses to be wherever he thought she might appear. Fortunately, he had the ready-made excuse of visiting Drum. Everyone in the village noticed how he timed his visits to coincide with those moments when Tiana was there, too

He couldn't get her out of his mind. He'd made love to many women in many places, and thought he'd fallen in love many times, but none of them seized his heart like this, not even Eliza. Tiana was spirited, but with her uncle's easy ways. She gave the impression of being wholly self-contained and soothed him simply by being herself, like a cool hand on his forehead. A roiling turbulence that was part of him for as long as he remembered seemed to disappear when they were together. When they were apart, he couldn't wait until he saw her again. He couldn't get enough of her and marveled at the feeling.

They fell into the habit of meeting at the well in the center of the village every day an hour before dusk. From there they'd stroll to an isolated place beside a small creek a half-mile outside the village. Laughing and teasing, serious and quiet, they spent hours talking about everything and nothing. Later, he barely remembered what they talked about, only that they talked. When they were together, time passed so quickly there was never enough of it.

He told Tiana everything. It seemed to pour out of him without inhibition or reluctance. He told her about his family, his father, his mother, and the war. He told her about Andrew and Rachel Jackson. He told her about his hopes, dreams and fears. For the first time, he talked about what happened with Eliza and held nothing back. He talked about what he thought that he might do with his new life, how he hoped to help the Cherokee and help himself at the same time.

He had never talked so openly and easily of such private things. With Tiana, it was as effortless as breathing.

———

DRUM'S HEALTH STEADILY IMPROVED, although he'd probably never regain his full strength. At first, it was all he could do to sit up in bed and be spoon fed hominy cooked to the consistency of paste. After a week, they carried him outside to his favorite rocking chair to feel the warmth of the sun on his face. Several days later, moving slowly and with care, he walked outside on his own, where he took the greatest pleasure of his life in watching his beloved niece and adopted son fall in love.

One morning in the late fall, as the colors in the trees died and the leaves tumbled to the ground to be crunched underfoot, Drum decided to move things along. He was an old man. This was no time for a long courtship. He couldn't wait forever.

Fall was Houston's favorite time of year. Most preferred spring, when the world began to grow again. But after the heat of summer, he always felt invigorated by fall, when the trees exploded with color and the earth seemed so clean and the air so crisp.

Drum was in his rocking chair on the porch, bundled in his robes. Houston brought the old man a cup of coffee made just the way he liked it, so heavily sweetened that it was practically syrup.

"Why don't you marry her?" Drum asked.

Startled, Houston's hand jerked and spilled the steaming black liquid over his fingers. He shook his hand, stuffed his fingers in his mouth, and danced grotesquely while Drum laughed and feebly slapped his knee.

"Why don't I *what?*" Houston asked, finally ceasing his manic gyrations.

"Everyone with eyes can see how you feel about Tiana," Drum said. "You're like a love-sick cow."

"They do? How? I mean ... who?"

"If you could only see yourself you wouldn't have to ask. It's time you found your dignity, what little you have left anyhow. Ask Tiana to marry you. It'd please me very much and please her even more."

"Has she said anything?" Houston asked warily.

"She doesn't have to. Everyone sees how much she loves you but you. I swear, you're still that boy I found lost in the woods. Maybe we *should* have named you Fool, after all."

The next day he met Tiana at the well as usual. They never planned it; somehow it just happened. As they always did, they walked down to the creek away from the village, where the ground was covered with a lush carpet of crunchy brown leaves.

Tiana sat on a moss-covered stump. Houston lounged at her feet, lying on his side with his head propped up in one hand so he could look at her while they talked. But for the first time there was an uncomfortable silence between them. Drum was right. He wanted to ask her, but he hesitated, mortally afraid that she'd turn him down. Worse, what if she laughed at him?

His fear made him impatient. He rose to his feet, brushed himself off, and walked a few steps to the creek. With his hands braced against the small of his back, he watched the clear cold water as it rippled over the rocks at the creek bottom.

"Tiana, I have nothin' to offer you," he said, still looking down at the creek. "I have no property and no money. I don't

even know how I'll make a livin'. But I love you, Tiana. And I
..."

"You have yourself."

She knew that he would ask her today, just as she knew
that one day he would break her heart. The broken heart
would come later and there was nothing they could do about
it. What they'd have for at least a while was worth all the
sorrow of the future.

She rose from the stump and seemed to glide toward him
over the carpet of leaves.

"I love you, too, Sam Houston. We will be together until
it's time for you to go. We will cry on that day, but until then
we'll make each other happy."

They held each other as if it was always like this.

"Lass, what do you mean about time for me to go'?" he
asked, whispering in her ear. "I've got to go to Washington.
You know that. But I'll be back soon enough."

Enclosed in his arms, she laid the side of her face against
his chest.

"You were meant for more than this place," she said.
"There'll come a time when the world will call again. Wanting
to be a part of that world is a part of you. When that time
comes, I can't go with you. What we have would not be
possible anywhere else. "

"No, Tiana, that's not ..."

She rose on her toes to kiss him into silence.

"For now we have each other," she whispered.

They sank down onto the bed of leaves. The soothing
gurgle of the creek and the love she felt for this troubled man
helped her forget the heartache that was busy setting traps in
her future.

Typically, Houston thought mostly of himself. It had been
a long time since he'd made love. What happened with Eliza
left scars. He wasn't sure he could make love to Tiana, no

matter how much he wanted it. He was afraid to try, but afraid not to.

She sensed his hesitation and instinctively knew the cause. She spread her knees and sat on top of him. As he looked up at her, the fading light through the trees dappled her lustrous hair. She leaned down and kissed him, brushing a strand of hair out of his eyes. He ran his hands over her back, pressed her down on top of him, and kissed her lavender-scented hair.

For that moment, all the ugly images and self-loathing left his tortured soul. The only sound was the rise and fall of Tiana's breathing against his chest as she placed him inside her. Her body began to stiffen as she slowly moved against him. He felt her thighs tighten. Her eyes closed and her face grew taut. He held her as close as he could without hurting her. He felt himself harden and swell. It made him cry out. His soul seemed to dissolve and burst from his loins in a white-hot glow obliterating the rest of the world. He felt bound with her in a way he never thought possible. They were locked together so that he felt the beating of her heart, the sweat on her skin, and the flush of blood in her body.

They would marry when he returned from Washington. He still didn't understand what she meant about leaving some day. Why would he want to leave? He felt as if all his life he'd been looking for what he had at this moment.

47

With a long skinny arm, Andrew Jackson flipped a letter with a broken wax seal across the desk to Houston.

"I thought you might find this interesting."

Jackson, Houston, and Secretary of War John Eaton were in the President's private quarters at the White House, gathered around the President's working desk, opposed to the desk in another room he used for public display and ceremonial occasions. Jackson, who was meticulous about his public appearance but relaxed about how he dressed in private, wore a comfortable old jacket and loose-fitting trousers that Houston recognized from at least ten years ago. With the President puffing on a long clay pipe while Eaton and Houston smoked cigars, smoke shrouded the room like a low-hanging cloud.

Always notoriously skinny, Jackson had lost weight. It worried Houston to see it. The old clothes hung on his emaciated frame as if they dangled from a coat rack. At a little over six feet tall, Houston guessed that The President didn't weigh a hundred and thirty pounds.

Houston's eyes widened when he saw the letter was

addressed to Vice President John Calhoun, a man with whom the President quarreled more and more these days. It was written by a Nashville lawyer named Leonidas Sides, who claimed to speak for "the moral and right-thinking people of Tennessee."

"The illustrious Allen family, along with other supporters of the President in Tennessee, was recently informed that the infamous former governor was seen to be traveling to Washington from his much-deserved wilderness exile," Sides wrote. "It would be most unfortunate if such a degenerate received a cordial reception from anyone connected to the current administration."

"Yes, it would be tragic, indeed, if such an illustrious Presidency came to a premature end after only one term as a result of the public outcry over the President's association with this villain," the letter continued. "However, should that unfortunate event come to pass, we feel that you, Vice President Calhoun, would be a more than suitable occupant of that high office and receive our steadfast support."

"Illegally openin' the mail, I see, even when it's the Vice President's," dryly observed Houston.

"*Especially* the Vice President's, when we can," Eaton said. "We read yours, too, Sam."

"I never doubted it, not that there's much of interest, or much of it at all," Houston replied.

"Can you believe these scoundrels actually threatened me, even if I'm not supposed to know it," Jackson fumed. "And notice how Sides didn't even refer to you by name, as if it isn't worthy of mention. Those people have more brass than a fine doorknob. Damned jackanapes!"

Despite his grumbling, Jackson seemed to take it well. Could he be mellowing in old age? The thought almost made Houston laugh, which he quickly stifled by coughing into one hand.

Houston had worried about how Jackson would receive him – or *if* Jackson would receive him - practically every day during the long trip to Washington. When Houston explained his relief, The President removed the pipe from his mouth and tamped down the ashes with a thin piece of wood charred black on one end.

"Good God, man, you of all people should know better," he growled. "I don't turn on my friends, even when they behave like damn fools. I thought you'd lost your mind, not to mention your courage. I wasn't the only one either. I know I was hard on you but what did you expect, flowers and compliments?"

———

BOARDING the riverboat Amazon in Little Rock, Houston steamed down the Arkansas to the Mississippi, up the Mississippi to the Ohio, then east to Pittsburgh, changing boats several times on the way. Although he did everything he could to keep himself occupied, he spent most of the lonely days and nights brooding about how he might be received in Washington. What if Jackson, or anyone in his administration, refused to see him? Especially at night, as he writhed restlessly in the narrow bed of his small cabin, the fear of such monumental rejection overwhelmed him.

From Pittsburgh he traveled overland by coach to Baltimore, a miserable, rain-drenched trip that saw them stop several times a day when the coach sank up to its axles in brown mud and the passengers clambered out to help heave it out of the ooze.

Why the coach out of Pittsburgh went to Baltimore and not directly to Washington was a mystery, but at least it gave Houston the chance to take the railroad from Baltimore to the capitol. He'd heard about it, of course, but this was his first experience traveling by rail.

Before boarding, Houston walked around the engine and carefully looked it over. Another waiting passenger explained that the nose pointed like a giant plow was called a cow catcher, meant for pushing the animals aside. The wheels were huge, almost as tall as Houston, and all manner of bewildering chains and rods ran from one end of the great iron beast to the other.

Advised to find a seat as far away as possible from the engine, which had a nasty way of covering passengers in the closest cars with soot and ash, Houston found a place on one of the benches flanking the center aisle in the last car. Fortunately he boarded early. By the time the train left there was barely room to sit or stand. The crowded car's thick air smelled of whiskey, tobacco, and pine-pitch smoke. Once they got underway, the car swayed from side to side as it rocked along on the uneven rails and the engine huffed out great billows of black smoke, along with an occasional shower of glowing sparks.

Houston collared a passing coachman and asked how fast they were going.

"For a minute or two, we'll top out at twenty miles an hour on the downhill grade," the harried coachman replied as he squirmed his way through the jammed car.

By the time they got to Washington, Houston felt like a well-cooked potato. Staggering off the train, he recovered his trunk from the baggage car, hefted it over his shoulder, and walked to his old standby, Brown's Indian Queen Hotel, where nothing had changed as far as he could tell, down to the same tired furniture and worn rugs in the lobby. The old place wore its vaguely genteel shabbiness the way an old man hangs on to a few remaining teeth. In the face of better and newer competition, the hotel's only advantages were its low rates and convenient location on Pennsylvania Avenue.

Houston sent a message to the President as soon as he arrived and spent a sleepless night waiting for a reply. The next day a messenger delivered an invitation to attend a diplomatic reception, an unmistakable sign of Jackson's friendliness.

After some thought, Houston decided to forgo the black claw-hammer coat that was typical at such events and appear as what he was - a citizen and ambassador of the Cherokee Nation. It was something of a risk because it called attention to the fact that when he became a Cherokee citizen he forfeited his American citizenship, although the United States had yet to figure out its exact relationship with the tribes. For all anyone knew, it was possible to be a citizen of both. Or were the tribes sovereign nations of their own? Some argued they were a lesser entity, like a protectorate. Maybe they fit no existing category? Official Washington used whatever definition was convenient depending on the issue at hand. Houston was among those who thought that the Supreme Court eventually would have to decide the issue when the right case came along.

Once Houston made up his mind he made the most of it, spending more than an hour trying on various combinations before settling on buckskin leggings, fringed moccasins that ran to his knees, a red shirt, and a fringed buckskin jacket decorated with a metal ornaments that clinked and tinkled as he walked. As a final touch, he wrapped his head in the distinctive Cherokee turban, a red and blue cloth.

When Houston met Jackson and Eaton in the President's private quarters before the reception, Jackson burst out laughing as he shook Houston's hand, drawing him close and pounding him on the back.

"Sam, I see you're as dull as ever." He stepped back and

looked Houston up and down. "You always did know how to call attention to yourself. I surely hope my scalp is safe with you. I believe there are a few who'd like to take it."

Houston flushed with pleasure.

"On the contrary, I'm yours to command, sir."

"We'll see about that," Jackson said, lifting his gray eyebrows skeptically. "I understand that we have a few things to discuss."

After revealing the Sides letter, the President briskly turned to business.

"It seemed best we talk privately before all this official clap-trap got in the way. What is this I hear about you wantin' to take over my Indian policy for me?"

While Jackson loaded more tobacco into his pipe from the humidor on the desk, Houston went over his arguments in his head. The opportunity came sooner than he expected, but he knew that he'd never have a better chance.

"Sir, it's not a case of my 'takin' over' anything," he explained. "The right word might be enhance, or maybe improve. I'm convinced that I can help grease the wheels for both sides, just as I did when I convinced Drum's people to move west."

"As I understand it, you *are* one of his people," Eaton put in. "A Cherokee citizen right down - or should I say right up - to that thing on your head. You look like some kind of oriental potentate."

Although he was surprised that Eaton knew about his Cherokee citizenship already, Houston kept his face expressionless. The information could only have come from Pilchard. He'd made a friend of the man, but Pilchard still was an officer in the United States Army and Sam Houston was someone to keep an eye on. Curious eyes were everywhere; it was a good thing to remember.

The Secretary of War raised his glass in salute.

"Not many white men could carry that outfit off.," he declared. "But on you I'll be damned if it doesn't look natural."

Houston didn't have his documents with him for the perfectly good reason that he didn't think he'd need them so soon. Working from memory, he ran through the highlights of his case denouncing the dishonest and incompetent Indian agents, along with the powerful men behind them known as the Indian Ring, a mix of bureaucrats, politicians, contractors, sutlers, and agents scattered from Washington to the Nations who always found a way to get around the most elaborate safeguards. He explained the proof was back in his room at Brown's and he'd be happy to get it to Jackson and Eaton at their convenience.

Moving easily and persuasively from one subject to the next, he proposed that he and Chouteau be appointed special government emissaries to help keep peace among the tribes and between the tribes and the white settlers already encroaching on the Nations. Chouteau wasn't part of his original plan, but he thought it through during the long trip to Washington and found no holes in the idea. Assuming Chouteau agreed, he'd be an invaluable ally. As Houston outlined it, they'd report directly to Eaton and have authority over all the Indian agents and all transactions between the federal government and the tribes in that part of the country.

He weighted his arguments toward what he knew would appeal most to Jackson.

"Chouteau is a man of fine intellect. You'd like him. He's honest, vigorous, and one of the clearest thinkers I've ever met. He can't be bought because he's already wealthy and he has the best practical knowledge of Indians of any man in the country, save perhaps myself. We'd make a formidable team."

"I have no doubt about that," Jackson agreed. "I've heard about that man and his family for years. If anything, you two might be a little too formidable for some tastes."

They went back and forth for two hours, with Jackson asking questions, Houston answering, and Eaton switching back and forth as he played devil's advocate.

As Houston knew from reading the Washington newspapers, the unofficial policy of Indian removal was well on its way to becoming official. The President vigorously supported a bill in Congress authorizing the usual exchange of land with the remaining Indians in the southeast, to be followed by the removal of every man, woman and child. Instead of dumping them somewhere without regard to other tribal lands, Jackson's plan called for a specific, but as yet unidentified, area to be set aside, with the land purchased from the tribes already there. Houston thought it typical that no one bothered to ask whether those tribes, wherever they might be, were willing to sell.

The problem was time. The state of Georgia had recently decreed that while all Indians in the state were subject to Georgia law, they were not protected by it, a damn peculiar ruling, in Houston's view. With that precedent, other states would likely take a similar position. Without any overriding federal policy the Indians would be left to the mercy of the states, which was no mercy at all.

Jackson bought a little time by sending federal troops south with orders to remove all white squatters from Indian lands by force, if necessary. He followed that up by talking old John Coffee out of retirement to try to convince the remnants of the Choctaw, Chickasaw, Creek and Cherokee to move west voluntarily, much as Houston did earlier, but on a much larger scale.

A few were amiable to the idea, but so far most of the remaining Cherokee stubbornly refused to leave. They reminded Coffee that Cherokee law made it treason for any Cherokee to sell land without approval of the tribal council, an argument weakened by the fact that such sales were common. Both sides got around it by calling it a trade instead of a sale. It fooled no one, but sufficed legally.

Jackson detested having to negotiate with the Indians as equals. For more than thirty years he argued that the federal government was mistaken when it allowed the Indian nations to operate as if they were a sovereign people within the borders of the United States, a poor policy for the simple reason that it didn't work. He reasoned that if the Supreme Court could be persuaded to rule that the tribes were something less than sovereign nations, then the federal government could do anything with them it wished. The President also questioned the logic that allowed the government to dispossess citizens of their property under the right of eminent domain, but prevented the government from doing the same to the Indians.

"They must be gone, sir, they must be gone!"

Jackson was getting worked up. Houston recognized the familiar signs: the blazing eyes; the way his skin seemed to tighten across his face; and the pugnacious set of his long jaw.

"It's for their own good. Their world has vanished. If they stay where they are they risk being destroyed as a people. We're obligated to remove this threat from within our borders. Treaties with Indians are an absurdity. They are subject to the laws of the United States, pure and simple. There's no other way, sir! There's no other way!"

When Jackson got cranked up it was pointless to argue. This was not the time or place to go tusk-to-tusk with the President of the United States.

"Sir, I'm confident our differences can be worked out," Houston said. "They always have. I'm simply offerin' my services to you, to the government, and to the tribes. You need someone you can trust out there. If just a fraction of the millions of dollars our government foolishly spent over the last twenty five years for the so-called benefit of the Indian population was honestly and judiciously applied this conversation wouldn't be necessary."

"From my long association with the Cherokee I have an insight no white man can match. From my service as an Indian agent, I'm familiar with the problems of the Indian Bureau. And from my time in public office, I know the considerations and responsibilities of government. I offer these unique qualifications to your service. It seems like such an obvious advantage that I really don't know what else to say."

Jackson rapped his pipe on the side of the desk, breaking loose a wattle of burnt tobacco that he cupped in one palm and dropped into a spittoon.

"You put it that way and it *is* obvious," Jackson agreed, his volcanic mood disappearing as quickly as it came. "But other aspects of this thing are equally obvious. At this critical time, you're askin' that I take on this so-called Indian Ring and remake the Bureau of Indian Affairs from top to bottom, discharging many of the agents available to me, men whose influence might jeopardize the bill I need from Congress. You want me to fill these positions with people of your own choosin'. I am also asked to appoint you to the position of Indian ... what did Johnny call you? ... *potentate* to oversee all this, a man who not long ago was governor of my home state, but forced to resign in disgrace before he was run out of office. A man who, I might add, still has powerful enemies. And you want me to appoint this Chouteau as your cohort, someone who seems more sympathetic to the tribes he's supposed to oversee than to the government he's supposed to represent."

Jackson's eyes bored into Houston with the full weight of his argument.

"Sam, are you sure that's *all* you want?"

"Sir, no mob ever ran me out of ...." replied Houston angrily.

Jackson reached across the desk and patted Houston's arm.

"Forgive me if I speak too harshly," he said. "But that is mild compared to what others will say. You might as well prepare yourself for it."

The President put his hands on the arms of his chair and pushed himself to his feet.

"Gentlemen, I must leave now to dress more formally so that I may attend this reception and say things I don't mean to people I don't like."

As Jackson left the room, he stopped for a last word, one hand resting on the doorknob.

"Sam, I promise that I'll consider everything you've asked, but beyond that I promise nothin'. You get your proof to Johnny in the morning. You are the first source credible to Washington, by that I mean the first experienced white man, to make these charges to this extent, even if they've been in the wind for a long while. You're concerned for the tribes. I understand that. I can even admire you for it, though most won't, you can take my word on that. But as President I am concerned for the whole nation, not just one part of it."

There *was* one more thing, but it was better to work on it with Eaton. Houston knew that for now he'd pushed Jackson as far as he could.

The government was about to open bidding on the contract to supply the tribes on both sides of the Mississippi with their treaty-mandated rations. Houston saw a chance to help them and do himself some good at the same time.

Each daily ration was defined as one and one-quarter pounds of fresh beef, or one pound of fresh pork, plus two quarts of salt for every hundred rations. But by the time it got to the tribes the meat was either rotten or a fraction of the amount stipulated in the contract. The existing contract cost twenty one cents per ration, too, so criminally expensive it was obvious that most of the money lined the pockets of the contract holders.

Working with Chouteau before he left for Washington, Houston came up with a way to supply high-quality rations at only thirteen cents per ration and still make a handsome profit. The rations would be delivered closer to the places where they were needed, too, instead of forcing the recipients to travel as much as a hundred miles to get them.

He started to talk it through with Eaton, but the Secretary of War waved him off.

"Hold it right there, Sam," he warned. "We'd be roasted over an open fire if anyone thought you had an advantage thanks to your relationship with the old man. If you and Chouteau are interested, submit a bid like everyone else and we'll consider it. We might even offer you a little *extra* consideration."

Seeing the disappointment cloud his friend's face, Eaton added, "Sorry, Sam, but that's the best I can do. These are tricky times."

"Of course, Johnny, I understand," Houston said. "I'll still land that contract, though, as long as it's fairly done."

"Are you implyin' we *won't* be fair," Eaton asked, bridling at the unintended criticism.

"Not at all," Houston soothed. "You know better than that. All I'm sayin' is that sometimes things get more complicated that they ought to be, especially here in Washington."

Eaton nodded, his irritation replaced by a bone deep weariness.

"Believe me, you don't know the half of it," he sighed.

48

As the days turned into weeks and the weeks into months, Houston found himself mired in Washington in ways that had nothing to do with the ever-present mud.

He met a dozen times with Eaton and his subordinates while they examined the proof of his charges and then followed it up with hours of excruciating testimony before various congressional committees and sub-committees, his patience wearing as thin as his finances. It was hard to imagine so many blowhards gathered in one place. At Eaton's suggestion, although Houston knew that the President was behind it, he argued that an outdated system was more to blame than any individual. That wasn't true - at least not the whole truth - but he owed it to Jackson.

He did find time to get away from Washington and meet with investors in New York City to arrange financial backing if he and Chouteau won the rations contract. He detested going cap in hand to stiff-necked popinjays whose only virtue was their wealth and their ability to look down their long noses at better men, but there was no other way. If they won the contract, they'd need seed money to get started. Chouteau didn't trust Washington and refused to put up a penny of his own.

As Eaton predicted, when word of Houston's bid got out it set off a firestorm. One newspaper charged that the President and Eaton were engaged in a conspiracy to fraudulently obtain the contract for the destitute Houston. Another claimed it learned from an "unimpeachable source" that "the immense profits from the rations contract would go to finance the disgraced Houston's plot to wrest a large portion of Mexico from its mother country."

Through it all, he spent as much time with Jackson as their busy schedules allowed. He wanted to tell the President about Tiana, but wasn't sure how the old Indian fighter would react. When he finally spoke up, Jackson surprised him once again.

It was late on a cold winter night with the snow piled high outside. Alone in Jackson's private quarters, they talked and drank toddies, watching the hot fire burn in the brick fireplace. At the end of the day the old warrior let down his guard. His long was face was etched in sadness and his skinny frame seemed to sink in on itself.

"Marry her, son," he urged. "Don't hesitate for a second. Even if you're not divorced from Eliza, I'm thinkin' you can still marry under Cherokee law. And if you can't, don't let that stop you. Hold on to her, Sam. If you love her hold on as hard as you can. I was fortunate to love one woman in my life but she was taken from me. I miss my Rachel every hour of every day. Never turn away love, Sam, it's too precious."

Houston rose out of his wing chair to put another log on the hot fire, a log it didn't need. He didn't want Jackson to know he'd seen tears in the old man's eyes, mirrored by the tears in his own.

49

SECRETARY OF WAR John Eaton's proclamation that from now on all payments to the tribes would be made in cash or gold brought an end to the government certificates that were so easy to manipulate. Eaton promptly followed that up by dismissing Du Val, Hamtramck, and three other agents.

And that, it seemed, was that.

Houston didn't let Eaton or Jackson know it, but he was bitterly disappointed. Cutting loose a handful of the worst agents was only a small part of what needed to be done to bring down the Indian Ring. Judging by the pains Eaton took to make it all look like McKenney's idea, it was obvious that in exchange for saving the man's reputation Jackson had his support for the Indian removal bill. Prodded by Eaton, McKenney also vowed to reorganize the bureau from top to bottom and do away with any "irregularities," which Houston assumed would come to pass at about the same time as the Second Coming.

With such a discouraging result after all his hard work and high hopes, Houston decided not to wait in Washington for a decision on the rations contract that still might be months away. It was time to go home, even if "home" was a simple Cherokee settlement far out in the Nations. With luck, the controversy about the Houston-Eaton-Jackson "cabal" might fade if he left town, too. Eaton was laboring under a terrible strain, anyone could see it. The good-natured man Houston had known for so long was haggard, short-tempered, and drinking too much.

Houston knew very well that he could travel all the way to the celestial kingdom in Cathay and it wouldn't help poor Johnny Eaton. The real problem was the Secretary of War's marriage to Peggy O'Neal. It was the talk of Washington, a scandal grown all out of proportion to the deed itself.

John Eaton fell in love with Peggy O'Neal the moment he set eyes on her working at her family's popular tavern and boarding house in Washington. He was one of many hopeful suitors who were devastated when the delectable Peggy married a young navy officer named John Timberlake. It was not a well-made match. Timberlake's duties kept him away from Washington for months at a time while Peggy stayed home to work at the tavern. A hip-swaying beauty who could make any man feel like he was the center of the world, half the men in Washington thought they were in love with her and more than a few of those were sure she loved them back despite her marriage. If you believed the gossip, she gave them good reason to think it.

When Timberlake died suddenly in the Mediterranean - a rumored suicide, although the details were vague - Eaton pounced. But he was too eager. So, it turned out, was the grieving widow. The couple married so soon after Timberlake's death that the gossip escalated instead of dying out, especially the rumor that they'd begun their affair while Timberlake still lived and that was why he killed himself.

Led by Calhoun's shrill crone of a wife, Floride, social Washington, including most of the foreign embassies, boycotted the couple, even to snubbing Peggy in public, an impossible position for a high-ranking cabinet officer. The boycott enraged, Jackson, who called it a "damned petticoat attack." Remembering all too well the unforgiving gossip about his own marriage, Jackson, who was fond of Peggy, saw it as another baseless attack on an innocent woman and it stoked the already poisonous feelings between Jackson and Calhoun. The only member of the cabinet who treated Peggy O'Neal Timberlake Eaton with courtesy was Secretary of State Martin Van Buren. Jackson's gratitude was so great that Van Buren would almost certainly succeed Calhoun as Vice President for Jackson's second term. Houston suspected that the clever little New Yorker didn't give a tinker's damn about Peggy Eaton, but cared a great deal about the vice presidency, and perhaps even the presidency one day, with Jackson's support.

Hard experience had taught Jackson and Houston that sex and politics were a combustible mix. Now Johnny Eaton was learning the painful lesson, too.

So Houston told himself leaving Washington was best for everyone. The place was a swamp in more ways than one and he was eager to escape. The self-deception allowed him to ignore what was in his heart: Even with all their worries, seeing old friends in high places emphasized everything that he'd lost. If he stayed much longer he'd begin to resent their success, and that was unthinkable.

He borrowed money, bought a horse, left a note for Jackson, who was away on a short speaking tour of New England, and quietly rode out of the capital at dawn.

———

To show the Allens and their contemptible allies that he did not fear them, Houston went out of his way to deliberately ride the entire width of Tennessee, stopping in Maryville on the way.

Elizabeth Houston was dying.

The woman who was so tall and strong in his memory was a frail and shrunken shell. She never left the farmhouse she helped build with her own hands and rarely even left her room as her mind wandered. She often spoke lovingly with her long-dead husband, as if he was at her side, and expressed the kind of tenderness that her son never heard in real life.

By now, Houston knew that his mother did her best with a hard life. If she seemed cold, it was because she didn't know how else to do what needed to be done. After her husband's death and the family's painful move to Tennessee, she watched her children die one by one. A daughter, Isabella, passed a few months after they arrived. A son, Paxton, died of tuberculosis. Another son, Robert, committed suicide as a young man. After a head injury when she was kicked by a horse, another daughter, Mary, spent most of her days cooing to the animals in the barn.

Elizabeth Houston's friends told him that of all the tragedy in her life, Houston's fall hit her hardest. He was stunned to learn that he was her favorite. Why didn't she tell him? Why didn't she say what she felt? There were too many whys and now it was too late to ask.

Fortunately, she didn't seem to remember that he *had* fallen as she feebly ran her skeletal fingers through his hair, the way she did when he was a little boy in Virginia. He was at her mother's bedside holding her hand when she died in her sleep.

More profoundly aware of his failure than ever, Sam Houston rode away from Maryville on a horse he borrowed the money to buy.

50

FROM OPPOSITE DIRECTIONS, *Sam Houston and Tiana Rogers slowly walk toward the small fire that brightly burned in the center of the council house.*

The dark-haired Tiana is heartbreakingly beautiful in her bridal "tear dress," a long dress made from different fabric swatches torn into squares and rectangles and stitched together.

His hair tied in a queue, Houston wears a roe-colored shirt, dark trousers, a black leather belt with a silver buckle, and brightly beaded ceremonial moccasins.

They each have blue blankets draped over their shoulders, blankets that represent their old ways of single life.

Standing beside the fire, as erect as old age allowed, Drum calls out, "Fire is sacred to the Cherokee. It is the gift of light and knowledge and has been with the people since the beginning of time."

Drum blesses the marriage union and asks the spirits that they have a long and happy life. At his nod, they remove their blankets to face each other and hold hands. The smiling couple listens as Drum says a solemn Cherokee prayer of continuance before they share a drink of crushed dried corn and water. They drink east, west, north and south, declaring their marriage to all the earth. The clay vessel is thrown to the ground and broken to seal the wedding vows. The fragments are quickly buried in mother earth.

A white blanket symbolizing their new unity is draped over the shoulders of the couple while Cherokee stomp dancers perform in the flickering firelight.

When the ceremony ends, Houston throws the white blanket over his shoulder. Hand in hand they leave the council house and walk into the darkness to their private shelter in the woods, one that he built by himself for their wedding night.

As they walk toward their future, he tells himself that he will do everything he can to make Tiana happy, and perhaps even find happiness for himself.

He had to make a living while they waited for word from Washington. Borrowing money and buying supplies on credit from Chouteau, he opened a trading post north of Fort Gibson, dealing in almost anything that he could buy and sell, including a few books, mostly Bibles, hymnals, almanacs and primers, gun flints, axes, tobacco, tea, coffee, scythes, rat traps, pewter candlesticks, Jew's harps, a variety of spirits and liquors, hollowed out cow horns for drinking whiskey and beer, some of them elaborately designed, and many kinds of dry goods.

Although he made the loan without hesitation, Chouteau made it clear that he didn't like the idea.

"You're no trader, Sam," he warned one evening as they drank port and smoked cigars on Chouteau's porch while watching the sun set over the Six Bull River. "This trading post idea is sheer folly. You of all people aren't meant to be some wretched little shopkeeper."

Houston called it the Wigwam. He knew that it wasn't much, but it wasn't permanent either; just a modest little enterprise to keep him busy and put food on the table until he heard from Washington.

He spent three weeks stripped to the waist laboring to build an L-shaped cabin that was big enough for the trading post and the small room where he and Tiana lived. The low-eaved roof was made of split-wood slats and the external log chimney sealed by clay mixed with moss. There were plenty of offers to help, but he wanted to build their home with his own hands.

It was Tiana who found the location, a small rise at the edge of a thick forest near the Neosho River overlooking an old military trail called the Texas Road. Houston liked to stand at the door of the cabin and watch the lightning of onrushing summer storms play in the distance, with the breeze coming in ahead of the storm feeling cool on his face. Cottonwood, ash, mulberry, and persimmon trees offered shade on hot days. Drum gave them a few pigs and cows and they planted a small apple orchard near the cabin because the pink blossoms reminded him of Tennessee.

Time passed quickly and happily. Tiana worked at his side building the cabin, tending the livestock, stocking the trading post, and planting the trees. As a relative to Drum by both adoption and marriage, Houston became active in the affairs of the Cherokee Nation as he began to do business with the Cherokee, the Osage, and even the garrison at Fort Gibson. He seemed so content in his new life that Chouteau wondered if he might have been wrong after all.

Best of all, he loved Tiana. Night after night they held each other by the fire in their cabin as they talked and teased and laughed and made love. He told himself that life would be better still once they got the rations contract. Until then, they happily drifted from day to day, as if living under a bell jar where the rest of the world didn't exist and the present was all that mattered.

One hot afternoon a rider galloped up to the Wigwam carrying a dispatch from Washington, the horse's hooves making little clouds of white dust on the dry road. The rider was impressed by his orders to deliver the dispatch to Houston and no one else. Pilchard might be a fat old wine sack who couldn't control his bowels, but as far as the messenger knew the major was supposed to see everything that passed through Fort Gibson. He wouldn't like being passed by, especially when it concerned a dispatch from the Secretary of War. The rider was only seventeen years old, but even his limited experience had taught him hat the less authority a man possessed the harder he held on to it, and that included boozy old men who farted too much.

Houston threw down the ax he was using to cut new wood slats to replace a bunch blown off by a violent storm that roared in two days ago.

"It's about time!" he cried. "Tiana! Looks like I finally heard from that old slow-movin' Johnny Eaton!"

Houston nodded his thanks to the rider. He knew that he should slip him a coin, even a small coin, but they had no hard money. After waiting a moment to be sure that he wouldn't receive a gratuity, the rider galloped away, his mail sack bulging, hoping for better luck at the next stop.

Houston sliced through the wax seal with the edge of his hand and eagerly unfolded the letter. Tiana came around the corner of their cabin just as his hand dropped to his side and the letter fluttered to his feet. As he walked toward a small stand of cottonwood trees down by the river, seeming to stumble a little with every step, she snatched the letter from the ground.

"Sam,"

"I wanted you to hear this from me before official notification reached Major Pilchard. I'm afraid there isn't any way to sugar coat this - you did not get the rations contract."

"I realize that when you resubmitted your bid as we asked it came in even lower than the first one, but we had no less than four bidders at roughly the same amount per ration. One even slightly underbid you, although none promised the quality and service that you and Chouteau guaranteed."

"But considering the controversy surrounding the contract, it was agreed that it would not be appropriate for a private individual or firm to be involved. Instead, the army itself will supply the rations, which places it directly under my authority. It also means that the President cannot fairly be accused of underhanded dealing in an alleged effort to give you the contract, although I am sure some will claim that it was only through their efforts that this so-called swindle was averted."

"In a fair and just world, you certainly would have won and we both know it. But you, more than most, know that the world is not always fair, and the righteous are not always victorious."

"I am deeply sorry, but there will be other days and other victories. I hope that you understand our position."

"Your obedient servant and friend,"

"John Eaton, United States Secretary of War"

For the first time since he married Tiana, Houston drank too much that night. He passed out in front of the fireplace, snoring gently with a jug of applejack cradled in his arms.

51

AFTER MORE THAN a week of brooding, Houston's mood began to lift. Looking at it logically, he understood Eaton's decision. He didn't like it, not at all, but he might have done the same thing. Any appearance of wrongdoing would only weaken the President and give strength to his enemies at a critical time. Jackson was engaged in too many important issues to let this one taint the others.

My God, he thought, the old man was fighting for nothing less than the existence of the union!

It was years, even decades, coming to a head. Most Southerners held to the notion that because the states came into the union voluntarily they could leave it if the union took a position contrary to their interests. Wasn't that why they fought the revolution? Didn't the United States break off from Britain for just that reason? After Congress passed a series of tariffs that the South regarded as beneficial to the North but harmful to its own interests, when the southerners in Congress begged for relief they were rebuffed by the northern majority. Believing that if the federal government could tax a state against its will, it could do anything against its will,

South Carolina threatened to leave the union. If it left, others would surely follow.

"No government based on the naked principle that the majority ought to govern ever preserved its liberty," wrote Calhoun in a widely quoted newspaper article. "An unchecked majority is despotism."

As a southerner, Houston understood the South's position without agreeing with it. He thought that something might be worked out if both sides would only bend a little, but Jackson would not compromise. The South's stance couldn't have been more opposed to the President's belief that states could not enforce laws they liked while nullifying those they did not, much less leave the union at their convenience. It didn't help that the clash between two giants was a long time coming. At this point, Andrew Jackson and John Calhoun couldn't agree on the sunrise.

Jackson bluntly stated his position during a speech in Boston: "If a single drop of blood is shed in South Carolina in opposition to the laws of the United States, I will hang the first man I can lay my hand on who is engaged in such treasonable conduct upon the first tree I can find."

With federal troops poised to move, and a warship, the Natchez, dispatched to Charleston harbor, South Carolina finally backed down, although emotions still ran high. No one knew what might happen next.

So Houston understood why Eaton made the decision he did. Jackson didn't need more trouble. Not now and certainly not from him, a man who already caused so much trouble.

But it was mortal hard. Despite their backbreaking labor, he and Tiana were as poor as church mice.

The second blow came with the devastating news there would be no official, or even unofficial, position for him here at home or anywhere else.

In another personal note, Eaton explained the reasoning:

"The truth is that you're too hot, Sam. It would serve neither you, nor the Cherokee, nor any tribe, nor the government itself for you to be placed in the position that you proposed, or anything resembling it. The attacks upon you - and thus upon everything you do - would be relentless. I'm afraid that your actions thwarting the Indian Bureau offended too many powerful people."

"I must say it did not help that, rather than let it all blow over and bide your time in silence, your intemperate newspaper articles stirred it up again. I would be less than honest if I did not tell you that I was personally offended. I assumed that we were friends of long standing, and yet you saw fit to attack me in print without warning or discussion."

"If an old friend may be candid, there are times when you are your own worst enemy. Life would be easier for you and the people who care about you if you didn't feel such a constant need to call attention to yourself. Apparently you see yourself as an Indian Thomas Paine crying out for liberty, but the truth is that you don't know when to keep your mouth shut."

Damn John Eaton to hell! He'd done nothing but write the truth, no matter what that contemptible coward thought.

Houston didn't know if any of the eastern newspapers would reprint the series of five articles he'd written for the Arkansas Gazette, but he hoped that they would and it pleased him mightily when they did. In his view, it helped opened the issue to the public far beyond what little he'd accomplished in Washington.

Yes, his words were harsh, perhaps even intemperate, he admitted, but the attention was gratifying. He criticized every President since Washington, indicted Congress, pilloried the Indian Bureau, and tore apart the inconsistent and bungling history of national policy toward the Indians. Perhaps he *could* have softened his words and still made his point. And it's true that Eaton *was* mentioned several times, but his was one name among many. The timing could have been better, too. He

BORN FOR THE STORM

could have waited a bit and still made an impact. A little patience might have been better.

No! Houston angrily brushed his doubts aside until once again he saw himself as a man deserted by his friends. People once spoke of him for the Presidency. Now he slaved to make a meager living in a tiny shack in the middle of a wilderness. Deserted by his friends? What friends? It was all illusion. He never had any real friends. They used him when they needed him and cast him aside when they didn't.

That, at least, is what he told himself.

And so his downward spiral began anew. Always susceptible to self pity, this time it overwhelmed him. Activity was the only solution, but he had nothing to do, at least nothing with any significance in his eyes. He not only embraced his self pity, he exaggerated it by drinking prodigious amounts of alcohol.

In the normal routine of the Wigwam, when Pilchard sent notice of a new shipment of supplies at Fort Gibson, Houston picked up it up in their buckboard.

The first time he got so drunk that he couldn't get back home began one afternoon when he stopped in front of the sutler's warehouse. Seeing Houston climb down from the buckboard, Pilchard waddled across the square to meet him. If anything, the major looked even fatter than on the day they met.

"Mornin', Sam," Pilchard said, wiping his sweating face with a red handkerchief that was the size of a small flag.

"How do, Major," Houston responded.

Motioning toward a private standing on a barrel in front of the guard house with an empty bottle in each outstretched arm, Houston asked, "What in blazes did *he* do to deserve that? Don't think I've seen that particular punishment before."

"Drunk on duty," replied Pilchard. "He'll be there 'till sunset, if he lasts that long. He's probably not drunk more than anyone else here, but he had the bad luck to pass out on guard duty, a fine irony considering what I've come to see you about."

Reading from an invoice pulled from one pocket, Pilchard called off the contents in a loud voice as Houston entered the warehouse.

"Four barrels of Monongahela Whiskey, one barrel of corn whiskey, one barrel of cognac, one barrel of gin, one barrel of rum, and three barrels of wine. That's quite a shipment."

As Houston hoisted a small barrel to his shoulder and carried it out to the buckboard, the officer unleashed another one of his incredible farts and muttered his ritual, "Ah, sweet relief."

"You're not selling spirits to the Cherokee, are you?" Pilchard asked. "You know I'd have to stop you if you were. Hell's whiskers, man, you're the one raised such a stink about it in the first place. How would it look if you of all people started selling?"

Houston slipped the barrel from his shoulder, thumped it down on the buckboard, flipped it on its side and rolled it toward the front.

"Don't worry," he explained. "This is my private stock."

Pilchard whistled. "Your *private* stock? By the blessed balls of Saint Peter, if that's the case then I admire your capacity, I surely do. I grant you, they're small barrels, but all that'll get you through many a cold night."

Houston offered the fat major a mock bow.

"Of course, I intend to accommodate my good friend the post commander," he said, his voice mockingly formal. "I might even be convinced to leave a few drams in his care for safe keeping."

That night Tiana found him on the road for the first time.

52

HE AWAKENED WITH A BUBBLING SNORT, taking in a snoot full of muddy water. He tried to roll over but had to settle for turning his head just enough to get his face out of the muck. His head seared with pain, his body ached from head to toe, and the world was awfully damned wet. He moaned, took in more of the gritty water, choked, and finally managed to flop over on his back like a fish floundering on a riverbank.

As best he could figure, he was sprawled in a big puddle of water somewhere on the road out of Fort Gibson. It was raining by the bucket, a gully washer where a man couldn't see twenty feet in any direction. Even now, with his face pointing toward the sky, he felt almost as close to drowning as he did face down.

He groaned and tried to rise to his knees. He got as far as one knee when the world started spinning. With a feeble bleat, he fell on his back with a splat as the muddy ooze swirled around his body.

The idea of drowning in a mud puddle sobered him up enough to realize that he was so spectacularly drunk that his mind didn't connect to his body. For that matter, he couldn't even feel his body. Everything below his head was numb. All he could do was lay in the water and mud and let the rain pound on him.

He remembered hoisting a few at Fort Gibson. Strapped for money, as usual, he brought two barrels of whiskey to trade. Pilchard suggested that they sample one barrel to make sure the United State government wasn't being cheated with inferior product. As post commander, his duty demanded no less.

He remembered how the feeling came over him again while they drank, only this time it was a greater melancholy than he had yet faced in the months of his decline. Of late, it took control of him more and more often, and each time seemed worse than the time before. He wished that he knew how to brace his spirit against it, but he did not, being deathly afraid of this eternity of days passing by, each one finding him more helpless to set things right.

He remembered being lifted onto the wagon so that he could go back to the Wigwam. He must have fallen off somewhere along the trail. It wasn't the first time. Tiana always came to fetch him. It took all of her strength to get him on the buckboard, his long legs dangling off the back.

The horse must have wandered off, buckboard and all. Not that it mattered. The old nag knew the way home as well as he did, unless the horse was drunk, too. He found the thought so amusing he started to laugh in the driving rain. The sound was a gasping wheeze, like a bellows with a hole in it.

He must have passed out again because the next thing he knew Tiana and her brother John were rattling up in the buckboard, the supplies he bought on credit still piled in the back and their horses following along behind. He wanted to wave and let them know where he was, but his hand wouldn't move. He tried to raise his head and shout, but only released a wet gurgle before his head fell back in the muddy water.

He heard Tiana cry, "There he is!" The buckboard creaked to a stop. He heard her lightly jump to the ground, followed by the heavy lumbering sound of her brother. John was mad. Even his squishy steps sounded angry. Strong hands grabbed him under the arms, hefted him up, and dragged him toward the buckboard, his heels making long tracks in the mud. He turned his head and saw the horse stare at him reproachfully. That horse never liked him. Not ever. He heard voices, but they seemed to come from far away.

"How many times are you going to do this?"

"As often as I have to."

"He's a worthless drunk. All he does is drink. You know what they call him now - Big Drunk. If it wasn't for you and Drum we'd throw him out."

Judging by the brittle sound in Tiana's voice, she was as mad as her brother.

"No matter how bad it gets, no matter how bad *he* gets, he's still my husband. If he goes, I go."

"You were better off without a husband."

"You don't know him. You're just like the others. All you do is complain."

The next thing Houston knew he was in the wagon, though he didn't remember being dumped there.

Tiana stooped to pick up Houston's old straw hat from the muddy road.

"If you're not going to do anything except whine then get out of the way and I'll take him home."

"Oh, all right." Houston heard the chorus of squeaks and creaks as Rogers climbed onto the wagon. "As many times as you've done this, you probably don't need my help anyhow. Sister, you deserve a better man. You deserve a better *life*."

As the wagon clattered down the road, his long legs dangling off the back and the wheels sinking deep in the bog, Houston's last thought before he passed out again was that he was no good for her, or anyone. Tiana's brother was right. She deserved better.

53

THE DEFEAT WAS HUMILIATING. The vote wasn't even close. Out of five candidates for three seats on the Tribal Council, Houston finished dead last. Worse, he had only a handful of supporters. It was personal rejection on a massive scale.

Sure that he'd win a council seat and wanting to be there when it happened, Houston and Tiana rode their old wagon to Drum's settlement. Like most days, his morning started with chicory coffee freshened with a little whiskey. By early evening, he was slurring his speech, sitting cross-legged in the same lodge where he and Tiana were married. Drum was there, along with Tiana, two of her brothers, the four other candidates for the three open seats, the current members of the council, and perhaps fifty other men and women all packed into the crowded lodge, some on benches, some standing in back of the benches, and some, like Houston, on the floor.

When Drum read the results aloud, Houston was stunned. How could they do that to him? Then he burst out laughing and fell back with his elbows on the floor.

"Well, damn it all," he mumbled. "The firs' 'lection I ever

lost. 'torney General, Congreshman, Gov'nor ... now I can't even get on a piss poor council out in the middle of nowhere."

Houston turned his head and took a drink from the bottle he kept inside his jacket, whiskey dribbling down the side of his mouth and staining his shirt.

"Turn *me* down!" he shouted to no one in particular. "Who the hell do ya think ya're? I chose to pursue life as a drunken trader and I failed *only* as a trader. Makes me qualified as anybody."

Laughing at what he thought was a fine joke, Houston started to get up off the floor but lost his balance and staggered sideways. Tiana reached out to help, but he angrily shoved her away. She would have fallen if her brother John hadn't caught her in his arms.

"You're nothing but a stupid drunk!" he shouted. "You're a disgrace to my sister and the man who gave you a home when no one else would have you!"

With an inarticulate shout, Houston dropped his bottle and charged, big hands clutching for his brother-in-law's throat. Moving quickly for a man his age, Drum somehow managed to wedge himself between the struggling men. Houston heard Tiana cry, "No!" But the whiskey dulled Houston's reflexes and Drum fell from a blow, taking Rogers and Houston down with him in a wild tangle as men jumped in from all sides, furious about what they saw happen to their beloved leader. Houston tried to rise under the avalanche of kicks and blows but only got to one knee before he was beaten senseless.

———

HE CAME to lying in Drum's feather bed with the sun streaming in the window. Keeping his eyes shut, he took careful inventory of his aching body. His right eye was swollen and painful. With the stabbing pain that seared through his chest every time he took a breath, he suspected that a rib was cracked, too. He was sore and hurting all over, but the rib seemed like the worst of the damage.

After a few minutes, he opened his gummy eyes to see Drum and Tiana at his bedside. One side of the old man's face was swollen and purple. Tiana held Houston's hand in both of hers. Her soundless grief tore at his heart.

"Oh, God, what have I done?" he moaned, feebly reaching for Tiana. "I'm so sorry. All I ever do is hurt you. They should have killed me."

She buried her head in her husband's chest as sobs wracked her body.

A week later, humbled, aching with remorse, and fully expecting to be banished, Houston stood alone before the council and made a long mumbled apology to Drum, the council, and the entire Cherokee Nation. The vote was close, but thanks to Drum's influence he was allowed to remain.

Afterward, he retreated to the Wigwam and refused to leave it. Not even Tiana's unconditional love could touch the depths of his self-loathing. He thought that he'd hit bottom before, but it was nothing compared to this. He'd made excuses all his life and blamed everyone around him for his trouble, but now he knew it for the pitiful web of lies and self-deception that it was.

He remembered what Talon said so many years ago about a man living so that fear of death never entered his heart.

Sam Houston knew the truth at last. He wasn't afraid to die; he was afraid to live.

54

It happened all too quickly.

A gold strike in north Georgia touched off a stampede by thousands of rabid gold seekers into Cherokee land in Georgia and North Carolina while both state governments stood by and watched it happen. Then the Supreme Court crushed the tribes' last legal defense with its ruling in the case of "The Cherokee Nation versus Georgia." In its long-awaited decision, the court held that the tribes were not sovereign states but "domestic dependent nations" that existed at the mercy of the United States.

And then Jackson finally got his Indian Removal Bill through Congress, a grim piece of work that voided all previous treaties and authorized the expulsion of the tribes remaining in the Southeast. Although any such movement was supposed to be voluntary, the government could use force, if necessary.

Houston saw tragedy in the making as clear as the sunrise. In one way or another, the bill would lead to slaughter, with thousands of Cherokee, Choctaw, Chickasaw, and Creeks forced to make the long march west at the point of an army bayonet. The weak would die along the way and the survivors would fall prey to the stronger tribes already living in the territory.

In response, the western Cherokee gathered to vote on whether to send a delegation to Washington. Drum was among those who argued that there was no other choice. The Cherokee needed more land for the thousands of refugees who would come sooner or later. Some way had to be found to care and feed them all, too. Even if a delegation couldn't head off disaster it might find a way to mitigate the worst of it.

Houston begged to be named to the delegation, desperately making his case at another contentious meeting in the council lodge.

"Who else has my experience?" he asked, looking around at the skeptical faces he knew so well. "Does anyone here know the ways of Washington better than I do? Can any of you call the President a friend? There's no one else and you know it. Please, I beg you, give me one more chance. I can help. I know I can."

The long silence that followed seared him like a hot brand. His eyes roved the lodge, pleading for support, even one voice in his favor. That they knew him so well was the problem. No one except Drum even met his gaze. The shame was unbearable.

John Rogers finally broke the silence. They hadn't spoken to each other since the fight.

"What would you tell them?" he sneered. "They already know how to drink."

Humiliated again, Houston lowered his head and wordlessly stepped back against the wall.

The meeting ran late into the night. Eventually a narrow majority voted to send a delegation to Washington, although few expected it to do any good. Some preferred to wait and see what might happen, while others argued that the Cherokee should move even further west to get as far from the white world as possible.

When it came time to vote on the four delegates, Houston did not have a single supporter.

But he had to go, if only for himself. He had to shake something loose. There was no other choice. They were penniless. With his ruined reputation, there was barely any trade. There was no money in farming and prices for skins were so low that hunting and trapping were no longer profitable.

If it wasn't for Drum's quiet generosity they'd starve. Tiana never complained, but he was dragging her down with him and he knew it. She did her best to hide it, but he saw the worry in her eyes. Her brother was right. She'd be better off without him. For both their sakes, he had to find something. He had to *do* something. And that meant Washington. It was his last chance. He felt it in his soul.

Sitting at their little table in the cabin after a sad supper of bacon, beans and cornbread, he asked, "Tiana, you do understand, don't you? Please tell me you do. I've got to go. I've *got* to. I don't know where my future lies, but I've committed too many wrongs here to ever recover. The council doesn't believe in me anymore. No one does. Why should they?"

He caressed her soft cheek with his big calloused hand.

"My beautiful Tiana. God help us, there's no other way."

She seized his hand and held it tight against her cheek.

"Do what you have to do. I've always known ...."

She gave a short choking cry and lowered her head to hide her tears. Helpless and crushed by sorrow, he got down on his knees and held her in his arms.

He never meant to hurt her, but hurt her was all he ever did.

THANKS TO DRUM'S quiet persuasion, Houston was allowed to accompany the delegation without being an official member of it. At least it helped defray his expenses. No one but Tiana knew it, but he planned to take a different route than the others. Traveling by horse, once they reached the Mississippi, when the delegation headed north he'd turn south toward New Orleans and hook up later in Washington. Houston wanted to see his old friend Ed White and sound him out about how things stood in Washington; how *he* stood, if he had any standing at all. White would know. He'd be honest, too. After that, he'd book passage across the Gulf, around Florida, and up the coast to Baltimore. From there, it was a short trip by stage or rail to Washington. He'd take two of their hunting dogs, sell them in Little Rock, and send the money to Tiana.

Houston packed his few things in an old buffalo hide bag, his once admired wardrobe down to two changes of clothes. He dressed in a calico shirt, deerskin leggings, moccasins, and an old straw hat. He still wore his long hair in a queue. When he looked into their cracked wall mirror that morning, he was surprised to see streaks of gray. What the hell, he thought. At least he'd earned it.

With his long rifle in one hand and the buffalo bag in the other, he was moving toward the door when Tiana stopped him. She got down on her knees, reached under their bed and surprised him with a present - a beautiful buckskin coat with a lush collar of wolf fur she made herself. She held it open while he slid into it. After fastening the polished wood buttons, she removed her bright red scarf from around her neck and gently tucked it into the top of the coat to protect his throat from the cold. He could smell her lavender scent on the scarf.

Tiana held him as close as the bulky coat allowed.

"I want my husband to be as warm as he is handsome," she said, reaching up to caress the side of his face with her tender hand.

Houston felt his emotions well up with the familiar gesture of affection. He'd tried to steel himself for it, but leaving Tiana was hard, the hardest thing he'd ever done. The hurt of it all but overwhelmed him. He knew that if he didn't go now he never would. Forcing himself to pick up his rifle and bag, he stepped out of the little L-shaped cabin, whistled for the dogs, mounted his horse, and started down the rise.

It was raining and the fog from the river bottom made it impossible to tell where sky and earth met. At the bottom of the rise he turned to look back at Tiana one last time. But with the fog and rain he couldn't see anything. Even the cabin was obscured. She was standing at the doorway. He knew that. But he couldn't see her.

It took every ounce of his self-control to keep from galloping back to gather her in his arms. Overcome by immense melancholy, he began weeping noiselessly as he walked away. What he felt was more than leaving Tiana, though that was bad enough. The tears seemed connected to nothing and to everything. They were compelled by their own accord, the sum of everything he'd seen, known, lost, cared for, and kept hidden all through his life. His youth, his loves, his successes and failures, all of life's hard complexities and impossible choices, every living moment, was condensed into the tears that flowed from his eyes.

And they did not stop for many miles.

55

HE WAS SURPRISED to find that his old friend's gracious two-story home on the edge of the *Vieux Carre* was next to the old Villars house, the place where he seduced Marie Villars and nearly broke his neck jumping off the balcony.

Claiming that he once knew the family - which was certainly true in Marie's case - Houston asked what became of them.

"They're all dead, I'm afraid," White replied. "There was a typhoid epidemic four or five years ago. First it took the old man and his wife, then their son, then the daughter Marie, a real beauty. Then her husband and *their* daughter, all of them gone within a few days."

Houston was silent as they walked, turning up *Chartres* from Esplanade, only a block or two from the river. Although he hadn't thought about her for years, in his mind Marie was ever young, forever the *coquette*. It did not seem possible that she could be dead.

He pushed the thought away and, not for the first time, marveled at his companion, a man who carried himself with the easy confidence of success. White's dark shock of hair had disappeared along with his shy nature. What little hair remained as fringe around his head he shaved every day so that he was entirely bald. Married with four children, the Louisiana Congressman was one of the most successful lawyers in the state. Although his family still owned their plantation down in Plaquemines Parish, when he wasn't in Washington White spent virtually all of his time in New Orleans. There was talk that he'd run for governor in the next election, and if he ran he'd almost certainly win.

"It's still a ways away but, yes, I'll be running, though I don't want word to get out just yet," he admitted. "The opportunity is there and if I don't grab it now it may never come again."

Walking shoulder to shoulder, they turned left toward the river and the great open market that Houston remembered so well. As was his habit with success, White wore all black. Houston guessed that White's rich wool overcoat was by itself worth more than everything they owned at the Wigwam. Houston wore his buckskin leggings, a shirt of linsey-woolsey, moccasins, and Tiana's coat. He lost the straw hat when a gust of wind took it while he was riding along the shore of the Mississippi.

It was a blustery day with a sky full of fat black clouds that seemed ready to burst. There wasn't much activity even on the docks on a day like this and the market was all but empty. He'd forgotten how cold New Orleans could be when the icy winter wind blew off the broad expanse of the gray Mississippi. The chill seemed to cut a man to the bone.

Although White already knew most of the broad strokes, Houston told his old friend everything that happened in the years since they last saw each other, and how he saw this trip to Washington as the last chance to straighten out his life.

"Leaving her must have been a cruel thing, but for what it's worth I think it was the right thing," White said. "If ever a man wasn't meant to be lost in the wilderness, that man is you. Of course, I'll do what I can to help. Money, contacts, anything, just name it."

Houston started to express his thanks, but White interrupted with a wave of his hand.

"Please, Sam, don't. Our friendship goes beyond that. I'll don't think you'll need much help, to tell you the truth. You had some disappointments and maybe lost your way for a spell, but you're still Sam Houston and that's not an inconsiderable thing to be. You certainly won't need help from a Louisiana Congressman as long as Andrew Jackson's on your side. And don't forget about your other friends. Polk still has your old seat in Congress. Buchanan's there, too. There's a lot of people say he's one to keep an eye on, though he's too weak for my taste. Eaton's out as Secretary of War. The scandal about that wife of his finally did him in. But I understand he'll be named ambassador to Spain. It's probably already happened. Jackson'll be re-elected, of course. Pretty easily, too. But he might lose some seats in Congress and that could make his second term difficult."

They stopped on the shore of the broad river, with the little wavelets washing up close to their feet. The air was filled with the fertile scent of rain and the chilling wind howled across the water. Houston felt it even through his heavy coat. Another New Orleans downpour was coming in just a few minutes. One of the country's largest and most cosmopolitan cities was at their back, but somehow the wind wiped out all sound. The feeling of two men alone, isolated, and utterly private was eerie, as if some invisible barrier separated them from the rest of the world.

"Have you ever thought about Texas?" White asked, breaking the companionable silence. "Things are breaking loose down there. I'm sure it's destined to join the United States someday. The only question is when. Too many Americans are pouring in and Mexico's too weak to hold it. You know the old saying: To populate is to govern. If I wasn't so well set up here I might take a look myself."

Yes, Houston *had* thought about it. He'd thought about California, too. God knows he thought about every possibility under the sun at one time or another. If he found a way to get there, he'd probably think about going to the moon. But he admitted that it was impossible to see beyond Washington. Anything after that was a void.

"Do you know what you'll do once you get there?" White asked. "Got something specific in mind?"

Houston shook his head.

"'fraid not," he admitted. "Ridiculous, isn't it? After all these years I'm no better off than when we met."

They turned away from the river and walked to a Canal Street restaurant that White that favored. It was time to get out of the cold, have a bottle of wine and a good meal. White paid for it.

Houston didn't sleep well that night knowing that the balcony where he last saw Marie Villars was just a few feet away. She couldn't be dead. She couldn't. It just wasn't right.

56

JAMES KNOX POLK was in a hurry. With its heavy eyebrows, his dark scowling face looked like a thundercloud as his short legs pumped furiously, eating up the blocks to Brown's Hotel.

He hopped up the steps and rushed through the double doors to find Houston lounging in the lobby, drinking coffee and reading the National Intelligencer, a sheet that was almost comical in its rabid hatred of the President.

Puffing from his rapid walk from the capital building, Polk gasped, "Good morning, Sam."

"Good mornin' to you, Jimmy," replied Houston cheerfully, placing the coffee cup on a small table beside his worn wing chair. "How's our representative from the great state of Tennessee?"

Polk nodded toward Houston's copy of the Intelligencer.

"Why do you read than rag? If you want fiction and fairy dust there are better places to find it."

"I remember something the President told me back at the Hermitage when we were all a lot younger," Houston replied with an amiable smile. "He said, 'You'll always know what your friends are up to. It's your enemies that need watchin'.' Reading the Intelligencer is one way to keep an eye on 'em."

He waved Polk to a chair across from his own. Knowing Brown's, the chairs probably hadn't been moved or cleaned in twenty years.

"I assume you're not here to check on my readin' habits. What's got you so agitated? You look like you're about to bust a gut."

Gratefully, Polk sat down. The life of a Washington legislator was not conducive to physical conditioning. The capital offered too much food and not enough exercise.

"Do you remember the contract to supply rations to the Indians?" asked Polk. "The one you didn't get?"

"It's not somethin' I'm likely to forget."

"Well somebody else remembers it, too," Polk said mysteriously.

It was Polk's manner more than what he said that jerked Houston to full attention. The resolutely self-controlled Polk never acted scattered and mysterious like this.

"What exactly are you talkin' about, Jimmy?"

Rather than answer right away, Polk waved down at a white-jacketed waiter and ordered a whiskey. As soon as it appeared, to Houston's surprised, he downed it in two quick gulps and immediately began coughing until his eyes watered.

"Why Jimmy, I didn't know you were a drinking man," Houston said, amused by Polk's helpless gasps and wheezes. "I seem to recollect that you were always the victim of water as a beverage. Isn't it a bit early in the day for a novice?"

"I'm certainly *not* a drinking man and now I remember why," wheezed Polk, who felt like he was on fire from his gullet to his gizzard.

Pulling himself together, he sat straight up in his chair, tugging his waistcoat over the small paunch he'd acquired lately.

"Do you know William Stanbery, the congressman from Ohio?" Polk asked. "He's a windbag of fantastic proportions, as pompous as he is stupid."

"Aside from the fact that your description fits half of Congress, no, we've never met," replied Houston.

In a speech to Congress earlier that morning, Polk explained that Stanbery resurrected the old controversy over the rations contract. Reading from notes pulled from his pocket, he quoted from the speech: "Was not Secretary of War John Eaton removed from office because of his attempt to fraudulently give Governor Houston the contract for Indian rations?"

The answer to Stanbery's rhetorical question was no, of course. Eaton's problem was his marriage. The scandal forced him to lay low for a while, if you could call being ambassador to Spain laying low. At least it got the poor man out of the country for a while.

But Stanbery didn't stop there, Polk continued. His speech went all the way back to Houston's brief career as an Indian agent, as he dredged up the old charges of slave smuggling and illegal whiskey sales, among other fabrications.

Houston felt a hot flush flood across his face.

"Jimmy, only a handful of people knew about that old nonsense. Calhoun disallowed all the charges. He never even let them get to the point where they were official. He rejected every one as the scurrilous lies they were."

"I know, I know," Polk acknowledged. "The point is that except for you, me, and the Old Man almost everyone who knew about it was, and still is, on the other side, up to Calhoun himself. I have no doubt that's where Stanbery got the material. It was much too detailed to come from anyone else."

According to Polk, Stanbery not only charged Jackson, Eaton, and Houston with fraud, but added a new twist to the old story by claiming the trio was linked by a long-standing thread of corruption that was "common in their benighted state."

It was, Stanbery bellowed in conclusion, "The Tennessee way of public service; crude, rapacious and dishonest."

"Why that bilious bastard! Where is he now?"

"I assume he's still ...." A warning rang in Polk's head. "Sam, you're not ...."

Houston rose out his chair, marched out of the hotel, down the steps, and out to the street.

"Oh, God no!" cried Polk. "Sam! Wait! You can't go off half-cocked like this!"

Polk pursued Houston down the crowded tree-lined avenue. Too small to physically restrain the larger man, he bounced around the massive Houston like a puppy yapping at the heels of an angry lion. In the next block Polk saw Cave Johnson, a fellow Tennessee Congressman and another old friend of Houston's, step out of Burch's boarding house.

"Cave!" Polk waved frantically. "Over here! Help!"

With Polk tugging on one arm, Johnson on the other, and passersby gaping in wonder, the trio marched almost another block before the Congressmen finally persuaded Houston to stop.

"Sam, this involves more than you," Johnson warned, maneuvering to block Houston's way. "Whatever you do, think it over first, that's all we ask. Don't do anything you'll regret. And for God's sake don't do anything to damage the President."

"I understand how you feel," Polk added, still clutching Houston's arm. "I wanted to box Stanbery's ears myself. I came to tell you about it because I thought you should hear it from a friend before you read about it in the newspapers. I never thought you'd take off like a damn Chinese rocket."

As angry as he was, Houston agreed to wait, but only if

Johnson delivered a note to Stanbery giving him the opportunity to deny or retract what he said, the formally recognized first step of a challenge leading to a duel.

"You write it and I'll deliver it, as long as you agree to hold your fire for now," Johnson agreed.

Polk rolled his eyes at such ridiculous bravado. He'd been challenged three times in his life and ignored every one. If he was ever challenged again he'd ignore that, too. He regarded the whole thing as a lot of childish nonsense.

Seething but under control, Houston returned to Brown's. He went upstairs to his room, scrawled out a note to Stanbery, and arranged for it to be delivered to Johnson, who would then deliver it to Stanbery.

The message was simple so there could be no misinterpretation: *"The object of this note is to ascertain whether my name was used by you in debate, and, if so, whether your remarks have been accurately quoted. I hope you will find it convenient to reply without delay."*

Until now, Houston reckoned his stay in Washington as a success, although it certainly began with failure. He couldn't to do a thing for the Cherokee. No one could. His lack of official status didn't help, but the Cherokee delegation was helpless, too. The President was intractable and the government held all the cards. The next few years would be disastrous for the Eastern Cherokee and there wasn't anything San Houston or anyone else could do about it.

Regarding his own future, he felt that he was on the verge of a breakthrough after meeting with no less than three New York City syndicates that were interested in investing in Texas land, with himself as their representative. California was still an option, but it was fading fast. The opportunity in Texas was too good to ignore. It was about time he made some serious money. Proximity was a factor, too. It could take six months to travel to California. Texas was only a month away.

As he understood Mexican law, in order to acquire land he'd have to join the Catholic Church and become a Mexican citizen, but based on everything he heard no one took either step seriously. To his mind one church was pretty much like another anyway. He sometimes wished that he believed in a merciful God and an afterlife where the dead lived on, but it just wouldn't come. He accepted the existence of God readily enough. If he was wrong there was no harm in it. But he had no sense of the nature of such a being, and certainly no sense that the Creator took a personal interest in Sam Houston, which probably was just as well, considering.

Once he got a foothold in Texas he might even get back into politics. Why not? Texas was a new world, a place where a man's past was not held against him. Ed White's reasoning was sound, too. Texas was destined to join the United States someday. It was inevitable. Those who were there at the beginning would have an advantage.

Even the President liked the Texas idea. It seemed to fit with something already on his mind. But, as usual, Jackson refused to divulge anything until he was ready.

So right now land speculation looked awfully good, especially using someone else's money, which was the only way he could do it. Houston didn't have a penny. His hotel bill was long overdue and the only reason Brown's didn't throw him out was his well-known friendship with the President. If it wasn't for Tiana's coat he might have frozen to death over the winter.

So Stanbery's speech couldn't have come at a worse time. Houston was confident that at least two of the syndicates leaned in his direction, but he knew that he wasn't the only candidate. Anything, no matter how insignificant, might tip the balance against him. It didn't matter that Stanbery's charges were false and the speech just more empty bombast. It was public perception that mattered. After three years in exile, much of it in an alcoholic daze, he finally had his hands on a real opportunity. He must not let it slip away. There might never be another.

Damn the man! This must not go unchallenged.

———

EVERY WASHINGTON NEWSPAPER ran a report of Stanbery's speech the next day, which guaranteed that other newspapers across the country would pick it up.

As good as his word, Cave Johnson delivered the challenge to Stanbery as soon as he received it from Houston. Alert to Houston's intentions and familiar with the ritual of the *Code Duello*, Stanbery refused to accept the note. Under the complex etiquette of the code, if he did not read the note, even if he knew or suspected what it said, then Houston could not call him out.

As Polk predicted, Stanbery wrapped himself in the cloak of legislative privilege, too. After keeping Johnson waiting for more than an hour, an unheard of insult for a fellow Congressman, Stanbery huffed, "I do not accept the note and I do not acknowledge the right of Governor Houston to demand that I explain myself, if that is, indeed, what the note demands. The right to debate on the floor of this great legislative body is sacrosanct."

Even Polk and Johnson admitted that Stanbery made a shrewd point. Congressmen were traditionally immune to prosecution as a result of what they said in Congress, no matter how offensive or libelous, and it was a violation of Congressional privilege to call a member to task for words spoken on the floor. Given the rancorous nature of national politics, it could hardly be otherwise.

"Good God, Sam, if that wasn't the case we'd have to walk around with pistols in our belts," laughed Tom Benton, who dropped in at Brown's for a drink with Houston when he heard the news.

Still representing Missouri in the Senate, the hulking, hook-nosed Benton was one of the most powerful men in Washington.

"Anything I can do to help, I will," promised Benton, pouring champagne into twin flutes on the table between them in the lobby. "But my advice is to let this nonsense go until it dies from neglect. Just ignore it. In a few weeks, no one will remember anything that worthless fool said."

Benton did have one piece of interesting news. Stanbery had armed himself and let everyone know it. In the face of Houston's hostility, the Ohio congressman claimed that he never went out without a pistol and a knife.

"I don't care if he totes a cannon," Houston told Benton, lifting his champagne in salute. "One way or another, I intend to introduce myself."

57

HOUSTON, Senator Alexander Buckner, and Congressman Francis Blair, both of Missouri, and Tennessee Senator Felix Grundy strolled two abreast down Pennsylvania Avenue. It was a balmy evening and they'd just finished a passable dinner of seafood from Chesapeake Bay paid for by the good people of Missouri, washed down by two bottles of wine paid for by the people of Tennessee.

Houston wasn't sure that Washington weather was pleasant at any time, but spring was closest to it. The brutal humidity of summer had yet to set in and the blooming cherry blossoms along the Potomac River were strikingly beautiful. While the city's dominant structures still were the President's House and the Capitol, in between them both sides of Pennsylvania Avenue bustled with a mix of brick and clapboard boarding houses, taverns, hotels, stables, and shops.

As they ambled down the broad avenue, Houston twirled a walking stick in his fingers. Cut from a hickory sapling at the Hermitage, it was a present from Jackson on Houston's birthday.

Without a word, Blair, a rat-faced little man Houston

never liked despite his unswerving loyalty to the President, turned on his heel and walked rapidly in the opposite direction.

"What the devil?" muttered Buckner.

Houston called out, "Frank, where you goin'?"

Buckner tugged at Houston's sleeve.

"Look up ahead and you'll see why he took off in such a hurry."

Houston peered down the avenue illuminated by the dim light of the street lamps. On the other side of the avenue a half-block away he saw a man of about his own size wearing a tall beaver hat. They'd never met, but some instinct told him that it was William Stanbery.

"Alex, is that who I think it is?" Houston asked.

"It is, indeed," Buckner replied.

Smiling with relief that the confrontation was finally at hand, Houston hurried ahead and caught up just as the Congressman crossed the street.

"Excuse me, sir," Houston asked, "are you William Stanbery?"

Stanbery turned to face the big stranger in buckskin.

"Why, yes," he said. "Yes, I am."

From behind Houston, Grundy yelled, "Sam! Be careful! Remember, he's got a pistol!"

Alerted by the warning, Stanbery's eyes widened as he stepped back, one meaty hand reaching inside his coat.

"Then you are a damned rascal!" cried Houston as he raised his walking stick and cracked Stanbery across the head.

The blow knocked the Congressman's beaver hat off, but the hat blocked most of its force. He turned to run, but Houston easily caught up, seized Stanbery by the coat collar, and with a mighty yank put him flat on his back.

As Houston flailed away with the cane, Stanbery rocked from side to side, crying, "Don't! Please don't!" He tried to protect himself by raising one arm over his face while struggling to draw his pistol with his other hand.

Houston tossed the cane aside with a clatter, grabbed two fistfuls of Stanbery's shirtfront and hauled him to his feet. Now that he was erect, Stanbery drew his pistol. He jammed it against Houston's chest, pulled the trigger, heard the snap, saw the flint strike a spark ....

Misfire!

Holding Stanbery by the shirt with his left hand, Houston's right fist sank deep into the Congressman's soft belly. When Stanbery doubled over as the air exploded out of him, Houston brought his right knee up and felt a satisfying jolt as Stanbery reeled sideways and fell to the ground, where he tried to scuttle away on his elbows, screaming for help. Houston calmly found his walking stick where he tossed it aside, seized one of Stanbery's ankles with the other hand, lifted the man's leg, and brought the cane down a half-dozen times on Stanbery's well-padded backside while the Congressman squealed and blubbered.

Breathing heavily, Houston let go and stepped back, walking stick still in hand. He saw Grundy standing with his back against a building and his eyes as wide as saucers.

"Felix, it's a fine evening, isn't it? Houston laughed and twirled the cane in his fingers. "A damn fine evening."

He stepped around Stanbery, who was whimpering and curled into a fetal position.

"And good evening to you, Congressman," he said as he started happily down the street. "I *do* enjoy your speeches."

58

MOST DARING OUTRAGE AND ASSAULT!

The headline in the Telegraph was almost as hysterical as the story beneath it. The newspaper babbled about Houston's close relationship with the President. It breathlessly summarized his colorful history and speculated about his return to Washington. After achieving a state of near hysteria describing the attack on Congressman Stanbery, it concluded by sorrowfully observing that the beating "could only mean that the thuggish tactics of Nashville have been transferred to Washington. The tragic result is that the courageous voice of truth was silenced by an assassin."

In all of its babbling, speculation, hysteria, and bizarre conclusions, Polk estimated the newspaper got perhaps ten percent of its facts right, making it one of the Telegraph's better performances. At the same time, it consoled its readers that they need not fear: "Our voice will not be silenced because we have not yet taken fear as our counselor."

"Well that's too bad," Polk muttered, tossing the Telegraph on a pile of newspapers at his feet.

Raising his voice, he added, "Sam, would you mind taking

that famous walking stick of yours and pummeling Pete Cavendish down at the Telegraph?"

From the other side of Polk's desk, where he was reading an account in another newspaper, Houston replied, "Jimmy, I think I've done enough pummelin' for a while. However, I'd be happy to loan it to you."

Polk and Houston were in Polk's office assessing the newspaper reports of what was already known as "the Houston street brawl." It wasn't all anti-Houston and anti-Jackson by any means. There were at least as many pro-Jackson newspapers as anti-Jackson newspapers in Washington and the hysteria, not to mention the inaccuracies, seemed about equally distributed on both sides.

As usual, the President did not back down. He told one correspondent that he would be "pleased to have a dozen Houstons to cudgel members of Congress."

According to the reports, Stanbery languished in bed with a concussion, a fractured left hand, bruised ribs, and complaints about "various welts and bruises elsewhere on my person."

Polk gazed at Houston over the top of a newspaper.

"Is 'elsewhere' where I think it is?"

"I believe so," replied Houston happily. "I'm sure I hit him on the elsewhere hard enough to cause welts and bruises."

"In that case," Polk grumbled, "the man probably has brain damage."

Even so, Stanbery was well enough to write a letter to Speaker of the House Alexander Stevenson:

"Sir,"

"I was waylaid on the street, near my boarding house last night about 8 o'clock, and attacked, knocked down by bludgeon and severely bruised and wounded, by Samuel Houston, late of Tennessee. I am confined to my bed and unable to discharge my duties in the House and attend to the needs of my constituents. I *communicate this information to you and request that you lay it before the House."*

Although not particularly popular with his peers, Stanbery became a rallying point for the President's foes. With his statement read into the public record, a motion was put forward for Houston's arrest. Although Polk shot to his feet to protest that the House didn't have the authority to do any such thing, the motion easily passed by a vote of one hundred and forty five to twenty five.

"Congratulations, Sam, you're a first."

Polk took a sip of coffee, his fourth cup in what was still a young morning.

"In the short history of our country, this has never happened before. Think of it: A former member of the House of Representatives is to be arrested by the House of Representatives, where he presumably will be tried. You should be proud of yourself."

"Believe me, I find it thrillin'," replied Houston, who was waiting in Polk's office for the Sergeant at Arms to serve official notice of his arrest, although he'd already promised not to leave Washington in exchange for his freedom until a verdict was rendered. "By the way, is any of this legal?"

"I doubt it, but I'm not sure. I don't know if anyone is," Polk admitted. "But I don't think we should fight it, my protest to the contrary. I was just being difficult. It's one of my specialties. There's no question that you did it, after all. There were many witnesses and Stanbery has the welts on his elsewhere to prove it. The President believes, and I agree, that it's best to keep the whole thing confined to Congress if we can, anything to keep it from the civil authorities. If it goes there, we lose what control we have."

As Polk saw it, in the most likely interpretation the attack was a violation of Congressional privilege. Stanbery intended for the House to vindicate him and penalize Houston, probably by throwing him in federal prison, and thus embarrassing the President.

"This being Washington, there is no doubt that the whole thing will deteriorate into a remarkable fiasco," Polk concluded. "There will be a long and noisy debate. Every question will be objected to and every answer righteously demanded, all of it interrupted by frequent votes on how to proceed, or whether to proceed at all. In short, this is exactly the sort of situation at which you used to excel and at which I have no small skill myself. It should be most enjoyable, except, perhaps, to you."

59

WEARING in his buckskin coat and carrying his infamous walking stick, Houston stood before Speaker of the House Alexander Stevenson in the House chamber, a cold and cavernous hall that was warmed by only one pitifully inadequate fireplace and filled with so many echoes and dead spots that it vexed even the most accomplished orators.

The spectator gallery was jammed, including many more women than usual, which was not difficult because most of the time there were no women at all. There were more newspaper correspondents fluttering around, too, and every Congressman was present in his seat, a phenomenon of such rarity that no one remembered the last time it happened. It took several minutes of gavel-pounding before Stevenson managed to beat the crowd into something close to silence.

Houston bowed toward the Speaker, a man he'd known for years, and waited while the formal arraignment was read for the record. He asked for twenty four hours to prepare a defense. To his surprise, Stevenson gave him forty eight.

RESPONDING to Jackson's summons to see him as soon as possible, no matter how late the hour, Houston bounded up the steps to the north portico of the President's House and rapped the silver head of his walking stick on the door leading to the entrance hall.

As usual, there was no guard. An elderly servant opened the door and ushered him inside. It never failed to amaze Houston that virtually anyone could demand to see the President of the United States. It was even more amazing that the President usually took the time to see them.

Jackson's health was deteriorating. Everyone saw it but no one was foolhardy enough to mention it in his presence. Among other maladies, he was losing teeth at an alarming rate. The result was a kind of increasing liquidity to his speech that made it virtually impossible for Jackson to give speeches at any length. Considering that the President still carried two pistol balls in his body, one near a lung, the other near his heart, Houston wasn't surprised at Jackson's suffering.

Driven by his iron will and rigid sense of duty, poor health did not stop the old warrior from starting early and working late. In addition to the mountain of paperwork that comes with the Presidency, he kept up a voluminous correspondence with friends, family, officials, and fellow politicians all over the world, sometimes writing as many as twenty letters a day. Easily the most paternalistic man Houston ever met, Jackson also took on the responsibility for any number of relatives, friends, neighbors, old soldiers, and anyone else with a reasonable claim on his help, too, as if the entire nation was under his personal care.

Houston was ushered upstairs to the President's private quarters. At almost midnight, the big house was quiet. As he walked down the hallway, his footsteps sounded unnaturally loud.

The President was in his nightclothes, but not yet in bed, sitting in a chair at a small table against the wall. Sticking out from beneath the nightgown was the skinniest pair of Scotch-Irish legs Houston had ever seen. He was reading from Rachel Jackson's old prayer book. Houston recognized it from the Hermitage. Almost from the day they married, Jackson wore a miniature of his wife around his neck. The only exception was just before bed when he removed it to read his prayers. At those times, he tenderly placed the miniature on the table beside the prayer book.

Houston backed out of the room and waited in the hallway to give the President privacy. After few minutes, Jackson rose from the table and in his bare feet padded softly over to the bed.

"Come in, Sam," he called over his shoulder.

Jackson wearily climbed into bed. He looked like what he was, a tired old man at the end of a long day, the latest of many.

"Pull that chair up here," he said, waving toward the chair he'd just left. "We'll talk about how to pull your chestnuts out of the fire."

Houston carried the chair to the bed and sat in it backward, so that his arms were crossed over the high back. Jackson leaned against a pile of pillows in a half-sitting position, his white hair standing at attention.

"First things first," he said. "Do you have any money at all? Don't lie to me now. This is no time for false pride."

Houston ruefully shook his head.

"No sir. I can't even pay my hotel bill."

"I didn't think so." Jackson nodded toward a small table beside the bed. "Open that drawer."

Houston pulled the drawer open.

"Take it out," Jackson said.

He lifted a leather purse heavy with coins.

"Get yourself the best suit you can find just as quick as you can find it," Jackson ordered. "I know you for the gentleman you are, but we must take care of appearances. You must not look like a border ruffian who spends his leisure time beating the daylights out of offensive Congressmen, however much they deserve it. Pay your hotel bill, too. Keep the rest for expenses. If you need more, tell me."

"Sir, I really ...."

Jackson made a cutting motion with his hand, his old signal that he was not to be interrupted.

"We have served each other for a goodly number of years. I know there were times when I disappointed you, just as there were times you disappointed me. That only proves the strength of our bond. Friendship means nothin' if it isn't tested. My Rachel loved you like a son, and you know how I feel about you. You served me with your blood, your heart, your wisdom, and your passion. Balanced against that, these few coins are a pittance. And what you did to Stanbery gave me the most pleasure I've had in a long time. Now, to work ...."

After consulting with Polk, Buchanan, Blair, and Martin Van Buren, the smooth little New Yorker, the President concluded that Francis Scott Key was just the man for Houston's defense.

Seeing shock on Houston's face, Jackson's wet chortle sounded like a slurp.

"Judging by the expression on your face, it appears you don't think much of him."

"Sir, I don't think of him at all."

He was bewildered at Jackson's choice of Key as his defender at the most important moment of his life. With the exception of his inexplicably popular poem after the bombing of Fort McHenry, Key hadn't accomplished anything of substance Houston knew of.

"In my opinion, Key couldn't defend a doll's house," protested Houston. "To be honest, I intended to defend myself."

"And you will, Sam, you will," Jackson agreed. "Whatever you think of him, and you are too harsh, by the way, Key is held in high regard in Congress. He is socially and politically connected to all the right people. He has a reputation for moral and legal rectitude, too. Did you know that as a young man he seriously considered becoming a preacher? Despite what you think, he's quite bright, in his way, and entirely above reproach. Having a man of Key's popularity and reputation on your side will help influence the weak-minded in Congress, by which I mean most of 'em."

"Sir, I mean no offense, but this case won't turn on the law," Houston protested. "I'm clearly guilty. This case will turn on what's right. Just because a man is elected to Congress doesn't mean he has the right to say anything he wants, no matter how false he knows it to be. Stanbery slandered me. I gave him a chance to apologize or explain himself. He did neither. He was armed when we met and I was not. No matter what the law says, this is a matter of justice. The truth will be my defense."

"And you're lawyer enough to know that the truth often needs a little help," Jackson said. "Let Key handle the legal niceties and make use of his personal contacts. You will do the rest, with our help. That will win us this case, plus the usual tactics of parliamentary obfuscation and inflammatory rhetoric, at which no one is more expert than Polk."

The President stopped to take a drink from a glass of milk that a servant left on the bedside table. The milk left a white ring around his wrinkled upper lip. Jackson wiped it away with the back of his hand.

"Do you know the *real* reason why you object to Key?" he asked.

"Well, yes, as I said, it's ...."

"What you were about to say has nothin' to do with it," Jackson gently interrupted. "Son, the real problem is that you don't want to share the moment. The light is shinin' on you again and, by God, you love it. I don't know another man who loves it more."

Although he felt vaguely insulted, Houston was reluctant to disagree. The President looked exhausted.

Jackson pushed himself up against his pillows.

"I have faith in you, Sam. Despite what you probably think, I always did. Key won't win this thing. I won't either. It will be Sam Houston. Just let me help you. Key's the man. I grant you, it's more for what he represents and who he knows than for what he is, and what he can do behind the scenes, but he'll do fine."

With the leather purse heavy in his pocket, Houston left the President's house and stepped into the Washington night. Walking the deserted avenue on the way to Brown's, he couldn't rid himself of the feeling that Jackson was wrong. But whether the old man was right or wrong didn't matter because this time he'd decide his own fate. If he won, well and good. If he lost, at least the whole country would know about it.

He would not go down without a fight. Not this time.

The President was right about one thing. It felt grand to be in the light again.

60

EARLY THE NEXT MORNING, Houston walked into the establishment of Jonathan Hobby & Sons, the best tailor in Washington, where he was fitted for a new suit. He promised Hobby a bonus if it was ready that night.

Luck was with him. The fussy old man was an admirer who declared his belief that most Congressmen richly deserved a crack or two on the head from time to time and he was proud to donate to such a worthy cause.

In short, while he overcharged Houston for the material and the work, he didn't charge for the rush in making it.

That evening, as Houston modeled Hobby's handsome creation before the full-length mirror in the tailor's cluttered back room, he felt himself expand with a sense of self-worth that he hadn't felt in years. The black suit was of the latest cut and emphasized his broad shoulders. He decided to keep the knee-length coat unbuttoned to show off the white waistcoat. When his measurements were taken, he noted with pleasure that his waist measured the same as it did ten years ago. He had his hair cut, too. The long queue was gone. Jackson was right. He should appear as a gentleman, not a brawler.

By God, he hadn't felt this good in years!

"You give 'em ten kinds of hell, sir," the admiring Hobby said. "They deserve it."

———

As HOUSTON SAW IT, the trial hinged on a handful of issues.

The prosecution would make it out to be a simple case, which, in some ways, it was. Sam Houston beat senseless a member of the United States House of Representatives as a result of comments made by the Congressman while speaking in the House. There was no denying it. He beat William Stanbery into the ground the first time they met. On that basis, there could only be one verdict.

The best defense was to do turn the accusers into the accused. The main point was simple justice, the notion that private citizens have the right to defend themselves against attacks made on them by overbearing Congressmen who play fast and loose with the truth. He'd only defended his reputation when he attacked Stanbery, a coward who hid behind so-called Congressional immunity from prosecution for libel and slander. Instead of meekly defending his position, Houston intended to challenge his accusers and demand that Congress show him this so-called privilege. Was it really the law of the land? Or was it an informal and entirely unfair rule adopted for Congressional convenience?

Another point was that Stanbery was armed and attempted to draw his pistol before Houston struck a blow. Congressional privilege aside, he could make a case all he did was defend himself. Stanbery was armed, he was not, and that was a telling detail.

The Congressman's accusation of a well-planned ambush was easily dismissed. The three members of Congress who were with him that night would testify otherwise. That they met on the street was luck and nothing more. Too, it was widely known Stanbery carried a pistol and if Houston planned the confrontation he certainly would have armed himself with more than a walking stick.

Finally, he'd also make the case that Congress did not have the right to do what it was doing. There was no mention anywhere in the constitution that the House could try a private citizen for a violation of its privilege, assuming the privilege even existed. The House gathered the evidence against him, it argued the case against him, and now it intended to judge him. In short, Congress was trampling the same separation of powers it was supposed to defend.

Confident of his ability to make a good argument on all fronts, Houston also knew very well that making a good argument is not the same thing as winning it. He had to be very careful and very clever. A little luck wouldn't hurt, either.

———

FRANCIS SCOTT KEY was everything Houston feared and less than he hoped. It looked like cleverness was out of the question.

A tall cultured man with narrow shoulders, wide hips, and a soft handshake, Key was handsome in a weak and undefined way, with a touch of gray in his dark curly hair and a classic profile he displayed at every opportunity, as if he expected it to someday appear on a coin. Visitors to his office often left with the impression that they spent most of the time talking to Key's ear.

But, as Jackson said, there were several things in Key's favor. Yes, he was respected, Houston admitted, though less for his law than his celebrity, and he was popular with Congress and the rest of official and social Washington. After so long in the capitol, he knew everyone and everyone knew him. He was a longtime Jackson supporter and almost embarrassingly enthusiastic in his praise of Houston.

The first time Houston, Polk, and Key met in Key's spacious second floor office with a big window revealing Washington's mud in all its splendor, Key could barely control himself.

"Governor Houston, we shall *smite* them hip and thigh," he declared.

"All we need is the jawbone of an ass," muttered Polk.

"What was that, sir?" asked Key, who was hard of hearing. "I didn't quite get that, I'm afraid."

"Just thinking out loud," Polk replied, keeping a straight face. "A legal point. We can go over it later."

Key had several ideas, none of which Houston liked, although they did show original thinking. He suggested that the defense be based on the idea that Houston's attack did not come out of what Stanbery said in the House, but from what was reported in the newspapers. While it did get around the idea of House privilege, there was one problem.

"The report in the newspapers was a verbatim account of what was said on the House floor," Houston explained. "One is the same as the other."

"Yes, but how were you to know that?" Key asked rhetorically, the way he asked most questions. "You were not there to hear it. We will carry the day, Houston! I guarantee it!"

Key gave the impression that he employed someone to wait within earshot and scribble down everything he said because he might produce a gem that must be preserved lest posterity suffer for its loss. Francis Scott Key rarely said anything. He pronounced! Houston had run into that sort of man before, someone who is used to being heard but not at all certain about being listened to and tries to make for it in other ways.

When Houston explained that he intended to turn the

accusers into the accused and challenge the right of the House to try him, Key raised a soft hand to his forehead as he struggled with the idea.

"But the President told me that you *preferred* to have the case tried in the House," he said. "If that is so, why do you wish to challenge the right to hold it there? It seems so ... so ... *contradictory!*"

Polk popped out of his chair and left the office before he burst out laughing.

"Where's he going so suddenly?" Key asked.

"Jimmy's not feelin' well," Houston replied, babbling the first excuse that popped into his mind. "A sudden disorder of the stomach. He didn't want to ... to discommode you with his troubles."

Getting back to the case, Houston tried to explain. "You see, Francis, the reason *why* we want the trial to stay *in* the House is so we *can* challenge it."

He was dismayed to hear himself mimic Key's dramatic way of speaking. If he spent much more time with the man, he'd emerge from the office as an idiot.

Key promised to think it over, although Houston wasn't sure that having Key think it over was the road to progress.

Polk met Houston outside Key's office and steered him into a tavern in the next block. Ironically, it turned out to be the O'Neal tavern. Although he knew perfectly well that she was out of the country with her husband, Houston half expected to see Peggy O'Neal Timberlake Eaton sashay through the place, swinging her extraordinary hips with abandon.

"Sam, I'd say you need a drink as much as any man in Washington," Polk said. "Anyone would after prolonged exposure to that man's great legal mind."

Standing at the end of the bar, Houston held his head in his hands.

"Jimmy, if that fool defends me I'm ruined," he moaned. "What was the old man thinking?"

"He likes Key and you know how he is, the most loyal man alive," Polk explained. "You're proof of that. Believe or not, once he gets a grip on a case, Key isn't a bad lawyer, and he's a very good speaker. The President's right. Let him deal with the minutia, you handle the heart of your defense, and I'll work from the floor. This case won't be won or lost on legalities. You said so yourself."

After a second whiskey, Houston began to feel better.

"Look at it this way," Polk said cheerfully. "At least it sends a confident message."

"And what could that possibly be?"

"No truly guilty man would *ever* hire Francis Scott Key to defend him."

61

FROM THE SECOND THAT Speaker of the House Stevenson brought his gavel down with a crack, the trial seized the attention of the entire country. There hadn't been anything like it since Aaron Burr's spectacular trial for treason a generation ago.

The public was so hungry for details it was as if the newspapers wrote about nothing else. Every day the gallery was jammed with the cream of Washington society. The brooding Junius Brutus Booth, the greatest Shakespearean actor in the country, even canceled a New York City run in "Hamlet" to attend. Houston saw the actor's scowling face hanging over the railing like a storm cloud every day in the same seat in the front row.

During the trial's first week, Houston received one proposal of marriage from a rich, elderly, and wildly eccentric widow, two threats on his life, and a variety of business and political feelers. He hadn't felt so alive in years. Polk said that it was like watching a flower open in the sunlight. He realized once again how desperately he missed being at the center of things. The President was right. God help him, he loved it. He loved it all.

Key opened with a long and surprisingly effective statement in praise of Houston's character. He described his client as "a patriot who suffered grievous wounds for his nation in time of war" and made the point that it was Stanbery, not Houston, armed with "one cocked pistol and a dirk."

Poised with his finger in the air as if posing for a statue, Key cried, "I ask you, is *that* the *raiment* of a peaceful man?"

Houston turned to glance at Polk at his desk and saw Polk mouth the word, "Raiment?"

After Key's opening statement, Houston handled most of the defense himself. It wasn't just that he refused to put his fate in Key's hands. He couldn't bear to passively sit and watch while other men decided his fate.

During his long examination of Stanbery, whose arm was in a sling, Houston inquired if there was proof that he, Jackson, and Eaton ever plotted to commit fraud.

With Stanbery pinned down for the first time, a half dozen of his supporters rose and objected to Houston's question as irrelevant. Polk countered by rising to *his* feet with the demand that the question be put to a vote. The defense won the vote and Stanbery was ordered to answer.

Speaking in a voice so low that Houston had to ask him to repeat himself so that everyone could hear, Stanbery meekly replied, "Not at any time was it my intention to accuse Governor Houston of fraud. It was my intention to make a point about character, to illustrate that fraud was a theoretical possibility *within* such character."

The gallery responded to the Congressman's feeble reply with a thunder of boos, which provoked Stevenson into repeated bellows for silence as he pounded away with his gavel.

Later, when the prosecution produced the cane Houston used to beat the Congressman, the defense produced the pistol Stanbery used to try to shoot Houston, along with the knife he carried in a sheath at his side.

On May sixth, after almost four weeks, Stevenson informed the defense that it was required to close its case the next day.

The Speaker called the House to order at noon. Towering flag-draped portraits of Washington and Lafayette hung on the wall in back of the podium. Hundreds of people were packed into the theater-style chamber. Every seat in the gallery and on the floor was filled. Spectators without seats jammed themselves three and four deep against the wall, where they waited for more than an hour for closing arguments to begin. As a result of a savage rainstorm, puddles of water were scattered on the floor and everyone seemed at least slightly damp.

Over his usual light breakfast, Houston and Key had argued. Piqued that he hadn't played a larger role in the defense, Key still wanted to stick to legalities, a man so bogged down in detail that he had no sense of the moment.

"I'm not speaking to the House, you damn fool," the exasperated Houston snapped. "I am speaking the nation. *That's* my jury."

If Key wanted to sulk, let him, Houston thought. This was the most important speech he'd ever make. Everything rode on his closing argument. It was not about guilt or innocence. It was about the public perception of Sam Houston and where, if anywhere, he would go from here.

He was never in his life afraid to make a speech, but he was nervous now because so much depended on what he said and how he said it. It had been a long time since he spoke at length, too. Until now, the give and take of the trial did not demand it. Were his voice and nerves up to it? He wasn't sure.

After a slow start, he knew that they were. As the moment lifted and carried him, he felt stronger as he went on. Tall and craggy, he radiated his old magnetism, pacing back and forth with impatient energy. He found his rhythm and let the speech flow in his rich voice.

"When a member of this House, entrenched in privilege, brands a private citizen in the face of the whole nation as a fraudulent villain he renders himself answerable to the party aggrieved," he said. "There can be no other way. These are not my rights alone, but the rights of millions involved here."

He admitted that as a former member of congress he was aware of Stanbery's so-called congressional privilege. But even if such a thing existed, didn't he possess privileges of his own, just like any citizen?

"I therefore addressed him a note demanding an explanation," he said. "It was my privilege to do so, however humble I may be. The Congressman did not deign to reply. He sneered that I had no right."

Houston stopped at the defense table to pour a drink of water and was dismayed to see his hand shaking. There was a commotion in the gallery above and a bouquet of flowers thumped at his feet. A woman's voice cried, "Better Sam Houston in a dungeon than Stanbery on a throne." He smiled, raised the flowers from the floor, pressed them to his lips, and bowed while the applause rained down and Stevenson demanded silence.

The distraction gave Houston time to pull himself together. He spoke of the rights of the individual. He spoke of the dangers of a corrupt legislature. He waved the flag. He dipped into Greek, Roman, British and American history. He quoted Shakespeare. He quoted the Iliad. He quoted the Constitution. He quoted the Declaration of Independence and Magna Carta. He spoke of Caesar, Cromwell, Napoleon, and the Apostle Paul. He spoke of the law. He spoke of religion. He spoke for more than an hour.

"Would it not have been strange that I should seek to dishonor my country when I have ever been found ready to suffer in her service?" he asked. "So long as the flag, that proud emblem of my country's liberties, and its stripes and its stars wave, so long as it casts sacred protections over the personal rights of every citizen ... so long, I trust, shall the rights of American citizens be preserved safe and unimpaired."

Skin tingling and with his voice stronger than when he started, Houston was afraid that he'd overplayed his hand until the gallery erupted with a window-rattling ovation.

When it was over, instead of returning to his seat at the defense table, he dramatically walked out of the chamber with his head bowed, not because he was weary, but because he thought it wise to seem to be weary.

The actor Booth fought his way down the stairs from the gallery, shouldered his way through the crowd, blocked Houston's path, and embraced him.

"Good God, man, and they dare call *me* an actor," he said, whispering into Houston's ear.

If he dropped dead this instant, Sam Houston knew that he would die a happy man.

———

THE HOUSE DEBATED four long days, with the vigilant Polk fighting every step of the way. But he could not prevent Houston's conviction by a vote of one hundred and six to eighty nine. After the vote, Speaker Stevenson announced that he would inform Houston of his punishment the next day.

The gallery was packed again as Houston bowed to the speaker and Stevenson bowed in return. After a number of comments about Houston's "remarkable character and high degree of intelligence," the Speaker concluded, "I forbear to say more than to pronounce the judgment of the House, which is that you be reprimanded at this bar by the Speaker."

Barely restraining a smile, he said, "I reprimand you accordingly."

62

THAT EVENING, at the celebration in the White House, Jackson threw his arm around Houston's shoulders.

"Your wrist doesn't hurt from that slap, does it?" he asked with a grin that revealed an impressive paucity of teeth.

"Extraordinary, isn't it?" replied Houston, still dazed by the trial's sudden end. "Sir, you know as well as I do that I was dyin' out. If they'd taken me before a justice of the peace and fined me a few dollars or thrown me in prison it would have killed me. But instead they gave me a national theater and set me up again."

Jackson nodded happily. "So tell me, Sam, what are your plans now?"

The idea had gestated for months. It was time to bring it out in the open and commit to it.

"I believe that I will go to Texas," Houston said. "There's opportunity there, and a chance for a fresh start."

"Why that's excellent news," A broad smile cut across Jackson's narrow face. "You know, the very same idea occurred to me."

Waving everyone else away, he pulled Houston over to a corner where they could talk privately.

"Now listen," he said. "I have some thoughts on that …."

EPILOGUE

SAM HOUSTON

AND SO SAM HOUSTON went to Texas.

At the Battle of San Jacinto, on April 21, 1836, Texas won its independence when Houston's army of eight hundred men defeated the Mexican army of fourteen hundred led by Mexican President Antonio Lopez de Santa Anna. More than eight hundred Mexicans were killed or wounded. The Texans had fewer than forty casualties, including Houston himself, whose right leg was shattered above the ankle by a musket ball.

In 1840, he married Margaret Lea of Marion, Alabama. She was twenty one, he was forty six, and they had eight children during a long, happy marriage.

After serving two terms as President of the Republic of Texas, when Texas was admitted into the union in 1845 Houston was named U.S. Senator. He left the senate in 1859 and was elected Governor, the only man to be elected governor of two states.

On March 4, 1861, Texas seceded from the union on the

same day Abraham Lincoln was inaugurated President of the United States. Houston refused to take the oath of allegiance to the Confederate States of America and was forced out of office for the second time in his life.

Sam Houston died of pneumonia in Huntsville, Texas, on July 26, 1863. He was seventy years old.

ANDREW JACKSON

After two terms, Jackson left the Presidency on March 4, 1837. The day before he left office, the United States officially recognized the Independent Republic of Texas.

He spent the rest of his life at the Hermitage, where he died on June 8, 1845 at the age of seventy eight. He is buried beside his beloved wife, Rachel.

TIANA ROGERS HOUSTON

They say Sam Houston saw her one more time and left her everything they owned except the horse he rode to Texas.

She remarried in 1836, to Samuel McGrady, and died in 1838. In 1904, her body was exhumed and reburied at the Fort Gibson National Cemetery.

DRUM

Respected and beloved by his people, he died in 1838, perhaps of the same epidemic that killed Tiana.

ELIZA ALLEN

Eliza remarried in 1840, to Dr. Elmore Douglas. She died in 1862. No portrait or photograph survived her death.

A LOOK AT: THE RISING
SAM HOUSTON BOOK TWO

He was never one to back down from a fight, even when the odds were impossible.

These are dark days for Sam Houston and the Texas Revolution. The Alamo has fallen, its defenders slaughtered to the last man. Goliad is lost too, four hundred men butchered after they surrendered. Texas is a land of rumor and chaos, and Houston, now general of the army of the new Republic, commands a ragtag force on the brink of mutiny.

His strategy—an endless retreat through mud and misery—is as unpopular with his men as it is with the politicians who question his every move. But Houston knows what they don't: survival is victory, for now. He will bide his time, shape his army from raw frontier men, and wait for the moment to strike back.

From the wreckage of his past—a disgraced Tennessee governor, a man haunted by scandal and heartbreak—Houston rises once more, older but as headstrong as ever, ready to gamble everything on one desperate battle at San Jacinto.

AVAILABLE SEPTEMBER 2025

ABOUT THE AUTHOR

Robert Wisehart was born in Indianapolis, Indiana, and now is fortunate enough to live in Santa Fe, New Mexico.

In between Indianapolis and Santa Fe, he worked for many years as an award-winning reporter and columnist for newspapers in Florida, North Carolina, Louisiana and Northern and Southern California, plus occasional flirtations with radio and television as an on-air commentator. Such is the changing world that three of the four newspapers no longer exist.

Later, as a freelance writer Wisehart did everything from write speeches to ghost books. He labored as a restaurant critic and for a brief time as a one of the dreaded horde of government consultants, two words that can mean almost anything but usually add up to not much. His work has appeared in more than 200 newspapers and 30 magazines, plus several digital outlets.

Wisehart and his wife, Dana, have been married for a lifetime and intend to make it a very long lifetime indeed. They have moved much, traveled well and Dana easily is the best thing that ever happened to him. Their two sons, Marc and Carl, live in New York City.